Destroyer

GUARDIANS OF LIFE SERIES

Destroyer

GUARDIANS OF LIFE SERIES

By
Anthony Segarra

Willow Tree Horizon Press, LLC
Fantasy Horizon Press
New Jersey

Cover art, inspired by the author's imagination, designed by Caitlin C. Segarra.

Library of Congress Control Number 2024938423
ISBN 979-8-9906232-2-4 (hardcover)
ISBN 979-8-9906232-1-7 (paperback)
ISBN 979-8-9906232-0-0 (ebook)

To my beautiful wife, Sheila, and our daughter, Caitlin,
thank you from the bottom of my heart
for believing in me every step of the way
and making my life complete.

CHAPTER 1

A New Day

As she stares intensely, like a hawk, and with no worries, every movement in the entire perimeter is silent. Rubbing her hands on the chipped wood of her kitchen window, which extends just below her knees, she breathes deeply but tries not to overexert herself as she embraces the smell of the autumn breeze. It captivates her, bringing with it the purpose and meaning that she misses so much.

Eva slightly moves her head upward, watching the magnificent sight of the sun gazing down at the ancient willow tree only a few feet away from her home. The enormous branches shield the blazing warmth this morning. Each branch sags deeply with its thousand tiny companions, barely touching the ground, as the colored leaves hang on for dear life. For so many years, she has watched this scenery, thick roots that consume her backyard, expanding into complexity that seems to intertwine as snakes ready to captivate their prey. The roots know many things, deep, dark secrets, as deep as their mother, who brought her into existence. A network of life, Eva continues to wander in thought, containing truth and understanding that sets itself apart from its peers.

Exhaling slowly, she turns her attention to her precious backyard, which she tries to keep organized. She is very skilled, but those roosters move about their business, picking on the grass and disrespecting her hard efforts. She maintains the entire backyard, which she enjoys, while they search for food that surrounds the dominating willow. The buzzing of insects annoys the roosters as they invade her vegetable garden. Despite occasional disappointment, she chooses to let it go. Time has gone too far, and still, it hasn't come.

"Finally!" she says with excitement. The wait is over. As the cool breeze creeps up, gently touching her face, she shrouds her shoulders.

"Air," she says quietly. She feels the silky air weaving over her body, now a bit more aggressive and captivating, and it makes her smile once again. It electrifies her, forcing her to let her guard down, something she doesn't like to do!

She closes her eyes, lifting her head to let the wind pass beneath her. It brings a gentle scent of pine and musty, rusted leaves, teasing her with a pleasurable sensation of peace. Breathing heavily, she tries to take it all in. She feels so desperate.

Aww, that feels so good. Why can't it be like this every day? she thinks, and sighs.

The eagerness of the element of Air is now forcing her resistance. She wishes she could walk out of this filthy kitchen, straight through the annoying, squeaky back door, and run with the wind. Just to let the wind touch her body would be so inviting, but she stands her ground and doesn't move an inch.

It is now teasing her; it whispers strange songs into her ears. It knows the pain that she keeps deep in her soul. It speaks to her, pacifying her. *The entity will not stop!* she thinks. The weakness still buried deep is surfacing, the entity's power once again stepping over her boundary.

She gives up, finally accepting, and she lets the Air do as it will, but only on her own terms. The wind is running wildly into her mind. Images of her past flash, and events of the present interchange quickly while Eva keeps in control—but it's not enough!

Eva is now breathing heavily with anticipation to tangle with the powerful Air's magic. "Your Grace, I can't," she whispers silently. The essence of Air whispers again into Eva's ear, playing tricks with her mind, flowing into her body, mind, and soul. It is ratifying sensational power.

Moments pass, giving her a hope she knows is hopeless. Faith she has nearly lost. She hears the rattling of the ancient willow responding to the wind. It, too, sways back and forth, enjoying the presence of the entity. The grass joins in the parade as the powerful Air captivates its tiny hairs. She sees the fallen leaves rolling with respect as they pass other animals in their path, a respect only known to the essence and existence of this world.

Eva decides to join the festivities and gives in to the celebratory mood. She leans out the window, grasping the ledge with both hands, cautiously trying not to lose her balance. Eva desires to experience the essence of the Air in its entirety, as she yearns to escape her monotonous life. The Air responds immediately to her intentions, the wind and magic flowing through her long hair, tangling it into small knots and wildly whipping it without restraint. The Air caresses her back, its touch light, and every tiny hair on her skin stands on end as it passes through. Eva feels its presence, acknowledging her pain and struggles.

As she accepts the Air's invitation, the images flow quickly into her mind in bright flashes. She opens her eyes and finds herself running wildly in the Evermass Woods, as she once did as a young girl, feeling free. Free from her pain. Free from everyone. The pain cleanses her soul. She has no purpose. The power she possesses expands into a radiance of life essence that surrounds her. Eva quickens her pace, racing alongside the wind. She can feel the Air's presence right beside her, lifting her slightly and propelling her with great speed toward her destination. As she moves, her long hair whips wildly in the powerful current of this magical force that the entity has infused her with.

"There it is!" Eva exclaims. Her cottage! Her home! She misses it so much. Her rightful place, but to many, it wasn't. "It's there!" It sits so beautifully deep in the forest, just tucked in and well hidden so no one can disturb it. She feels his presence! Father is working hard in the yard that faces the Glory Wind Mountains. She is so pleased. Suddenly colorful birds appear. "I'm right!" Her heart starts to ache and pound with joy! "Yes! Guides are sent to join in the celebration of my long overdue return!" she exclaims. She urges the entity to hasten, embracing the powerful force as it carries her swiftly, like a baby. Together they sweep over the rugged terrain with ease, headed toward the Edqualdern River, an exotic waterway.

"The king is dead!" A voice suddenly breaks into her mind with a piercing pain. "The king is dead!" the unexpected voice screeches, which causes the image in front of her to change rapidly.

"No!" she screams. Then a white flash, and her peaceful serenity begins to evaporate. *I was so close*, she thinks in regret. In agony, she tries to grasp the vision again, but the entity departs, and the silent willow tree stares at her with the familiar kitchen surroundings. Feeling frustrated, Eva tries to regain her consciousness, and the familiar smell of the old, musty wood returns.

She nearly tumbles over the windowsill, she notices, but is able to press her hands firmly on the windowsill to prevent herself from falling. Fully aware now, she wipes tears from her cheeks and feels foolish. Eva smiles as she quickly blinks her eyelids and straightens her hair.

"Well, this was embarrassing," she says to herself, regaining her posture. She imagines the looks on her neighbors' faces if she had fallen off the window ledge. She would be the talk of the day, she thinks.

Taking a deep breath, she stares toward the annoying scream that rudely interrupted her pleasure. A town boy is running across her front lawn, frightening the hens and leaving a trail of leaves behind him.

The boy, Eric, is now running toward the Aberses' home. Couldn't the mayor find a more suitable way to communicate with these people? Eva ignores the drama and closes her eyes once again. Just a few moments of peace are all she wants. Moments pass in silence, but she opens her eyes with sadness. She was doing it again, trying to be somewhere she knows is impossible.

She sighs, releasing the window's latch, and stares at the weeping willow as it fades behind the shutters. *What an extraordinary sight of the tree*, she thinks again. The power it brings, ancient. It looks so drearily sad and weak compared to the others around it, but Eva knows its power. Not even the wind dares to test its strength and capabilities. Sometimes she feels like the willow is a part of her, but now she lets the thought pass.

Adjusting her favorite long, blue nightgown, she immediately returns to her exhausting routine. Time has passed quickly, and she retrieves her flowered apron, which hangs next to the fireplace. Personally, it does not suit her taste; it's old and poorly made, but she adores the thoughtfulness.

James will arrive soon; she hurries to prepare. She washes her hands in a pail of water beside the fireplace and retrieves a heavy frying pan from the stone hearth. Though the pan is old and worn, Eva has never replaced it because it has been in her family for generations. Her mother tried to teach her how to cook, but Eva had never been interested. Eva stares at the old frying pan, thinking of her mother and the memories it holds. She loves her mother dearly.

Smiling, Eva recalls the one time James wanted to replace it, claiming it looked like a large piece of charcoal. "If you enjoy going through my things, then it is only appropriate that I should remove your junk from your room," she had said, knowing that would make James think twice.

As Eva breaks the first egg into the frying pan, she notices the old layers of burnt oil, accumulated over decades of use, deeply ingrained into the cast iron. The egg simmers quickly, revealing patches of the original iron beneath the blackened layers of seasoning. These layers, built up over years of cooking, tell the story of its long history. Each new layer becomes a part of its ongoing legacy.

Now her thoughts wander to the unexpected news of the dead king, announced by the town boy.

"Good morning!" A cheerful, familiar voice greets the room.

"Good morning, dear," Eva replies as James strolls casually over to her while she removes the old frying pan from the fire. He kisses her lightly on the cheek, but his gaze is fixed on the scrambled eggs. They instantly upset his stomach, despite the pleasant aroma of sizzling oil and the scent of eggs swirling in the air. His piercing headaches have been coming more frequently lately.

"You're not thinking about the frying pan, are you?" Eva asks.

"Oh, no," James replies.

She smiles and says, "Sit. Breakfast is ready."

"I'm not hungry. I was thinking of going for a walk," he says.

"Headaches again? I'll make some tea. Now please sit," she replies, quickly removing her apron and reaching for the teapot and herb basket from the fireplace ledge.

"But...," James protests.

"Sit," Eva says.

Reluctantly, James walks over to the kitchen table, taking his usual place at the far end. He places his palm under his chin and stares at the long, handcrafted mahogany table that his father made. The table is a masterpiece of perfect workmanship, and he can still picture his father working in the backyard as millions of particles fell over his hands, with a small mist of smoke hovering in the sunlight through the window. It had taken his father months to finish the table, and he had been so proud when he brought it in, along with its four matching chairs, as a token of pride in this kitchen. Each chair had its own unique characteristic, carefully carved differently and shaped to be mismatched and smooth as the top polished table. It was unusual, but his father had been a strange man.

The ritual morning observation of James's stepmother, Eva, begins. He can't help but notice as she drops strange herbs into the hot teapot. Her nightgown is absolutely beautiful, made entirely of silk from her shoulders down to her ankles. It seems a little strange to wear such luxurious nightwear in the early morning, he thinks. The top half of the gown hangs on a thin, black silk thread that lightly overlaps her shoulder. As she continues to fuss over it, the strap keeps fumbling over, and she keeps putting it back in place. She works diligently by the fireplace.

Moments pass, and Eva walks over to James, steadying his tea. As the cranks of the window shutter reveal her long black hair and slim pale face, she moves with grace and continues her work, wearing a fearless expression. Her high cheekbones and piercing sky-blue eyes exude a captivating confidence, reminiscent of a goddess.

She sits in her usual spot across from him, just behind the fireplace. The sunken, deep stone wall is darkened from years of burning, revealing various utensils hanging from the top ledge.

"Your headache won't go away if you let the tea sit to cool, dear. Now drink up," she says.

He stares at her miracle tea as it steams in his face. Its strong scent enters his nostrils. It smells like earthy, fresh soil from fertile manure. The herbs are not familiar to him, but soothing. James drinks it with anticipation; it is one of Eva's mysterious creations, and it works wonders with his headaches.

James nearly finishes his drink, pretending to still be sipping as he stares at Eva's peculiar hands. The silver rings on two of her fingers are carved with symbols for the Water and Earth Elements, but that is nothing compared to her elegantly colored nails. The striking violet-blue shade matches the teacup he holds; it's a coincidence. In the city far east of here, it's not unusual for women and men to have such vibrant nails. Unfortunately, Lepersteed doesn't allow for such diversity, spreading rumors of witches among them. However, Eva is an exception; she claims to only follow the Guardians of Light, not Dark. It's a good thing she doesn't go out often.

"Feeling better?" she asks.

"Uh, oh, yeah," he lies.

Eva quickly stands up.

"Good, now I'll warm your eggs a bit and—"

"Eva, please don't worry. I'm not hungry, and I know how to cook my own meals. Besides, I used to prepare meals for us. Remember? I appreciate your concern for my headaches and everything you do to help," James says with a warm smile. As he rinses his cup, he accidentally knocks his chair over, causing Eva to become annoyed. She watches him separate the larger dishes to make room for her precious teacup in a small bucket, despite having told him multiple times to place it securely on top of the fireplace. Like most young kids, he seems to have no common sense.

Eva places the teacup in its proper place and tosses the eggs from the frying pan into the fire. "Fine, you can start breakfast tomorrow; I would enjoy that," she says, still a little irritated.

"I am sorry, Eva. I didn't mean to offend you. It's just this pain; I cannot seem to get my bearings," James says, feeling guilty. He looks up at her with pleading eyes, hoping she'll understand.

She sighs, placing the frying pan securely on top of the fireplace's ledge, along with her other collections of ceramic pieces.

"I know, dear," she says, her emotions getting the best of her. She places her right hand gently on James's face, feeling the pricks of his perfectly shaved beard. A thought crosses her mind—he's growing up so fast at eighteen years old. She strokes him lightly, staring at his tanned face; she can sense clear evidence of his tension. She gently strokes his wildly curly, light-brown hair, smiling at him, while his intense hazel-green eyes meet hers quizzically.

So many memories, she thinks. She can feel his eyes pressing on her.

"I see your headaches don't let you sleep well. I'm sure your appetite is not very welcoming," she says sympathetically, rubbing his broad shoulders. He is much taller than she is, and she remembers always comforting James when he was young. His hair has always been wild and full of life. He has grown into a strong and handsome young man, like his father, but everything about him is identical to his mother: power and trust. He has hands that look as if they could break any bone, yet he is gentler than any person she's ever known…except for one.

James notices Eva's sudden change of demeanor and asks with concern, "Eva, are you all right?" She turns around quickly, trying to hide her emotions, and wipes the tears from her face before answering.

"Go into town and buy some bread from Mr. Tyler. I would like to prepare lunch early. I like his new recipes. As a matter of fact, buy two."

"What's wrong? What's bothering you?"

"Always with the questions!" she snaps, moving away and picking up the frying pan, preparing to wash it. "Questions that have always seemed to cling on to you since you were five. Now would you please get my bread!"

James, confused by her reactions, decides not to challenge her and heads out of the kitchen toward the front door directly in front of him. Just before he heads out the door, Eva interrupts his progress.

"Dear, after you are done, can you please go to town and find out what happened to the king? It seems His Excellency is dead. Be sure you're quick. I prefer my bread moist."

James can hear her voice echoing with the rumbling of dishes as he stands frozen at the door, as if someone has thrown a stone at his head.

"What?" He swings around angrily. "Where did you hear this? When? Why didn't you mention it before?"

He stomps back into the kitchen.

"Calm down, young man," Eva says, wiping her hands on her apron and facing the distressed boy. "I heard it from the mayor's messenger boy just before you came in."

"But why didn't you just tell me when it happened? You always put news aside when you feel it isn't important...but this, Eva! Wouldn't you think it's extremely important? Our king is dead!" He raises his voice.

Eva quickly places her hands lightly over James's mouth, preventing him from saying more.

"James, I'm concerned about it too. I was merely worried about your headache and didn't want to press the issue on you so soon," she says calmly.

"But you should have told me." He lowers her hand, trying to stay calm.

"It just slipped my mind, that's all...Now that the news is finally out in the open, and your headache should be rumbling like a stampede of horses, can you please get my bread and the information we are seeking?"

They both stare at each other for a long moment. Even the smallest insect dares not disturb the storm that has suddenly entered the kitchen. James should have known. In the past, Eva never cared about politics or any individuals besides her own affairs. What mattered to her was the two of them. Of course, when his father was alive, she cared for him dearly. James remembers many conversations with his father, and they all amount to the same thing: Eva adores them. Ever since his mother died giving birth to him, according to his father, Eva has changed dramatically.

Eva is the only mother he has known, and he loves her dearly for all she has done for him and his family. However, that doesn't justify what she has just done.

Angrily turning around, James stomps out of the kitchen.

"Fine!" he says. "I'll get the bread, and maybe stop by to get the information about our dead king, since it's not on your priority list!" He slams the front door, causing the small, wooden, painted family portrait of James as an infant, Eva, and his father to drop, revealing a clean spot on the wall where it once hung.

CHAPTER 2

Protection

DISAPPOINTED, EVA REMOVES her apron, placing it in its usual spot, and sits comfortably. "So young," she says, tapping her fingers on the table. "That temper that lingers, it's so frustrating." She retraces the events, analyzing what went wrong, but all that comes to her mind are memories. She smirks slightly, then a creeping feeling in her stomach aches, accompanied by the need to release tears, but she holds them back.

She recalls how unique James's parents were. The wonderful times they spent together, enjoying each other's company, free-spirited before the Northern Nation stepped into their affairs and destroyed their lives. Her hatred toward elves is very clear; just thinking of them angers her. They are very selfish, saying humans are merely irresponsible and worthless. Regardless of their expertise and skills, elves view humans as imbeciles. This personal resentment toward humans goes way back to when the Guardians were very involved in these lands. The war between humans and elves persisted for generations, ignited by the actions of a single beloved Guardian. However, the destruction brought by the conflict altered the appearance and culture of the elves. Despite this transformation, a few noble elves from the royal elven nation managed to escape in time, retaining their integrity. Seeking refuge in the in-between realm, they demonstrated their trustworthiness and willingness to adapt.

Eva gazes at the fallen picture by the front door, her focus on the family, except for one member. She recalls her first encounter with Leeran. Initially skeptical yet curious, Leeran quickly recognized Eva's unique qualities. To her own surprise, Eva sensed her abilities for the first time, and Leeran accepted her into her home. They grew close rapidly.

The aching feeling reaches Eva's heart; she feels a tear and tries to massage the pain to soothe her sadness. She recalls the countless times Leeran put her hand on the willow tree, crying hysterically, begging the powerful Guardian of Earth to give her strength and power to protect her unborn child—she knew what was coming.

Eva tears away from the memories, stands up, walks toward the window, and opens the shutters again to let in some air. Taking on a new sight beyond her yard, she stares at the beautiful landscape, noticing the high mountains with a shadow of snow at the peak, flowing and shielding the town of Lepersteed.

It was her fault, she thought in sadness. She should have seen the signs sooner; she underestimated the elves' cleverness, especially dealing with the Aldoron Elves. It was a miscalculation on her part, mainly due to other affairs, or perhaps the Guardians intended for it to be so. There is nothing she can do now; the event has passed and was fulfilled.

"I'm so sorry, Leeran," she whispers, spying a small, upright tombstone that rests next to the massive roots of the willow tree. Sam, overwhelmed with grief, couldn't bear the pain of losing his beloved wife and carved an unfinished stone.

Eva sighs, missing Sam's company even though he spent most of his time working on various projects around the house to keep his mind sane. Sam and Leeran were extraordinary individuals, kindhearted, graceful, and well intentioned. However, Eva doesn't value these traits as much as she used to. After Leeran, everything changed for this family.

As she gathers the dishes and wipes them with her old hand towel, the same one she used to try to bring down Leeran's fever, she remembers how all her efforts failed, and Leeran eventually fell into a deep, coma-like sleep before passing away a few days later. The ancient magic that was used to place the curse on her was too powerful for Eva to undo. It required years of preparation and mastery of the element of light, something only a rare YassPa Elf could achieve. The dark elements are easy to conquer, but light elements require patience and dedication.

Leeran slipped away quietly from Eva one day, preventing her from detecting the devious merchant that confronted her at the market near them. Little did Eva know that when Leeran returned home, the magic stayed dormant in her until it revived, spreading quickly like a growing vine, making it unstoppable. If Eva had more time and resources, she might have been able to stop it. Fortunately, James was spared.

After placing the towel by the basin and removing her apron, Eva prepares to put the clean dishes in the cabinet above, remembering how Sam became depressed after Leeran's death. She tried to comfort him, but his love was so strong that he was lost. Their son, James, was only seven years old when his father fell ill. No medicine can stop the essence of love, an unknown, raw, and unforgiving force that grows in power. It can cure, curse, and destroy. Eva witnessed its effects on Sam herself. Love is either rewarding or unforgiving, and no one can control this powerful element of both light and darkness.

Suddenly Eva feels a warm, vibrating sensation spreading through her body, and she immediately calls forth her defenses. A powerful presence is approaching her home, breaking through her concealed barriers. She slowly releases her magic, not wanting to catch the intruder off guard, and uses a counteractive spell to repel the new presence. She then relaxes and exhales deeply, knowing who the intruder is.

Eva waits patiently, returning the dishes to the small cabinet by the fireplace when the front door latch opens by itself, revealing a wicked old man. "Just let yourself in, Radion," she says sarcastically without looking up. "Can you please pick up the picture frame next to you?"

The man squints his eyes in the dark hallway, trying to scan her location before rushing inside, ignoring the picture frame. Eva shakes her shoulders and arms to ward off the chilly air that follows Radion. Smirking as she watches him from the corner of her eye, she continues to search for vegetables for lunch preparation in the icebox.

Mumbling curse words and digging under his cloak, Radion retrieves old documents. He reveals a bundle of worn, torn papers within a black leather book. He stumbles to the kitchen, leaving the lingering scent of manure behind him. He waits silently, extending his arms and holding the book toward her. Eva sniffs the air, and her mood changes quickly as the smell of manure fills her nostrils.

Staring intensely at Eva as she places the vegetables on the oak wood table in front of him, Radion breathes heavily, and sweat drips from his scarf. Eva finally observes his appearance. Radion is wearing bright red trousers and a yellow, raggedy shirt, accompanied by colorful scarves around his neck. Despite his beautiful, smooth, dark skin, his overgrown and unkempt gray beard makes him look aged. Being outside has given him a slight tan, which seems to age him even more.

For a few moments, neither of them says anything, waiting to see who will speak first. Finally, Radion slams the old leather-bound book onto the table, and dust springs out from the ancient pages, almost touching Eva's face. Eva tries very hard to hold her patience. Sam's beautiful oak table can handle many impacts, but slamming something onto it without respect is like a dagger to her heart. How she hates men showing no respect.

"We should move quickly," Radion says.

Eva continues to stare at Radion, unsure of how to respond. "The next time you come in here covered in dirt and slam that book on my table, I will personally take the book and turn it to ashes," she says firmly, keeping her voice low. "And why do you smell like that?"

"It's a long story. Did you speak to him?" Radion asks.

Eva gives Radion a stern look. "Speak to him about what?" she says, retrieving her clean teacups from the sink and returning to the fireplace. She sets them securely on top of the mantel.

"About what?! Is that all you have to say? Didn't you hear…the king is dead!" Radion exclaims, opening a clearly marked page of the old book and placing his long finger on it. "It's here, in the Ra Les—"

"Lower your voice," Eva interrupts. "Give me a moment."

Eva closes her eyes, concentrating, and raises her hand slightly, focusing on the Earth Elements magic around her. Slowly, she releases the magic that stirs within her reach. The sensation of magic fills her body with an electrifying feeling and sends it to its destination. The faint, ghostly light surrounds her hands, finally dissipating after a few moments.

"I thought you already secured the area," Radion says.

Eva responds, opening her eyes and turning to face the wrinkled old man. "The Vertex alerts me of magic entities. I simply enchanted it to include non-magical beings. You have no idea how nosy my neighbors are."

"Umm…" Radion sounds unconvinced.

"So, what do you have to show me in the Ra Leslar Var?" Eva approaches the old book.

"Look here." Radion presses his finger on the old parchment papers with ancient writing. The pages are worn, and the binder is barely holding itself together. "Version Par 50, translated elvish tongue, the Destroyer proclamation." He reads to her, pressing on the specific paragraph for her to follow.

"Thus thy night, more than anyone foresaw, I see thy sky burn, and thy King is no more! Evil will strive again, as it once did before. Thy proclaimed Destroyer, burning inside, where they will try for more. Hear me now! I foresee! He shall see light, thy proclaimed Destroyer, will now, once again, be born!"

"I am familiar with this passage," Eva says, moving away from the book. Unalarmed by the passage, she returns to the rest of her clean dishes. "I know the king is dead. I just sent James to obtain more information."

"Why did you send him, Eva? Don't you see? The passage clearly states that the boy will be burned to death. We have to stop him!" Radion paces around the kitchen, waving his arm behind Eva, waiting for her to face him.

Eva sighs and finally turns to face the old man. She can feel his narrow, brown eyes watching her closely. He must have been a handsome man once, with smooth, dark skin, but now his face is weathered with deep wrinkles that speak of long years spent in the sun.

"He will be fine, and you have misinterpreted the prophecy. The burning version of the Destroyer reveals the magic he was born with, and those are the headaches he has been having for the past few weeks. It is trying to manifest. I'm not sure why the passage includes evil mixed in with his magic, but I am sure it will all be clear soon enough."

"How can you be so sure?" Radion says, feeling unconvinced.

"Well, I did study in the same place you did, after all," she says sarcastically. "Besides, he is my responsibility," she adds, and decides to head out of the kitchen.

"Where are you going?" he demands.

Radion watches her intensely as she stops just before the second window by the doorway, which leads to the dark hall and stairs that lead to the sleeping area. She turns slightly, and the sun settles on her fair, smooth skin. The beam electrifies her, and he cannot help but fixate on her. Her stern complexion and her long, silky, black hair. The town is right; she is a deadly woman to the local men.

"First of all, change your tone if we are to work together. Second, you need to clean up. Something tells me there's more to come, and we should prepare quickly." Then she exits the kitchen and picks up the picture frame as she ascends the stairs, disappearing into the darkness of the hallway. Everything is now silent for the first time, and the birds chirping from the backyard quickly soothe Radion's growing temper and anxiety as he reaches for the old book beside him.

⋯✦⟹ ⟸✦⋯

James keeps his pace, approaching the Fisherman home with mixed emotions. He loves Eva, but her sinister ways of viewing situations just don't make any sense. She could be the most giving person, but also the most ruthless and selfish. Remembering his urgency to find more information, James walks quickly, passing the enormous farm and making sure he avoids contact with Mr. Fisherman. Mr. Fisherman enjoys watching travelers pass his turf, ensuring information doesn't pass him by.

Normally James would spend a few moments with Mr. Fisherman while he showed off his flocks, but today is not the day. Mr. Fisherman, known for his skills in breeding farm animals, became popular among his town and beyond this region. James sees him exiting the horse shed and going about his usual routines while James picks up his pace. He feels regret for the old man. His children are grown and gone, and nature has taken a toll on him. For most farmers, age gets punished while tending to nature.

James walks in silence while dirt picks up in a floating cloud behind him, nearly covering his existence as the old trail begins to take form, revealing the shape of the forest. The forest looms in a heavy mist, forsaken looking but untouchable in its ancient beauty. The town of Lepersteed has only one forest, and the folks here refuse to enter it, although it is the quickest way to the town hall. He doesn't mind, as the forest holds a special place in his heart. It captures a unique beauty that always soothes his stress.

At eighteen years old, James feels the pressure to settle down, run his farm, and perhaps even get married. He knows the locals gossip about him, as his best friend Ethan often tells him. However, James can't shake the feeling that now is not the right time for him. Ever since his father's passing, he feels out of place and uneasy, especially with the persistent headaches he experiences. He feels different from everyone else, and maybe even thinks he might be sick. The idea of settling down is far from his mind.

His headaches are growing stronger, and he knows it's not normal. Eva always tries to help him by providing herbal medicine, but she insists it is normal. Something is trying to break him inside his head. It scares him!

He passes children, all of whom are barefoot and dirty from the mud, throwing pebbles at each other. They stop as they notice him passing and scatter back to their homes. The kids were obviously daring each other to enter the forest, he thinks. He never had a chance to develop socially when he was young. Eva made sure visits were controlled, and venturing outside was not allowed. Only a few friends came to visit, but they never returned. Eva made sure of that. As he got older, Eva had no choice but to loosen her chain.

He really enjoys the outdoors. The fallen leaves are everywhere now, and the air chills his arms during this season. The smell of hay, fertile ground, and spices mixed with the fresh autumn blossoms overpowers him.

James finally reaches the large oak tree that blocks his path, leading into the Miser Forest. The ancient tree appears forbidding, with its massive bark crumpling like parchment and as large as his arm. The roots spread widely and intertwine for miles, forming a natural barrier that makes it difficult to proceed directly. He searches the tree and finds a small passage, squatting before squeezing through the puzzling roots. Each time he ventures forth, it seems the tree conjures new vines, adding to the challenge of his adventure.

As he figures out his new pattern, he finally makes it through, and his back is now behind the tree. He wonders if the ancient oak finds this amusing as he cleans off the thorns, revealing scratches with blood slowly coming down his arms. It's a bit unnerving to come this way, as he knows nobody bothers with this ancient path, but he really enjoys exploring.

Thinking silently as he continues to pull the thorns out of his shirt, he recalls a childhood legend of Miser the fairy creature, who was assigned to guard this forest from thieves. Eartha, the great Guardian of Earth, punished Miser for neglecting his responsibility to guard the forest and turned him into this oak tree. It is said that this forest contains hidden, rare plants and herbs personally created by Eartha herself that cannot be found anywhere else. Apparently, Miser was busy with humans when witches from the forsaken mountain slipped into the secret layer and found the Guardian's prized possessions. So he doesn't mind a few scratches that give the tree the purpose it so desires. He smiles and moves on.

As he makes his way into the forest, the view before him never ceases to amaze him. It's as if he has been transported to another realm. The beauty and colors of this forest are so captivating, it feels alive! Walking on the old, paved dirt path, he hears scattering everywhere, assuming they are small creatures, but he has no clue. The distant sound of the familiar waterfall continues to provide him with the soothing peace he so desires. The aches in his head seem to subside slightly as he admires his surroundings. The fresh smell of the air and the exotic, bright lavender and red flowers near his path have grown wildly; he never dares to pull out. So different from home. He has seen maps of this region from the town hall, and this forest is vast, with rivers, lakes, and caves throughout. He remembers his father telling him stories as a youngster that venturing beyond the path is dangerous.

"Boy, there are fairy folk that live there, waiting for intruders. Evil is every-where. Magic lives in there, always waiting for intruders…Don't stray from that path!"

He finds it amusing that his father was among the many who believed in the myths and legends to keep their children at bay.

The path comes to an end, and beyond the ridge, towering ancient trees reveal a small opening. James finally emerges from the forest, landing on a pile of neatly gathered leaves. As he steps onto the cobblestones, he pauses, surveying the area around him.

CHAPTER 3

Unexpected Stroll

"STRANGE," JAMES MURMURS.

Normally, people would be covering the entire area, conducting their business, exchanging goods, and shopping in the various markets. Lepersteed, although poor, is a thriving little town known for its farming. Many come from far and wide since it sits between the High Mountain and Miser Forest. They provide valuable agriculture and beef in the region.

James quickly passes Vincent's Butchers, which is closed. It's possible that Mr. Vincent hasn't had a chance to open with the sudden news in town. He ignores Mr. Tyler's Bakery; the smell of fresh bread has instantly taken him by surprise, which rumbles his stomach.

"Wait up, James!"

James quickly looks back at Mr. Tyler's Bakery to find Ethan running toward him, chewing sloppily on Mr. Tyler's famous bread as James continues his path, ignoring the call. Ethan finally catches up with him and quickly matches his speed.

"Hey, would you wait? Didn't you hear me call you?" Ethan says, still chewing.

"Yeah, I'm just in a rush," James responds.

"Where are you going?" Ethan takes another bite of the golden loaf—he is being rude—and then tears off a piece for James.

"No thanks. Did you steal that?" James asks.

"No way, I'd never do that," Ethan says, smirking. James lets it go, not in the mood to challenge him. He sighs.

"I'm going to the town hall," James finally says.

"Oh, it's really a mess there, with the king being dead and all," Ethan says.

"So I heard," James says sarcastically.

"What's wrong?" Ethan asks, concerned.

"It's just that E…" James pauses for a moment to avoid confusing him. "It's just my headache. It just won't let up."

"Can Eva mix you some of her tea?" Ethan mumbles while chewing, and tosses the last piece of loaf into his full mouth.

"She did…look, never mind that. So, what did you hear about the king?" As they slow down, they find themselves facing a large crowd only a few feet away. Villagers from various parts are there: farmers and merchants. The children are scattered all over, in the way of the adults, and are being yelled at by them to find another suitable area to play.

I don't know," Ethan says, spitting on the ground and wiping his skinny hand on his mouth. It's a bad habit James has known him to have since he can remember. "Well, they say he may have died by unknown forces—witches, or possibly dark wizards and sorceresses that lurk silently in the dark. "Would you cut it out, Ethan? You know perfectly well there hasn't been any wizardry or sorcery since the time of Olen!"

"Right, we've got witches. I was just trying to cheer you up. Anyway, they're saying he died of natural causes, in his sleep," Ethan says.

"I don't know about that. Don't you think that's strange? I thought he lived a long time, like his family."

"I know. I thought it was unusual too. I guess we never know when people are actually sick. Maybe the royal family is becoming like us…" Ethan trails off. "Well, at least we've got witches who could help our race," he says sarcastically.

"You know we can't trust them."

"Whatever. Better them than me." Ethan turns his attention to the crowd and notices familiar faces standing in front of the town hall. "Hey, there's Abela and her friend. Let's go."

James sees his girlfriend Abela wearing a simple, off-white dress that extends just above her ankles. She is a bit younger than him and should be turning seventeen next week. Her face still has that slenderness and particular beauty it's had since they were young. They call her baby face. Her hair is wildly curly and long, just below her shoulders. They have been close friends and eventually became a couple, so close that he senses she is restless and ready to move to the next level. He catches her off guard and tries to distract her. It's the best he can do right now, but he knows it can't last forever. He really adores her, but it seems terrible to commit himself to marriage. It just doesn't feel right. With this unusual headache that comes every so often, it's like something deep inside grows in fear that he shouldn't be with her right now. He's not sure why. He really loves her, but oddly, it's not right to see her now.

James pulls Ethan close to his face. "I'm not in the mood right now. Do you know another way in?"

"James, you know she'll be upset if you ignore her."

"I'll deal with her later." James releases Ethan; he is three times his size and out of line. He feels anxious to get into the town hall, also known as the Lady Tavern, and find out what's going on.

"Sorry, buddy. Well?" James says.

"Me?" Ethan grins as if James is insulting his intelligence. He places his thin hands into his deep, large pockets, looking around cautiously. His best friend is so awkwardly odd. Looking at him, he seems so obviously sinister. His distortion seems to give it away, with the several fights he has endured. But that's not true. He's skillful with his hands. His large, seaweed-colored eyes look heavily lifted, pressing against his long face and making him seem out of place. Ethan is about James's age, and he tends to follow his own ways, like not caring about his unkempt, long, pitch-black hair. You can always spot him in a large crowd, always pulling his hair back, which reveals a crooked nose that sticks out, having never healed from all his troubling days. People don't find him very attractive but they do find him very intriguing because he is a gifted talker. The town folks refer to him as Snoop, the one that can get things. But James knows another side of him. His longtime scarecrow friend has a good heart and is more loyal than anyone he has known. He totally trusts him.

"You should know me by now, James," Ethan says as he searches for other hidden parts in his baggy pants.

"Fine, genius!" James says, already annoyed.

Ethan grins as he surveys the area, motioning for James to follow him swiftly and quietly. They retrace their steps, halting just before the weathered facade of the old bookshop. Leaning against the cracked brick wall, Ethan engages

James in a casual conversation, all the while keeping a watchful eye on their surroundings. Satisfied that they are unnoticed, he grasps James's arm and steers him toward a narrow alley adjacent to the shop. Rats scurry away from mounds of garbage that litter the ground, filling the air with a putrid stench of decay. As they reach the far end of the alley, the acrid smell of urine and excrement assaults their senses, warning against any further exploration. Ethan, seemingly unfazed, maintains his composure, signaling to James that they should remain focused on the task at hand.

He swiftly ushers James into a corner where a narrow gap between the walls reveals a small structure in the distance. Ethan effortlessly squeezes through the gap, gesturing for James to follow suit. James struggles on his first attempt due to his stockier build, but after a moment's effort, he manages to push through, feeling the rough brick scraping against his cheeks and eyes. Slowly they navigate the narrow, dimly lit passage, nudging aside rats in their path. The putrid smell assaults James's senses, threatening to overwhelm him, but he grits his teeth and focuses on holding his breath. Spiderwebs, thick with dust, brush against his face, hindering his progress. After what feels like an eternity, they emerge into a sprawling garden, the foul odor replaced by the sweet fragrance of autumn flowers. Gasping for air, they brush dirt off their clothes, relieved to be free from the confines of the narrow passage.

"Are we…"

"Yes, behind the town hall, in the back garden," Ethan says, cleaning the rat droppings off his boots.

"How did you know about the gap between the buildings?" James asks.

"Uh, you know, I enjoy exploring new ways to escape. I'm sorry it wasn't easy," Ethan replies, pointing to the small scrape on James's face.

"It's okay. I did ask you to find another way in…I guess it's a consequence for ignoring Abela," James says, shrugging it off.

They both laugh.

"So, how do we get in?" James asks.

"Come on," Ethan says, skipping like a child and leading the way.

They stroll through a small garden maze adorned with various white-and-yellow roses, a tribute to the Guardian it honors. Upon reaching an open clearing, they behold a magnificent statue seated upon a stone bench. It is the Guardian of Water, depicted with exquisite craftsmanship, her figure seemingly alive with the power of the sea.

"The Lady of the Sea," James murmurs, his voice filled with awe as he studies the statue's delicate features, reminiscent of an elf. Her visage, as smooth as the ocean's surface, boasts finely sculpted ears with subtly pointed tips. Her cascading hair merges seamlessly with the flowing water behind her, creating an ethereal illusion of movement. With arms outstretched toward the heavens, she exudes an aura of grace, control, and boundless might. Simply gazing upon her leaves one breathless.

Like many, James is familiar with the legends surrounding these enigmatic beings known as Guardians, who once traversed these lands. Tales of their sight-inducing madness are widespread, yet James recalls Eva's skepticism, reminding himself of the importance of verifying such stories through multiple sources.

Regardless, the reverence for these Guardians, embodiments of Water, Air, Fire, and Earth, permeate every facet of life. James knows there are also Guardians of Darkness, though he isn't sure what their elements might be. Though mythical and unseen, their significance is undeniable, symbolizing the essence of existence itself. Light and dark magic, intertwined with the elements, shape the world in ways both mysterious and profound. Despite their elusive nature, the Guardians are universally admired for their contributions to the tapestry of existence, their presence serving as a testament to the enduring beauty of the world.

James and Ethan stare at the intricately detailed structure momentarily. A rusted plaque states, "A Gift from King Rockhammer." If James is not mistaken, that's a dwarf name. No wonder the statue looks extraordinary. He has never seen that type of stone crafting, a stone that's difficult to carve, which could only be handled by dwarves. Folks here say they have been extinct since the period of Olen.

As a hummingbird alights upon the statue's head, diverting their attention, Ethan takes James by surprise. He surveys the Guardian's naked body, tracing the contours of its perfectly sculpted form with his slender fingers. "Umm," he murmurs, a sinister smile playing upon his lips, "they feel..."

James punches him. "Will you cut it out and have some respect!" He pulls Ethan away. "You're lucky she's not here to drown you!"

"Sorry, buddy, you're right. I should have respected her," Ethan says, mesmerized by her bare body like a little boy while rubbing his left arm.

They reach the end of the garden, which leads to the back door of a small building structure. "This door will lead to the town hall's wine cellar," Ethan says.

James notices that it is bolted with a thick chain and an ancient-looking cap lock. "I assume you have a way in?"

Ethan smiles and reaches deep into his pocket, retrieving a small, handmade key chain with various keys, some of which look very old. His friend is very resourceful. Not knowing his little adventures, he is a collector of keys. A strange hobby, but very effective now that they need to get in!

"Not a problem," he says, his voice barely a whisper as he carefully waves the clanking key ring. The metallic jingles fill the air, but he remains focused on the task at hand. With deliberate precision, he selects a long, crooked, thin metal item from the ring and places it meticulously into the ancient lock. The tension in the room is palpable as he listens intently, his senses attuned to every creak and groan of the old door.

There is something peculiar about this door, something that makes his skin crawl. It's as if he's searching for more than just a way inside; he's searching for answers, for secrets long forgotten. His hand trembles slightly as he moves the key randomly left and right, his movements so silent and graceful that he seems almost transcendent, like a ghost in the night.

Time stretches into an eternity as he continues his delicate dance with the lock. Beads of sweat trickle down his forehead, evidence of the mounting pressure. The atmosphere in the room grows thick with anticipation, the silence broken only by the faint sound of their own heartbeats pounding in their ears.

And then, a faint click.

The latch releases, and with it, the heavy chains fall off, clattering to the ground in a cacophony of noise. The door swings open, revealing an impenetrable darkness within. But before they can fully comprehend what lies beyond, a mystical cloud substance begins to coalesce, swirling and pulsating with an otherworldly energy.

The cloud takes shape, revealing an ancient-looking dwarf, his weathered face etched with lines of wisdom and hardship. His piercing eyes gleam with an otherworldly light as he brandishes a colossal club, ready to unleash its devastating power. The sight sends a chill down their spines, their hearts pounding with primal fear.

Instinct takes over, and both James and Ethan stumble backward, their eyes locked on the menacing figure before them. Panic sets in, and they feel the urge to flee, to escape from this surreal nightmare. But just as they are about to turn and run, James's hand shoots out, gripping Ethan's arm with a strength born of desperation.

"No! We can't run," James whispers urgently. "There's something more to this. Something we need to uncover."

Ethan's wide eyes meet James's determined gaze, and a flicker of trust ignites within him. He nods, silently acknowledging their shared conviction. With their fear momentarily suppressed, they brace themselves, ready to face the unknown and confront the secrets that lie within the grasp of the ancient dwarf.

Together they steel their nerves, their resolve solidifying with each passing second. They know that whatever awaits them on the other side of that door, their lives will never be the same again. But armed with curiosity and the unbreakable bond between them, they step forward, venturing into the depths of uncertainty and into the heart of an enigma that will test their courage to its limits.

James stops suddenly. "It's magic, some kind of mist magic," he says. The mist reforms to reveal a dark, ghastly shadow trying to attack them. They stare in fear but relax as it reforms into a gnome creature they have never seen before. Exhaling, James pulls Ethan away from the mirror that is blocking the entrance. They slip through into a dark room. The smell of fresh wine fills their nostrils, and it is both sweet and inviting.

They carefully walk in, keeping themselves low and out of sight. Large wine barrels are scattered in a mazelike fashion. They notice a stairway leading upward.

"What the hell was that at the door? It wasn't there before!" Ethan says, trying to pretend he isn't terrified, leading James toward the dimly lit staircase.

"I told you, witch magic. Some sort of tricking reflection to warn off thieves like you," James says.

"Witchery stuff, I hate it. Well, it didn't work; I got in."

"Sure you did," James responds, and they both giggle.

James stumbles over a wine crate in their path, setting off a chain reaction among the lined crates. The loud crash fills the air, fracturing the tense silence. Their hearts race as they fear the consequences of their noise, but they find solace in the absence of immediate danger. With renewed determination, they push forward, mindful of the obstacles that still lie ahead, their mission driving them ever onward.

"And here we go again," Ethan says.

He slips around James, waiting for him to catch up and cleaning off the cobwebs from his hair.

"You know, there are better things than locks for a hobby," James snaps.

"Hey, you stick to your farming and let me do my snooping."

CHAPTER 4

Searching

THEY REACH THE top of the stairs that lead into a dim room with a huge table covered in disorganized, overflowing documents. James heads to the table quickly but stumbles again, this time over a smaller crate, and almost falls on top of Ethan. Ethan falls back with the weight of his big friend, but James catches him in time.

"Yeah, you should definitely stick to farming," Ethan says.

"Very funny."

"Next time just wait for me and have a little patience. I'm the one leading this expedition."

"You're right...I'm sorry."

"Oh, lighten up, James. I was just kidding. You should really clean your face; you don't want your girlfriend's lips to get dirty," Ethan says.

James gives him a threatening look, ready to punch him again.

"Okay, okay...let's go."

James stops Ethan at the table as he rummages through the documents. He's not sure what he's looking for. There aren't any clues as to what's going on. The town seems deserted, and obviously everyone is here seeking answers. James wants to know how King Argus, king of the human race, died. The family leader who possesses the power to protect them from sinister witchery threats is now gone. There must be something out of the ordinary in these documents that can explain his death.

James notices a crumpled paper on the floor and unravels it as he reads it aloud. "Look at this. It was signed by Raymul, the king's High Druid. He's sending a representative to keep order. Why would he do that? Don't we already have a council person for the king?"

"Lower your voice, buddy," Ethan whispers. "I already saw the stupid letter."

"You mean you read this earlier?" James asks.

"Yeah, remember, I was here earlier. I snuck in from the kitchen," Ethan replies, signaling toward another door at the far side of the room.

James looks at the door and then back to the crumpled paper. "Did you throw this out?" he asks.

"No, I put it back. Like a normal thief."

"Never mind. Look, you know as well as I do that we send delegates who are approved by the king. How could Raymul send someone? It doesn't make sense! Shouldn't the Argus family be declaring his daughter as the rightful heir to the throne?"

"Lower your voice." Ethan tries to pull James away, but his hands are too small to wrap around James's arm. "Who cares about that governing stuff anyway? It's not like we're really paying attention or getting involved. Besides, you know everyone here is just a puppet."

"It makes all the difference. Something is not right." James continues rummaging through the documents. Ethan manages to pull him away.

"They are royals, James. You know, majestic royals, they say. I'm sure they'll figure it out. Anyway, why would you care about that family? We're not magic-born or conquerors of elements; otherwise, we'd be at that Witch Mountain."

James sighs. "You're right, Ethan. Lead the way."

Ethan stares fearlessly at his best friend, ready to face anything. He knows this place is all about politics and actually feels sorry for James, a simple farmer boy who is both headstrong and benevolent at the same time.

"Now listen carefully: stay low, and try to follow my lead. Please don't bump into anything," Ethan says as he slowly cracks open the door.

"I can't believe we're doing this, sneaking around," James mumbles.

"It's not my fault you have girl trouble," Ethan says, smiling.

James nudges Ethan. "Just go ahead."

Ethan signals James to watch his every move and wait for a signal. He crouches low and slips underneath the long wooden workbench filled with crates of meat, cheese, and pots scattered along the way. Seeing these items suddenly gives James a stomachache, causing it to rumble loudly. Ethan freezes, looking back at James, and signals him to keep quiet. James signals back with a profanity, indicating that he has no choice.

Ethan continues through the obstacles. He is so skinny that he slips through as easily as a snake, not disturbing anything in his path. While James is waiting, he hears a slight chopping sound—they are not alone. Two servants are working across the room, gossiping quietly while cutting meat and throwing it into a huge pot. The smell of stew suddenly fills James's nostrils, and his stomach rumbles again. However, his headache seems to oppose the idea, as it suddenly escalates.

Ethan approaches another door a few feet away. He reaches for a broken piece of brick from the wall and throws it at the opposite wall, where it knocks two heavy pots hanging from the wall. A loud crash follows, making James jerk his head above the bench, causing it to shake and knocking off all the items on top.

The servants scream, startled, and run to the other room, throwing utensils behind them. "Is everything okay?" A rugged old man appears, and they both quickly stand to greet him.

"Yes, Mr. Pickner," Ethan quickly says, changing his look to appear like an innocent boy. "We're just checking the noise too. Seems to be a loose nail," he says, showing the old man where the pot fell. "Looks like Maggi and Erill went into the next room to get supplies to fix it."

James feels lightheaded from the constant pain and struggles to maintain a straight face as he stares at Mr. Pickner's thick, bushy eyebrows. The area around the old man's weak eye is scarred and wrinkled, with the damaged left eye slightly off, gazing in another direction.

"You don't look good, boy." Mr. Pickner stares at James.

"I'm fine, sir. Just shaken by the noise, that's all."

"A strong boy like you, shaken by such noise; what's bothering you?"

"Nothing, sir."

Mr. Pickner sniffs deeply, spits on the floor, and wipes his mouth with his dirty shirt. Ethan jumps back with disgust.

"Well, I'll be telling Zefer we need to replace those old rusty nails. What a big racket. Right, boys?" Both Ethan and James nod in agreement.

"So, Ethan, you just appeared out of nowhere, saving the day, huh?" The smell of wine suddenly fills the air, and James turns to catch his breath. "Keeping an eye on you, boy."

"Which eye are we talking about?" Ethan says.

James kicks him, says, "Cut it out!" and pushes Ethan to proceed into the tavern.

"Yeah, sure, you're lucky James was there to save your ass!" Mr. Pickner yells back as he enters the kitchen.

James and Ethan stand in front of the large common room, which is also a tavern. Broken benches from previous fights are scattered all over and occupied by people, half of whom James already knows. Old wooden tables that can barely hold themselves up, with flasks scattered everywhere. Farmers, merchants, and many with their partners are all huddled on top of each other, mumbling and yelling. The air is thick with the smell of wine and vomit, overlapping the smell of an overly crowded tavern, especially today. James has never seen the common hall like this. It must be madness with the sudden news of the king.

"We made it!" Ethan says, smirking as he prepares for his next sinister plan.

"Good plan." James observes Ethan, not approving of his smirk and whatever intentions he has.

"I'm thirsty. Do you want a beer?" Ethan says.

"No, you go. I'll catch up with you later. I see several people talking with the mayor."

James and Ethan maneuver their way to the large serving bench where the mayor is overwhelmed with elderly people from the town. James moves closer to get a glimpse and a word or two about what's going on while Ethan provides a distraction, moving inward to order some beer.

"When do you think they'll find the princess?" asks a man with white hair wearing a huge apron covered in baking flour. It's Mr. Tyler, the town's baker.

"I don't know. I think they are searching for her," responds Mayor Zefer.

"I'm telling you, he's responsible. They're saying he's a witch or maybe a wizard, an Andord—you know," says a hoarse-voiced old man with one tooth.

"Nonsense, no wizard. It's all myth. Anyway, how can the king appoint a witch, especially an Andord?" says Mrs. Pepptrier, a woman in a high, flowing hat scattered with wilted colored flowers, setting off a pattern of unique fashion.

"It's not like Raymul could resume control when Princess Celestia is the rightful heir to her duties. Besides, the Argus family is the only one capable and bound to protect us. Raymul is not royal blood," says Mr. Tyler.

"Well, I think it…" Mrs. Pepptrier stops speaking and turns quietly to speak to the mayor. The group suddenly redirects their attention away from the mayor. The short, stumpy, overweight man, with his dark hair combed perfectly, is staring at James with an annoyed look on his face.

"What are you doing here, James? You should know better than to listen to your elders." The mayor catches James by surprise.

"Sorry, sir. It's just that I was waiting for Mr. Tyler. Eva wants to know the recipe he's using for his bread," James lies.

"Odd. Why would she want to know my recipe?" Mr. Tyler stands up at the mention of his name and walks toward James.

"I don't know…you know how she is." James shrugs his shoulders.

Looking composed, Mr. Tyler crosses his arms and traces his long mustache with a floury hand while contemplating. "That's quite complimentary coming from her. Tell her to come by later today," he says, smiling as he walks away.

Yes, sir. Will do," James responds, noticing the mayor staring at him intensely, not buying his story.

"I'm sorry for interrupting, sir," James says as he pulls away, but a short, stumpy hand gently pulls him back.

"Make sure you don't start spreading what you heard, boy. We already have enough going around here to spread more panic. Do you understand me, young man?"

"Yes, sir. My lips are tightly sealed. Oh, by the way, what's an Andord?" James asks.

"An Andord is a wizard that once roamed the land with the Guardians. It's a fairy folk story, nothing more."

James nods and begins to pull away, but he accidentally knocks down a person behind him. The huge man jumps back up, his red, gleaming eyes staring angrily at James. It's Mr. Lumer, a retired blacksmith, wiping the dust from his shirt.

"So, what do we have here?" he yells, causing the room to settle down.

"Sorry, Mr. Lumer. I wasn't paying attention," James apologizes.

The blacksmith boldly takes off his shirt and throws it on the floor, revealing a massive upper body that was built over the years working with steel. The black-smith has a reputation for placing fear in everyone that confronts him. They say during the wars, he lost his mind making unstoppable weapons for the king's guards. He grabs James by his shirt and drags him closer. Although James is well built too, he feels like a rag doll as the man hisses at him. "Don't let it happen again!"

"Oh, cut it out, Lumey," says a young woman next to him.

"Stay out of it, Roxy!"

He shoves James, and the entire tavern's attention is now on them. "Tell your mommy hello," he laughs.

Ethan suddenly appears, helping his friend, but James is already filled with anger. Insulting him is fine, but his mother is another thing! Pushing his way past Ethan, he leaps forward to the drunken man and punches his massive chest. He doesn't even budge! The men are ready for a brawl when the mayor intercepts them. "That's enough!"

The girl jumps onto the blacksmith, hugging and kissing him fiercely. "Oh, sweetie, he's nothing like you!" she says.

"Yeah, I know," he responds, rubbing his chest with a sudden surprise that it hurts. "I'll get him next time," he says, turning away with the woman as another person shoves their way into James.

James stares at his buddy Mores, who deliberately pushes Ethan out of his way. His friend looks bewildered. James's head suddenly blasts in pain, and he stumbles backward, holding his head in agony.

CHAPTER 5

Revelation

Ethan suddenly jumps up, shouting, "Rats! Mores, what's wrong with you?" The entire tavern falls silent, anticipating a fight. But instead of retaliating, Mores shoves Ethan, pushing even the mayor away when he tries to intervene. Then, with a look of anxiety, Mores grabs James and holds him tightly. Suddenly, James falls to his knees as his headache intensifies to an unbearable level, and he starts yelling.

Ethan tries to assist his best friend but is surprised to see Mores, who is only half his size, holding James. The crowd starts to gather around them, and James struggles to break free, gasping, "I don't know...my head...it's in my temples... the pain is worse...it's different...Ethan!"

In the heat of the moment, Mores effortlessly drags James toward his face, causing James's heart to race with fear. Mores is one of James's friends, usually a quiet and reclusive figure who keeps to himself. His appearance is disturbingly off, almost demonic, with a snow-white face and blood-filled eyes that send chills down one's spine. Normally reserved, Mores's sudden aggression is shocking. His gaunt features and hollow eyes suggest a malevolent force lurking within him, creating an eerie emptiness that seems to radiate from his very being. As James meets Mores's unsettling gaze, he feels an overpowering sense of dread that only intensifies the fear already gripping him. Suddenly, Mores tilts his head with a suspicious look, as if he is trying to sense something in James. In an instant, Mores lets out a piercing, shrill scream that brings the entire tavern to a sudden halt, with all eyes now fixated on the commotion.

Ethan tries to pull Mores away from James, but Mores clings to James with surprising strength. Mores then lunges at Ethan with his other hand, throwing him across the room as if he were a rag doll. The tavern erupts in chaos as the blacksmith returns and tries to intervene. He watches in amazement as James appears helpless in comparison to Mores's average height.

"Ha! Who's the fool now?" the blacksmith taunts.

"Mr. Lumer, please...help, something is not right!" James pleads.

"All right, boy, that's enough." The blacksmith yanks Mores away from James, tearing James's shirt.

As James and his bewildered friend face the blacksmith, James struggles to comprehend what has just occurred, but his headache is still spinning out of control. He feels lightheaded and starts to lose his balance. Ethan joins him, grabbing his arm to hold him up.

"Are you all right?"

"No."

Then, out of nowhere, Mores lets out a scream, but it's not a typical human scream. It sounds almost like a crow's scream, a howling animal. A long, high-pitched yell that sends shivers down everyone's spines, causing them to cover their ears in surprise.

Mores then pulls the large man toward him with both hands, with ease. He then firmly pushes his chest in the opposite direction. The blacksmith's entire upper torso snaps loudly in half. Intestines splatter, spraying blood all over the area and showering everyone with gore. His waist stands erect with the upper part of his body barely attached, twitching wildly.

Chaos erupts. A stampede of people throws themselves everywhere. The tavern typically holds hundreds of women and men, but the scene seems like a scattering of rats, scurrying in all directions, leaving the horrific display alone in the room.

Ethan tries to yank and break James out of his trance. Mores tries to lunge for them, but the area is blocked. They leap toward a mountain of fallen people and back over the servicing bar, momentarily hiding under the cabinets. They stare at each other, realizing they are bathed in blood. The scattering of people yelling increases in the room as others huddle. James can see his friend focusing and analyzing the area, watching for movements and an opportunity to present itself. On the other hand, James is dazed and shocked. His headache pulsates on the side of his temple, and he tries to digest the events that occurred.

Then strange screams erupt again, but from a different location! He senses something is coming from the tavern's entrance. Deep inside his gut, they're warning him. He now knows they're searching for him.

"Why me?" James says, panicking. His head continues to pulsate in pain, now contracted with the emotional fear that consumes him.

"What are you talking about?" Ethan asks.

"We have to go now. It's me they are looking for!"

"James, what the hell are you talking about? Mores looks sick or something, maybe possessed. Why would he be—"

James interrupts and grabs him.

"Ethan, I can't explain it. Something is very wrong with me. I just feel it! Let's get the fuck out of here. We need to get to Eva! Go!"

They scramble on top of the counter, and the long shelf along the wall holds their weight. Jugs of beer spill off the wall behind them as they run toward the kitchen door, only a few feet away. James slips and lands on top of an elderly man trying to pursue the same direction. Ethan ignores the poor fella, trying to pull James away as they finally push through the kitchen door. James quickly blocks the door with the huge shelves next to it with ease.

"Quickly, back to the office!" Ethan leads, but James quickly pulls him back. "No…you can't come! He will kill you! He's after us!"

"What are you talking about?"

"Didn't you see his eyes?"

"What are you talking about? Like I said, he just went crazy…Remember, his pops just passed away!"

"It's not him anymore, Ethan. I just know it."

The cooks scream as James scrapes on the floor, quickly reaching the back door. He can see fear in their eyes as he reaches the doorknob, unable to open the door. Frustrated, James bangs on the door.

"Someone there?"

On the other side, James hears someone unlocking the door. When it flies open, he finds Mayor Zefer, looking frightened. He grabs James and slams the door shut, leaving Ethan behind. James tries to open the door, but the mayor stops him.

"James, he'll be fine. It's you they want." Astonished, James is about to ask why when the mayor quickly places his hand over the top bookshelf by the door, mumbling a strange language. His hand starts to glow, and James backs away, frightened, not sure what is happening. A set of books disappears, and Mayor Zefer quickly retrieves a small, wrapped gray rag and thrusts it into James's hands, urging him to move quickly.

"Give this to Eva." The mayor is shaking, and James feels the moist sweat from his hand as he releases the item.

James stands transfixed, unable to comprehend what he just witnessed, when he hears the door being thrashed open. Mayor Zefer shuffles James down the cellar stairs, and when he turns to face the plump man, they only share confusion and fear. Sweat pours freely down James's face, the salty taste lingering on his lips. Suddenly he senses fear in the mayor, but oddly, he also senses death in the air. He starts to protest, but Mayor Zefer simply indicates for him to be silent; danger is near.

He can't believe what is happening now. Just a few moments ago, everything had been normal. Now the rumors of magic and witches are real, and even the mayor he has known all his life is some sort of magical being.

"What's going on?" he manages to say.

"Just get the hell out of here!" the mayor yells. "I'll hold them down!" Then he pushes James further down the stairs, and James's foot breaks through the wooden step, pinning him. At the same time, the door slams shut behind him.

James hears the mayor scream as the door crashes open from the room. "For Olen!" Flashes of light brighten the doorway where he stood, followed by the sound of liquid splattering. James feels a warm fluid drop on his left cheek from the bottom of the door. Once again, more flashes brighten above him.

Instantly, James yanks his foot from the stairs, not caring about the pain that follows. As he tumbles over the wine crates again and tosses them aside— the ones he can see in the dark wine cellar—the room suddenly becomes bright when James realizes his pursuers are at the top doorway, trying to locate him. But James has already opened the cellar's back door, running out and fumbling into the garden's maze while clutching the mysterious wrapped item.

◦➤═◉ ◉═◄◦

Back at the cottage, Radion finishes analyzing the Ra Leslar Var's prophecy. He can't count the times he has gone over this ancient book, but he can't find any additional information regarding the dead king. Frustrated, he lets the matter rest and stands from the table, walking toward the window. Hoping to relax his temper, he opens the shutter, and the inviting, cool breeze swarms into the kitchen. He thinks about how responsively the air flows in this particular home, even though Lancaster is situated in a region of dry air. Nevertheless, it is very refreshing.

Observing the beautiful landscape that Eva and James worked so hard on, he looks at the strange, ancient willow tree erected in the center, overpowering the entire background. It's an unusual spot, he thinks, when all the other trees seem to grow away from it. He remembers spying on the family and seeing James's parents spend hours in the backyard doing typical farmer routines in these parts. But what had caught his constant attention was Leeran holding her womb and praying to that willow tree. It was obvious she was attracted to Eartha, the beloved Guardian of Earth. He also observed the strange practices of the mother where she would dance wildly around the tree, which forced Sam to pull his wife back into their home. He couldn't blame James's father; such things would label his wife as a witch in this simple town. But sometimes he would see Eva convincing Sam that these practices were normal for women wishing to express themselves. It didn't make sense, but who was he to judge pregnant women?

The thought of Eva turns Radion's stomach sour. He senses her immense power and wonders why the council chose her to watch the Lander family. Radion had spent years studying the family, searching for the coming of the Destroyer. Suddenly, Eva appeared, and they worked closely together for five years. Radion questions why she was selected, and he regrets not taking the proposal to lead the council. The idea of being involved in politics turns his stomach inside out.

Radion thinks about the events that led to Eva's involvement. She claims to have studied in Kumartal, the ancient city of witches, and that her expertise was needed. Despite his numerous visits to the city, no one had ever heard of Eva. Witches are clever and stick together in common causes and studies of the Dark elements of life. Radion knows Eva possesses extraordinary sorcery abilities, similar to those of a young Andord wizard. It would take a human up to a century to master such abilities of Light elements, which rules out that theory.

Unless, of course, she studied with the elves, which is impossible. The elves do not interact with any human, except for one family belonging to the dead king. The Andord were at one time plentiful but have been dominated by elves since the time of Olen.

Suddenly, a sweet voice interrupts Radion's thoughts. "Ah…ah, daydreaming?" Eva says. "So, are you ready now?" She walks in gracefully, wearing a long, plain, gray wool dress with a light-blue knitted shawl over her shoulders. She's carrying a large, empty sack.

Radion asks, "What's taking the boy so long?" as he closes the ancient, delicate book and slips it into his robe.

"I'm not sure," Eva responds. "I suspect he's still in the town hall with Ethan, perhaps getting into trouble." She reaches for her frying pan and spice jars, packing them into the sack. Radion watches quietly, obsessing over her long, midnight-dark hair, which is neatly braided.

Radion asks, "Where are we going?"

"Just preparing," Eva says.

"Don't you think James will notice something particular going on?" Radion inquires. Eva turns around, revealing her stern yet strikingly beautiful features. "Are you challenging my judgment, or do all men enjoy undermining women's expertise? We are just as equal."

"There's nothing wrong with my question," Radion insists. "You know I need to know."

Eva steps closer to him, and he sniffs the scent of berries, making him sneeze loudly. He notices the smirk on Eva's face; she is truly a witch by nature. Radion apologizes and says, "I won't interfere, but that doesn't stop me from advising."

"Of course," Eva responds. "After all, we are scholars. I value your advice, as always."

"I know, my apologies," Radion says. "The council keeps reminding me. I just want to be sure we don't lose focus. We worked so hard, and we must protect the boy at all costs."

"Good," Eva says. "Now, on your way out, can you prepare the horses and—"

Eva freezes as the window shutter flies open, startled by the sudden rush of

Air that sweeps through the room. Gasping for breath, she quickly rushes to the window. Radion takes hold of her, sensing her unease.

Eva's sudden outburst startles Radion. "Death!" she mumbles in a low-voiced language that Radion doesn't understand. "We must find James now!"

"What's going on, Eva?" Radion asks, his confusion growing.

But Eva ignores him and rushes toward the front door, heading for her horse. Radion quickly snaps out of his confusion and follows her in the same direction. As they run, he notices the old willow tree swaying in their garden to his right, even though there is no wind. He thinks how strange the presence in the Air was, but now it's gone. Radion's unease grows as he wonders what Eva's warning could mean.

•→══◑ ◑══→•

James bursts out of the alley, stumbling over piles of garbage and feeling sweat dripping down his face. The taste of salty blood fills his mouth. He moves cautiously into the street, scanning in every direction for any signs of Mores or his pursuers. As he tries to calm his mind, he replays the sinister events in his head.

"Why would they attack me? And those bloodshot eyes Mores had, they looked demonic. They were so sinister and evil that just looking at them made my bones chill. Which only means…witches are back."

He continues to scan the area as he walks along the small shops, noticing the sound of glass crackling under his feet. The entire storefront is in ruins, with broken glass and furniture scattered everywhere.

"For the love of Earth," he mutters.

Then a raging scream echoes, and James pins himself against the wall. "Mores, they did this. None of this makes any sense." Suddenly, he thinks of Eva. She will be in danger. He feels an urgent need to get home, so he moves cautiously into the main marketplace. The smell of rotten meat hangs in the air, and many of the tents are ripped apart, as if a stampede had run through. James lies low near a tent, observing the chaos and trying not to attract any attention. The entire tent is destroyed, as well as the surrounding area. A sadness washes over him as he thinks about all the hardworking people who will now have to work twice as hard. He wipes his face with his left hand, the other hand still clutching the mayor's item. He notices that his hand is severely cut, and the cloth is soaked with blood. Ignoring the throbbing pain, he continues moving forward. Suddenly, someone grabs his shoulder, and he swings around in anger to confront his enemy.

"Wait! It's me!" Ethan hovers over him, eyes wide and ready for an impact. James loses his balance and falls.

"I could have knocked you out! What are you doing here? Go home!"

"Just follow me, okay?" Ethan reveals an unexpressive face and a swollen left eye that looks like an oversize plum. James follows him to a tent at the far edge of the market, where vegetables are laid out neatly on a wooden table. He knows this table belongs to the Rema family. They enter the tent, finding it untouched, and take cover, trying to conceal themselves in the back, where boxes of unopened items are stored.

"What now?" James asks.

"There are others like Mores."

"No kidding," James replies sarcastically.

"When I was finally able to leave the building, I noticed unusual activities. I saw Bob and Tammy talking with Mores, and then they ran off together. Can you believe that I thought they hated each other?"

James looks away, concerned.

"It seems like something is possessing our people," James says.

Ethan is taken by surprise. "What do you mean? There haven't been any witches in these parts for years."

"I don't know, I just feel it. I can't explain it; it doesn't make sense. Do you know that Mores killed the mayor?"

Ethan opens his eyes wide in surprise. James can see his long face, now scared. For the first time, he looks frightened. His friend is tough on his own terms, but this time he's shattered.

"Ethan, listen to me: go home and stay there until this is sorted out."

"No way, buddy; besides, no one is home. Mande is out visiting her sister, and she won't be back for a few weeks."

Mande is Ethan's aunt, his only living relative. James often hears stories from his friends about how she is ruthless and doesn't care about anyone, especially her own nephew.

"Okay, go now. Check to make sure Abela is safe, then head home quickly to Eva and stay with her until I get there. I'm not sure why they are looking for me, but I don't want to put anyone in danger," James says, worried about his friend's safety. "I'll try to divert them...You got it?"

Ethan is about to protest, but James shuffles him out of the tent. He feels a twinge of regret for pushing him, but he knows how stubborn his friend can be.

"Okay, let's move," James says, feeling anxious about luring his pursuers away from his loved ones. He runs in the opposite direction, leaving his now confused friend behind.

CHAPTER 6

Reborn

JAMES FINALLY REACHES Miser Forest without being followed. The smell of pine and moisture from the wet ground enchants him and soothes his nerves. He constantly looks back to make sure he isn't being followed and tries to keep pace as the forest grows more intense. After a few moments, he finally calms down and tries to catch his breath while he rethinks his next move.

Suddenly, he realizes that something is terribly off. He has walked these woods numerous times, but today is different. Then it occurs to him, as he slows to a stop and looks around suspiciously, that everything in the forest is completely quiet. Not even the singing of birds or the rustling of animals is heard. Even the trees seem to stand still, not letting the autumn leaves fall from their stems.

He starts to panic and runs again. His instinct tells him that something is distracting the forest's existence and that the forest seems to take notice. He's not sure why, but he can sense that the forest is afraid, perhaps waiting for whatever lurks to pass.

From a far distance, a comforting sound alerts him: the stream of the Miser River. It is the only natural thing that seems normal, so he runs toward it. He thinks of Eva, his only family member, and the danger she may be in. The urgency to get away and protect her is inevitable, so James presses on faster.

Finally he stops at the edge of the river. James holds his head tightly as the headache returns with a vengeance, pounding hard. The excruciating pain becomes so unbearable that he gasps for air, feeling nauseous.

From the corner of his eye, just a few feet away, he sees leaves swirl, and slowly, a distorted figure emerges. The area suddenly becomes foggy and dark.

James's knees buckle as the figure alters its shape into a dark, ghostly individual, revealing only its bloodshot eyes that resemble Mores's!

He tries to focus, but the escalating pain from his headaches makes it impossible to wipe the tears from his eyes. The sensation is a piercing force, as if it's trying to break out of his skull. The ghastly, transparent figure starts to shape a mouth and emits a piercing scream before quickly moving toward James.

"Noooooo!" James screams as the creature merges with him.

He feels a cold sensation throughout his body, like a chilling breeze that makes all his hair stand on end. Shaking violently, James feels an alien entity trying to break into his head. He falls to the ground, rolling from side to side in pain, trying to shake off the powerful being taking over his body. He knows this thing is trying to possess him, and he tries with all his strength to resist, screaming and pulling his own hair, not knowing what to do.

Suddenly, a new feeling springs to life: a tingling sensation creeps up his spine, making his bones shrivel, while the other Evil controls his will. Every bone seems to crumple, and his heart pounds so fast that it feels like it will explode. Something deep inside James awakens. A burning sensation now fills him, and he can't explain it, but this fire feels good, so he seeks more of it. The new Entity now embraces the demonic invader inside him.

He continues to embrace with hope that this wild entity will aid him when suddenly something becomes alive in him. Grabbing his chest, he is sure it isn't the demon; it feels worse. A sleeping giant finally awakens from deep inside. He holds it tight as the magical entity takes him over, targeting the shadowed dark magic.

As the shadow's essence attempts to take over James's body, a sense of wrongness pervades. James feels the essence striving to escape and tear away from him. He stands his ground, crouching as sweat pours down his face, feeling every ordeal within. With determination, he pushes the demonic shadow out of his body. Now, as the shadow rips away from him, it emits a scream of agony. James watches as it tears into shreds, continuing its escape.

A fire inside him wants to destroy the thing escaping from his body, trying to consume his soul. They both fall, tumbling, and the fire consumes them both as the demon creature turns to ashes, leaving James untouched.

As he lies down, not moving, the sweet taste of sweat and dirt enters his mouth. He pants wildly and stares at the clouds, bewildered at what just happened. The headache is completely gone, but he feels weak and hot and can't move. Something is quite different. He feels something alive in him, something he knows will change him forever.

As he tries to get up, feeling dizzy, someone grabs him.

"What?!" James manages to say, falling back as someone immediately grabs him to steady him.

"Hold on, boy," the person says.

James looks up and sees a familiar, wrinkled face.

"Radion! You can't…you have to go…they want me," he says weakly.

"Take it easy, boy," Radion says as he carries James away from the river.

James can hardly believe the old man's strength, but something else catches his attention. He can barely make them out, but he's sure of it: three individuals are watching them intently from a distance away.

"Radion, you must get away, they—" James gasps and vomits.

"Shhhh, you're sick. You need your strength. I saw what you did," Radion says.

Just then, they hear the sound of galloping hooves coming toward them. Eva appears on a black stallion, with another horse following closely behind. She dismounts and runs toward them. James's head starts to spin, and darkness overtakes him.

"Radion, stop them before they alert the others!" Eva says, kneeling beside James and stroking his head.

Radion leaps into action, heading toward the three strangers in the distance.

Eva waits, scanning the area to make sure no one else is nearby, as James regains consciousness and mumbles in pain.

"Eva…what are you doing here?" he asks.

"Dear, please don't speak. You're very weak. I'm here to take you home," she says.

"But…"

"Shhhh, rest," she whispers softly, gently placing her hands over his eyes, and soon he succumbs to sleep.

As she tends to him, she notices a rag in James's hand. Retrieving it, she finds a small, handcrafted stone relic engraved with the symbol of a wave, symbolizing the domain of Water. Such relics are rare; the only person she knows who could possess this is the mayor, who works closely with her. The relic is a protection spell used to discreetly cover their tracks, a valuable tool indeed. She carefully tucks it into her robe, knowing its usefulness may be crucial in the days to come.

Eva calls out to Onyx, and the horse responds instantly. She uses her magic to help James onto the horse, checking the area again to make sure no one is watching, and they quickly ride away.

⋆⟫═◉═⟪⋆

"I can't believe this...What are the Shadowlen doing here?" Radion says as he runs, dodging through an obstacle course of rocks and mud. James's friends are the ideal target, close to him and weak-minded, he thinks. It's unmistakable that his friends are being consumed by these deadly creatures. It's been a while since he last saw the Shadowlen. He notices they are running back into town. He must get to them before they get there! He runs as fast as he can, recalling how the Hawthorne sisters from the in-between realm assisted in disposing of the last of these sinister creatures more than twenty-five years ago.

He was a youngster then, only forty years of age when his Guide sent him to the witches' homeland. While he was there, the prophecy never provided any clues about these lost soul creatures or the reason for their return to the living land. He studied them from other sources that the witches kept hidden in one of their vaults. The creatures infuse themselves into their victim, consuming their entire soul until the victim rots. Once the victim is lifeless, they quickly find another suitable person before their own soul dissipates.

He realizes he has caught the attention of one Shadowlen, and it slows as it enters the heavily concealed path beyond the high grass. Radion slows down too, watching carefully not to be led into a trap. He senses a deep emptiness in his heart, a clear sign that they are near. He exits into a vast, open area that seems to be used as a resting place for travelers who once passed through this forest. Several circular stones clearly show that once, firepits and ashes kept travelers warm. It's clear to him that a battle is about to begin.

Radion quickly moves to the center, readying himself and watching all angles intensely. He knows they are watching behind the thick trees, and he can feel the area is dead silent, with not even an animal in sight. He thinks slightly about how James ripped the demon out of his soul, burning it with some unknown magic, and it was astonishing! He couldn't recall anything in history with that magnitude of power, the ability to destroy a magic substance of the element of death. Only witches known to study the elements of darkness can forcefully remove a Shadowlen, but not destroy them! Even with that success, the victim will never be the same. The Shadowlen should have killed James, but it seems the creatures now have someone to fear.

The battle that he thought he would never see again begins. The three Shadowlen stand in a triangle formation, at least twenty feet away from each other, seemingly wanting to ensure they have the upper hand. They speak in unusual gestures that worry him. It appears that a lot has changed since he last confronted these evil beings. A sense of sadness overwhelms him as he stares at the individuals before him—friends of James, who are now doomed to have their souls consumed and never see hope again. He has known these kids since they were young, good-hearted people building lives of love and hope. The range of mixed emotions he feels suddenly saddens him deeply.

"They don't deserve this!" he screams.

The first attacker, Bobby, the baker's son, a once-smart youngster, leaps with a screech that frightens him. He lashes at Radion's cloak as he smoothly swings in the opposite direction, displaying the Shadowlen's clever abilities. Instantly, Radion sends a flash of wind, aiding himself and pushing the creature further away. The second boy, Mores, is nearly on top of him, smashing into his chest, taking the air out of him as he gasps. Rolling quickly on the ground, he anticipates the third Shadowlen to come, but he can't find her.

Their fighting techniques have improved, like prowler cats, he thinks. But Radion is one step ahead when leaping toward Mores. He summons the magic of fire, conjuring a blazing whip that moves swiftly at his command. Tricking his opponent, he slashes Mores instead. The top half of his body splits into two halves. Flames consume the poor boy, and he scrabbles with pain. No one can withstand this sinister whip. It can only be summoned by Radion, finished by a powerful being, and is a truly precious gift from the royal boy Jarin Argus himself, the nephew of the late King Argus.

Ashes fill the air. Now the girl, named Dema, screams in anguished pain.

She appears to be from the Lomter family as she swiftly extracts blades seemingly out of thin air. Radion recalls from his past readings about these blades from the dark realms that the pain they inflict is unbearable. The taste of the darkness of these elements is unpredictable. The intensity of the pain from the blades drives the victim to the brink of madness, where death seems a preferable release. Rather than resorting to his usual recourse of casting a spell—a practice in which he's adept—Radion instinctively calls upon the protective power of Water from the nearby river. It's a maneuver that he hopes will lend him some relief. This skill demands every ounce of his strength; he isn't inherently magical by birth, but through diligent study, he has learned to harness the spells of both Air and Water and possesses a basic understanding that a skilled human wizard can attain only through relentless study and practice.

Surprisingly, the power of Water responds, spinning wildly yet in control as it hardens a barrier between him and the coming blades. On impact, the unexpected occurs. The blockage rushes toward Dema, consuming her by entering her nostrils, and she explodes into pieces. The water swallows the flying flesh and blood, appearing as a tentacle that snakes through the air, preventing the region from being painted with blood.

Radion stares in amazement. *How could that be?* He looks around, dumbfounded, to see if he is being aided by someone, an elf perhaps. *No one*, he thinks and senses. Now the last Shadowlen, Bobby, stands before him, which, according to the laws of dark elements, is the last, strongest link of the three. Radion must be extra careful. When these demons come in groups, the last one to exist contains power that prowls for a limited time to freely seek its next victim and can summon more of its kind. The boy screeches so loud it rattles Radion's spine, and he takes off in another direction. He heads back to town, perhaps looking for a stronger victim. A simple, weak-minded person can suffice its needs!

Radion races, trying to gain momentum to stop the creature, but he is so weak after calling forth Water. He stops, trying to think fast, and the only thing that comes to his mind is terrible, but at this point, he has no other option. He slaps his hands together, rubbing them hard and concentrating on the wild magical element in the vicinity, Air, which he has no right to control. The spell calls forth a long electric rod, which illuminates before him. A creation of Air acts well with the power of fire, which, as he just learned from his Guide, he shouldn't use unless in dire need. He throws it toward the running Shadowlen. "Forgive me, Eartha!" he yells in great sorrow.

The electrical rod expands into a large, uncontrollable, reptile-like mass, not what he was expecting, as it destroys everything in its way. Massive old trees come down instantly with its touch as the magic cuts cleanly through the bark. The rod finally reaches the Shadowlen and destroys the boy instantly upon contact. Body parts scatter as it explodes in the air, a bath of blood splattering in all areas. With that, the fire element consumes the area, leaving it practically in ashes. A heartfelt sadness aches in Radion. Again, a powerful gift, taught by none other than Argus in one of his visits to their hidden compound. Jarin, he is called, human and royal-blooded, with magic-attribute-born abilities, only among his royal family, which he can easily control.

He feels dizzy all of a sudden, aware of being exposed and exhausted from electroshock. The Shadowlen hovers where the boy once stood, its dark, shadowy figure very distraught, and out of formality moves toward him. Radion's heart sinks down to his stomach; he knows what's going to happen. Because of his weakness, it is preparing to consume him in mind and body. He quickly concentrates, reaching deep within himself, feeling the inner pit, and calls forth, with the last of his strength, a Shanter spell. This barrier protection of the Water element can be used against the Shadowlen's attempt. He only needs to hold on until the dead demon can relinquish itself and go back to the sinister realm of death.

Radion slowly opens his eyes to find a shapeless, demonic, ghostly thing with red eyes up against his face, trying hard to penetrate his magic. Its breath smells of mold, and it sends an icy cold feeling to break his concentration. The creature pulls away, howling in disappointment, as its time is up, and the ground where it stands suddenly opens. A swirly black cloud appears as the Shadowlen disappears into the dark realm.

Exhausted, Radion looks out at the forest in shock, realizing that everything around him has disintegrated, and dark smoke from the burnt grass hovers in the air. He had no choice but to use this powerful magic, but he knows the Miser Forest is ancient, and it will adapt quickly with the aid of the elements of light.

His eyelids feel sticky, and he blinks slowly, bringing his hands to his chest to feel his heart pulsating rapidly. He takes a quick look at his surroundings and finds a clear path to Eva.

CHAPTER 7

Mystery

EVA SUMMONS THE Inferior, an Air magic that swiftly moves the caster from below, but it isn't going as fast as she wanted. She continues to look behind her, but no one is pursuing them. James is securely tied to Onyx as they continue to pick up speed. His face is covered in blood and sweat, and she can sense death nearing.

"I'm sure you would love that, Your Grace of Darkness," she says sarcastically. She lets it pass out of respect. The Guardian of Death would welcome her thoughts, as she would like her impassive thoughts to lead into the dark elements the Guardians so eagerly need.

She presses her hand on his hand, trying to calm the heat, but the fever is so intense. *So, it was the Shadowlen,* she thinks. The prophecy referred to these dark creatures; they needed to confirm James as the born Destroyer, and they needed to consume his soul to do so. But they didn't suspect James was the direct heir to Olen, the only one who can destroy them.

She's close. The magic quickly slows as Onyx descends to the ground, which is only a few inches from her hovering position. Finally the magic disperses, and horse hooves touch the ground with a hovering sound of wind as the dirt lifts in the air. As her eyes adjust, she finds Ethan standing before them with his mouth open.

Eva quickly dismounts Onyx.

"Ethan, I'm glad you're here. Help me untie him and bring him to his bedroom quickly!"

Ethan, still with his mouth open, shakes his head in shock at what he just witnessed.

"How did you—"

"Are you going to stand there?" she interrupts while untying the ropes on James's hands. "Or are you going to help your friend? He's dying!"

Ethan quickly helps Eva, and they both remove the ropes and dismount James from Onyx. Eva can feel the heat from James's body as she rushes toward the back door of the house.

In front of James's room, Eva suddenly halts and quickly takes out an item that resembles a long fingernail with a black feather covering it, then places it on top of the door.

Ethan gasps.

"A witch's trick of some sort," he says, panicking. *Only a true witch would carry such a sinister-looking thing*, he thinks as he struggles not to let go of James's feet.

Eva sees his distress.

"It's only for luck, Ethan. I've obtained many objects on many journeys, which I don't have time to explain right now. Quickly!"

Eva gives Ethan instructions as they lay James on the bed, and he quickly exits. She starts clearing the room, as hand-painted crafts and collections of outside junk overcrowd the floor from wall to wall. James seems to have every-thing from various nails, pins, and rocks to assorted wood. He is known as the town junk collector and an excellent carpenter, which he quickly practices. She looks over to James while he lies still, realizing that the room is cramped with his belongings.

Suddenly, Ethan reappears, holding towels and checking James's progress. The room is slightly lit by the lamp on the small, dark, scratched wood table. "Now," Eva says, "stay with him and take off his clothes, all of them. He must be completely bare. I will be right back." She quickly exits.

"James, are you okay?" Ethan asks.

"Ummmm," James replies as he twists and turns, sweat pouring down his face.

Ethan removes James's clothes and throws them on top of a pile of leathery books next to his bed. Another of James's obsessions is his love for reading. Ethan never comes into James's room, except for that one time he snuck to his back window, attempting to wake his friend to help him with a prank. But Eva was already beside the window and asked what he was doing there. He always wondered how she got there first. He was very careful and planned well. Now it makes sense. She is a witch…that can make horses fly!

Eva returns with a steaming pot. "Take the tea, lift his head, and slowly pour it into his mouth—it's very hot, and I don't want you to burn his throat," she says, shoving the hot pot into Ethan's hands. Holding the smelly pot with his other hand, he then realizes something. *That was quick*, he thinks to himself, amazed at how Eva managed to prepare a steaming pot of tea so quickly.

"Why did the room need to be picked up?" he asks.

"You seem so distracted; besides, it desperately needed to be. I don't like to leave unkept rooms," Eva replies.

Ethan frowns.

Eva lifts her dress and positions herself on top of James's lower body, leaving her left leg over the bed. Ethan gasps, as it is unheard of for an unmarried woman to sit on top of a naked man. She ignores Ethan's reaction, as it is necessary to call forth the spell that requires both bodies to be exposed in some manner. Eva extracts a small jar from her dress and begins applying a green ointment on James's body, using a towel to spread it thoroughly with all her weight. She quickly rubs it all over his upper body and slows down as she reaches his legs, avoiding his lower abdomen. The entire body needs to be covered; it's the only way to consume the magic that's burning inside him, she keeps reminding herself. Eva then applies the ointment on herself, momentarily distracted by James's masculine body. She last saw him naked when he was only six years old, and obviously he is not the same now. She continues to concentrate, reciting the ritual so the fever can find its way into her. Just several moments, and it will be done.

Meanwhile, Ethan finishes pouring the liquid into James's mouth, observing the strange ritual with nervousness. He concludes from the way it smells that it must be some sort of medicine. As he puts the pot down on the floor, he notices that Eva's lower body is covered in the same green substance as James's. He is convinced that a witch is living among them. To top it off, she is beautiful. He knows his best friend is doomed, perhaps placed under some sort of spell. *He is going to die*, Ethan thinks, based on what he just witnessed.

"Now, please take it back to the kitchen and get another bowl of fresh water," Eva says, realizing Ethan is too distracted and confused.

Eva finally finishes and stands next to James, sweating. She senses that the fever is leaving him. Ethan takes the pot and looks back at Eva's peculiar treatment before slowly exiting the room.

"James, can you hear me?" Eva whispers softly, sweat dripping down onto her dress.

"Evaaaa," James replies.

"Shhh, the fever is breaking, just rest."

Slowly, Eva kneels next to James and carefully removes the green substance from his body. She can see every scrape, bruise, and gash on James's naked body. His muscular chest reveals the most substantial cuts, which she goes over a few times to clean the wounds.

Finally Eva finishes, regains her posture, and walks toward Ethan, who is itching to run. She must look terrible; the fever is already escalating, but she can handle it. The young, cunning boy smiles at her; anyone else witnessing what just happened would have run away in fear, but not Ethan. He stares intensely at her, ready for anything, and one hand is poised to release a hidden knife. He always seems to be in the wrong place but at the right time. Eva never understood why he was so attached to James, given how different they are. While James is responsible, Ethan tends to get into trouble with authority. Yet, she senses a great loyalty and trust in him, as always. She never questions fate, and it seems that fate is at work here.

"Ethan, can you cover him with the blanket in his closet? Watch for any signs of discomfort and let me know. I'll be in the kitchen," Eva says.

They both turn when they hear the front door shut.

"Eva!" a distressed man yells.

"I'll be right there, Radion," Eva says, feeling rushed, then turns to face Ethan. He is bruised up and has a black eye and dirt all over his face, making his nose more noticeable. "I love him...as a son, nothing more. And no, I'm not a witch. Besides, that's an ugly stereotype word for someone who simply studies the dark elements, which are equal to the light in their own way."

Ethan is confused by her reply. He never told her what he thought. His heart starts pulsating faster as he asks, "So what are you?"

Eva simply turns and stares at James. Ethan could have sworn he saw a tear running down her face, but he isn't sure, because she seems to be burning up with a fever, just like James had been.

Exhaling, Eva gives Ethan a stern look. "Who do you think I am? I'm the same person you've always known for all these years, Ethan. I've always been family."

Ethan doesn't know what to say, so he stays silent. Eva continues. "If I were you, I'd clean myself up. You're beginning to stink up the room. What were you kids doing out in the woods anyway? Don't forget to cover him," she says before leaving the room.

⊸═◦═◦⊷

"Where's the boy?" Radion asks as Eva enters the kitchen.

"He's fine. He's resting in his room," she replies.

"We have to go, Eva!"

"I know. Just give James some time to recuperate. I gave him some Lyle herbs that should help."

Eva moves to the sink and begins to wash herself with fresh water. The fever is already escaping her.

"So, what are we going to do?" Radion asks, looking out the window for any danger.

"As soon as the fever lifts, and hopefully by morning, we'll set out for Ander Plains for shelter." Eva pats her face with a towel.

"Eva, they might be here before that. You know the news will have spread by then, and every Council guard will have arrived. Besides, the Shadowlen already know, which means we'll have unfriendly visitors in no time."

"Did you stop the ones we encountered?" she asks.

"Yes," he says reluctantly, recounting the close encounter with one of the lords of the lost souls, who led a pack of followers from the powerful realm of the Guardian of Death in pursuit of James.

She notices his change in tone and asks, "Are you okay?"

"Yes, yes," he says, moving his head away and looking out the other window to check his lookout. "Now listen to me, Eva. A lot has happened in such a short time. I didn't have time to prepare. The boy is suffering, and he doesn't realize how much is at stake. For the love of Earth, he is the Destroyer. Do you know what this means? Everyone will be looking for him. He is our final hope!"

Eva stares at Radion for a few moments. His gray hair seems to be stretching out more, and his wrinkles carry more layers of dirt than before.

"Pull yourself together, Radion. We are responsible for him. I need you to stay out until morning. We must stay within my barriers for protection and let the town settle down before we make our next move. You know everyone will be spreading rumors and looking for any signs of strange behavior. We usually have a good reputation. I will be ready then. Make sure no one wanders near the house. I don't care how you do it, just keep them away. If the Shadowlen wander by, I will know it. You're right. The time is finally here."

"All right, you don't have to treat me like a boy!" Radion says.

"Well, you seem to act like one," Eva replies.

"I will go, but I think we should make a detour to the dwarf realm. We need warriors, and they will help as they once did. We need to cover our tracks too," Radion says.

"No need to worry about tracking, I have a relic that will help," she says.

Radion is about to say something but closes his mouth.

Eva raises an eyebrow and turns to the back door. It's already getting dark, and she knows it's the perfect time to do what she needs to do. She grabs her sack and heads toward her garden. Immediately she walks toward the ancient oak tree.

As she enters the backyard, she waits until she feels Radion isn't watching and places her hand on the rough bark. Her hand sinks into the deep ridges. It seems so small and weightless compared to the power of this tree. She looks up at the ancient tree, taking in its grace and might. Underneath its branches, it feels like it's cradling her to give them privacy and keep anyone from looking at them.

"The time is now, my beloved messenger. Thank you for all that you have done and for helping this family find your settlement. My heart aches now for what I am about to do. I must relieve your ties and protection tomorrow. Please do not take this as your final purpose. Continue to thrive and take hold of what you see fit. One day the Leeran family will return to these parts, I promise you. Now goodbye, my beloved, and send my message."

She releases her hand, and the tree rumbles slightly beneath her foot, almost as if it's showing respect to the person it's talking to. The tree sends her a unique blessing. The feeling is soothing, accepting, understanding, like the elements of air she felt this morning. Slowly and gracefully, leaves start to fall lightly on her face and the perimeter. Not too many, but enough to know that she is also aching and crying for her family's departure. She feels the connection, as always. This ancient connection she knows, feeling a heaviness in her heart. Eva turns away sadly, knowing the new purpose that is laid in front of her. The past she was comfortable with is no more, replaced by an unknown future. She walks toward her small garden, where she needs to extract important herbs and remove others permanently with her magic.

CHAPTER 8

Obsession

IN THE FAR western land from Lepersteed, in a kingdom called Selcarth, the high advisor holds firmly onto the fireplace mantel with one hand, leaning heavily on the stone ledge. He tastes the sweet sweat flowing from his head. The sensation of touching the sinister, leafless plant that sits alone on the mantel with his other hand fills him with a strange pleasure. Planted in its own pot, its jet-black branches, sharp enough to prick, dangle freely above the old fireplace. The vibes from the small, lifeless tree flow through him, taunting him with the allure of forbidden knowledge. It's an unexplainable feeling that he finds addictive. The tingling runs up his spine as he softly rubs the branch's black bark. Though it appears dead, the gauntly living thing was acquired from the dark realm and is a rare plant that's held strong in his family for generations. It's the only connection he has to the forbidden entities of the dark elements.

Reluctantly he releases the mantel, feeling a sense of regret. He has an insatiable thirst for knowledge and power, and the greed to seek them out is all-consuming. The dark elements are known to seek out their master and offer their magic to anyone who is willing to learn. Raymul is one such individual, born into a family that accepts the dark elements over the light. As a result, many of them have become powerful sorcerers. He may be an Andord, but he's a special one— a Darken Andord—known to many.

As he walks around his royal bedroom, observing the grand architecture and many rich relics, he can't help but feel content with his life. He is one of the richest and most influential people in the land, second only to the king.

Thinking of the king, he smiles to himself and laughs quietly, his gaze now fixed on the elegant yet sinister plant. The king is an overly protective ruler who values the land and its people above all else, especially his legendary, pathetic family. But that's all about to change. The tree has taught him a clever plot, and the king is dying as they speak. His family's healers are making useless efforts to save him. The tree has given Raymul a way to get what he wants.

He had accepted the task many years ago when he was still learning to become a Tomentor, an elfish term for "Givers of the Elements." The dark tree had insisted on it. For years, he carried out its bidding, but now he couldn't remember the original reason why. With new tasks mixed with old ones, nothing seemed to make sense, leading to the downfall of the once-powerful magic dueler in the realm.

Pacing around his bedroom, he debates whether or not to touch the dark plant again. His hand shakes and aches with desire, like a drug he can't let go. But he needs to regain control. Reluctantly he sits on the corner of the bed, sinking softly into the plush feathers carefully woven by the castle's seamstress. The candles around the room softly glitter, inviting him to take a nap. However, he can't stop glancing at the dark plant, which is so inviting. Its roots have grown out of the golden pot, as if the tree is searching for something but not daring to touch anything other than itself.

He asks if he can plant its roots outside the garden, hidden from the others. The tree screams and insists that it belongs to him only. He lies down, sinking softly into the plush bed. He stares at the mosaic painting before him, depicting the sea flowing swiftly into an enchanted open cavern beach, a landscape he has never seen before. The breeze is visible in the sky, integrating with the sun's fire, blazing upon the colorful landscape. This tapestry signifies the powerful elements of life. The castle contains thousands of such illustrations, along with the royal Argus family portraits. Interestingly, he hasn't come across any that represent the dark elements, which are an essential balance between the two essences.

As he closes his eyes to relax, his mind wanders. Studying the elements is not an easy task, except for the fact that the dark elements tend to reveal themselves easily to those eager to learn. Humans have adopted many attributes from the dark elements due to this, but many assume that dark elements refer to evil and witchcraft, which is quite wrong. This makes them a foolish race. However, the king and his Argus family legacy, the only human family born into magic rather than learning it, have ruled over humans for centuries by interweaving their bloodline to keep their magic pure. An Argus seems to acquire one special dark or light element and can quickly learn any magical elements of light and dark in a short period of time.

The royal Argus family commands great respect in the region, but not from all. The elves hold a deep hatred toward them, despite the Argus family's similar magical traits since birth, which were previously thought to be unique to elves. The reason behind this animosity is unknown, and it has been this way for a long time. In the past, before the time of the Destroyer, elves shared their knowledge of elemental forces with all races, including humans. However, mastering the elements of light took years due to their complex nature, unlike the dark elements, which could be acquired quickly. Due to their shorter lifespans, humans could not master the light elements as fully as the elves, and they became more drawn toward the dark elements. This may be why the Arguses, who can adapt to both, are so powerful and dominant. They are also born into magic and have a longer lifespan than the average human.

Eventually the elven nation, Umta, which is now the largest known elven community in the north, distanced itself from human magic wielders known as Andord, who were too eager to master the dark elements. The Andord then formed their own cult, which was eventually considered witchcraft by most races, and they settled in what is now called Witch Mountain. However, the Argus clan never intervened and remained immune to these historical events, continuing their ritual of bloodline and rule.

In the post-Destroyer era, Kumartal has emerged as the City of the Witches, or as they refer to it, Witch Mountain. It has thrived as a hub for individuals of all races seeking to learn, apprentice, and master the arts of the dark elements. The dark elements are essential components of life and are governed by the Guardians. Despite the struggles and wars of many years past, Kumartal has established various schools and academies dedicated to educating those who wish to understand and harness the power of the dark elements. However, the elements of light are not practiced there, as the teachings of those elements were lost to the passing years and are not readily accessible to humans, only to a select few elves and dwarves. Of course, the Argus clan is an exception to that rule. It's said that elves are the only race known to have exiled themselves. Since the time of the Destroyer, no elves have been seen, but interestingly, it's been rumored that they have been sighted in some human towns, accompanied by Argus. Moreover, some Argus youngsters are training in Kumartal, studying but highly protected by the headmasters. The Arguses never leave their home-land, especially—Raymul is sure—Princess Celestia. Something is brewing, and Raymul can feel it in his bones.

Feeling restless, Raymul removes himself. He can feel the tree pressing on his back, seeking his eagerness.

"Not yet," he tells the demonic-looking thing.

He knows that if he continues his transition with the elements of death, it could trigger the element of Earth. The Guardian will be aware of the intrusion into life.

He sighs. So much planning needs to be done. She says the Destroyer, the incarnation of Olen, will soon be among us, and time is of the essence.

"I'll be back, my sweet," he says, now looking at the shining stem as it hangs loosely from the handcrafted, ancient pot. "You know I need you; the time will come when all will be revealed, and we shall be one." He smirks as he enters the lounge, closing the heavy door behind him.

His lounge is far from being as elegant as the king's chambers, which are now overcrowded with flowers, presuming his death. As he pours himself a glass of wine, he feels completely satisfied that King Argus is out of the way and will soon be dead. The only thing left is to get his daughter to cooperate, and then everything will be set in motion. They will rule the realm together. She promised that all would bow to him in the kingdom of Selcarth.

"Sir!" a rusty voice interrupts his thoughts, and a six-foot soldier abruptly enters the room.

"Yes, Pennaldo," Raymul responds calmly.

The tension in the air is palpable, as they both despise each other. As the rightful protector of Princess Celestia, Pennaldo must now answer to Raymul as the head of state until the heir takes over in her father's absence. Raymul enjoys the moment, waiting for Pennaldo's response with a smirk on his face.

"Forgive me," Pennaldo says. "The beloved king is still sick, and the gracious queen has not yet returned."

"Commander," Raymul quickly interrupts, ignoring Pennaldo's response. "Have you found Princess Celestia?"

"No, sir...Your Grace," Pennaldo replies. "My scouts are searching. My princess is still missing. But I'll find her; I always do."

"Do you always have to be so dramatic? It was your doing that she slipped out."

"She is gifted; they all are. But I'm her protector, and I can sense that she is okay."

"I'm sure she doesn't need protection, Commander," Raymul retorts.

It's strange how he can sense her well-being. The entire family is peculiar, and this connection between the princess and the most powerful head commander is something he can't quite put his finger on. It must be some hidden magic that the family possesses.

Raymul walks confidently toward the burly man, showing no fear as he approaches. Despite the significant size difference between the two, Raymul places his finger firmly on Pennaldo's chain mail.

"Then I expect you to find your beloved princess soon, or it will be your responsibility. Do you understand?" Raymul stares intently into Pennaldo's piercing blue eyes, and a brief moment of tension passes as their gazes lock. Pennaldo's thick eyebrows furrow, and the veins on his massive neck pulse heavily behind his long, wild hair. He is fully armored and a broad man, though not very tall.

Finally, Pennaldo breaks the stare and turns to exit the room, leaving Raymul to relish the pleasure of treating him like a fool. But before he reaches the large oak doors, Raymul calls the commander back.

"Go find Mr. Eila and tell him to meet me in my chambers at once, Commander. He can be found at the corner of Mistwood Lane, where he typically purchases daily fruits for the princess."

Pennaldo scoffs at the mention of Eila. "Are you referring to the witch?"

"I would be careful saying that to him," Raymul warns. "And yes, he does come from the ancient city of Kumartal, but they are scholars of magic. You should know that, Commander!"

"Of course, Your Grace," Pennaldo says, showing some respect as he exits the room. Left alone to continue his scheming, Raymul plots his next move to solidify his hold on the kingdom.

The sun finally dips below the horizon, and the shimmering light reflects on Muran Lake, which separates the castle from the bustling city. Suddenly, a gentle knock interrupts Raymul's fascination with the tree, and he quickly wipes the sweat off his face before leaving the window and pushing back his long, black hair. He heads toward the receiving lounge, and the light knocking continues.

"Yes?" he says.

"Are you looking for me, Your Grace?" asks a middle-aged man as he enters the room. He wears a slightly plush, well-groomed long cloak and is lightly tanned from being outside. His eyes are oval and dark, and his fingernails are painted beige. His balding head is adorned with a red headband that matches some of his garments, and he wears a necklace with an upside-down golden triangle, each point representing the Guardians of Death, Ice, and Void. The circle in the middle represents the Guardian of Fire, which connects them all, with distinct lines coming out to each point of the triangle. He performs a theatrical presentation that most sorcerers like to do to simulate some of the arts they study in the city of Kumartal.

"Yes, Eila, please come in," Raymul says as Eila enters the living area. "I need you to go into the bedroom and clean it up; it's absolutely filthy," he finally says.

Eila's eyes widen in surprise, and he responds, "Typically, cleaning isn't my duty. I usually prepare the fruits for the princess and our king." He looks around the room and notices the strange black plant sitting on the mantel. He is puzzled. Its roots are overgrown, and he feels uneasy. Why would Raymul place this unusual plant in his room?

"What is this plant?" Eila asks in concern as he feels a slight intensity from it.

"That's why I asked you to go clean up my room. I purchased that plant a few weeks ago. It seems strange, and it's overgrowing onto the mantle. Can you remove it? You are the expert in the arts," Raymul explains.

"I am not familiar with the Earth elements, but I have to say, this doesn't seem to fit the capital of the element of light. Let me see if I can remove it," Eila says.

Eila bows respectfully to Raymul and enters the room, approaching the bare, black tree to take a closer look. He raises his hand and a white, shimmering glow manifests as he attempts to analyze its origins.

Raymul patiently waits until he hears a blood-curdling scream. He rushes into the bedroom and finds Eila staring at the Sintra plant, its branches oozing with blood.

"My, my, Eila. It seems you couldn't resist the plant's beauty," he remarks, gently moving Eila's hand away from it. As Raymul looks at Eila, he notices the veins in his arms are slowly turning into a black, ink-like substance. Although his eyes show no fear, they are frozen in time as the substance pulsates in his pale face.

As Raymul taps into the elements of Void, he wills himself strength to transform Eila into the creature he desires, known as a Rockfear. Infusing him with the properties of Void and Death, he channels dark energies through his body. The veins sprout from his skin, snaking around his limbs as he focuses his power on Eila. His form begins to contort and shift, his features distorting under the weight of the transformation. The essence of the Rockfear seeps into his bones as he convulses in agony, his screams echoing off the walls of the room. Raymul stands back, watching as the transformation takes hold, his heart heavy with the knowledge of what he has done.

After the transformation is complete, the creature that was once Eila stands before him, his eyes now glowing with an inner fire. The Rockfear's intelligence and ferocity now reside within him, and Raymul can feel the connection between them growing stronger by the second.

He turns to face the Sintra plant and says, "Thank you, my love," as he opens his will to the sinister plant. Slowly, he can feel the passionate love of the plant once again shocking his body, waiting eagerly to take form and give in to Raymul. The sentry's voice comes to him, saying, "Raymul, do my bidding. Send your pet to find your destiny." Raymul opens his eyes and releases the sensual magic that intertwines with his own. It's a sensation of discomfort as he severs the connection between the plant and his soul, a feeling he seems unable to let go of.

"Yes, my love, our destiny, and we will rule once again!" he exclaims.

Raymul turns to face the creature, which is now sitting, already anticipating his next command.

"My pet, go find the princess and bring her to me alive. You should know her scent and her ways. You've confided in her many times. Do whatever it takes;

kill the others that follow her. We don't want any witnesses. Do my bidding, and we shall prosper!"

The Rockfear jumps up, unfurling its wings and flashing its form around him. Its large hooves and wide face with sharp teeth stand out as it balances on one powerful leg and small but mighty arms, appearing poised and ready. As its name implies, the Rockfear is a master of crawling and camouflaging on any solid substance. It squats low to the ground as the bedroom window abruptly flies open, and a gust of wind rushes in. The creature brims with anticipation and excitement as it takes to the skies, soaring high into the clouds to fulfill its master's wishes.

The voice returns again, giggling deviously and slowly in Raymul's head. "What's so funny, my internal love?" he asks.

"Just pleased, my Raymul. You've done well. Come to me; I need you," says the voice.

Raymul feels his heart pump again, and his magic aches in pain for the death element's magic that resides in the Sintra plant. He closes the bedroom door and gradually removes his bathrobe, walking naked toward the Sintra plant. He places his hand tightly around the intertwining, smooth, black, shiny bark of the small dead plant, and the magic consumes him instantly. Everything around him disappears as he is lost in the darkness.

CHAPTER 9

Acceptance

JAMES LANDER STANDS a few feet away from the cliff that overlooks his hometown of Lepersteed. A deep sadness overwhelms him as he sees the quiet little farmland so peaceful and at rest. Smoke rises from the chimneys in every section of his town, from the congested marketplace to the scattered farmland homes, indicating that the homes are warm and content. So many unanswered questions fill his mind once again. Eva is very insistent that they must leave if the town is to survive. He leaves everyone behind, even without saying goodbye to Abela. But he knows that by being present, the Shadowlen—or as Radion refers to them, Soulshiver—entities from the realm of death that would decay over time as they consume the victim's soul, would hunt again and destroy anyone who came between them.

James looks dejectedly at the rock beneath him, wishing that this were just a dream. Ghostly creatures hunting him—why? What do they want from a farmer like James? Looking past the horizon where the sun is just barely over the town, James wonders how strange it is that Eva has come to his rescue, and how all of a sudden, his headaches are completely gone. Many times, his father had specified that Eva was a member of the family and that he should trust her and follow her lead. But now, how can he always trust Eva? James knows she is very capable but feels odd that there is more that she is not telling him. Some dark secret. Now that he is no longer home, he feels uneasy and different. Those Shadowlen that tried to take over his mind unleashed something he can't figure out, like nothing he's experienced before.

He slowly surveys the landscape, which is filled with small trees and continuous rumpling hills. Leaves now float and flick about everywhere as the slow wind brings in a misty hint of winter to come.

According to Radion, Eva acquired the rag when he went into unconsciousness, a state prompted by the mayor's request to deliver it to Eva. It's some sort of relic, Eva mentioned, that will hide their progress as they venture into an unknown destination.

"Hey," Ethan says from a distance.

He notices that Eva is sitting gracefully on a rock, clothed in a long, heavy garment to keep her warm. She is still staring out into the woods, lost in her thoughts and worries, ignoring them all. She is deep in thought.

James waits until Ethan joins him, positioning himself on the rocky outcrop that leads out to the cliff below.

"How do you feel?" Ethan asks, taking the same view as James.

"I'm fine," James replies with a light smile. "Thanks. You know, you still have time to get back. There's no need for you to come with me."

Ethan shakes his head. "I told you; I'm not leaving you alone. We're in this together."

James nods, grateful for Ethan's steadfastness. "I appreciate it."

Ethan turns to look at James and asks, "So where are we headed?"

James replies, "Eva says there's a safe haven for us. She knows a place where we can regroup and figure out what our next move should be."

Ethan then asks, "And you trust her?"

James hesitates before responding, "I don't know. There's something she's not telling us. But for now, we don't have any other options. We have to trust her."

Ethan nods in agreement, his expression uneasy and concerned. James notices this and asks, "What's wrong, Ethan?"

"I don't trust her either," Ethan admits.

James looks at him in shock and concern. "What do you mean?"

Taking a deep breath, Ethan explains, "When Eva came back with you, it seemed like the horses you both were on were floating slightly above the ground, as if the air was propelling the horses to move faster."

James is taken aback by Ethan's statement and raises his voice. "What are you talking about?"

Ethan continues, "I'm telling you, James, I saw you come out of thin air. And Eva was doing some sort of bewitching on your body, adding some gooey substance and chanting words I've never heard before."

Instantly, James clenches his fists and steps forward. "I don't know what the hell you're talking about, but keep Eva out of this, okay?"

Ethan stands up awkwardly and yells, "Fine! I was only telling you what I saw!" Then he turns around and bumps into Radion.

"Take it easy, boys," Radion says, smiling amusedly.

Ethan stares at Radion blankly; he looks very old and wise, wearing a long, blue cloak that drapes over his shoulders down to his leather boots. Ethan sniffs and moves out of his way.

"I guess he can't take a little humor," Radion says as he walks up to James and puts his arm around his shoulders, leading him away from their small camp. "I'm sure you have many questions. I will try to answer them the best I can."

"You're only an herb seller. How could you possibly know what is going on?" James points out.

"Looks can be deceiving; nevertheless, it can be uncomfortable," Radion says, fixing his heavy cloak into position, indicating he's not enjoying the new look. He looks well groomed and clean. His beard and hair are both braided. "You were right to point out that I am only a merchant, but your anger and confusion have clouded your judgment, not allowing you to see through the misunderstanding of what is really going on. You see, I have known you all your life. As a matter of fact, I have known your family for quite some time—"

"But how can you—" James starts to interrupt when Radion indicates for him to be quiet and sits him on a small stump that is shaded by a large tree. Radion situates himself next to James.

"You have to learn, boy, not to interrupt a conversation. Sometimes it's wise to absorb all information first before making your statements. Your temper doesn't help you. It's a trait that's run in your blood for years. A magic of relief that's waiting to explode. Try to relax and forget what is happening now. Focus on the beauty of these surroundings instead. It can help you control your temper."

James is stunned by what Radion is telling him, and he's very confused. He lets it pass and opens his mind to listen more.

"Good. Now, what's on your mind?"

"Who are you?"

"For starters, I am not a merchant but a scholar. I have been monitoring your family for years."

"You're not telling me more, are you?"

"I don't want to overwhelm you right now."

"Is Eva also a scholar or something else?"

"James, Eva loves you very dearly. I cannot speak for her. If you have any concerns, don't you think it's best to confront the main source?"

"You're right." James feels disappointed. He doesn't know where to begin asking Radion. There's so much confusion, people dying, the mayor, his best friend—why?

"Listen," Radion says, sensing James's confusion. "Let me tell you a story that might bring you some comfort." He strokes his long, white beard as he reflects on the wriggling memories that overlap in his mind.

"The dark times of our world were many years ago, long before your time and that of your ancestors. It was a time when the balance of the elements was terribly off, and the Guardians of Light, Water, Earth, Fire, and Air were cautious because the Guardians of Dark saw an opportunity to share their forces with the light. The Shadowed Sorcery, composed of individuals who mastered the art of the elements, joined forces with other races to restore balance, but their efforts failed, leading to countless wars and fury.

"Finally, the elves, leaders of magic, sought the aid of the newly formed wizards. However, the wizards were not well regarded due to their recent discovery of magic. Together with the Shadowed Sorcery, they fought for one hundred years. Yet all seemed hopeless, as the Dark Lady Zarma and his minions escaped a realm governed by dark elements. Our realm then took on a different form.

"The Enchantress Guardian of Water secretly called forth the mighty wizard Socrater, and through her magic, she was able to influence race in our realm to forge a mighty sword that would aid in sending the dark elements back to their world. But this sword had to be held by a nonmagical being to set forth a balance and had to contain a small part of each Guardian of Light's soul."

"The mighty wizard, assisted by close friends, sought out the legendary King Olen, a fearsome, strong-hearted individual with a love for all. King Olen accepted the task and sought advice and instructions from the Guardian of Water. Within a few months, the mighty sword known as Vertmor was crafted from a rare metal extracted by the dwarves from the dragon nest deep in the mountains. It was in this nest that the dragon lived, breathing fumes into the ancient rocks where it slept. The elves shaped the sword with their master skill in weapons, and finally, the fairies placed magical properties into it to withstand the powers that were to come.

"King Olen, aided by his new sword, embarked on a long journey to obtain the promised partial souls from each element of light. After obtaining the powerful orbs, he journeyed to the far lands where the realm rips, over the sea of the east, where a mighty battle took place, and King Olen destroyed the mighty Zarma, and she fell back into the realm where the balance could be restored.

"All was well, for King Olen had established the balance of the elements, and all knew that greatness would come to the mighty king. He used the sword as a guide to keep the element proxies of magic in order, which he did so well.

"However, these glory days were only the beginning of something new. The magic elements seemed to strive for more, and the balance of light and darkness took on a new form. The Shadowed Sorcery, scholar-witches by name to most humans, and wizards acquired new properties and learned to control them, while the elves blamed the wizards for intruding on the elements and enhancing the magic properties. King Olen fell under the spell of the sword's magic, and he later used the sword for unnecessary tasks.

"Socrater, Olen's close companion, warned him that the sword must be used with purpose, compassion, and love, not hate, greed, or denial. Olen, torn by the sword and his rage, denounced all wizards and banished them from his kingdom. He later cast out his family and abruptly used the sword to kill innocent beings. Darkness fell upon King Olen's kingdom a few years later, and rumors escalated that his kingdom would soon see its fate.

"Socrater, with his unique gifts, decided the fate of Olen and all that followed. He entered the kingdom and took Olen's only two-year-old son, scaling the castle walls and flying away like a bird with the child cradled in his arms. Olen, obsessed with finding his son, searched the royal room the very next day, destroying everything in his path. Some say he was upset his son was missing; others say he meant to kill his child. Olen's beloved wife tried to stop him, but he turned the sword on her, destroying her soul along with everything within her. Lacking magical abilities, Olen's actions triggered a chain reaction, causing the sword and the souls it contained from the Guardians to unleash devastation. It turned against Olen, consuming his being and soul. The Guardians of Light lashed out in pain and anger at Olen's kingdom, with Fire burning the living, Air destroying nonliving things, Water washing out the kingdom's existence, and Earth concealing it in shame.

"Some people managed to escape the kingdom's destruction. Those who remained were consulted by Eartha, who was ashamed of Olen's lack of magical ability. Eartha, the leader of the Guardians of Light, took this ordeal seriously and brought new life to the kingdom of Olen. Meanwhile, Socrater saved Olen's heir and concealed him, raising the boy with the help of his companions. They watched over him, and he later married and had many children. The family grew, and Socrater and his companions, now known as the Rachar—the protectors of Olen—watched for signs that the magic of the sword that consumed the Olen family had returned. One sign was a child of the Olen family born with blue eyes that later turned sea green, indicating that the magic of the elements was a carrier to the next Olen child. Prophecies surfaced, and rumors spread that evil would strike again and Olen the Destroyer would return, but stronger. The balance of the Guardians of Light and Dark still needs to be restored."

Radian stops and waits for James's response, but the boy simply looks away and stares at his town for a few moments before saying, "Thank you."

Radion stands up and walks in front of James, tears slowly coming down the side of his unshaven beard. "As I said, don't make radical assumptions. We will talk again. I will leave you alone now."

James looks up with a determined face and a newfound understanding. "Should I call you by another name besides Radion from the Rachar?"

"Radion will be fine," Radion replies. "I would appreciate it if you kept the Rachar concealed for a while." And with that, he walks away, thinking to himself, *We don't need to alarm people like Ethan.*

⟶▭◯▭⟵

Onyx responds to her master's command and gallops right off the massive, open field where the everglade forest lies just ahead. The forest can be seen from miles away, deep, dark, and forbidding, with various assortments of trees and birds flying in and out of its top surface. It spreads out over fifty miles, with numerous mountains and lakes. As Eva and her party approach the massive trees that perfectly layer side by side, as if they are protecting themselves from outsiders, all sounds stand still as they stop a few feet ahead. The forest is heavily guarded because it is very ancient, and the one who claims it is the mountain dwarves' lord. Eva dismounts Onyx and waits for her party to catch up. She sees James's expression strain as he approaches beside her horse. He has changed so much since his first encounter with the Shadowlen, and she can feel his power slowly escaping and reaching out all around them. James dismounts his horse and acknowledges Eva without a word, staring.

It has been two days since they left home riding, stopping for short periods of time to eat and sleep. Eva prepares the fire while Radion starts preparing dishes for the cold meal they have stored. But since their departure, James has not once confronted Eva with any questions or remarks. The conversation with Radion seems to have worked. Although a deep unease has built up inside her because she wanted to tell James herself, it is better this way. There are many things James doesn't need to know right now.

James stares at Eva for a few moments, wondering what she is thinking. Suddenly, his magic flares like a blood rush, seducing her soul and wildly trying to capture Eva's mind without his control. James isn't sure what he is doing and is still naive to his new abilities, which forcefully try to seize Eva's mind. Strangely, his mind is completely blocked, abruptly, without cause. It subsides and pushes back quickly. Eva now stares at him and asks, "Are you okay, dear?"

James exhales. "I'm fine."

"James, I know you're confused and want answers."

"Just tell me one thing; are you part of the Rachar, from the City of Witches?" James says.

"Yes, I was educated in both cultures, light and dark elements," Eva says sternly.

In that instant, the wind branches quickly between them, and James looks around wildly, saying, "Something is coming."

"What's wrong?" Radion notices James's reaction and joins them, with Ethan trailing behind.

"I don't know. The breeze sort of excited me with its touch, somewhat like a tricky warning, and I could sense magic in the air—like it's coming toward us."

Radion looks hard at Eva. "What do you make of this?"

"It's part of his nature," Eva says. "James, can you try to be specific about what you felt?"

"It's sort of a sweet taste feeling. I can't explain it exactly, more like a rush and anticipation…"

From the sky above, a swarm of crows flies in an orderly fashion, bringing screeching sounds. Five out of what seems to be a dozen have left its flock and descend slowly, magically transforming into human forms. The beings land and place their hands on the floor to prevent themselves from falling. As the male individual stands up, he throws back his long, black cape-like garment, which appears to be made of a leathery, bat-like skin, allowing assorted colored knives on his waist to be revealed. Stepping forward toward their party, the male stands at a height of six feet, with long, black hair framing his determined features. His eyebrows are slender and oval-shaped, adding to his unusual appearance. Eva cautiously approaches the group, which now consists of two females and two males, all similarly dressed in black leather attire and carrying an assortment of knives on their bodies, some even in their hands. James quickly jumps to protect Eva, but Radion pulls the young boy back. "It's okay, boy. They're from the city of Kumartal."

Ethan pulls up next to James, holding a sharp knife in his left hand. "What are they?" he asks.

"They're known as the Malij, the assassins," Radion replies. "I'm surprised that our young man here," he says, looking at James to his right, "would sense such devious beings."

"Great, now we have super witches," Ethan adds.

Meanwhile, Eva meets with the Malij group casually. The head of the group, the male who was the first to land, steps forward toward Eva and kneels. As he does, a curling fog-like substance forms around his hand, slowly enveloping it. Eva recognizes it as a binding spell, a method of magical constraint developed by the elements of death and ice, commonly used by the Malij group. "Mistress, we are here to assist and abide by your bidding. Our empress sends her goodwill and hopes you will accept." He hands her a small, rolled parcel.

Eva quickly reads the parcel, which is clearly sealed with magic and can only be read by the addressee.

My dear Eva,

Although we had a misunderstanding the last time we met, I reconsidered your request. Please accept my finest warriors to assist you. They are gifts for our misjudgment. We hope that you will bring the Olen descendant to Kumartal so we may further evaluate his mysterious capabilities and advise him in these dark times. My regards to you and your faithful subjects.

Empress Samatar

Eva wills her magic, and the parcel disintegrates in her hand. "I see she finally sees the importance of this mission, but she is mistaken that I need aid, especially from your group. You may stand."

The male stands and looks at Eva with a stunned but fearless face. Despite his lack of expression, Eva senses an underlying shock in his demeanor. "No offense, but I am not very fond of your practice," Eva adds.

"No offense taken, my lady," the male replies.

"What is your group name?"

"We are called the VaTem Vartum. My name is Perlarn. Would you like me to introduce the rest?"

"Not right now. Let me see your hands," Eva says.

Perlarn lifts his black cloak, revealing two distinct symbols on each of his hands. Eva places her hands over the symbols—a single eye on top of a small crescent moon and a hand in a golden sun. She releases her magic and places it onto Perlarn's forearms. Perlarn examines his trademark, the crescent moon symbol, which no longer shines as well as the empress symbol to his right. He looks up into Eva's eyes and smiles.

"I don't like group links; it tends to complicate missions. I want to be sure you don't have a direct link with your grievous empress at this time, which I'm sure she anticipated I would do," Eva explains.

Perlarn says nothing and waits.

"Your knife, please," Eva requests.

"Excuse me, my mistress?" Perlarn asks.

"You heard me well," Eva responds.

The other members of Perlarn's party look uneasy and start to talk among themselves. Perlarn retrieves a small, red blade hidden deep inside his cloak and hands it over to Eva. Eva instantly wills her magic to control Perlarn and his advising party. Perlarn's group tries to resist the magic hold, but Perlarn tells them not to advance. The magic contact finally takes place, and Eva commands her magic will of the element of fire. The empress symbol is replaced by an oval sky-blue symbol. She then releases the hold on Perlarn.

"I thought you didn't like torture, mistress," Perlarn says as he covers his right hand and adjusts his black cloak.

"I don't. I just thought burning you instead would prevent the predictable sound of your screaming. I know the cult follows the passion of the Guardian of Death. I need to ensure that it doesn't cloud your judgment or my mission," Eva replies.

Perlarn bows. "As you wish."

Radion observes the unusual interaction between the Malij group and Eva. He knows that once the empress releases the Malij and assigns them to assist someone, they are very valuable. Only a powerful sorceress links themselves to a Malij master, an act that requires tremendous will and strength. The Malij are very faithful to one leader and, once linked, can be very deadly. It's a strange custom these Malij practice—magic of control and a thirst for death or, should it be said, blood. Radion now knows that Eva is more than what she seems and vows to find out who she really is or who she is really working for.

James watches intensely, not understanding the unusual situation that has transpired between his stepmother and the strange new assassin witches. He steps forward toward the group casually to give Eva a hand. The leader of the group quickly looks into James's eyes and bows suddenly, followed by his group, saying, "Your Highness."

"What the hell are you talking about?" James answers back angrily.

"Dear, it's only a formality. They only show respect," Eva explains.

James yells out, "Okay! Now I see that we really need to talk, Eva! I want no part of this king Olen, magic, or whatever you want to call it. As a matter of fact, you and your magical people can take this title and thing inside of me!" He grabs his own shirt in frustration and anger, feeling outraged. The only thing on his mind right now is to run. He takes off. He can't believe that he is now a "Your Highness," and the surprise and fear have completely overwhelmed him. Ethan chases after James, amazed at how much faster he is than normal.

Radion joins Eva. "What happened?" he asks.

"The formality seemed to bother James. Radion, go after him and see what you can do. I'll speak with him once we're in Mount Rocksmear," Eva responds.

Radion peers into her eyes and says, "I see that there's more to this than meets the eye, Eva. We'll speak later." Then he takes off after James and Ethan.

Eva sighs, feeling tired and frustrated. Her identity is slowly being questioned and eroded, and she hates it when people try to overlook who she is. It's something she's worked hard to overcome over the years, and now someone is questioning her identity again—Radion. She must try to address this with him. This sorcerer, with whom she recently worked on a project, is very intelligent and talented, but he's also a thorn in her side that she needs to carefully remove.

She turns to face Perlarn, who is watching her with a curious expression. This is another issue that she must address—Samatar is once again trying to take matters into her own hands. They've conflicted numerous times about what's best for Destroyer to come, but now Samatar has made a move against her, using her spies. Eva smirks at Perlarn, waiting for her command. Little does Perlarn know, Eva is planning a surprise for Samatar once she's done. Eva then focuses on the magic group that is waiting for her instructions. She has to make a choice—if she keeps them, it could mean interfering with Samatar's plans. She could simply cast them off, but that would only add more suspicion to Samatar's plans. Eva thinks for a few moments and decides to accept the empress's invitation. Now she must figure out how to best use their unique skills without interfering with her plans. The link she placed on Perlarn was the first step, and she plans to manipulate the Malij to suit her needs, adding fire to Samatar's plans.

CHAPTER 10

Escape

JAMES RUNS INTO the forest, feeling the trees looming over him as he enters the dense surface. Each tree seems twisted, massive, and old, with no two looking alike. He walks carefully, moving the high grasses aside and steadying himself by touching the tree trunks. Their bark is decayed, evoking a sense of sorrow and disgust as James touches them. He quickly retracts his hand, feeling odd about how he reacted to the tree. Perhaps he's just exhausted and overwhelmed. He continues, finally emerging into a wide-open area, still surrounded by trees but more manageable. James settles down on a stumped rock and pulls back his curly brown hair, which blocks his view due to sweat. He reflects on Eva, who is the only woman he has known as a true mother figure. She cared for him and advised him wisely, but he now feels only confused. She deliberately kept his family secret from him, a vital piece of information she should have shared. James looks up, seeing the branches intertwining above him, and thinks to himself, *She's planning something.* His father had assured him that she was trustworthy, but how? James wonders why the crow beings bowed to him and called him a king. "King to what, to them? Ha, I can see it now: James, the farmer ruler of the witches," he says to himself. They don't know what they are talking about. James continues to survey the area around him, observing small mammals and squirrels going about their business, perhaps searching for food for the upcoming winter.

He shivers suddenly; he left his cloak behind and feels foolish for being careless. The birds sing in the background, soothing his senses, and he is calmed by the beauty of the landscape. A huge mountain looms in the distance, forbidding and towering over a thick, heavily dark cloud. "I guess this is the work of the

Guardian of Earth." James observes the flowing colors around him. It is a true miracle. Suddenly, a small voice interrupts his thoughts.

"So it's true." James spins around, looking for the source of the voice, but no one is around. Only the ticking of the birds and the overpowering trees. The rustling of the mammals makes itself known as footsteps; is he losing his mind?

"Over here!" The voice comes from below. James looks down and sees three squirrels. The one in the middle is much taller than the other two beside it. Strangely, the middle squirrel, which is unusually light and different from the others, starts to squeal at the ones behind them. James watches as the smaller squirrels bow and scurry away.

The remaining squirrel has a lighter fur tone, and its forest-green fur and small feet are quite different from what James usually sees. Its tail is well groomed and bushy, with a golden ring attached to it! James does a double take on this. He is astonished to see that the squirrel also has tiny gold rings on its small claws and is wearing a brightly bronzed medallion of some sort. The creature looks unnervingly humanlike as it stares at him, and James can't make out the medallion, but it seems to be a carving of a tree.

"Are you talking to me?" James finally says after a few moments.

"Yes, my name is Merel. I am here to witness you," the creature responds.

James backs away, feeling uneasy and unsure of what he is seeing. He thinks he might be losing his mind.

"You are not losing your mind, young one," Merel says, seemingly reading his thoughts.

"Are there other creatures like you that can speak too?" James asks.

"No, they follow me," the creature replies, referring to the other squirrels that had skittered away moments ago. "I am from Her Grace's realm of Earth. I was asked to witness your coming and report to Her Grace and those who asked if you have returned, although we are still waiting for Her Grace to return too... That's funny, right? That kind of rhymes."

"Actually, it doesn't," James says.

"It sure does! Your return and Grace waiting to return," Merel replies.

"Whatever, why are you talking to me?" James asks.

"I told you I am a witness."

"Okay, you're a witness—now what?"

"Oh, nothing. I'll be going now."

"Wait, how is this possible that I could talk…," James asks, trailing off.

"I don't know. I told you I'm a witness, so I witnessed. Now I will go and tell the others that I witnessed…ha! That rhymes too. Witness, witnessed. Ha ha!" The shrewd creature laughs and holds its belly, supporting itself with its shining rings on its claw. "You will be safe in these realms of the dwarves' clan. You will not have any unexpected visitors from the realm of darkness. It's an agreement that has always been before."

James looks perplexed as the little creature laughs again about the rhyming, which is clearly not a rhyme, but he decides not to intervene.

Suddenly, the squirrel dashes away as James is about to say something. "We shall meet again, young kin," Merel says, disappearing into the trees.

"I wouldn't go that far," Radion says, emerging from the trees behind James, a few scratches spread on his wrinkled face, indicating that he was tired of searching for him. A few moments later, Ethan emerges behind Radion, looking bewildered and panting heavily after being lost.

"Did you see that?" James asks Radion.

"See what?"

"It was a strange-looking squirrel. It was talking to me."

Radion looks around.

"It's gone now, but I swear, it was an unusual-looking animal. It seemed to act with human expressions and was wearing tiny jewelry, and it was talking to me," James says.

"What are you talking about, James?" Ethan says.

Radion looks perplexed and seems to be deep in thought before speaking again, while James waits patiently for his response.

"There are only two people that I know of who can talk to animals, and they are Argus born. But an actual special animal? I've never heard of that. I've read that Guardians have enlightened creatures that can cross dimensions and visit other realms, but that's just a myth. Perhaps your mind is playing tricks on you, James. Magic tends to manifest itself, and you haven't received any training to guide you," Radion explains.

"No, it was there. I felt it too. It was strange, almost as if I connected with it and felt its curiosity. I can't explain it. Also, earlier, when my mind trailed off toward Eva, suddenly it was disrupted, almost as if it were blocked—"

"Be careful, James, when using your magic of the element of Air. It's powerful and deceiving. It takes decades to master. Invasion of the mind could lead to uneasy, mixed emotions that are tied to reality and unreality. That's why we sleep and daydream. It's a balance that is meant to be. Infusing your mind into someone else could upset that balance and make you consume the person's mind that you're trying to connect with. It's best to leave the mind alone until you learn to capture the essential aspects of what is needed. Besides, it's better to enter a mind with the host's permission for easy access and cooperation between the two."

Ethan listens intently. "You can read minds too? Shit, all this magic crap you got! That's awesome! I have a few people I'd like you to check, James," he says. James can see the excitement light up Ethan's face at the prospect of this new thought.

"It will never happen, buddy," James replies.

"Ah, it was a nice thought," Ethan says, resigned.

Ignoring his friend's disappointment, James turned to Radion. "Can you talk to animals and read minds too, Radion?"

"No, some elves could, and as I said earlier, Argus born. Arguses are gifted with some of these traits and possess them naturally. It has always been a mystery why and how this family is gifted with these magic-born properties," Radion explains.

"Um, that's why they run things. Remind me never to speak to an Argus, don't want them entering my mind…it wouldn't be pretty. Maybe you should run shit too, James," Ethan interrupts.

Both James and Radion give Ethan a sharp look.

"Okay, okay, I get it," Ethan said.

"So I am an Argus?" James asks, looking down.

"No, remember the story. You are a descendant of Olen. Your ancestors' bloodline was infused with the orbs provided by the Guardians after Olen took his wife's life. You are the first born with this manifestation of magic, a reflection of the orbs that are trying to take root. It needs to be contained and controlled, just like those who study magic but are not born with these elements. The elements of life contain both light and dark elements. The dark elements tend to be more easily learned and studied, while the light elements are the more elusive ones that take decades to master. Magic-born individuals are rare, like the Arguses, who grow into their magic. The Argus family is born with the properties of light and can easily acquire the dark elements too. Although you were born with these properties, you were not magic-born. Your abilities are an expression of the elements from the orb given to King Olen, which is totally unique. Two separate factors at play."

James looks perplexed as he listens to the story, his gaze wandering as if he were distracted.

"Let's talk about your encounter later, James. Eva and I can help you with your magic and the illusions you're seeing. Your family was very special and unique too," Radion says, trying to reassure him.

"I'm sorry I ran off. I just needed some time for myself," James apologizes.

"I understand," Radion replies, sitting next to James and waiting for Ethan to calm down.

"Are you okay?" James asks Ethan.

"Yeah, if it wasn't for Radion, I would have gone crazy. This place is huge and confusing, and the tree doesn't make any sense. I started to feel sick after a while," Ethan says.

"The tree and its surrounding area are meant to keep intruders out," Radion explains. "People who are not familiar with Mount Rocksmear usually get lost and die here. There are dangerous creatures in here that could kill you."

"So you're familiar with this area?" James asks.

"Not really," Radion admits.

Ethan jumps up suddenly and exclaims, "So we're lost!"

"Relax, boy. I never said we were lost," Radion says calmly.

"How the hell do we get out of here?" Ethan asks.

Radion takes a deep breath and turns to face James with a concerned expression. "You should train your loyal subjects to be patient and trust your judgment. Also, choose your companions wisely. You don't need Ethan to complicate things for you."

"What do you mean?" James asks, curious.

"You know exactly what I mean. Just keep it in mind," Radion replies, then turns his attention back to Ethan.

"I will call a Guide," Radion says, ignoring Ethan's protests.

"How?" Ethan persists.

"I will use this rock we're standing on as a communication beacon and alert the mountain dwarves we're here."

"What?" Ethan exclaims.

"Please, Ethan. Let him explain," James interrupts.

Ethan lets out a long sigh. "It seems all we do is talk and hear these silly stories from this old man. Obviously, they are old wives' tales."

Ignoring Ethan's comment, Radion continues. "Thank you, James. The ground we're standing on is a network to the homeland of the dwarves. We're on top of the ancient city of Yanter."

Ethan is about to interrupt again, but James signals for him to hold his tongue.

"As I was saying, the mountain dwarves are skilled and resourceful. They can penetrate rocks and metal to create weapons more powerful than any we know. During the wars, they needed to conceal their homeland and came up with the idea of burying their mountain underground. With the help of the beloved Guardian of Earth, they were able to hide the mountain from the dark lords. It cost the lives of thousands of dwarves, but they accomplished the task in just a few decades. Today the mountain holds a unique mystique that can never be reproduced. The dwarves also formed alliances with the forest around them to protect their homeland from outsiders."

"Did they ever want to bring their mountain back to the surface when the war was over?" James asks.

"They tried, but the task proved to be impossible, and eventually they had no choice but to adapt to a life of hiding. However, over the course of centuries, a complex network of tunnels was formed that spanned various mountains and lands. This network became a lifeline for trade, allowing the dwarves to travel swiftly and efficiently between destinations. It was one of these tunnels that led to the kingdom of Olen, with whom the dwarves forged a strong and loyal alliance. Thanks to Olen, trade between humans and dwarves flourished, and the two became mutual friends.

"Sadly, this friendship came at a cost. The destructive actions of Olen caused catastrophic damage to the dwarves' tunnels, leading to widespread floods that claimed many lives and destroyed countless small cities within the network. In a desperate bid to save Mount Rocksmear, home to thousands of dwarf families, they were forced to make a painful sacrifice. They sealed the tunnel leading to Olen and even went as far as to sacrifice their own to seal the city of Yanter, which had a population of over thirty thousand dwarf families.

"The devastation and despair that the dwarves had to endure during this time broke off all ties with the humans, leading to a permanent rift between the two races."

"What makes you think they would want to help me?" James asks.

"Here we go again, more talk, no action. At this rate, we should just stand longer and let these shadows take over. At least something would be different," Ethan interrupts.

"Cut it out, Ethan, or I'll knock you out!" James warns.

"Good luck with that. If you could catch me," Ethan smirks.

Radion shakes his head at the two boys. "The mountain dwarves are an incredibly resilient people. Their unyielding nature is a fundamental part of their magic and culture, shaping them into who they are. They've managed to keep their true values intact and not let the deceitful ways of humans affect their judgment. While they can never forget the past, they eventually learn to forgive. You can think of them like a rock. You can chip away at the surface, but the core remains intact, and it takes a considerable amount of effort and time to chip away at it. It's something that is rarely accomplished."

James nods, accepting Radion's explanation before setting out into the dense, congested forest. He stares into the blocked view of darkness, where the trees seem to loom over him, ancient and forbidding, unlike anything he has ever seen before. Each tree seems to take on its own unique shape and definition. Thick vines, as wide as his thighs, snake around the tree bark like earth veins escaping the ground. It's clear that there's magic at work here, as if the forest is protecting itself from intruders.

"Radion, why do I feel like they don't like me?" James pauses, trying to choose his words carefully so that Ethan won't overhear. He gazes out into the forest, gesturing toward the trees.

"What do you mean?" asks Radion.

"You know what I mean. From the story, it seems like they want nothing to do with me. I could sense the sorrow and disgust when I touched the trees," James replies.

Radion strokes his long, gray beard thoughtfully. "Interesting. I never suspected that the Guardian's feelings could have any effect on them. However, it's known that her emotions have an impact on all living things. I imagine that her feelings haven't changed, but they can be forgiven. James don't let the past dictate your present. There were many speculations about what happened to your ancestor. Some say the magic was too much for him, or that the darker side of his nature simply took over. Others say he was deceived and manipulated. Whatever the truth is, it doesn't define who you are. You're a unique and special individual. You won't succumb to the same fate as your ancestor—that's not logical."

"What do you think caused my ancestor's fate?" James asks.

Radion turns away from James, directing his gaze toward Ethan, who is listening intensely. He thinks to himself, *It doesn't matter now. Ethan, like James, is a unique individual and will eventually need to know the truth about himself, if he hasn't figured it out already.*

At that moment, Eva emerges from the forest with someone by her side. "Are you okay, dear?" Eva asks, looking at James with concern.

"I'm fine," James replies, staring intently at Eva. Her appearance has changed, but she still maintains her balance. Her long hair is braided similarly to Radion's.

"I'm glad to see that everyone is accounted for," Eva says glamorously, looking toward James and Radion as she adjusts her cloak. "Firstly, I would like to introduce some new members to our group, the Malij. They have been sent to assist us if necessary."

"Do we really need their assistance, Eva? I thought we came here to ask the dwarves for help," Radion objects.

"The Malij can be useful for protecting us against unknown magic, and their skills are different from ours. We could use that," Eva explains.

"So who is in charge here? Is it Eva or Radion, or is it you, James? You seem to have magic powerful enough to take out an army," Ethan interrupts.

Eva looks at Ethan with a disapproving look and says, "Why does anyone need to be in charge? A person with a focused intention and mindful observation should guide others, not force them to do their bidding. The ground you walk on is the creation of Mother Earth, and she doesn't set terms of taking charge but provides the necessities for people to appreciate and lead on their own."

"I'm sorry, madam. We've just spent too much time talking instead of getting help from my friend," Ethan apologizes.

"I understand. You are naive, but you are a powerful friend to my James," Eva acknowledges. "Radion, did you notify your friends?" she asks.

"I was about to, but I got sidetracked," Radion replies.

"As always," Eva sarcastically remarks. "Please do your inviting." Eva then moves closer to where James is sitting and says, "Walk with me a bit. It will be a while before someone else comes."

James rises from his seat and follows Eva into the thick forest, while Radion finds a log to sit on and places it onto the rock stump where they were previously seated.

Ethan mutters to himself, "Here we go again, blah blah blah."

CHAPTER 11

Kumartal

THE HUNCHED CREATURE surveys the towering structures of the city of Kumartal, situated near the eastern shores of the Atlantea Ocean, before him. Despite his ability to sense both the living and the dead worlds, he is amazed by the organized mastery of magic displayed by these beings. Observing the various towers, statues, and structures illuminated by the city lights, he senses a strong magic holding the city together, including a dark magic that detects beings like him. As the sun settles behind the castle-like structure before him, he needs to be careful not to trigger the city's protective magic. Although he is impressed by the magic creatures' advanced skills, he knows they are not perfect, for he is a magical creature born of the Guardians of Death and Void, a far more powerful magic than that possessed by the city's inhabitants. He spots a loophole in their shield near the odd oval structure at the end of the city and concludes that he only needs to be within a few feet of his destination to achieve his goal.

He waits patiently, sorting through different possibilities. He could easily reveal himself and fight his way in, but that would only slow him down and possibly force his target to be moved elsewhere. He does not want to displease his master, who has promised him other means to accomplish his goal. He needs a diversion.

Moving away from the rock that had concealed him, he unfurls his wings and flies over to a small swampy area, where he lands on a rock stump and settles down like an unmoving stone. He observes the area and releases a small portion of his magic, causing a crocodile to approach, along with some toads, snakes, and a bobcat. He examines these pitiful creatures and smiles, for he has a special ability to alter and control other beings. He focuses on each animal and wills his magic. They must know he is coming to their city and are preparing, but they do not know he has company. He turns his eyes into a glowing sunset red and enchants the creatures to do his bidding.

⊷═◉═⊷

Empress Samatar stands behind the black satin drape, which flaps over her balcony facing the courtyard of the Hall of Guardians. A golden statue, representing the first scholar of Kumartal, stands in the center room, surrounded by Guardians and benches. There is a commotion going on below. She gently places the earplugs in her ears to hear and uses the magic relic to listen to the conversation between the four Malij guards and her faithful servant, Kerfort. They are preparing for an attack from the west, and a disturbance in the dark realm has just been revealed. It seems that Kerfort finally believes the bastard seer who has been warning them for two years. Samatar smiles as she removes the earplugs from her ears and tucks them into her satin robe. *So, it seems that the prophecies are being revealed,* she thinks, *the coming of the Destroyer.* Samatar moves a few steps back, making sure she is silent and not heard eavesdropping. Casting her magic, she gracefully draws the drapes closed, veiling her sight of the towering stone pillars that define the ethereal allure of the shimmering City of the Witches. As the drapes gracefully fall, they gradually obscure her view, until finally they block out the mesmerizing sight entirely.

Satisfied, she returns to the overly stacked bronze table that is overflowing with parcels and antique-looking leather-bound books. She picks up the copy of the Ra Leslar Var, stares at it, and holds it tightly against her flat chest. She has compared countless prophecies with their own books, and they are almost identical. The creature that awaits them will come and take the princess away. The wicked seers also saw this. According to the ancient witch, "her own faithful servant will turn against her." She feels its presence, and she knows who created it. It was forged with the assistance of the beloved Death and the obsession of the gracious Void. These Guardians, just like the others, are pillars and governing entities of this realm, entrusted with responsibility since the beginning of existence to protect the essence of life and maintain balance between the dark and light elements. They are entities of fairies and gracious beings of their own beauty and presence, whose essence is incorporated into all aspects of the surrounding reality. Both are incredibly powerful, as are the counterparts of Earth and Water. Their presence permeates the fabric of reality, shaping the very essence of the world we inhabit.

The creature that awaits them is known as a Rockfear. Just as the name suggests, it is fearless and extremely intelligent, and it can conceal itself on any surface. It is a warrior of the realm of Void, in a different form, since this one takes on the form of the princess's servant. It has its own unique magic and can access a gateway to the realm of Death, which they are known to do. Besides being a powerful warrior, it can consume souls and alter creatures of lesser minds, using the elements of Void with ease. But the city is prepared for any dark magic and can protect itself. However, the creature is no lesser mind, since it was once a human form. It adapts to the understanding of human ways and thinking, making it very dangerous for them. It will find a way to overcome their defenses and prepare an attack. According to the ancient books, the Rockfear's power rivals that of a hundred men, making it incredibly formidable. Additionally, its ability to control minds adds to its persuasive prowess. According to legend, it is one of the most powerful creatures ever known to Kumartal. Nevertheless, Samatar will wait. Just catching a glimpse of this creature would be magnificent. Very rare, they seldom turn up, and it takes immense efforts and magic buildup to call forth this creature.

She knows that Princess Celestia is doomed, though the princess herself is unaware of it. The old witch of the Miser Forest, also known as the bastard seer, foretold this. Samatar laughs to herself, placing the leather book down, fixing her dark cloak back on her shoulder. Raymul is an overly eager one who doesn't understand the ways of the Guardians of Dark. The Guardians are indeed very powerful and are always willing to give, except for their own souls, but they always want something in return, unlike the Guardians of Light.

She walks toward the side window and gazes at the horizon, spotting Ra Tomaraz School looming to the right of her view. As the sun sinks into the darkness, the school's silhouette emerges against the fading light. Its gothic architecture rises tall and imposing, adorned with numerous windows that glint in the diminishing sunlight. From this distance, she can make out the imposing spires and fluttering flags, each representing the three elements of Death, Void, and Ice. Among them, the flicker of flames at the school's center adds a subtle, ethereal glow to the scene.

The sight evokes memories of her days in the school's dormitory, where she delved deep into the mysteries of light and dark magic. Those were captivating and inspiring times, as she effortlessly mastered the intricate arts. Though politics never held her interest, she recognizes its importance in achieving her ultimate goal of leading the people of Kumartal.

She has undergone many experiences, leading her to create an underground society to revive the lost witchcraft called the Shadowed Sorcery. The society has many members, including Deryn, a powerful sorcerer living in the slums of Passear, and her followers, practicing healing and spells. To keep a watch, she recruited Deryn into her society, knowing her capabilities. Though scholars may not approve, she takes pleasure in using the term "witch" to describe them. For Samatar, "witches" and "sorcerers" both cast charms, spells, and rituals by the Guardians of Life. However, Eva holds a different opinion.

She can no longer trust Eva, ever since she recruited her into the society. Eva always goes against her judgment, but she possesses exceptional abilities. They had studied together for many years, and Eva is also a wizard with capabilities. Eva has never disclosed how she acquired her powers, but it appears that she might be classified as an Andord. Wizards were thought to have disappeared during the Olen era, and only a handful remain today, but they are nothing like before.

What intrigues Samatar is that Eva is the only woman she knows of who can will her soul, a practice that only wizards know. She brought her into the society because it would benefit their cause, but something feels off. Eva is concealing something, and she can sense it. She tried using secret spells and charms, but nothing was revealed. Even the old woods fairies wouldn't provide even a tiny clue, which gave her further reason to distrust Eva.

As soon as the door closes behind Samatar, she feels a sense of unease. She turns quickly to find Kerfort waiting for her. He is only five feet tall and very broad, with long hair combed neatly straight and a beard matching the length of his black hair.

"Sorry to disturb your meditation, Empress Samatar," says Kerfort politely.

"What is it, Kerfort?" Samatar asks, walking swiftly over to her congested desk, lifting her cloak, and sitting down promptly.

"May I?" Kerfort asks, pointing to the tall flask by the door containing the magic dust of Isqu.

Kerfort grabs a handful of the dust, which irritates Samatar since he only needs a pinch. However, being a mountain dwarf, they are known to be rough by nature. Kerfort tosses the dust in the air. "Spectral Veil," he says, and the dust stops in midair and compresses into a miniature window that represents a moving tapestry of the outskirts of the city wall.

"As you can see, my dear, it's impressive," Kerfort says, placing his finger on the gate's wall and running it up toward the swamp. "The creature awaits. I suggest we align our forces here," he says, placing his finger in the middle of the tapestry. "That way, they will go head-to-head against the creature before it attempts to enter our defenses. At the same time, we can send out other warriors around the city to make sure it doesn't send any other surprises."

Kerfort then places his hand into the dust and concentrates, swirling it within, and extracts his hand. When the dust tapestry reveals the ancient swamp forest, Kerfort points to the top left of the swamp, where a rocky mountain of death—the musky water—lies. "Sources tell us that the creature is a male from the unforeseen underworld, and he waits within these rocks. I could send our best warriors to confront the creature now and set traps." Kerfort starts to shake with excitement. "We will blast the creature back to where it came from, along with all its sinister followers, and then—"

"Wait, my dear Kerfort," Samatar says calmly, leaving her arm on her chair and her stumpy hand against her face, with her black fingernails pressing against her wrinkled cheek. "Don't you think you're being a little too overly excited? We've dealt with many unnatural phenomena in the past. Besides, don't you think we should first find out why this demon decided to take on the surface world?"

"With all due respect, we shouldn't have this thing near us, especially with you and Princess Celestia in our debt. It's from the Void realm, unsacred and unwanted. It should be destroyed and sent back. I'll take it on and smash it into pieces. I won't allow this thing to set a foot in your presence," Kerfort says as he faces the tapestry and points to the mountain location. He pokes it, causing the magic to be disrupted. Suddenly, Kerfort takes a deep breath, composing himself. "Mistress, excuse me. We can take it on and take what is needed, or maybe we can destroy it…something to that effect," he says, acting confused.

The empress stands up and moves over to the short dwarf. He has a young and fierce face with hardened features, wide and aggressive looking. His hair is long, as with any typical dwarf, well-groomed, black, and beautifully braided down each side of his shoulders. His hair shines brightly against the candles in the room. His broad, blue eyes stare intensely, and his nose stretches halfway across his large mouth. His skin is dark but light on the brown side, revealing a rosy cheek. This is one of her closest friends, a high-ranking lord of the mountain dwarves of the city of Yanter. They are a unique species and can be beautiful or ugly but rough and forbidding creatures in the realm.

"My Kerfort," she says, putting her small hand on his shoulder, causing his chain mail to rattle. "Remember, we are a city of reason and learning. It should come naturally to us." Samatar stands quietly for a moment, staring at her faithful friend. "When was the last time you mated?"

"Uh, maybe six months? I don't recall, Your Grace," Kerfort replies, looking nervous and unsure.

"Well, I think you are well overdue. Go find a mate and come back to me in a few days when you are in a solid state of mind. The magic is clouding your judgment."

"But Your Grace, I will be fine—besides, we have potions that can subside the pain," Kerfort protests.

"I know, my dear friend, but I need a determined warrior with strategic abilities and reasoning ready at this time. Go, find your mate quickly, and release your Traversintul."

Kerfort bows, swirls his hand, and commands the magic dust back to the flask, then turns to leave. "Kerfort," Samatar says as he opens the door.

"Yes, Empress?"

"Please find a partner."

Suddenly, he starts to shake and squeeze in excitement. He tries to control the Traversintul sensation that suddenly overtakes him. Kerfort realizes that he has broken the empress's solid wooden door latch, which he holds in his enormous, stubby hand. "I'm sorry, my empress," he says, trying to take hold of the wooden latch. "I will fix it as soon as possible," he adds, feeling embarrassed by his lack of control.

"It's quite all right. Now hurry," Samatar replies.

Kerfort runs off anxiously, still holding onto the latch.

Samatar smiles with understanding and sadness. Mountain dwarves are such unique and wonderful beings, unlike humans and many other species. The mountain dwarves have special needs and magic that are seamlessly integrated into their entire city. Since the time of the city's destruction, they are expanding and adapting their magical skills in a desperate effort to avoid extinction, a situation that deeply saddens her. Their queen demands that they reproduce, as there are too few female dwarves left. They are a highly skilled clan, but their numbers are dwindling. The Destroyer saw their near extinction. Kerfort is at the height of adulthood, and his mating cycle magic is uncontrollable and must be enacted before it kills him. He needs to mate naturally, as the curse put upon his people prevents any natural cycle of birth that needs to be monitored by the City of the Dwarves. The situation is further complicated by the fact that finding any partner, especially a female, is extremely challenging. Females are not only few in number, but they are also burdened with the responsibility of leading the dwarf race. Only one out of three hundred dwarves has a child, and biological mating does not make a significant difference. The survival of the dwarf race depends on finding a solution to this crisis.

Without proper mating, the mountain dwarves' population will gradually decrease and their strength will weaken over time, making them vulnerable to their enemies. The unique magic that runs through their veins could also be affected, leading to a decline in their overall abilities. The dwarf people were once renowned for their mastery of magic and skilled warriors, but without proper reproduction, they could face extinction, and their legacy could be lost forever. The City of the Dwarves recognizes the importance of mating cycles and created a system to monitor and control them, ensuring the continued strength and growth of their people. However, the Destroyer's actions disrupted this delicate balance, leading to chaos and endangering the entire dwarf race.

⊷⟹ ⟸⊷

Jessie leans against the Eternal Tavern on the deep end of the city walls. He chews on a Parslee elven-tobacco stick, waiting for the signal to release the beacon magic. He is young in his group, just graduated with honors, and the first in his family to attend the Ra Tomaraz School to study dark elements. He needs only three more years of training in the real world to become a young sorcerer. He imagines himself wielding magic, an obsession he has had since he was young. Despite his mother's warnings about the city's witchlike past, Jessie wanted to learn magic in the best city known to humankind, Kumartal.

Looking out into the filthy street, Jessie observes a beggar rummaging through an alleyway for scraps. He has been told that the western gates of Kumartal are very dangerous, but he has mastered proactive charms that can overcome offensive magic. Lost in thought, Jessie absorbs the cluttered buildings tightly packed together, broken brick floors, and puddles of dirty water. He spots a few brave rats scurrying by, joining the beggar in search of food. This section of the city has various famous areas, such as the Kingdom Rights Hall, a beautiful and richly decorated area where the best potions, every known magic book, and magical relics can be found. Every time Jessie walks by the polished gem floor with assorted pine trees by its side, he is amazed by the display of building structures, shops, statues, and gardens. He yearns to explore it all, but he knows he cannot gain access to that section of the city because of his probation as a Yugster, an elven word for "one of magic."

As a storm begins to brew, Jessie feels a sense of disappointment as he waits for some sort of phenomenon that he's been told might occur. However, what he's waiting for was never exactly explained. Standing there, Jessie notices a couple of toads hopping quickly toward him, followed by several more appearing and jumping to various locations. He's transfixed as they reveal an unusual shape and size that he's never encountered before. While this area is known for its strange reptiles, these toads are unlike any he's seen; they're three times the size and covered in sharp scales reminiscent of a dragon. Their bulging eyes seem to be filled with veins, and a milky glass orb protrudes from each toad, emitting a disgusting, watery odor that fills the alleyway.

Jessie shakes his head in amazement and shock when the toads freeze and start to push their hind legs back, as if preparing for an attack. Jessie is confused when one of the oversize toads opens its mouth, revealing its fangs. He has never heard of toads—or any species of its type—having fangs. In that instant, the toads croak loudly and spit a liquid red substance at Jessie's face.

He screams as the substance burns his skin as if a knife has slashed it. Jessie tries to remove the liquid by rubbing his face, but it isn't on his skin anymore. Instead, it has penetrated his bone, leaving a burning pain. Panicking, Jessie tries to run into the tavern, but he feels more substance being splattered onto his back. With each contact, a running, burning pain breaks his skin and rips into the surface of his bones.

Jessie reaches into his pocket to retrieve the beacon bird and his short staff, but instead, he only pulls off pieces of skin from his thighs. What is happening is beyond his comprehension. Jessie gasps for air and falls to the wet, slippery floor, which is covered in his own blood. He is trying desperately to find the beacon, with only one eye left, when the two demonic toads jump on him, biting into him like vultures. In his last attempt, and in agony, Jessie is thinking of how his mother argued with him not to go to the witch tower when everything turns dark.

CHAPTER 12

The Argus

MEANWHILE, ON THE academy campus in the city of Kumartal.

"Come on, cuz!"

"I'm coming, and stop yelling at me!" Larmari replies as she gallops as fast as she can, dodging the civilians who are apparently running for shelter. All the shops and market stalls are boarded up and closed, and they are the only two on the streets at this early evening hour.

"Just like all Gloomreaver, slow," Jarin remarks, amused as he gallops beside her on their bloodhounds.

"Cut the crap and tell me what's going on," Larmari says impatiently.

"I don't know. They said they need us at the front gates, that the magic holding the gate has weakened," Jarin responds, looking at Larmari while her long hair flies wildly behind her from the speed of their ride.

"You're not doing this again, are you?" Larmari asks suspiciously.

"Don't be ridiculous. You know I can't do something like that here. The professors would have picked up on the magic residue," Jarin says, rolling his eyes. "And that doesn't explain the magic that is now being broken down at the front gates," he adds.

"That's impossible. The magic in the gate has held up for centuries," Larmari argues.

"Yeah, I know. But do you really think that magic that old can hold up forever?" Jarin retorts as his hound jumps over a barrel, nearly knocking him off.

"Jarin, did you ever read your textbooks? Magic never weakens," Larmari responds.

"Yeah, whatever. So why are they asking us to help protect the city? Why don't they just send out the Malij?" Jarin asks.

"Maybe there's some sort of phenomenon happening that they need additional help with. I'm not sure. I'm not a psychic or seer," Larmari says.

"You're the brainy girl here. You should know," Jarin says, grinning and pushing his wild hair back from his face.

Larmari swiftly rides her hound and raises her hand, causing a large wine barrel to move out of Jarin's way just before he impacts it. The barrel crashes against one of the small, dark buildings, and he quickly maneuvers his ride to avoid getting wet. He nearly falls off his bloodhound but manages to jump quickly, with ease, as the magic he generates guides him safely onto the hound's back. They both erupt in hysterical laughter.

"Too bad, I would have enjoyed the taste of wine right now, thanks," Jarin says as he quickly looks back at his cousin.

"What are cousins for?" Larmari replies with a smile.

As they approach the front gate of kingdoms, they see multiple Malij crouched and waiting for an attack. Larmari also notices some hidden on the rooftops and behind trees. The High School Masters, also known as the HSM, are scattered in groups, conversing with each other, while a few are taking positions on the limestone centerpiece statue of King Olen the Destroyer. Suddenly, a voice behind them yells, "There you are!" A young lady in a gray satin robe with a hooded black cloak steps forward, accompanied by a slim elf wearing a similar cloak but with black trousers and a white top. "What took you so long?"

"Mistress Lyla and Professor Ref." Both Jarin and Larmari jump off their bloodhounds and indicate for them to stay off to the side. They quickly approach their professors. "We are sorry, we were a little distracted," Larmari says, looking at Jarin with an uptight expression.

Jarin takes a quick survey around the area, looking perplexed. "Excuse me, Mistress," Jarin interrupts, "but why do you need us? Is it the elements of light you seek from us?"

Mistress Lyla stares at them, concentrating, and Jarin can feel that it's not just about the barriers, but a sense of protecting them. "We could use your help," replies Mistress Lyla, "but we felt we needed some bystanders to assist us. Don't you agree, Professor Ref?" She gives Professor Ref an odd look for approval.

"Yes, Mistress Lyla," agrees Professor Ref reluctantly.

Mistress Lyla continues to stare at Professor Ref, indicating that he must speak. The elf sighs and turns his attention to Jarin and Larmari. "Young Graces, this is a very serious matter. Your assistance may be vital, but we may be putting you in great danger. However, Mistress Lyla and I have concluded that these phenomenal beings are from the realms of darkness. We are not sure which realm, and we need young minds that are clear about what they can do and eager to help with a contract on what needs to be done quickly. Since you two are the best students in your union group, we know your family can withstand and help our city, but we need you somewhere else to aid us. In other words, while we handle the confrontation, we need someone to oversee the creatures' behavior."

Jarin and Larmari look at each other with confusion but decide not to say more. Their abilities are uniquely different from everyone here, but they listen with respect to their assignments.

Professor Ref continues, "Your education has prepared you well, and your reputation, besides being royalty, speaks for itself. However, let me remind you that you have much to learn. Your royalty means nothing in our domain, and you must take this event very seriously, or you both will be killed. Now listen carefully; I have activated a portal designed for your family on top of the Evergreen Library, just in case things get out of hand. It will take you directly to your home. The library will only answer to you or your family. It has always been only in the interest of the royal-blooded Arguses to allow anyone within its surroundings, created by the Guardian of Earth."

Larmari gasps with excitement, and Jarin's green eyes widen with surprise as Professor Ref points toward the Gothic structures a few kilometers away from the main gate, well hidden behind the reception building. They can see high, earthly spears looking outward that sit on enormous tree trunks and the structure of an old house that sits inside the huge tree.

Larmari recalls the famous legends from centuries before them that said the Guardian of Earth once needed a place to stay and asked the empress if she could stay in their city. Eartha built this structure for her to keep intruders out while she meditated and studied for a few decades. No one knew why, but she requested certain books, relics, strange planters, and access to certain individuals while within the structure. When she completed her work, to show her appreciation and gratitude, she left the earthly structure to the city as a gift. Since then, it has become a library where the city keeps the most important archives, scriptures, books, profiles, and lord heaven knows what else. The magic still existed when the Guardian took temporary stay, a very protective magic.

Only high scholars, royals, and, of course, the empress can access the building. Rumors say that when the Guardian was here, she actually linked the structure to her secret earthly Guardian lair for when she needed to leave in a rush. The structure stands high and forbidden, with flowers and vines all over. It is very dark green, but there is no sign of grass in the area. No stairs or doorways exist; magic is needed to enter and exit the ancient library.

Cleverly and unexpectedly, since the departure of the Guardian of Earth, the library actually does not provide entries, but strangely only allows the true bloodline Arguses in and out with ease. It is said that for years scholars tried countless times to enter but were only allowed around or on top of the structure. Since then, the library has been forbidden to everyone. It makes sense that their professors here are able to make a portal and ask them to go into the structure to protect them, even though they don't believe the cousins need any protection.

Professor Ref continues, lifting both eyebrows to show his boredom and turning his attention to the students. "When danger approaches, I expect you to escape through the portal, nothing more. While you are in the library, seek some ancient books about these oversize frogs and their acid venom, and anything else that may be useful to help us. Only when it is safe to do so, bring me these books. Try to be observers only, and keep your magic at bay. It may distract these creatures' attention. If it is not possible to get these ancient books, send us a beacon with any important findings that may help us improve our situation. Is that understood?"

"Yes, Professor," Jarin and Larmari reply in unison.

"Good. Now hurry on."

Jarin, born with natural senses of the element of Air, can feel the elf's dislike for his family, but he doesn't know why and decides to let the matter drop.

Jarin and Larmari quickly run to the bloodhounds and take off. The library that the mistress referred to is located at the far edge of the city, away from the main entrance gate. They pass the dormitories, each with its own gargoyle guarding and protecting the young children inside. The gargoyles are strong and forbidding-looking, and with their own magic, they can instantly transport you to another location. This keeps the students safe when curfew has been initiated.

One of the gargoyles stomps near them, warning them not to interfere with the building it's protecting. Larmari and Jarin laugh, knowing that they usually don't stay with these students. They have a separate housing near the city castle that includes larger and more experienced guards. However, they both prefer to stay with other students. Unfortunately, that's the life they have to abide by. They both know how to get around these stonelike creatures and guards. Celestia and Aberra can speak with animals and showed them a secret tunnel, created by a Stonewyrm creature, that can easily access most areas, except for the Evergreen Library, which is oddly inaccessible.

As Jarin and Larmari ride through the streets, they soon spot the Evergreen Library as they pass Enlightenment. The duo speeds down the road on their bloodhounds, passing various bookstores with a wide range of items on display. As they pass by a voodooist shop, they enter a well-manicured grassy area filled with parallel rows of assorted trees that lead them straight to the library, just a few hundred feet away.

After fifteen minutes of travel, Jarin and Larmari finally arrive at their destination with the help of their trusty bloodhounds. They dismount their creatures, which hail from the realm of Void and are a hybrid between a horse and a jackal. The bloodhounds are loyal but constantly thirsty and hungry, so the pair send them back to their stables to rest and eat.

Larmari is struck but not surprised by the sight of the massive tree in front of them, its bark as large as the homes in the area, with roots resting on a couple of stones that define the whole city. Despite the village that developed around the tree over the years, making it seem out of place compared to the surrounding ancient and historic city, the tree looks vibrant and alive, standing out against the landscape. Despite being warned that the area is dangerous and off-limits, Larmari looks around and senses that the information is unusually misinformed.

Jarin nudges Larmari and says, "Hey, snap out of it and come back to reality."

Larmari responds, "I was lost in my thoughts."

"Do you believe the professor's request?" Jarin asks.

"Obviously not," she says.

"Yeah, I sense something, especially from Professor Ref," he says.

"I agree."

A small wooden sign is held aloft by a glimmering reflection of a wood fairy floating and hovering with enchanted grace. The fairy, a magical illusion crafted from elements of air, adds an ethereal touch to the scene. The sign instructs visitors to the Evergreen Library. It politely requests Evergreen Guardians to curb their transportation and leave footwear behind, while advising scoundrels, mammals, and amphibians to ensure cleanliness before proceeding. Other beings are asked to consult with their headperson before entering, emphasizing that only those with permission may enter. Additionally, all inquiries and comments must be related to the Enquire Hall located in Charm Place.

Ignoring the directions due to their circumstances, they approach the enormous, Gothic-looking library, which sits atop four ancient, oversize trees. The bark's size and appearance suggest that it has been there for eternity, compared with the other small and puny trees surrounding it. The vines integrated into the structure escape wildly around the surface, beautifully enveloping the trees and completely engulfing the structure that stands hundreds of feet high. Various exotic flowers and bird nests add to the area's ambiance and surround the tree.

The tree seems uncharacteristically placed in the dark and looming city, yet it looks magically placed in this area.

"Now what?" Jarin asks. "Do we find an entrance or something like that?"

"No, silly, we have to make our presence known," Larmari replies.

Jarin waits for a few moments, feeling restless. His cousin also possesses unique abilities related to the element of Water, including intrusion, intellectual smarts, and control over the elements. He quickly grows impatient.

"Hello! Anyone up there? We're here!" Jarin yells.

"Not like that!" Larmari exclaims. "Don't you know anything? Just say who you are."

"Okay, brainy, so how?"

Larmari thinks for a moment, trying to think of the appropriate words to say.

"Any day, Larmari."

"Shut up. I'm thinking."

"Stop saying that. I'm not a young kid!"

"Fine, then, grow up, because you act like one. Now let me think."

"Fine, then think. That's all your magic is about anyway—thinking."

"Fine." Larmari exhales and continues to power the correct phrase.

After a few moments, Larmari makes her way toward the center of the massive structure. Jarin observes that she has grown up a lot since he last saw her; she is seventeen, only one year younger than him. She is now a fully grown woman with long, flowing brown hair and delicate features. Her wide oval eyes and other traits resemble those of her family. She wears a crescent moon shirt, symbolizing her studies in dark elements—a departure from their family's natural talent in light elements—and an off-white cloak that hangs just over her ankles. The cloak matches her family's pearl stone necklace, signifying her position in this realm.

She stops and looks directly at the vines, raising her hand to touch the massive network of harmony. "My name is Larmari Argus, and this is my cousin Jarin Argus, also a descendant of our ancestors. We request entrance to your beautiful fortress by the request of Mistress Lyla, the High Master of Kumartal, City of the Witches."

Suddenly the ground shakes. Jarin flies next to Larmari, expecting the worst to happen. A long ladder made of twigs and vines appears, ascending to a small opening under the structure. Jarin mounts it and is stunned.

"That's it! All that crazy talk and intrusion, and we get a stupid-looking ladder! I expected a grand entrance!"

Larmari easily discerns Jarin's expression. He always enjoys displaying his emotions, giving him a wild appearance. He is quick to react rather than analyze. He wears the black-colored shirt of his studies of fire, which depicts a flaming fist. Born with attributes of the elements of light of Air, Water, and Earth, same as her. He wears short, baggy trousers hanging over his knees and a long, blue cloak. His dark-brown, curly hair is wildly unkempt, and his pale-toned skin is smooth as the moonstone. A small blue stone earring dangles from his left ear, glinting in the moonlight. He also wears an off-white stone necklace, like hers, consisting of over five hundred small chipped pieces of flat stones compressed tightly around his broad neck. Each Argus necklace has special magical properties that could alert family members through a network unique to themselves. It detects unusual distress or danger. It is their family's unique magical relic, passed down from the elves, so they say, color-coded to represent their family lines and royal background, just like elves. Only the royalty's children and specific members wore them when away from home.

"You should lower your voice and keep comments to yourself. Eartha is not forgiving, and she wants specific requests on an individual basis. She is a very simple person, and material things are irrelevant to her. Remember your studies on the Guardians? Eartha is obsessed with how she set up these specific libraries," Larmari says.

"Well, I thought it was too simple," Jarin replies.

"Let's just go," they both say, and head toward the vine rope when they are interrupted and sense that someone familiar is coming.

"Hi, Jarin and Larmari," their cousin Celestia greets them, accompanied by a group of youngsters.

Jarin is taken aback. "What are you doing here, Celestia? You shouldn't be here!"

"Watch your tone with our princess, cuz," Larmari admonishes him. Another voice joins in from behind Celestia, that of a young girl with long hair that reaches almost to her ankles. It is obviously Aberra Argus.

"You know we don't need any formalities when we're together. What are you doing here, brother?" Aberra adds.

"I should have known my family would sense our distress," Jarin retorts as he starts to walk away from the twig ladder.

"Look, I think you guys should go. Mistress Lyla and Professor Ref won't be pleased to find you here, Celestia," Larmari says.

"I go where I please. Besides, I heard there was some disturbance, so we wanted to see what's going on," Celestia replies.

Two young children, around ten years of age, step forward. "Yeah, you heard her!"

"Who are they?" Jarin asks.

"They're my cousins, Aluiz and Dario, from the Onars side of our family," Celestia explains. "Don't you remember?"

"Oh wow! They've grown so much since the last time I saw them. Hey, cousins, how are you doing?" Jarin exclaims. After their greeting, they all hug each other one at a time, enjoying the warmth and smiles and sharing each other's emotions and passion, a tradition that the family has been doing for generations.

Wait a minute!" Jarin says suddenly, unable to believe his eyes as he looks over his family and out toward the woods, waiting impatiently. Suddenly, another indistinct figure emerges from the bushes a few feet away from them.

"Is that you, Sakeris?" Jarin exclaims with excitement. A tall, shadowy figure joins them.

"Yeah, Prince Jarin."

"Ah, the one and only Sakeris!" Jarin jumps at the individual and gives him a tight hug. He is a towering figure, wearing a long black cloak with matching trousers and a plain shirt. Despite being outside, his massive body and stone-looking face are noticeable. Assorted knives in his belt glint in the sunlight, complementing his shining boots. Sakeris and Jarin slap hands again and hug tightly for a long time. They are the same age and not blood-related, but the family has accepted him as their own, and they are bonded together. "What the Death are you doing here?" Jarin asks, pulling away. "I thought you were still in training."

"Must you curse?" Aberra chides. They all join in the enjoyment of welcoming Sakeris to the group with hugs and smiles again.

"Hey!" Aluiz and Dario join Sakeris, playfully hugging and wrestling with each other, as Jarin also joins in. The identical twin brothers are dressed in matching royal outfits with dark red, neatly groomed hair and cloaks that hang below their waists.

"That's enough, everyone!" Celestia interrupts, knowing they will spend most of the time talking and not focusing on the main purpose of their meeting. "Listen, I asked Sakeris to come with us to distract the Malij for me. We heard that you were called into some sort of duty, and I wanted to make sure you were okay, since our family is in danger. Raymul is looking for me, and although Kumartal has assured my safety, I cannot risk the safety and well-being of my family. Dad is almost at the brink of death, and I believe Raymul is meddling and has something to do with what is happening to my family."

"We understand, Celestia. Father and Uncle are on their way back home. We will get to the bottom of this; you know we always do," says Larmari.

"Yeah! How's Auntie doing?" Jarin asks.

"Mom is still in Zimeris. The priests are trying desperately to reverse the spell, but they haven't had any luck. She's well hidden and protected with our family's help—thanks for asking."

"All right, so why are you here, brother?" Aberra interjects, her eyes fixed on Jarin. She and Celestia share a similar born magic of the element of Earth, which he believes to be the most powerful element of all. In addition, they both possess a rare ability to communicate with creatures of all types, a skill that is scarcely known among humans and creatures in these lands.

Jarin responds to Aberra, and Larmari swiftly adds to their story as they recount the events leading up to their gathering. Suddenly, they hear a loud crash and yelling coming from not too far away. They quickly prepare to confront the source of the disturbance.

"Quickly! We can't do this right now!" Celestia yells. "We need to go to the library as instructed. Up the ladder, everyone!"

They all start climbing the ladder, but Sakeris doesn't move from his post. "Come on, Sakeris!" Aberra says with one foot on the vine leading upward to the treelike structure. "What are you waiting for?"

"I heard Larmari say that only royals can enter the Evergreen Library," Sakeris says, disappointment etched on his dark, tanned face as the moon shines upon him.

"Do you guys ever use your brains? You're part of us, therefore our family," Aberra responds. Suddenly, a loud crash and screams fill the air, accompanied by large fires hovering over some buildings.

"Come on, we're wasting time!" Aberra yells, and Sakeris quickly jumps on the ladder behind her. As they hurry upward, Sakeris can see the ladder disappearing beneath him as he steps on the next visible step with his leatherback boots.

"Hurry! The magic is losing hold! It knows you're not an Argus!" Aberra yells, feeling Sakeris's boots as he tries to move them away on the skinny vine.

"I thought you said I'm family!" Sakeris yells as she leaps to the top, almost reaching him. He realizes the stress Aberra is feeling. Aberra looks almost identical to her brother Jarin, with a distinct and smooth, fair face and curly, light-brown hair, like her cousins. She could almost pass as Celestia's sister too, but they are actually cousins.

"You are family, but the magic of the tree only seeks to protect blood relatives of our family. But you're with us; trust me, just come on! Quickly, I don't have time to explain it, Sakeris!" she says as she pushes him ahead of her. Sakeris is surprised by her strength as she lifts him with one hand, and he feels a strong force pushing him upward as the ladder disappears below her feet. He shakes slightly and stops, causing her to bump into him from behind.

"Ahhh, Sakeris! What the heck are you doing?" Aberra yells at him.

"I want to help you," he yells back, noticing a strange, oversize frog circling the lower perimeter they had just escaped from.

"I don't need your help; I know how to handle myself," she replies, pushing him and causing him to lose his balance. However, the wind cradles him like a baby and swiftly escalates him above. Jarin grabs him easily with one arm, as Sakeris dangles in the air while Jarin holds him, despite Sakeris being twice his size. Then Jarin pulls him in. Aberra is already inside, looking at him with annoyance, while everyone surrounds him, patting and hugging him. The door below them seals instantly.

Sakeris takes a deep breath and looks around the group, thinking to himself, *What a strange family this is*. He smiles with joy at the thought of being a part of them.

CHAPTER 13

Chaos

THE TOWERING FRONT gates of Kumartal rise over two hundred feet tall, their bark-heavy wooden surfaces crackling with powerful magic. More than a dozen Malij stand at various positions around the gates, including a few menacing demons off to the side, their personal staffs at the ready in case of any surprises.

Suddenly, the magical barrier of the Kumartal Gates dissolves, and within moments, an enormous creature bursts through the wall. The demons waiting off to the side cast out blazing red fire in an attempt to consume the creature, but it advances unharmed, heading straight for the main entrance walkway of Yester Street. The wall of fire created by the front defense magic, which appears to resemble an oversize crocodile, fails to stop the creature's progress.

Mistress Lyla and Professor Ref exchange concerned glances, realizing that they have never encountered this type of creature in all their years of study and have no indication of its background. The creature reveals its mouth, which is filled with a variety of deformed fangs that overlap each other in a horrifying display. Its voice is a terrifying, guttural sound that sends shivers down the spines of all who hear it. The creature's black horns start small and unassuming at the upper part of its mouth but line perfectly down to its double tail.

The creature's oversize arms allow it to move quickly, much like a centipede, as it begins to destroy the magical gate. Mistress Lyla and Professor Ref quickly move back to take their place with the other demons. Two young Malij assassins, guided by the wind magic, leap into action, wielding swords in one hand and long, black leather whips in the other.

One of the Malij, Adric, jumps onto the creature's neck, attempting to strangle it with the sharp horns on his body. However, the creature's scaling skin proves impenetrable. The other Malij, Terfford, wraps the Sunford around the creature's mouth and casts a spell, hoping to restrain it. But the creature snaps its mouth open, ripping the famous Sunford whip out of his grasp and grabbing hold of the young Terfford. With a single snap, the creature tears him into two pieces and tosses him aside.

Despite their valiant efforts, it seems that the Malij are no match for this formidable creature. What will happen next?

Laya, from another Malij group, screams in horror as she sees the two pieces of Terfford's body lying before them. In that instant, Professor Ref raises his black staff and summons the magic of Death. He calls out, "Soulbane's reckoning!" A stream of dark light escapes the staff and lands on Terfford's body. It stirs and mounts together, with half of its body destroyed and blood still oozing, and leaps back toward the creature. Professor Ref lowers his staff, with a tear flowing down his cheek. "I'm sorry, Terfford," he says.

While Frank, from the HSM, tries to hold on to the creature's back, three other Malij appear and join him, flipping and leaping toward the creature. Meanwhile, the zombie Terfford leaps toward the creature's mouth, where it bites off his arm. Terfford does not slow down, continuing to fight the creature even as it chews him up and swallows him whole. The Ignisbane's Fury, a curse fueled by the element of fire, is invoked by Frank as he raises his staff, directing magical flames at the creature's face. However, to his surprise, the fire seems to have no effect on the target.

As the creature advances with five of Malij on its back, one of the Malij calls forth his mind magic and summons over a thousand crows, confusing the creature as it snaps at the wilding birds. A couple of Malij fly off the creature's back. One of them flips and lands perfectly on his feet, guided by ice magic that he created before landing. The other, caught off guard, lands and stumbles, with both legs snapping. Suddenly, five white-dressed witches materialize out of thin air and carry the fallen Malij to a secure location, healing the broken bones with their potions and magic.

Another white-cloaked woman materializes next to Mistress Lyla holding an ancient, leather-bound book. The old lady, Deryn, from the slums in Kumartal, opens the hovering book, which glows dimly in the dark, and recites a spell. She casts out a small, silvery substance that hovers over the creature's body like a soft blanket that descends slowly. The demonic crocodile can't move where it stands as the magic dust settles over its body.

Immediately after, Mistress Lyla and Professor Ref, along with three other witches, raise their short staffs. The assorted-color staffs glow and then unite together, emitting a blast of green light that shines out and uncoils around the creature and the three remaining Malij trying to cut it down. The glow instantly turns into ice, consuming the creature like a giant statue of rock.

After a few moments of relief, the group is approached by Mistress Lyla and the wrinkled old woman, Deryn, leader of the Shadowed Sorcery witch society. She asks why they didn't call for their assistance, to which Mistress Lyla replies that they were just fine on their own. As they talk, Mistress Lyla notices a strange necklace around the high witch's neck, adorned with small skull bones that glow in the moonlight. She also observes the woman's weathered face and shaggy gray hair, wondering about the unique magic she seems to possess.

Meanwhile, the remaining Malij gather around the frozen crocodile sculpture, examining the creature and those who froze with it. One of the Malij transforms into a crow and flies up to the top of the sculpture, returning to human form and indicating that no one survived. More witches arrive on the scene to tend to the wounded, but suddenly the ground begins to shake.

Something is stirring in High Witch Deryn, and a new threat has arrived. Mistress Lyla and her group of enchanters and witches are gathered around the frozen crocodile when Deryn shouts at them to leave immediately. She sends forth a blinding light that forces the group to jump away, and as they do, a massive, hideous serpent emerges from the crocodile, quickly grabbing a group of witches and swallowing them whole.

An overgrown bobcat appears in front of Mistress Lyla and her colleagues, revealing its oversize teeth and claws. Deryn quickly grabs the two professors and indicates that it's time to retreat. A portal appears behind them, and they are tossed into it like rag dolls before it seals shut.

Deryn stands back, staring at the beast. She realizes that it was a trap and that the creatures are intelligent, altered in mind. Only one creature could have done this: a Rockfear. The creature leaps into the air like a monkey, revealing its shining fangs and enormous claws. Deryn is mesmerized by sudden fear, but then the creature disappears into thin air.

✦━◉ ◉━✦

Back in Eartha's library, Jarin peers through a large, rusty telescope that he found in the artifact room. "Would you believe that shit? Those creatures actually overcame the Malij," he says to Sakeris.

"What the hell are you talking about?" asks Sakeris as he yanks the telescope away from Jarin's eye, trying to locate the incident.

Princess Celestia moves toward the center room where Larmari is engrossed in a book.

"Relax, boys," she says to Jarin and Sakeris. "Are you done, or should I throw a dog bone so you can wrestle over it?"

Larmari asks Celestia if she has been able to reach Netaha. Celestia shakes her head, indicating no. She has been trying to communicate with the animals in the lair to spread word about the danger outside, but they are duty-bound to stay put. Celestia needs Netaha's unique abilities to communicate with spirits and the undead in order to help locate the creatures' origin and isolate the ancient books that Larmari is sifting through.

Aberra approaches them, two squirrels on her shoulders speaking slowly into her ear. "Did you find anything, Larmari?" she asks.

Aberra quickly relays to Celestia what the squirrels told her. "Did you hear them?"

"I know, Jin and Jan told me," Celestia replies, petting the squirrels gently. "Something about the Destroyer being reborn. We'll talk about it later, Ab."

"Those two mice are gossipers," she says as she quickly peers at two mice scurrying away.

"No," Larmari finally responds to Aberra's earlier question, continuing her search by placing enormous books on top of wooden tree stumps that are part of the library's structure, resembling grown treelike formations. She skips rapidly over the oversize, vine-covered book labels, such as *Far-Seen Creatures* and *Be One of Them—Coded: Reptiles*, searching eagerly for a clue to halt the crocodile.

Across the Evergreen Library room, Celestia stands and yells at her two younger cousins, who are climbing a large oak wood bookshelf with careless-ness, standing on a leaf ladder, and throwing books down as they scan the titles.

"Nothing yet," they both reply.

Celestia looks disappointed and worried, staring at her two younger cousins. "Great, they haven't found it yet, and now we have two new creatures: a bobcat and a serpent. I can't understand why there is no reference to these particular scaly looking creatures, not a single clue."

She knows that the Evergreen Library room contains the most populated and enchanted books in Eartha's library. Books from the entire world can be found here, from the smallest known magical thing to the greatest magic ever known to humans. Every subject is covered in this small room, only two hundred feet wide on each side but magically containing millions of various particle-sized books. Some books were even written by Eartha herself, but no one knows or has been able to recover them in this enchanted room. When the Guardian of Earth departed, she concealed those ancient books in this room. Demons, witches, and even elves have tried many magic techniques to reveal their hiding place, but with no luck. It would be their luck that the answer they are seeking is in one of Eartha's reference books.

Celestia wonders why Professor Ref is relying on them to find some sort of solution. Just because their royal blood gains them access to this library and many peculiar sections in this treehouse doesn't mean they are the only young apprentices in these parts. They are powerful in ways that are magical and can easily control the elements, but there is still much to learn. If her mother was well, she would tear Professor Ref's skin apart for putting them in danger, espe-cially the young ones.

Celestia's younger cousins, Dario and Aluiz, have finally joined her at the window overlooking Jarin and Sakeris. They are tossing a telescope back and forth while arguing and trying to see through an unfortunate incident at the main gate. Celestia stares down at Dario's reddish hair while he clings to her right side, and Aluiz clings to her left arm, taking in the surroundings of Eartha's study room with wide eyes. They are both handsome, like the rest of the family, with similar features, and their magic hasn't surfaced yet, as it usually starts to grow at age thirteen. Although they are afraid now, their purity will soon change that. Just like the rest of the Argus family, they are born into the elements of light and can easily learn and adapt to both elements of dark and light at a very young age. After thirteen, their magic will manifest itself, and it will slow their growth age compared to other humans, almost comparable to an elf but with a lifespan two times shorter. An Argus can live up to two hundred years. Celestia's great grandmother lived nearly to 220. Celestia is only fifteen years old, but due to her innate magical abilities that slow her growth compared to a typical human, she is equivalent to someone in their twenties in terms of maturity and knowledge.

Celestia takes a quick glance at Jarin and Sakeris, watching them be themselves, and smiles. She admires their closeness and knows they are inseparable.

"How's Saram?" Jarin asks Sakeris while Celestia listens.

"She's good, just off on another mission."

"Um."

"What? So you know about her mission too," Sakeris says with surprise.

Celestia approaches Sakeris and tenderly places her hand on his cheek. Having known him all her life, he has always been a constant presence, offering help in countless ways. He holds a dear place in her heart and is cherished by her family.

"Of course, we understand, Sakeris," Celestia says as she steps back, withdrawing her hand from his gentle face. "Jarin is simply being overly protective, not just emotionally but physically as well. It's the vigilance that comes with being family, always watching out for each other, even those without the gift of magic."

"That's right. My sister told me, silly. I'm glad you found someone after Tramisha; she really broke your heart," Jarin says.

"Yes, crows are bigger gossips than you know," Celestia says as she walks toward Larmari.

Jarin continues, "Why haven't I met her, Sakeris?"

"She's afraid of you all."

"Then you should let her know we don't bite."

"Really? Cuz, you are the most intimidating person," Celestia teases.

"Ah, cut it out, cuz. You know what I mean," Jarin says.

"Listen, bro." Jarin turns to his dearest family member, Sakeris, his expression serious. "Love is a powerful emotion. It can be for or against you, good or evil, and it can make you feel unbalanced. You see, the elements of light and dark magic can both have a role in love, perhaps a little of both, making it unpredictable. Love can manifest and come with desirable or undesirable qualities, heavily weighing on either good or evil causes, and it can tip the balance of the elements."

Sakeris looks at Jarin quizzically. "What are you talking about?"

Celestia interrupts their conversation. "He's saying that if you don't feel the same way for her and she's in love with you, you should be honest and straightforward. Don't play with her feelings, because it could lead to unexpected outcomes."

Larmari joins in. "Jarin just wants to make sure you won't get hurt physically or emotionally because of her studies in the dark elements. You men are all the same, complaining about the simplest things!"

Sakeris moves back toward the window, saying, "What do you know about my feelings? I know how to take care of myself."

Jarin places his hand on Sakeris's broad shoulder. "You know I love you, man. I'm here if you need anything. Just do me a favor and trust your gut feelings. Your first instincts are usually right, as my dad used to tell me."

"I know," Sakeris replies.

Aluiz and Dario chime in with agreement, saying, "So meeting her will tell you more about this."

Celestia smiles at her youngest cousins and walks out into the center area.

The Eartha studies room is vast and extremely garden-like green. Every piece of furniture, the windows, and even the books are manifested from some sort of Earth element. Strangely, the room is very bright, and the sun seems to make its way there through the leaves on the ceiling, magically, as if they were outside. Celestia turns to stare at Larmari, who is sitting on a shaped tree trunk. Her pale skin stands out against the oak-wood polished desk, which looks as if it grew out of the ground on the perfectly cut grass they're standing on. Celestia then turns her attention to the beautiful willow tree trunks in every corner of the room. The trunks are massive and seem to form the foundation of this room only. The vines spread out wildly with assorted flowers of all types. The room is also occupied by various small mammals, birds, and insects that roam freely, interestingly not disturbing her and her family. It's as if their presence is known to them, and they are free to access any items and books. There are countless corridors that lead to other odd rooms throughout this vast, ever-changing, beautiful, and earthly library.

Princess Celestia is distracted when she sees Jarin and Sakeris once again arguing over the telescope. Celestia smiles lightly as she moves her brown hair from her eyes. Her cousin Jarin loves Sakeris like a brother, and Sakeris is well known in their family. The only ones missing here are Netaha, their second cousin, and, of course, Jarin's wife Ramara, who is five months pregnant and glowing as ever. A few months ago, she confidently declared that she is expecting a boy. But of course they all knew that already because of their magical connection. The entire family adores the coming of new children; it brings hope to the region and continues to expand their love for one another. They will be wonderful parents.

Celestia looks away, tears starting to flow down her face as she reconciles her thoughts of her father once again. How she misses her parents terribly, especially knowing that her father is ill. She wants to see him one last time, but he insisted on her coming here.

"My beloved daughter, you must go to Kumartal and seek safety there. Once you are there, seek information about the Destroyer, for he will once again strive to restore what was broken. Our kingdom must be reborn once again."

"But Father, I cannot leave you here by yourself. Mother is not here; she won't be back until they find a cure. I can't leave you here alone; I won't do it!"

"My dear, you have your mother's fire and our soft heart. Understand it tears me to see you go, but the woods fairy revealed to me my destiny and that I must see it through, my demise and my kingdom befallen. My dear, I will not be here anymore." Then King Argus placed his soft hand on Celestia's heart and said, "And I will be here always."

"No! Dad, don't say those foolish things; how can you trust those fairies?"

Celestia could see her father's brown eyes filling up warningly with tears. His long, wavy hair, a mix of black and sandy strands, settled lightly on him. "Don't make this hard for me, my love. You know the woods fairies have been supportive. Besides, since the day you were born, your mother and I sought to protect you always. You know your background; you must guide our people. Since I am in danger, I cannot bear to know that you are here in danger too. I know Raymul has something murky planned with the Guardians of Dark.

"My daughter, you must help our people," the king said with a grave expression. "First, I need you to seek out your cousins. Pennaldo will look after our people and keep a watch over Raymul for now; no one knows he is an Argus."

Celestia felt a sudden, overwhelming pain in her heart and ached with grief. Tears welled up in her eyes as she reached out to embrace her father. The two of them cried in silence for a moment before the king gently pulled his daughter back.

Reaching into his robe, he produced a small, red stone, perfectly oval in shape and radiating a faint glow. Celestia had heard of this stone, but she never thought her father actually possessed it. He took her delicate arm and opened her palm, revealing the precious gem. As soon as it touched her skin, it glowed faintly before releasing a burst of red light that enveloped Celestia's chest before fading back into the stone.

"This stone was handed down through the Argus generations. It's unique compared to the other stones made by our families. We don't know its origin, but it's been handed down for generations. It can only be given to another Argus bloodline when the holder knows their time is coming to an end. It's a powerful love stone; some say it possesses a unique love of our family generation all combined, and it aids the holder in unpredictable distress. Others say it protects the Argus family from evil. It's a beacon of our love for you, a way for you to reach us if you are in terrible danger. Keep it close to you, my beloved daughter. When all is said and done, give it to your children and share the love we had, and all the Arguses had, and pass it down to future generations. I believe this stone gets stronger with each passing love, and I know it possesses other properties that we and all past generations were not able to understand."

Celestia stared at the smooth oval stone in awe and then touched the chipped, off-white necklace engraved with her family crest that she wore around her neck. She was also carrying the legacy of her royal bloodline in this unique necklace, a beacon to alert her parents of her ordeal or danger. Now she held an additional special stone, one that would protect her like a shield against magic and non-magical things. The stone glittered in the room, reflecting its core. It was simply beautiful, more stunning than any ruby she had ever seen. She closed her hand over it and brought it to her chest, feeling its warmth spread through her body.

"Father, why give me such a precious gift when you should use it to protect yourself and Mother?" Celestia asked her father, feeling confused.

The king smiled at her and replied, "Why do you think the Arguses are so unique? It's because we have an extraordinary bond and love for each other and the people we protect. Our family believes in love as the true foundation for those to come. This stone was specifically made for our bloodline, and although there are others, our love is strong and extends to others, especially our children. It would not be in my nature to keep the stone when I know you may need it more when I am not here. You and your mother are the only two people I love more than anything in the world. I know your mother would agree with me. So carry the stone, wear it, and pass it on when the time comes."

He paused and then continued, "Now, it's time for you to go." The sun was setting over the High Mountain in the far east. "When you see your mother, tell her I love her so much. I will miss her dearly."

Celestia felt a sudden pang in her chest and threw herself into her father's arms. They both cried for a few moments, and then he spoke softly. "I know you will be okay; I just know they will find a cure. I love you, my Celestia," the king said.

"I love you, Daddy," Celestia replied, feeling both sad and grateful for the precious gift and the love she had just received.

Celestia keeps staring into the library, absentmindedly stroking the small red gem on her neck, a sad smile on her face. She's been holding back her emotions, trying to remain strong and focused. Celestia is the youngest cousin here, alongside her cousins Dario and Aluiz from her mother's side of the family.

Sakeris notices Celestia's tears and asks, "Hey, are you okay, Princess?"

Celestia shakes her head, realizing that tears are streaming down her face as she looks out the window where Jarin is now using the telescope, still stroking Dario's hair. She exhales slowly and quickly wipes the tears with her robe, then smiles at Sakeris, who looks at her with deep sadness.

"Yes, I'm okay. I was just thinking," Celestia replies.

"Your father is a great man. We all love him. I am deeply sorry for what happened to him and your mom, my princess," Sakeris says.

"Thank you, Sakeris. You know, you can always call me Celestia," she says.

"I know, it's just that this training with the Malij is very particular when it comes to formality. I'm sorry," Sakeris says.

Celestia smiles and hugs him. He has grown so enormously that her arms don't reach around his built body.

"It's okay. I just missed you all," she replies, reaching out to touch his smooth and tanned face. His eyes, small yet captivating, still hold the beauty of the small mark on his wide nose—a reminder of a story passed down by his mother.

"So, how are your parents doing?" she asks, a smile gracing her lips.

"All good," Sakeris replies.

"May I ask you something?" Sakeris begins, and Aberra joins their conversation. Two squirrels sit nearby, watching intently. Eventually, one jumps on Celestia, though it fails to distract her. "What is it about your family—this strong connection? You all seem to only stay and marry within one another. It's kind of odd. Why do you all do this?"

Sakeris appears uneasy, prompting Aberra to break the silence.

"Our family's bonds run deep, but it's not by our own choosing. It's the magic we're born into that dictates our fate, even in matters of love and marriage," Aberra explains.

"I always thought your family had arranged marriages," Sakeris says, surprised.

"No," Celestia interjects firmly. "Our souls are bound to another Argus without our consent. It matters not who the biological partners may be. Love discovers our soulmates when the timing aligns."

Sakeris is visibly taken aback by this revelation, his expression betraying surprise and confusion.

"What about this 'Destroyer' character you're all talking about? Are you connected to him, like your magical thing?" Sakeris asks.

Celestia and Aberra exchange knowing smiles.

"We're not connected to the Destroyer in any way," Celestia clarifies, her tone solemn. "Though he does have a place in our history. He is a descendant of Olen, and his ancestor married one of our own. It marked the first time an Argus fell in love with someone who wasn't magically born. The family was thrilled for Terbara and chose not to intervene. Our ancestors believed it signaled the end of the magic bond. But then, the unexpected occurred."

"He killed her," Sakeris interjects, his voice heavy with understanding.

"Yes," Celestia confirms. "It was a chain reaction across races and our beloved Guardians of Light. The Destroyer's actions were destructive and changed the order of nature. Our family had never before lost any of our ancestors to violent death. Races were destroyed or altered. Humans, elves, and dwarves were nearly wiped out. Our family of mostly humans born into the element of light magic paid a heavy price, nearly killing our existence. Some of our family went mad and committed suicide because of the shock of the soul elements of light that killed our beloved Terbara. Only a few strong survivors remained."

"Our ancestors," the two younger Onars twins say.

Celestia smiles softly, looking down as the two younger Onars twins speak.

"Yes," she confirms. "The strike of one of our own Argus by King Olen severed our connection, and even his own descendant was eventually taken from him. Our family became so small, the human race was also nearly wiped out, and they declared us as rulers and protectors of the human race because of our unique abilities that could protect the few remaining humans. Since then, we have protected our people. We don't know anything about the Destroyer, nor do we care about his intentions. We focus on the prophecies, and our family will do what we can to protect our race."

Looking at the squirrel sitting comfortably on her shoulder, Aberra chimes in again, "According to our sources, the reborn Destroyer seems lost and out of place. He has unique properties related to the essence of the Guardian soul."

"So, based on what you just told me, he is dangerous," Sakeris says, staring quietly beyond the library, lost in thought. The group falls into a long silence. The entire area is silent except for the scraping of various animals that scurry here and there in the library.

"I need to ask, am I bound to you all?" Sakeris says.

"Not in our family ways, but more in a protective means," Celestia clarifies.

Suddenly, Jarin yells, "Oh shit!" as he jumps back from the window, dropping the telescope on the grassy area within the library. Everyone jumps up; even the animals run and fly away into hiding, and deer scoot and jump past the group. They all stare at the window, where an oversize green toad is pressing its face against the glass. The toad looks demented and is oozing a greenish liquid that sizzles as it hits the edge of the window. The magic of the evergreen tree is obviously blocking its entrance, but it continues to pound away without success. Fizzing steam emanates from the window as it continues to try to break through the barrier.

"What the fuck was that?" Jarin says as he pulls out a small rod that expands into a long staff. Flames erupt on each side of the tips as he readies himself for battle.

CHAPTER 14

Rocksmear

IT HAS BEEN a couple of hours since they entered the strange tunnels, and they have not seen daylight yet. They finally reach a secure area after walking on foot for what seems like hours into the night. James walks beside Ethan with Eva and the Malij group behind them, and the old wizard leads the way with the strange-looking dwarf. Despite hearing stories about these tunnels being massive and intertwined, James is surprised to see how tightly and neatly they are packed. The tunnels are limited and polished, with a smooth gray rock floor. Occasionally, James catches small glimpses of other dwarves winding within the tunnel walls. These dwarves seem to adjust in the dark, giving James an eerie feeling that he is being watched or observed.

The group encounters a young, stocky dwarf wearing a white robe adorned with unfamiliar symbols. His long, black hair is braided and tied with white fabric matching his robe. Unlike the rest of the group, he has distinct features such as nicely trimmed eyebrows and a wide nose. He appears pleased to see Radion, whose robe flows and features a volcanic mountain erupting and a dragon breathing blue fire. The group walks through the tunnels with the dwarves using their arms for support. The dwarves wear blue trousers and off-white shirts hanging over their broad legs, with neatly tied black hair in small braids. James notices the dwarf carrying his torch looking over his shoulder with concern for their group. The dwarf wears a large, golden medallion with simple circles coming outward, and a large silver knife hangs off his black leather belt. However, James feels a sense of nausea whenever the dwarf looks at him, due to his large eyes that are widely spaced apart with black pupils and a nose as wide as his mouth. The dwarf gives no expression except when he smirks to reveal his perfectly shaped, boxed teeth, which stand out against his peach, rough-looking skin. Of all the strange people James has met, the dwarves are the strangest—but they are neat-looking.

James begins to wander off in thought, recalling the story that Radion recited about Olen. It was clear to him that he was the next descendant of Olen, a powerful wizard lineage that apparently runs through his blood. James feels somewhat different from an ordinary farmer—he is quick to learn and has a strong affinity with all entities around him. Sometimes he can even sense the air, water, and trees whispering to him. At first, he thought it was a quirk, but now it all makes sense. It is said that Olen possessed the powers of the element of light, which encompasses Air, Water, Fire, and Earth. It was these powers that labeled him as what he was known to be, the Destroyer—a name that will now stick to James as the descendant of Olen. James shakes his head as they continue their trek through the unchanging caverns into the dwarf realms. He questions why he was selected and what he is supposed to do. He asked Radion numerous times, stating that he is not fit to be a wizard. Radion assured him that time is needed, and he will know what to do. Nevertheless, he is just a farmer boy. How could those ancient-looking dwarves claim that he is the king?

"Did you see those feet?" Ethan whispers, bringing James back to the present moment. James realizes that Ethan is looking at him with concern, trying to change his mind and bring him back to current affairs.

James exhales, relieved to see Ethan, his best friend, always looking out for his best interest. He then peers slowly at the advising dwarf's feet, trying not to be too obvious. He can see that the boots only cover the tops of the dwarf's feet, revealing what appears to be heavily calloused and leathery black skin. It's strange to see how he walks so differently on the rocky floor, with his feet seeming to stomp every so often.

"Yeah, strange, isn't it? They don't need to cover the bottoms of their feet," James responds, pondering the curious nature of the dwarves.

Ethan points out, "Not only that, but the bottoms of their feet are almost a stone texture."

The dwarf suddenly looks back, catching James and Ethan in conversation. James nudges Ethan to be quiet, and the dwarf makes a grumpy sound before smiling and facing forward again.

"Weird," Ethan mutters. "Everything okay between you and Eva? You two were in the woods for a while."

James replies, "Yeah, everything is fine. I really don't want to talk about that right now. Sorry, Ethan, it's just that I have so much on my mind."

"I understand. When we get to the dwarf city, we should go to a local tavern, get a few drinks, and just relax. I mean, you need it more than I do. Or should I say, we both need it. I could use a nice wyvern ale if they have any there," Ethan suggests.

Ethan turns to face his best friend, and James notices that his nose is healing, and the bruises are fading away. They had shared personal secrets for so many years, but this time, James couldn't say much.

"I'll definitely take you up on that offer," James says, and they fall silent as they continue their trek through the rundown tunnels that lead downward into blackness.

As James walks down the long stone hallway, he notices Eva talking to an unusual group of Malij. He scans his back and wonders why she is still hiding things from him. The entire conversation they had earlier still echoes in his mind.

"Why did you lie to me?" he asked Eva, his voice rising. "I thought I knew you; you were like my mother, the mother I always knew. How could you hide such evil things from me?"

"Please lower your voice," Eva replied, looking around. "Eartha doesn't like distractions in her creation. And yes, I did lie to you. I was protecting you from the Dark Guardians." She sighed, revealing her beautiful face that shone vividly against the dense trees around them. The sun was setting to the east, and its light filtered through the branches, casting a goddess-like aura on her.

"Why are you protecting me? My father never mentioned such silly things!"

"Your father wasn't well since your mother passed away," Eva explained. "Your parents knew who they were and why I was here. They hired me as a wizard and guarded their secrets. But when your mother died, it signaled that darkness was coming. We thought it was best to keep you from knowing the truth and complicating things."

"What does my mother have to do with this? You told me she died of a rare disease."

Eva looked away slowly, gazing emptily into the silent forest. It was as if James had opened up deep wounds in her, and the forest felt her pain and agony. She closed her eyes, and a tear fell from her face, hitting her blue robe lightly. When she looked back at James, her eyes were filled with tears.

"My dear, I loved your mother so much. We go back a long way. I tried everything I could, but I was tricked." She paused, trying hard not to recall the terrible ordeal from her past.

"She was murdered by a powerful elf who introduced rare poison into her bloodstream while she was carrying you in her belly. Knowing that they were also trying to kill you, she quickly altered the blood flow to prevent the poison from reaching you. Unfortunately, it was too late for her, and she passed away while saving your life. Your father eventually found me, and we were able to deliver you in time."

Eva moved away from James to gather herself. James came up to her, placing his broad hand on her delicate shoulder. "I'm sorry, Eva. I'm just confused, and I wish you didn't have to bear this burden alone," he apologized. He felt foolish for believing Eva's story, but he now understood why she didn't tell him earlier. "It's just this idea of Olen and me, or should I say my family, being linked to it. I don't want any part of it," James declared, his silence breaking. He waited for Eva's response, but the forest had gone completely quiet, as if it were eavesdropping on their conversation.

"How did this happen? Who did this to my mother?" James asked suddenly, feeling a surge of anger.

Eva wiped away her tears with a stained blue napkin she had retrieved from her pocket. "Your mother would have loved you so much. She asked me to take charge and accept you as my own. I told her I couldn't do it, but she insisted," Eva revealed, ignoring James's question as she recalled the painful past.

Eva smiled at James, gently touching his face. "We will talk later, my dear. We have company," she said as a dwarf emerged from the woods.

"James, look." Ethan interrupts his thoughts, bringing him back to the present.

James feels his heart race for a while but then spots a bright opening ahead. Dwarf guards surround them, but this time they look different. Some are fatter, shorter, and have various hair colors and styled beards. They are no longer walking in small tunnels but in large, long chapels, bunkers, and more dark tunnels carved out of rocks. Each tunnel leads to a thick stone door engraved with strange symbols. The stone walls are carved with statues of distinguished-looking warrior dwarves, and the ceiling is made of arched and corundum rocks. Candles with a strange blue light flicker in the rocky cradles, providing a soft light for the entire cavern. Moreover, certain areas seem to contain small puddles of lake water and carved, rich benches, revealing some evergreen grass and flowers that bring beauty to the cavern. James is confused because he cannot understand how growth can exist within these caverns.

All the warrior dwarves stop to look at the newcomers. They have similar features such as large mouths, more prominent eyes, and perfect teeth, but they are different in their own way. As they continue their parade, they walk toward the center chamber, where the floor is carved with a strange, circled symbol that glows faintly in purple and is gated with an elevated, heavy golden robe. Four heavily armed guards stand on each side, each dressed in distinguished clothes of dark red, light blue, off-white, and a sea green color marked with the same symbol on the ground. James's guide walks over to the dark-red-clothed person and begins talking with him in silence. James and his party wait, and the confusion around them intensifies as the dwarves around them keep talking among themselves, only eyeing James and Ethan. An uncomfortable feeling starts to rise as James senses an unpleasant resentment toward him.

The guard standing by the gated rope suddenly steps back a few feet in a very formal manner. They turn around and bow down, their faces touching the floor as they mumble. A bright glow shines in the exact color of their robe and surfaces from their body, floating slightly to the center of the gated circle. The glow then recedes and is absorbed into the center symbol, revealing a pointed star.

James notices a huge carving on the stone wall to his right depicting two triangles side by side, with one of the triangles upside down. There is a circle in the middle of each triangle with a line connecting each point to the circle.

James stares curiously at the carvings.

"Strange-looking symbols...looks to me like if you merge these two triangles, you get a star," Ethan says.

"Very good perception, Ethan," Eva says from behind him.

"What do they mean?" James asks.

Radion chimes in, "The triangle on the left represents each point of the elements of light. Earth is on top, Air is on the bottom right, and Water is on the left. The upside-down triangle on the right is their counterpart and equal. Death is on the bottom point, Ice is on the top right, and Void is on the left side. The middle circle on both triangles is the element of fire. They call her the bridge and access to both realms. Each point of these triangles is governed by a Guardian. The Guardians of Light are on the left, and the Guardians of Dark are on the right; these are the Guardians of Life. Yes, Ethan, combining the two signifies mastery of the elements, but very few can master both. Elves are known to understand the light elements well, given their longer lifespan. Dwarves live long but have a shorter lifespan than elves. And, of course, humans cannot master the elements of light, except for the Argus clan. Humans have shorter lifespans, and the dark elements are eager to pass through our realm, adapting easily and tending to influence humans more readily. Humans often lean toward the dark elements, as they perceive them as more liberating compared to the light elements. The study of dark arts is often associated with witchcraft, while the light arts are termed wizardry. And then there is you, James, possessing a soul aligned with the light."

"Witches are evil, then," Ethan says.

"And this, Ethan, is where you are naive," Eva says sarcastically.

"This is confusing; I'll stick with stealing," Ethan says as he walks away.

Radion faces James and warns him to be prepared when entering the lair of the dwarves, as their welcome may not be entirely friendly.

An elderly dwarf emerges from one of the open corridors. He seems frail and weak as he slowly makes his way toward them, eventually stopping at the glowing star symbol in front of them. James thinks that someone needs to support him or find him a seat. The old dwarf has a long, well-groomed beard that is completely white. Another dwarf, the opposite of the older one, appears full of energy and life. He wears a dark blue robe with an upside-down triangle as he quickly walks to the top right point and stands ready on it. The point symbolizes the jagged mountain, which represents the element of Ice. The energetic dwarf signals to the older one that he is ready. The older dwarf realizes that he must begin.

James realizes what Radion was referring to—mastering the elements of light, which took years and likely the entire life of the older dwarf, while the young dwarf, who appears to be his age, is adept at dark elements.

The older dwarf raises his hand, and a slow, shimmering light appears, causing water to ripple from all sides of the cave. James has no idea where the water came from since the entire cave is closed off with no visible signs of water or life. The water converges in the center of the star, and the younger dwarf quickly extends his arm, forming a beautiful archway of ice around the flowing water. The water then transforms into a transparent, waving substance, creating a doorway that could lead to the other side of the cave. Both dwarves rotate their hands in different fashions, murmuring to each other. The archway begins to glow brightly, and in a flash, it creates a solid, see-through wall that displays a bright city beyond it.

Ethan gasps and faces James, stunned and afraid. "Interesting. It's some type of complex lock between the old guy and the young one to open a gateway," Ethan explains.

"Yes." Eva joins them by the archway as they gaze out at the city. "In the city of Rocksmear, dwarves are the masters of locks and doorways. Their city has been completely sealed and protected since the time of Olen. It takes two dwarves of precise cooperation to open its doors for visitors, using the correct locking sequence. And to complicate matters, it requires skill from both elements of light and dark, which the dwarf nation adores," she explains.

James and Ethan both stare at the doorway, unsure of what to do and afraid to proceed. The old dwarf, now limping from standing too long, says to them, "You don't have much time, lads." His voice is raspy. One of the warriors, fully armed with weapons, helps him back toward a small passage that leads to darkness. The younger dwarf quickly walks back and stares directly at James, pausing for a few moments with what seems like anger and no fear. His features are young, with a broad face, dark skin, and powerful-looking upper cheeks.

"Be quick and stay out of the way!" He raises his voice.

Eva places her hand on James's shoulder as the dwarf looks directly at her and sniffs loudly, pushing his robe back and following the older dwarf into the darkness.

"It's okay, dear. We need to proceed quickly. We don't like to keep the portal open too long; it leaves the city vulnerable," she says, nudging them to move.

"Wait! Isn't there another way in? I mean, I don't mind taking the long route," Ethan says, stopping with sweat pouring down his face, looking anxious and frightened.

"Yes, there are other ways to get in if you wish to get your soul sucked out and be killed before attempting to enter the underworld. Besides, we don't have weeks. We're pressed for time, and I don't like to keep the queen waiting. Now let's get moving," Eva replies, and they begin to walk through, followed by the Malij assassins.

"But I don't—" Ethan protests before one of the dwarf warriors pushes him through. Ethan feels a hard thump on the side of his head, as if someone has thrown a chair and it landed on his head. The impact is so strong that his blood rushes to his head, causing him to feel suddenly lightheaded, and he faints.

Instantly, James reacts and reaches for the dwarf guide, but before he can, he is stunned by a quick-tempered warrior who lashes out at him. He can't move. "James, please." Radion suddenly appears in James's mind. "Ethan isn't hurt; it's a dwarf technique to temporarily stun an individual."

"Would you let go of me?" James says out loud, struggling to move. A few nearby dwarves look at him strangely, as if he were a lunatic. "In a minute," Radion replies. "Listen, the dwarf people are very quick to judge, and their temper is very loose. They are very protective of their home, especially the women and their queen. James, please, just pick up Ethan and apologize."

Reluctantly, James stands up, staring hard at Radion and then at the guide. He realizes they are surrounded by warriors. What's interesting is that one of the Malij seems poised to attack, holding a short sword strapped behind him. "These are the Ironfist warriors, the queen's personal guards of the city," Radion says as he too stands up, slowly readying his hand in his robe to pull out a weapon.

James proceeds slowly, pulling back his curling hair and pulling up his trouser pants before bending down to pick up the pale-looking Ethan. Ethan leans swiftly on James's sweating arm, and then James stands up slowly and walks over to where Radion waits patiently. James bows to each Ironfist warrior and recites Radion's statement when he is done. "Forgive our behavior, for neither I nor my companions knew and have yet to learn your customs. If you would please let us proceed so we do not burden any more of your time while you continue to protect your queen and the prosperous city she governs." In an instant, all the dwarves smile and nod at each other, and the air seems to lighten when the dwarves continue with their duty. The guide steps forward, smiling, and leads James slowly to the milky funnel.

James feels the magic power slowly engulfing him and Ethan. James feels like he's being drowned upward and at the same time like he's being stretched thin. Everything around him disappears, and only the swirling of the funnel gate surrounds him. Within moments, he feels himself snap back like a rubber band, though his body seems to be intact throughout his journey. Slowly, the milky funnel dissipates, and his head stops humming after he enters the magic gate.

He slowly puts Ethan down on the rocky floor and looks outward, completely breath-taken by the extraordinary view before him. They are standing on top of some kind of tall pedestal as white clouds hover slowly around them, and the sun's rays beam into what appears to be an enormous dome above them. Small cracks and scattered openings in the dome allow light to shine through, revealing a dozen golden beams of light reflecting off the clouds around them, the stone dome, and the massive city below.

James can't resist the temptation and has to stand up and blink a few times to take it all in. The landing post they are standing on has over a thousand steps that lead downward to a vast expanse of assorted stone homes, countless arches, bridges, and a network of sparkling rivers. The surrounding trees seem to blend seamlessly with the environment, glowing and producing a shimmering effect by a glamorous waterfall toward the end of the city. Thousands of tiny beings are bustling about, and the city is alive with houses, animals, children, workers, and a sense of community that James has never seen in his whole entire life.

Oddly, James takes a double look and notices that there are no dwarf females in the busy area. All are males and youngsters, and some are couples; others are workers and warriors, all wearing various types of clothing in different fashions. The city is absolutely stunning, decorated with assorted statues, water fountains, overly structured rocks, and a variety of trees and plants. Mountains are scattered all around, and as James looks farther out, the city seems to stretch on for miles, at least three hundred leagues. The stone buildings grow larger and more Gothic-looking the farther he looks, eventually leading to an enormous and peculiar tower at the back of the city, not far from the heavy waterfall that falls and filters the network river, which includes a shaky and unusual growing ruby substance all around, and tunnels beside it. Flags on top of the continuous stone towers must be at least a thousand feet tall on top of the perfectly carved stone structures. The queen must live in that astonishing castle.

James hasn't blinked since he first saw the breathtaking view before him, but he suddenly senses something new stirring within himself, something forbidden and magical. Despite this, James lets the feeling pass.

"Beautiful, isn't it?" Radion says.

"Yes," James responds. "I've never seen such beauty and attention to detail in the craftsmanship." James turns to face the old man and notices how relaxed and at peace he looks, as if the place they've entered has rejuvenated him. "How could such beauty be captured inside this mountain? I mean, the sunlight coming through, the clouds roaming freely, and the river filtering life."

"It's a very old city, James. It existed before even my time and the time of Olen. They say it was once occupied by fairies who served the Guardians and unified the magic that exists today. But as time passed, they moved on. Fairies don't like to feel oppressed or pressed upon, and they tend to be private. Therefore, the Guardians commanded them to move on. Some fairies disappeared due to this, especially the Turlock, known as the swamp fairies. Nevertheless, they moved on into different isolated areas, eventually becoming permanent residents of these areas. They devoted their time to protecting the magic that resides beneath these precious grounds and stone. Over time, wars sprung out, and eventually, they became darker. No one knows why, but the powers of Eartha and the beloved Guardian of Air assisted the dwarves in protecting their city by establishing the dome mountain you see. It was accomplished just before the first Dark Wars. The dwarves grew accustomed to this closure, and soon they depended on its protection. They built tunnels and passageways that led to various places, including the city of Olen. With time, the city became a network between the dwarves and the outside world."

"Where are the females?" James finally asks.

Radion sighs slowly. "That, my boy, is a long story."

"A story that doesn't need to be told right now," Eva interjects, urging them to move forward down the path.

"He should know," Radion objects.

"Okay, I'll explain it quickly," Eva says. "Your ancestor killed an Argus and caused an imbalance in the natural order of things. Since the sword he acquired from the Guardians of Light carried a piece of their soul, it erupted and distorted their existence. It was not your doing, James, please understand that. However, for the dwarf race, the disruption meant that fewer females were born naturally, making them a vanishing being. Once a rare female is born, she is aggressively protected by the queen and raised separately. Dwarf females are valued as rulers, a promise of their continued existence in this world. It's a burden that these females must endure, a huge responsibility whether they choose to find a male mate or not. Dwarf society is a cohesive race where females and males are equally capable. Because of the elements of light, the dark elements were able to force their way into the living world and caused chaos for the dwarf race. No one knows why the Guardian of Void specifically targeted the dwarf nation. Regardless of the outcome of this ancient race, the dwarves have adapted and maintained their existence and managed to try to reproduce their kind with the aid of magic."

"They are like a bee colony," Ethan says aloud, finally regaining awareness.

James gives him a quick, disapproving glance.

"But it's true; look at them. The males work and give their lives for the queen and females as they protect their only means of existence," Ethan continues.

"Good observation and interesting interpretation, Ethan," Radion says.

"Okay, that's enough; they are waiting for us," Eva interrupts, noticing the Malij assassins appearing from behind the group. They were following the dwarf warriors through the shadowy caves and now look around intently, astonished to witness the thriving, brightly lit city for themselves.

CHAPTER 15

The Meeting

THEY WALK THROUGH countless passages, through cave stone homes of various sizes and heights. Citizens bustle through them, laughing, moving, mixing with birds singing, trees swaying, and small, comforting breezes that occasionally come through. It feels as though they have entered another realm of experience, another world. James has heard stories that other realms exist besides their own. Each realm is different and governed with various purposes of life.

As they stop a few times, warriors change shifts and exchange greetings as a new group of warriors replaces the earlier ones. Young dwarf males are running wildly, throwing a heavy rock around, playing some sort of sport as they pass through a grassy area. The youngsters seem to use their bare feet as they kick the small boulder with ease, while the opposite team tries to catch the rock and tumbles on top of each other. Adult dwarf males are screaming and maintaining order to keep the boys from hurting each other.

It breaks his heart to see that his ancestor's actions caused a disruption to their existence. However, he agrees with Eva that they seem happy and contented. What was once known is not known to the new generation that never experienced what was before.

It feels like hours as they continue to walk, pausing occasionally to rest. They pass through a bustling intersection teeming with dwarf citizens. The scent of ale immediately fills James's nostrils, signaling the presence of a nearby tavern. Inside and outside the tavern, screams and laughter mingle in the air. Some dwarves are visibly intoxicated, while others watch with keen interest, navigating through the crowd with ease. A few individuals even spit at James as he walks by, though others offer smiles and slight bows. As he observes the scene, an unsettling sensation gnaws at him, urging him to react, though he's uncertain why. A gentle breeze brushes against his skin, sending a shiver down his spine. He realizes he wants to delve into their thoughts but suppresses the urge, recalling Radion's warning against interfering without consent.

As he's lost in thought, Radion catches up with him. Finally, he feels relieved that the air has stopped feeling intimidating. He can see Radion's expression immediately change, his dark face brightening in the twilight of the trees around them, and he smiles.

"This is such a magical place. I am still in shock at the beauty of this thriving city. I could never imagine a mountain possessing such glory," James says.

"Yes, my boy. It is just as unusually beautiful as the elf city, in my opinion, maybe even better."

James falls silent for a moment, and Ethan intervenes. "What about the strange rivers? Some look sparkly clear, and others look forbidden. Is it safe to drink from them?"

"They are the creation of none other than the Guardian of Water. They help preserve life here and provide special properties to keep the dwarves alive. The Guardian's heartfelt sadness for the dwarves is necessary to channel her magic through the stone walls, purifying the water and providing the means for them to survive and stay protected since the destruction caused by her sister, the Guardian of Void."

"I thought you said they are counterparts, opposites," James adds.

"In magic, but all Guardians are sisters and brothers, belonging to the fairies. They lead and promote life, the existence of light and dark in balance," Radion says.

"To a certain extent," Eva says sarcastically, walking together with the Malij assassins in front of them.

"That's true," Ethan says, agreeing with Eva. "Look what the Guardian of Light has done. It seems to me like they alter the balance."

"Not by choice, Ethan," Radion says.

"Why are you telling us this?" James finally asks.

"It's important that you understand the nature of magical elements and who governs them."

"Great, we are getting a crash course on Guardians, volume number one," Ethan says jokingly.

"All right, Ethan," James says, nudging him and causing him to lose his balance.

"Then why do the Guardians treat us differently? I thought they governed the magic that produced the well-being of all creatures and existence in this world. It seems to me that they are constantly on top of each other rather than fulfilling their purpose of existence," James says.

Radion doesn't say anything for a moment, watching James analyze his thoughts, and smiles at him with pride and admiration.

"You're right, James. They are busy worrying about others and themselves, but I can assure you that they are doing their jobs. Both the Light and Dark Guardians are very important, and their sole purpose is to ensure that magic is properly protected. They will never do anything to harm its existence. It's not part of their nature to destroy magic; they simply can't do it." Radion pauses to catch his breath and recall his thoughts.

"Fairies, on the other hand, are a different story. There are higher forms of classified fairies that are very powerful, some more powerful than the Guardians. Fairies can alter magic and change existence if they choose. The woods fairies have been around since the existence of this world, and they have involved themselves with the Guardians and humans. Even today, rumors have it that the royal Arguses have ties with these fairies and possess special inner powers, unfamiliar to any wizard and witch. Our scholars believe that these Argus descendants are somehow linked to the gracious Guardian of Earth and possess unique capabilities and magic only known to them since Terbara Olen."

Radion pauses for a moment, lost in thought and analyzing what he has just said. Seemingly forgetting where they are, he mumbles to himself as he tries to convince himself of something.

"Arguses are indeed unique in their own fashion," Radion continues, returning to the topic at hand. "We have yet to fully understand their ways, how they are able to propagate their kind, and how they can sense one another. Their love and mutual protection are so otherworldly, even though humans possess the capacity to love and care for their families just like a mother and father would. But the Arguses take this to an extreme when it comes to their own bloodline and entire clan. Just like any king who wants to ensure the existence of an heir, these Arguses act like a pack of wolves, protecting their own and their mysterious ways. They stick together and protect one another like no other family. And, of course, the secret magical abilities they possess when a new Argus is born are unparalleled. I have never seen such hope, love, and unique magic in any human. They are almost like elves but purely human. Yes, these Arguses, who I believe are somehow integrated into the fairy world, have been a big asset to the Guardians and humans ever since the early times of Terbara Olen. She was a powerful Argus and secret sorceress who possessed one of the most powerful stones of her ancestors."

"You mean to tell me that the legendary Queen Olen is actually Terbara Argus, the wife of King Olen?" James asks in disbelief.

"Yes," Radion confirms. "Terbara Olen possessed a unique stone of her family legacy," he continues. "Some say it was a gift from an ancient ancestor of the Arguses, a simple farmer who obtained it from a fairy. Others believe he stole it from one of the Guardians. We don't know, James. These stories tend to be myths. What we do know is that the stones only answer to the bloodline of the Arguses, which makes them unique and royal.

"But in my opinion, it was the very stone worn by his wife that drove King Olen to madness and led him to kill her, as well as cause the eruption of the realm," Radion states grimly. "It's possible that the power of the stone was too much for him to handle, or that it corrupted him and made him use Vertmor— the sword imbued with the souls of the Guardians—in ways he shouldn't have. We may never know for certain, but one thing is clear: the Arguses have always been the protectors of this stone, and it holds a great deal of power and significance for them."

"Do I have any ties with Argus, then?" James asks suddenly.

"I'm not sure what you mean. I already told you that you have unique properties," Radion responds.

"Then what am I?" James raises his voice in frustration.

"Calm down, buddy." Ethan puts a comforting arm around James.

"Boys!" Eva intervenes. "Let's focus now. We are nearing our destination," she says from the front.

"They are already taking us down, so let's proceed." At that moment, the

Malij join Eva, and the group, including five dwarf warriors, is escorted down the rocky staircase. As the city draws nearer, it becomes more elaborate. Citizens become fewer, and those walking around these specific parts look more regal. Warriors of many types, young and old, some in robes and many in fashionable colors, wield magic and carry symbols of the elements of light and dark.

As they walk through the city, the guards, initially dressed in light armor, are replaced with heavily armored warriors wearing shiny steel mail and carrying huge weapons, which seem to be bigger than the dwarf warriors themselves. Many of the warriors are covered in their own helmets and don't notice the group as they parade through the city, slowly approaching the magnificent castle made of stone that climbs at least a thousand feet high. James can see tiny figures along the castle wall balcony, and flags bearing the symbols of both sides of the elements of light and dark are hung everywhere. A gargantuan fire, centered in the far distance, reveals a white stone as tall as the huge gates, unaffected by the fire that engulfs it.

All around James, as they near the castle front, are massive stone doors, each one carved with many unknown dwarven statues showing powerful figures. He is astonished by the watery network all around the entrance, almost as if the water were protecting the castle itself, with a blazing, fiery stone in the center of the courtyard. An older dwarf dressed in highly golden clothing stands in front of the blazing fire, and the entire courtyard is magnificent, a guardian in itself, with strangely glowing trees all around them. Both Radion and Eva bow to the dwarf, and James and Ethan follow along with the Malij assassins.

The old dwarf approaches them, smiling. He seems to be wearing a golden bracelet of moons and has long, silver, braided hair that is perfectly neat. His face shows years of aging, yet it's firm and strong. He comes forward with two powerful dwarf warriors joining him side by side. They look more dangerous than anyone James has seen, even more deadly because they are dressed in armor, totally black and red, with huge hammers and spears that shimmer like the glowing trees that surround them. The old dwarf claps his hand on his chest in front of Radion, and they both hug and laugh.

"Radion," he yells richly, "it's been too long. What brings you and the lovely lady here to our beloved land?"

"Your Majesty, thank you for having us. We request a present from your queen. We need assistance from the mighty mountain dwarves." Then Radion looks directly at James. James's heart starts to beat faster as Ethan looks confused. "The prophecy of the Destroyer," Radion says. "The Destroyer is reborn!"

Then James notices that Eva and Malij are kneeling and bowing down to him. At that moment, the silvery river flows through the cavern so brightly that it causes the entire dwarf kingdom to shine with it. Immediately after, the silvery river bursts up and sprouts high along with the flame at the dead center of the courtyard. The wind joins in, capturing both water and flames, as everyone in the entire courtyard kneels, including the king, before James. Ethan is not sure what to do and finally submits, slowly kneeling before James, confused and unsure of what's happening. The river quells the flames, and the wind suddenly floods and rushes through everyone like a gust leaving through the cracks. Whispers and sweet praise fill the air in silence, but it is enough for everyone to understand its unique whispers.

"OooooOlen...they come indeed."

At the same time, the earth beneath them rumbles, and the trees wilt lightly, inciting sadness and rejection, which only James can sense. All stand quiet for a few moments. James feels weak and shaken; suddenly, he feels dizzy. The overwhelming introduction and valiant magic that suddenly submerged and surfaced around him makes him feel a warm feeling in his head. He feels Eva's gentle arms trying to hold him up as the blood rushes to his head. Then suddenly, the area starts to spin, and everything goes dark.

James lies on the peaceful beach, with the sound of the waves and the sun shining on his face. As he stands up, the familiar headache returns, but it doesn't bother him too much. He looks out at the ocean, which is aggressively waving and slamming into the rocks on each side of the log he's sitting on. The ocean's smell is so inviting, and the birdsong in the deep blue, clear sky is calming. James feels the soft sand beneath his feet, which is as light as a feather. He picks up a small handful, noticing it's a pure light beige color with no other substances mixed in. He smiles, feeling unexpectedly happy.

Looking down, James realizes he's shirtless and wearing only his torn brown shorts. He quickly stands up, wondering how he ended up in this beautiful place. The blue waves flow gently through the sand, creating a peaceful and respectful atmosphere. He realizes he's alone and looks around, noticing a motionless, dark cave behind him and a pillar covered in sand that appears ancient. The pillar reveals three waving cave symbols with a point on top. The rocks around him are a mix of blue, pink, and purple colors. He sees no signs of life around the area but notices the cave behind him seems to be an extension of Rocksmear, as he can see the mount's peak through the cave entrance.

Feeling lightheaded again, James hears a faint noise, sounding as if someone is calling him. Suddenly, the voice is in front of him, and James swings around to find a ghostly, beautiful woman's figure shimmering like the water's waves. She slowly transforms into a solid fleshly woman with white, silvery hair. Her skin appears solid now, but James can tell it's not flesh like his own. The woman is completely bare but not in human flesh, rather a flesh of the sea behind her. Slowly, her bare body is covered as the sea pushes up her body, turning into a long blue robe, covering her substantial flesh. Her hair is now covered by the sea waves, turning from white to golden, waving in the same constant motion as the waves behind her even though there's no wind where they stand. James feels a mist of wetness on his face, which is refreshing and cool, making him want to embrace it entirely. Feeling strange, he steps back, not understanding what's going on. The stranger touches his face, and a rush of coolness touches his skin. A purity of love and life suddenly rushes through his nostrils, and she says, "Olen, you have returned, my love. Come to me, so much to do."

"Who are you?" James yells, suddenly submerged in the salty water, trying to speak as he begins to drown. "Come to me!" Then James screams as he's swept up entirely by the salty taste of the ocean. The life force is so strong it overwhelms him, and he cannot think. He's drowning, feeling this overexposing sensation of hope, power, and need, and he screams again.

James wakes up suddenly, nearly pushing Eva off the stone bed. Eva jumps and quickly gasps for air. James says, "It's okay, it's me." He sits up and notices that he isn't wearing any clothes but is covered in an oily substance. He looks at Eva, feeling embarrassed and wondering what she was doing.

"You had another fever; the magic in you is taking over again," Eva says, concerned. "Is there something you need to tell me? I know this is a lot for you in just a few days. I am so sorry you have to endure so much of who and what you are. But please know that I am here for you and will do everything in my power to help you through this. Olen has passed down his legacy magic to you, but with training and understanding, the magic could be useful and help you in the long run. I know you regret leaving everything behind, but you must trust me and always remember your family. Your parents adored you, as do I. Please tell me, what did you see, James?"

"How do you know he saw something?" Ethan interrupts, standing near James.

Eva ignores Ethan's response and waits to hear from James.

James looks at Eva with confusion. She is very wise, but he knows that there is more to her. He trusts her as his parents did. "Something about her reminds me of you," he says. At that moment, Radion appears, looking surprised and concerned. "Are you okay, boy?" Radion asks.

"We all care for you, my dear. Tell me what she said," Eva says, gently placing her hands on his overgrown beard.

"The Guardian of Water, she waits for me," James replies as he removes Eva's hands.

Radion raises his hand with joy. "Now we have a purpose!" he exclaims, jumping up and heading out of the small stone house.

CHAPTER 16

Selcarth

IN THE HUMAN kingdom of Selcarth, Kelvin is once again up at the crack of dawn, admiring the beautiful sunrise above Castle Taeron, where the royal Arguses resides, far in the distance from his farm. Although his family doesn't live within the city, he enjoys being outdoors and supplying the city with his farm's produce. Kelvin smiles as he feels the cool breeze on his face, signaling the arrival of early fall. This is a typical morning for Kelvin, a farmer who rises early. The autumn breeze carries a tapestry of orange, red, and brown leaves from the trees, signaling the approach of winter in the coming months. The morning air brushes gently against his face, bringing a sense of ease and allowing him to savor this part of the season. Kelvin loves fall because it marks the end of the busiest agricultural period, and he and his family can finally take a much-needed rest at home after providing crops to those in need. As he walks toward his farm, Kelvin enters the gutted area where the six-foot corn stalks tower over him at over one hundred paces away. He smiles, feeling excited to work on his land and partner with the grace of the Guardian of Earth, thanking her for a wonderful crop this year. He searches for his basket and heads into the maze to gather corn.

Suddenly, Kelvin hears his son calling out to him. Just like Kelvin, his son is always eager to work on the land. Kelvin hears rustling behind him, and his son emerges, strong but still so young. "Pa, why are you out so early? Mother said you should rest. I can take care of the crops today," his son says, attempting to take the basket from his father's hands.

Kelvin looks at his son's face, so soft and delicate, reminding him of Angela when they first met. He was his son's age, twelve years old, when he fell in love. His son has that same look, a sense of innocence and love. Kelvin slowly places the half-full basket on the ground, using his knees to support his back. "Spying again, son? It's okay. I didn't want to wake you up. Besides, you should be out playing with your friends. You've already helped me a great deal," Kelvin says, smiling at his son.

"Pa," Sammy says, approaching slowly, his stern face softening. "You're not doing well. The healers said you're overworked and need to rest. It's been two weeks already, and you're complaining about your back. You should let me handle things," he says with concern.

"There's nothing wrong with my back. It's just a cramp from last night," Kelvin replies.

"From last night? Come on, Pa, you're pushing yourself too hard. I don't want to find you here with a broken back."

"I'll be fine. Go back inside now and tell your mother there's nothing to worry about." Kelvin insists.

Sammy exhales loudly, feeling frustrated, before turning around. "I'll come back later to check on you. I'll let Mom know, but she won't be pleased. You know she'll come out and get you."

"Sure, sure. I'll worry about that when she gets here. Go enjoy the day. It's going to be beautiful," Kelvin says with a smile as Sammy quickly leaves the area in disappointment.

Kelvin searches his basket, and as he slowly bends down, the pain in his back intensifies. He grimaces in pain and tries to ease it with his hand. Confused, Kelvin grips one of the corn stalks for leverage and pulls himself up. As he stands on his two feet, he uses the stalk for support and slowly makes his way back home, feeling the pain increasing with every step.

Suddenly, the pain bursts into a new, intense agony that spreads throughout his spinal cord. Kelvin tries to move quickly away from his post, but the pain paralyzes him, and he cannot move. He tries to yell, but the pain continues to stab him, and he tumbles over. Feeling regret for not listening to his son, Kelvin tries to pull himself back up but cannot feel his left arm, and his right leg goes numb. He stumbles again, landing flat on his face, and the cornstalk serves as a makeshift bed for him.

Kelvin yelps in agony, feeling the pain spreading all over his back and a pressure in his chest, as if he's having a heart attack. He flips over onto his front,

146

grabbing his shirt with his right arm, and rips it off. The pain subsides in his back but quickly moves to his chest, and he yells in agony, moving around like a madman. He feels his heart being pierced as if it's being attacked, but not by an ordinary attack, as blood starts to spurt out of his chest.

Feeling the pain subside and the bruising quickly coming through, Kelvin feels lightheaded, and the blood rushes to his head. He sees the sky slowly getting darker, and the pain fades away. He feels relieved as everything turns white.

Kelvin lies on the ground, covered in dirt and twitching. The crows notice the fresh scent of blood in the area and start to descend toward the lifeless body. As they approach, a new entity suddenly appears, slowly emerging from Kelvin's nose. It's a small, carbon-red insect with three tentacles and skin that easily melds into Kelvin's body. It moves to the human's lower lip, using its tentacles, and opens his mouth with ease, revealing five slimy caterpillars, each about half the size of their mother. They quickly obey their mother's command and jump off the human body, walking toward the next unharmed home.

A centipede-like insect with a detached head, resembling a gopher, climbs up the cornstalk. It looks around, sensing someone approaching quickly. Sending a small signal ahead to her offspring, a signal only their kind can detect, traveling for miles—she then leaps and grasps onto the stalk with her powerful tentacles, holding on effortlessly with her tiny hands. Using her wax-like skin, she secretes a glowing germ substance that allows her to slide down rapidly before disappearing. Her task in this area is complete, and now she must return to the city from which she originally emerged.

Mistress Mila hurries up the ancient steps toward the bedroom, finally reaching the heavy mahogany wood door. She lifts the golden hook and knocks softly, then waits patiently for a response. "Come in, Mila," the voice beckons from inside. She lifts the golden knob and pushes the door open.

Raymul is standing by the window with his back to the door, draped in the king's favorite red satin cloak. Mila can see the symbol on the cloak that represents the Guardians and the truce between them but forgets herself and rushes inside without a second thought.

"Your Grace! I was finally contacted," she exclaims. Raymul swiftly turns around, and the satin cloak flows like the wind and settles over his body. His eyes are wide and red, showing that he has not slept in weeks. Mila senses magic stirring in him, the kind that comes from the sinister tree.

"It's the swamp witch," Mila says softly, her voice barely above a whisper.

As Raymul watches, he sees Mistress Mila's body start to shake and tremble uncontrollably, as if a great force is taking hold of her. Her skin turns pale and clammy, and her eyes roll back into her head as she starts to convulse. Her once-beautiful hair starts to writhe and twist as if it's alive and trying to escape her scalp. As the transformation continues, her hair grows longer and thicker, turning black as night and taking on a life of its own.

Her features begin to contort and twist, her nose and chin elongating and curving into a sharp point. Her lips thin and curl back over her teeth. Her eyes snap open, now glowing with an eerie green light, and she lets out a bloodcurdling scream. The transformation is complete.

In her place stands Gitma, the swamp witch. Her skin is now a sickly gray-green and covered in warts and pustules. Her hair is completely gray and coils around her like living serpents, and her long, spindly fingers end in sharp, black claws. Her clothes have been replaced by a ragged, tattered robe made of animal skins, and she carries a gnarled staff carved with dark symbols of ancient power.

Raymul can feel the power emanating from Gitma, like a dark, oppressive force that threatens to overwhelm him. He knows that dealing with this powerful being comes at a steep cost, and he steels himself for what he knows will be a difficult negotiation.

As Gitma approaches the king's chamber, her deformed ears, resembling those of an elf but burned to a charcoal-black color, emit a foul swamp smell. She lets out a sinister laugh as she walks around the room, not acknowledging Raymul's presence.

He watches cautiously as Gitma places her hand on the door to the king's bedroom but quickly recoils and gasps as if burned. Raymul knows that Gitma is not to be trifled with, and he must be careful in his dealings with her.

As Mila had not been aware that she was to bring a message, Raymul realizes that she was actually a beacon leading him to the swamp witch. Despite the danger involved, he must seek Gitma's wisdom and knowledge, but at what cost?

Gitma, the swamp witch, lets out a sigh before reciting in a sinister tone, "Behold thy darkness be folded, their darkness once again will prevail. Yes, the Destroyer is born once again!" She cackles loudly and flings the heavy door open with ease, not giving Raymul a second glance.

Raymul follows cautiously, not wanting to provoke the powerful creature but also not afraid, knowing that the sinister tree will protect him. The room is filled with the stench of musk, and it feels as if they are in the middle of a swamp.

Gitma turns to face Raymul and speaks with a mocking tone. "So, you shall seek the darkness through, Raymul. Do not underestimate the cunning of the dark Guardian of Death. It is very protective and giving, but it always comes at a price."

She suddenly throws herself on the floor, mumbling and wilding about, before practically throwing herself on the ground like a child searching for something. After a moment, she stands up with a sly smile on her face.

"A powerful creature indeed, but it seeks a greater purpose," she says, smiling knowingly, as if she knows something more. She raises her skinny, wriggling hands toward the tapestry pictures of the entire kingdom of Selcarth that hang on the walls, positioned above the mantel. "All will be doomed, for I see thy kingdom so high in sickness, and life will be tarnished before me."

Gitma looks back at Raymul and says with a slaying smile, "So, what can I do for the deliverer of darkness?" She then turns and ignores Raymul, walking back to the recessed room and waiting for him to close the door. Raymul knows that he has to tread carefully when dealing with Gitma, as her knowledge and power come at a steep price.

"Why do you call me that? I'm not a delivery witch. I am destined to be a new king, fulfilling my duties to my beloved Guardians of Darkness," Raymul declares with a sense of pride and conviction.

The witch smiles, revealing her stained teeth and filthy appearance, making Raymul feel sick to his stomach.

"Of course. What question do you seek an answer to? My time is precious and will require a suitable payment," the witch responds with a sly grin.

Raymul locates a small chest underneath the table and lifts the top, revealing gold, various relics he has accumulated over the years, and rare stones.

In seconds, a small, sea green orb extracts itself from the chest and floats into the witch's hand. It hovers for a few seconds and then flashes as it disappears.

"You fool! You've given up such a precious stone. You have no idea what it is or its true value," the witch admonishes.

"I don't care. Is that payment sufficient?" Raymul asks, hoping to conclude the transaction quickly.

"Yes. With that stone, I can answer a few questions you wish. But be warned, for any unanswered question, what I have acquired will not be returned," the witch warns.

"Fine, fine," Raymul responds, relieved that the witch did not take the entire chest. He only gave her an emerald-green gem that was given to him many years ago, which he considers worthless, as it holds no powers or value. If it makes the witch happy, it is her loss.

"I don't have much time. Unless you want me to return your mistress rotten," the witch says, reminding Raymul of the stakes.

Raymul places the chest back underneath the table and casts a magic spell on it. He then quickly walks over to the witch, holding his breath as he prepares to ask his question.

"How can I destroy the Argus stone?" he asks, hoping the witch's answer will lead him to success.

The witch chuckles. "You can try all you want, but the Argus stone cannot be destroyed or stopped. It's a powerful magic that even the strongest beings can't undo. And as for your title, you may call yourself whatever you want, but the fact remains that you are part of the darkness, and you always will be."

Raymul grits his teeth, frustrated with the witch's lack of help. He needs to find a way to protect himself from the Argus stone and its power. "There has to be something I can do," he mutters under his breath.

The witch smirks. "Well, there is one thing you could try. There is a legend of a powerful amulet that can nullify any magic. It's said to be hidden deep in the Forbidden Forest, but no one has ever found it."

The witch ponders for a moment, tapping her chin with a bony finger. "This amulet could serve as a compatible component to the Argus stone. If they're worn together, it could counteract the stone's protection. But be warned, the

Argus stone is ancient and could react violently if threatened. It could destroy everything in its path." She chuckles wickedly.

Raymul's eyes widen at the prospect of a solution. "Where is this Forbidden Forest?"

The witch chuckles. "As if I'd tell you. You'll have to find it yourself. And if you do manage to find the amulet, there will be a price to pay. Everything comes with a price."

Raymul nods, determined to find the amulet and protect himself from the Argus stone. "I'll do whatever it takes."

The witch cackles. "That's what they all say. Good luck, Prince of Darkness."

He knows the journey will be dangerous and fraught with peril, but he is willing to do whatever it takes to protect himself and his reign as the new king.

"Are you trying to accomplish something by removing the scarce stone from Princess Celestia, which is impossible?" Gitma asks.

"Why, yes," Raymul responds, slightly impressed. "I want to marry her."

The witch once again laughs widely and moves closer to Raymul, looking into the bloodshot eyes of the man who wishes to achieve a goal that she knows will fail.

"Marry her, you will not succeed, for the Argus stone will assure this. It will protect her and will counteract any force and unwillingness. It is a powerful love stone whose essence was transferred from one generation to another. You cannot harm the princess with any form of magic, for the love stone will protect her in all ways. The stone knows her true heart and the will of her ancestors," the witch explains, smiling.

"I know it is not marriage you seek; for you to obtain this ground that was forged by the gracious Guardian of Earth, the princess must submit it directly to you without any force, but willingly," Gitma continues.

"How do you know I need this land?" Raymul sounds surprised.

Gitma's eyes focus on the black tree sitting on the mantel. Its branches are hardened like needles that can prick at any part of the plant. It looks deadly. Then she giggles and looks back at Raymul.

"I see darkness unfolding," the witch says.

"What do you mean?" he asks, puzzled.

The witch looks at the green stone he has given her and smiles.

"This will be the end of our conversation, young giver of darkness. Love is not needed to obtain the land. Instead, persuade the young Argus in a way to take away the love of her people," she says, laughing loudly, and her voice finally fades away.

As the power of the swamp witch fades, Mila's body convulses and trembles. Her eyes roll back, and her fingers twitch as if in a spasm. Gradually, the convulsions subside, and the rest of her hair returns to its normal state, except for a few strands that remain tangled and disheveled. Mistress Mila blinks and looks around, disoriented and unsure of what has happened. Then recognition dawns on her face, and she remembers everything. Her features gradually soften and return to normal as she looks at Raymul, her fear replaced by relief. Without a word, she turns and runs out of the room, needing time to process the traumatic events that just occurred.

A guard enters the room quickly.

"Are you okay, Your Grace?" The tall female guard stands before him. Her body is fully armored, similar to Pennaldo's, but she is slightly shorter. She is one of the guards that protect the Argus royals but, in their absence, is sworn to protect him.

"I am fine. Have the guards found the Destroyer?" Raymul asks.

"Yes, a boy, young and naive. It seems he is not aware of his powers. He is accompanied by Radion and a female companion we are not familiar with, but sources say she controls the Malij assassins that accompany her. They entered the dwarf kingdom. You know we are not—"

"I know the law of the lands, Kimba," Raymul interrupts.

He thinks to himself, *The Malij is accompanying Radion, that's an odd companion.* He has heard stories of the old wizard Radion, traveling to many parts. Rumors say he is a scholarly observer watching the Destroyer's family, while others say he is a personal professor of the Argus clan, especially the young Jarin. The mixed companion from the City of the Witches is strangely mixed with the Destroyer.

"Thank you, Kimba. Where is Pennaldo?"

"I don't know; he said he is seeking our princess."

Raymul then turns to the window and sees that the horizon is rising for a new day. He needs to sleep now; it has been a few days without any rest, and he needs his energy to prepare for his next plan of action. The tree sits teasingly on the mantel. Slowly, sweat comes rolling down his face. He whispers quickly, "Not now, my sweet. I need my energy."

Raymul looks at Kimba while she stares at him oddly. Her short hair and fierce face are a stark contrast to the black tree on the mantel.

"Your Grace, are you okay?" she asks, looking at the unusual plant.

"I am fine. It's just the strain of our king not being here and suffering from that unknown sickness. It's very tiresome to run his kingdom," he lies.

"I know. We miss him dearly, especially Pennaldo. He is torn by his responsibility to find the princess and to protect her, as we all want to do."

"Right," Raymul says, wanting to get to the point. "Go find Pennaldo; bring him to me by this evening while I rest."

Kimba bows and leaves the chambers.

Looking around, he notices a pile of fruits and bread from the previous day sitting undisturbed. He is tempted to take some, but he has lost his appetite and walks back to his chamber to go to bed. But she calls him again, and he finds himself in front of the lifeless black tree once more.

CHAPTER 17

Ancestor Stone

JARIN STARES OUT the window, which is completely covered with oversize frogs attempting to breach the force field around the library. He can hear their croaking from the roof and knows that the entire library is occupied by these creatures and who knows what else. Although the library is bright inside, from the outside it seems as though the sun has just surfaced for a new day. They've been here all night trying to figure out what's going on, but Jarin has a gut feeling that they were deliberately put here. He's not sure why, but his intuition is usually correct.

"So, have you figured out a way for us to get out of here?" Jarin paces back and forth, occasionally glancing out the open window where the dragon frogs are waiting for his return. The fortress prevents these creatures from entering the library, since Eartha magic is very strong and would not allow any entity to enter without consent or means to destroy. No wonder the professor wanted the royals to stay here. Or is it something else? His family is far from needing protection for this city. They are more than capable. Strangely, his cousin Celestia is here at the same time, wondering if this was part of the plan or a way for their uncle to warn them about something to come.

Jarin's father is a powerful seer who uses his magic to protect the family, and his uncles are also powerful with the elements of Earth and Air, which protect the kingdoms. Jarin knows that time is short for his elder uncle, Celestia's father, who fell ill with some strange magic, but the Argus stone did not protect him. His aunt also fell sick and was taken away from the kingdom to the land of Zimeris to be healed. He wonders how the Argus stone counteracted the protection of his uncle unless his uncle intended it that way to get his cousin out of the kingdom and here. There are so many unanswered questions, but for now, they are all together, which makes them a powerful and deadly family. Jarin is determined to face whatever opposes them and his people.

"Jarin!"

"What?"

Larmari looks at her cousin with concern. She knows he analyzes things well but wants him to stop. "Would you relax and come over here?"

"I'm thinking, okay?"

"Oh, I didn't know you could use your brain."

"Okay, smarty-pants. Figuring out those things out there is like some witches' brew of dragon, and what the heck do I know? Can you put your face back into those books and find out how the hell we get to the roof without being fried?"

Aluiz and Dario start to get anxious, and Aberra tries to calm Dario while Celestia does the same for Aluiz, turning to face Jarin.

"Jarin, cut it out. You're scaring the young ones."

"We need to get the hell out of here. Why can't we just confuse those creatures out there? It would make things so much better for us. Better yet, let's just deal with them and take them out."

"Jarin, would you relax and lower your tone? I know we are all stressed," Celestia says sternly, which quickly shuts Jarin down. "Besides, we can't do anything at all since we are in Eartha's library. We have a task."

"Yeah, right. I don't believe it anymore. Do you see those creatures outside?"

"I agree with Jarin. It seems the focus point of the creatures is us, since they are congregating in this specific area," Larmari finally says as she leaves the study area and joins the group.

Sakeris moves forward to block Jarin's view. "I know what you said before, but please calm down and respect the princess." Jarin stares at Sakeris and stands tall, ready to confront him. Aberra raises her hands and signs, "Great. Should I get the swords?"

"Sakeris, stop playing the hero. She's just my cousin."

"He should stop worrying about what's happening and join us to work out a plan." Celestia moves Sakeris to the side, facing Jarin.

"All right, you guys can't take a joke, can you?" Jarin pleads down next to Aberra, where the family stands waiting in the oval tree located in the back of the library.

Aberra smiles at Jarin and laughs. "Too bad. I was hoping to see who would win the fight. I was betting on Sakeris."

"Aberra, you know Sakeris will never hurt me. We go way back." Jarin sniffles and returns to the group.

A few moments later, Celestia and Aberra return to the table after occupying Aluiz and Dario with some squirrels who were willing to play with them.

"Okay, Jarin. Yesterday, you suggested some sort of bait. Did you mean the animals here to lure them away?"

"Not exactly. Eartha would not allow that. She treasures animals, and if they are hunted for anything other than food or for destruction, she would not be pleased. Besides, she might open the floor beneath and eject us from the library."

"What about a decoy? Maybe we can magnify ourselves using some sort of illusion," Larmari adds with renewed anticipation.

"No use," Sakeris says from his post at the window, one hand on a black silk knife. He stares intently out the window, anticipating an attack. It's an attack all Malij were trained for—protection.

"I summoned my magic, but I couldn't even get a small fire started. It seems this fortress is blocking any magic summons within this library."

"Has everyone given thought to another back door to move away from these creatures?" Aberra asks.

"What about that weird-looking door over there?" Sakeris points at the far side of the library. It is heavily decorated with glowing brass and golden outlines. There is a huge star at the center of the room, with distinctive circular lines that connect into each point of the star.

"No!" both Celestia and Aberra exclaim.

"That's a realm gateway," Aberra explains. "Our furry friends said it will alter and wipe out your memory while entering into another realm."

"Yes, Guardians can go freely into other realms as they please, but it's only meant for fairy kinds," Celestia says.

"Although strangely, one human passed through a few years ago, according to Jin," Aberra continues, looking at the squirrel that runs between them as it quickly darts at Celestia and Aberra. "He dropped some sort of relic from his hand, screaming as his memory was wiped, and ran off into the library as it ejected him below," Celestia says.

"That's unusual. I hear that other realms have magical properties and are governed differently from each other. How could one human pass through? Do you know where this relic is?" Larmari asks.

"Yes, the animals here at the library keep it safe," Aberra replies.

"We don't have time for this," Jarin interjects.

"I agree. I have a feeling that those creatures out there are after us or me since my parents fell ill. We should leave this area and bring the danger away from the city. I could be the cause of this disturbance and don't want to hurt any more citizens," Celestia says.

"I agree with Celestia. If Professor Ref wanted to protect us, he would not have sent us to a library to search for answers. He would have created the portal on the spot and sent us back home. I think it's more than you, cuz. I believe it's the library he wants too. You said it yourself, Larmari; Eartha only allows our family here at will, and anyone she sees as family too, like Sakeris. We should go; Celestia is right. We are bringing danger to the citizens here. Back home, our family will address this issue."

"Larmari, are you sure there isn't anything referring to these dragon-like creatures?" Celestia cut in.

"No. I went over numerous volumes last night. If it hadn't been for Aberra referring to them as scaling dragons, I wouldn't have picked up that they're protégés of dragons. It was then that I consulted with Aberra for her expertise. We concluded that all dragons have a weak point, but we wouldn't know where to start with these unique creatures," Larmari says.

"Then we should fight them," Sakeris replies.

"We don't know anything about these strange creatures. We need to be sure what we are dealing with before we take action. Jarin is right; we must get out of here. I don't like the idea that the purges can move and control us at will. For one thing, when Mother gets better, we will make sure that things will change around here." Celestia sighs, looking over her shoulder to see if Aluiz and Dario are okay and then returns her attention to the meeting. It is already getting late, and she is sure Aluiz and Dario are hungry.

"We should rest and get something to eat," Larmari says.

"Ahh, not fruits again. I'm tired of eating veggies and fruits," Aberra says, standing up and moving out of the room.

"You don't say. I could use a nice piece of steak and mashed potatoes with corned beef gravy spilled all over my plate," Jarin exclaims, as Sakeris joins in and says, "Yes!"

"You're disgusting," Aberra says.

Celestia, Aberra, and Larmari walk away with Aluiz and Dario, who are hungry, as they gather food for themselves. Sakeris is about to join them when Jarin pulls him back calmly.

"Are you okay, buddy?" Jarin says.

Jarin can see his longtime friend, who he has known since they were young-sters, staring blankly. Sakeris has a darker tone than he does, with a much bigger and taller body. But his face looks older, tired, and mixed with emotion.

"You know you shouldn't speak to Celestia like that," Sakeris says.

"Sakeris, lighten up. This Malij thing has you too wound up. She's my cousin; I respect her just as much as I respect my entire family. I love her as much as I love you, buddy. It's in our blood."

"But you know—" Sakeris interjects.

"Yes, I know. She, or should I say, the daughter of King Argus, is destined to join the ruling of our human race, so the legend says. Ha, I think it's a bunch of hogwash. We all know, Sakeris. Just because she comes from the line of legacy doesn't mean she's any less my cousin, for you as well. You should remember that too, Sakeris. She already has a heavy load on her. Sometimes being reminded that you're a normal person too can make a big difference. Sakeris, you're our family. Treat her like family, not a title. Believe me, she needs it now more than ever."

Sakeris smiles and exhales. He turns to face Jarin, who is half his size and looks stocky and strong. All Argus bloodlines have unique features: fair skin, smooth features, and most of all, unique eyes. They possess long eyelashes and wide eyes. If you put all the Arguses together, you would say they are related by the unifying similarities of their eyes. Sakeris knows that Arguses are extremely powerful and very royal in the entire kingdom. They carry with them a legacy that no one understands, not even him, despite being so close to the family. All he knows is that this family possesses unique abilities and must be protected for generations to come. They are like a cult only known to their kind.

"You're right, I'm sorry. It's just that the training emphasizes so much pro-tection, especially for royalty," Sakeris finally says.

"Royalty, royalty. I wish they'd stop labeling us that. I'm tired of people bowing and seeking protection from us. We are already marked and reminded daily, especially with these necklaces we have to wear."

"Well, you are an important line. These necklaces only alert your parents of danger," Sakeris says, touching the necklace given to him by King Argus.

"I know. Too bad we are not really in any danger. Otherwise, Dad would have been here, reigning death and sending these professors to Arches Waterways."

"Yeah," Sakeris adds. "Too bad we can't use these necklaces to our advantage, other than alerting our parents. You know, it wouldn't be so bad if I could link with my girlfriend." He smiles shyly.

Jarin's expression suddenly changes after Sakeris's comment, as if he has been enlightened with a bright idea. He smiles like a boy about to get into trouble and jumps up to kiss Sakeris on his forehead. Sakeris pushes him away, feeling embarrassed. "What?"

"Sakeris, you are a genius." He runs off to look for Celestia and the rest.

Back at the garden hall, Celestia, Aluiz, Dario, and the girls are inspecting the auspicious and exciting fruits when Celestia hears Jarin yelling her name. He flies into the hall, and since they've been trying out various fruits, the remains are scattered all over the ground, causing Jarin to slip and tumble over a bush. Everyone laughs with glee, and Celestia thinks this is good since she's been so stressed and concerned for her family. She joins in, and Jarin picks himself up, almost tumbling, with bits of strawberries all over his face. Aluiz and Dario are hysterical.

"Funny," Jarin says, wiping his face with his hand and sticking out his tongue at Aluiz and Dario. They mimic his actions and laugh. Jarin then rushes to Celestia to share his idea.

"Listen, I have an idea. Well, Sakeris inspired it," he tells her.

"It figures," Aberra says, causing Jarin to give her a stern look. "Look, Celestia, you're the bearer of the Argus stone. My father told me it's an ancestral thing. Since we can't communicate with it, maybe you can communicate with our dead families. They could tell us what to do so we can get out of this greenhouse that's making me feel too earthy." Jarin changes his position and adds, "No offense, Eartha. Sis."

Larmari stands up with new anticipation. "He's right, Celestia. You know that

Netaha was unusual with the dead spirits, but her magic to speak to them daily was powerful magic. She told me a few times that the dead used to speak about the stone as ancestral souls, and each soul is a piece of every ancestor since the beginning. Good thinking. I knew you could use that brain of yours," she says, tapping Jarin's head and then sitting next to Celestia. "Since this could also be an ancestral stone, maybe you can talk to them and ask for help," Larmari suggests.

"Has anyone ever thought that maybe we can't use the stone at all?" Aberra interrupts. "It seems our beloved professors are preventing any communication to land on our parents. You know that our parents would not be happy with the situation that they are handling here. I don't think Celestia's stone will work either if ours are not working properly."

"You know, Aberra is right," Jarin says, with Aberra stepping up behind him. She looks slender, with long, black hair and, almost identical to her brother, the same oval eyes. "Dad told me that this school is running on a thin thread. I bet the suspicious ones want to make sure we are safely put away, or should I say locked up, until they clear up the problem they are facing now."

"So they must have locked us up here together to keep us away, prevent our magic from working, and our necklaces to simulate that we are okay," Jarin adds.

"But Celestia came by as a surprise. Maybe they didn't anticipate that she would be wearing her father's Argus stone and didn't have time to make the appropriate changes," Larmari suggests.

"But the Argus stone is different, from what I understand," Sakeris speaks up. He is leaning against the wall at the front entrance of the garden, startling everyone. His skill to sneak around is not anticipated by the group. "Celestia, your father once told me that your bloodline runs very strong, especially with your mother's."

"Well, let's do it," Jarin exclaims to everyone. "So I can get the freaking death out of here and set fire to those witches' asses when I speak to Dad. I would love to see the look on Professor Ref's face when Dad walks down the Everest Ferrano Hall."

"I don't know," Celestia says sadly, touching the smooth, red stone that her beloved father gave her. The polished stone stands out perfectly, oval and glossy, reflecting the dim surroundings of Eartha Garden. "My father told me it's a love stone that seeks to protect me. I'm not sure if I can use it as a way to communicate with my ancestors. Maybe I can go out and alert someone since the stone should protect me?"

Everyone looks shocked, and they all respond with "NO!"

"We cannot risk that, Princess," Sakeris says. "How do we know if the stone is false?"

"I don't know about it being false," Celestia responds.

"I assure you it works properly, but we cannot take that chance with you, Celestia," Aberra says.

Aberra sits beside Celestia, with Aluiz and Dario joining in on her lap. Dario fusses over Aluiz, but Aberra picks up Dario and places him on her lap.

"Celestia, Dad mentioned that the Argus stone was special and dedicated only to your line. It was a protection stone to protect the rightful ruler. He also said that each generation marks some kind of love onto the stone, something he didn't quite understand. Maybe Jarin is right, since that mark or maybe a soul is somehow locked into the stone, you can talk to our ancestors for help."

"You're right, Aberra," Celestia says. "Thank you for your kind words. I'll try. But how? My dad never indicated that I could connect with the stone."

"Try using the properties of the dark element of Ice we learned. Maybe you can gain possession of the stone. It works with beings as long as the channel you are trying to possess is willing to open. I don't see why the stone wouldn't open itself to you," Larmari says.

"But the stone is not of flesh and blood, and besides, we can't do any magic here."

"We can't do any matter of defense, but we may be able to do magic on ourselves. It doesn't matter."

"If Aberra is right that your stone was conspired by souls, that should be sufficient enough to be a living entity."

"Okay, I'll try. Do you know how to take possession, Larmari?" Aberra says.

"No, but I think Netaha does, and she is not here."

"I know everything about possession. I once almost took possession of a boy that got on my nerves. But when my parents found out, they sent me to learn about socializing with my peers," Aberra says.

"Oh, that explains it," Sakeris says. "I was wondering why your mom decided to send you down here."

"What can I tell you, Sakeris? I'm unique." She turns her attention to Celestia and kneels down, looking very tall with her long, brown hair. She, too, possesses the unique look of the Arguses, except she has her mother's slender, picturesque nose. But the eyes once again give it away, just like Celestia and the rest of her family. They all possess long, beautiful, black eyelashes, a look of sorrow, simplicity, and love.

"We need to get you prepared, mentally. It can be dangerous if you don't know how to subject and release the connection. Are you sure you are up to this?"

"Yes."

"Maybe we should try something else," Sakeris interrupts, looking concerned about the safety of the princess.

Jarin puts a hand on Sakeris to indicate that it's okay.

Aberra smiles, revealing a sincere pleasure that makes Celestia wonder what she is up to now. "I have a few tricks up my sleeve."

"How long?" Jarin adds.

"As long as it takes," Aberra lashes out at him. "I need to prepare a few magic potions. I noticed a sanctum room next to the gateway door. I need to go there, maybe in a few hours."

"But we cannot produce any magic here," Jarin persists.

"Correction, my pain-in-the-butt brother. We cannot produce any magic that leaves this library. What we are doing is producing something that stays here."

Then Dario and Aluiz stick their tongues out at Jarin, giggling, and run off, waiting for Jarin to chase them in another game, which he does. He runs off after them, saying, "I'm going to get you," laughing as he chases the young ones around the library. Other animals start to run with them as they enjoy the action. Sakeris looks at them as Jarin hides behind the treelike bookshelf and remembers what he told him. Just be cautious and enjoy your family around you. He can see the stress being lifted as the younger ones start to laugh while they throw eggshells at Jarin, and Jarin pretends he is being hit hard and falls down. The two young ones jump on top of him as the squirrels pretend they are pushing them down. Sakeris smiles and decides to pick up the fallen eggshell and throw it at the young boys, and they shoot up, ready to tackle the newcomer.

CHAPTER 18

Snooping

ETHAN WALKS ALONE through the corridor that leads out of Yemter Tavern, where he had mingled with some dwarves. It has been two days now, and he has journeyed silently through the city of Yanter, in Mount Rocksmear, grasping all possible escape routes and hiding spots. The corridor is dark but unusually clean, with not a single fly in the alleyways. It is the first time he has encountered a city of speedy hideouts and such neatness. Not a single piece of garbage is left unattended. The short buildings seem to be well taken care of, and Ethan tries to find some sort of breach or crack in various buildings but cannot find any. It seems the dwarves are very particular when it comes to their construction, and everything is perfectly shaped. Ethan is fascinated with the architecture and various statues that are scattered throughout the city. The dwarves seem to take pride in their skills in stone-carving.

He exits the corridor that leads to the back way of the tavern and finds himself at the center of Mithril Market. From what he has picked up in the past two days, this market is a central point where one can find weapons, armor, and exotic gear. Ethan continues his trek toward the end of the street, and a guard stands in his way and slightly bows to let him through. Ethan wonders why the guard seems to take him so lightly even though he looks like a strange, alien being to them and is good at stealing things. Either the guards are aware of his party's arrival, or they are taking this city too lightly. Ethan is not sure, but he has a feeling that he is being watched—not by the dwarf, but by a hidden entity that resides in this glorious city.

He finally makes his way up the various stone homes and arrives at a central bridge that reveals a liquid substance of royal reds and azure blues that seem to intertwine but not touch each other. He crosses the bridge and climbs the oval stone steps that lead to a special tavern, an arrangement of stone homes on top of each other. On the first level, he rushes to the center stone wall, which has a golden plaque over the stone door. Ethan cannot read Draconic, but he assumes this room is of great importance because the other rooms have silver or bronze plaques. He is about to hit the heavy door with his palm when James opens it.

"Hello, Ethan."

"How did you know I was at the door?"

"I just knew. Please come in."

Ethan enters the strange royal room, and every piece of furniture is polished and glittery in stone. The smooth, silvery marble reveals various artifacts and decorations, all made of gold, silver, and even diamonds. Although Ethan was in this room a couple of days ago, he can't help but marvel at the gold and diamonds that glitter so vividly. A temptation to grab an item, even the golden vase, runs wildly through his mind. This room is like a living treasure chest.

"Ethan?"

"Oh, yeah, right." Ethan takes a deep breath and tears his face away from the stone desk that holds the golden vase.

"Where have you been? I wanted to talk to you."

"You know me, James. I like snooping around. I hate to be in a place if I don't understand the network of things. I just had to find things out—you know, passages, secret places, and the like."

"You should not be doing that here. I don't think that a nose punch will be temporary when it comes to these dwarves. It looks like more of a permanent fixture on your face."

"Ahh, don't worry about me. I know what I'm doing." Ethan takes a seat on the hard stone chair that faces the stone bed. Everything seems to be so glamorous, but it is obvious that these dwarves don't like to decorate with fabric and flowers. Ethan waits for James to join him; he can see that James has changed since they left home. He looks worn out, and his muscular upper body has lost some sense of dignity. It seems to him that James has lost his innocence and looks tired and confused. Although he never combs his curly brown hair, it seems messy and unkempt. James walks slowly over to Ethan and sits on the flat stone bed that faces a small balcony. He is still wearing the same clothes: brown trousers and a dirty gray shirt. Ethan can see that the dwarves provided him with royal clothes—a blue raven top and matching silk trousers, and a black cloak with golden trim. James doesn't seem to take this king thing lightly.

"So, how are you feeling, buddy? Did you rest enough?" Ethan asks.

"Not good. I keep having strange dreams about the Guardian of Water. She is so persuasive and demanding." Then he looks directly into Ethan's small eyes. He looks all cleaned up and completely healed of his scars. His crooked nose still stands out, with his hair now overlapping his eyes. James is glad his friend is with him; he wouldn't know what to do if he weren't here to keep him sane.

"Look, I've been meaning to tell you—I'm really sorry for snapping at you when you told me about Eva. Everything was so secretive to me. I just couldn't believe it when you told me."

Ethan slaps his skinny hand on James's leg.

"Hey, don't worry about it. I understand. I would have felt the same."

"You shouldn't have come alone, Ethan. This is not your simple, everyday adventure. You could be killed. I'll talk to Radion—I'm sure he can arrange for your safekeeping to go back home."

"Don't be silly. You know I have nothing back home, no family, not even a partner. Besides, I think you need me here. Who else will give you gossip?"

They both laugh and hug.

"Thanks, buddy. I owe you one."

"You bet your butt you do. So, have you heard anything yet about this queen we're supposed to meet?" Ethan asks.

"Not really." James stands up and heads toward a stone-engraved door, pulling it open with his strength to retrieve some fruits. "It's been two days, and not a single escort has come so we can meet the queen. Radion keeps telling me that we have to wait until we're called. I don't know what all the fuss is about; I just want to get going already, and I'm tired of looking at stones around us."

"You know, James, I got some information that the queen is a peculiar ruler, and the king is simply the messenger and overseer of the army. From what I gathered, the queen is too busy with her own affairs and people and doesn't have time to worry about external affairs. The king takes care of anything that concerns the other race."

"Do you know why the queen is taking so long to see us?" James says, irritated. "I must speak to her about this unknown journey."

"I don't think it works like that. According to what I gathered, her main concern is her people only. You're simply a stranger, nothing more. The king can relay the message to her, but the queen makes decisions and has the final word."

"What's the purpose of having us come into their realm? Do you think they're keeping us captive?" James asks.

"The system works very differently with the dwarves I observed, buddy. It's possible the king is assuming that we will remain until they study our intentions and perhaps relay the information to the queen. She may want to keep us here when she's ready to speak with us. I went to various taverns and made the same observation: all the males are simply moving along their ways of life, coupling together and moving the system accordingly, while the females are not prevalent but highly regarded as superior to the males that move the city accordingly. Like I said earlier, they seem to follow an unusual trait, like a bee colony. I hear talks among the dwarves that the king and queen interact for a common cause. They rule together but in different aspects, without overstepping each other's boundaries."

James is surprised by the intelligent comment from Ethan. He has known Ethan all his life and can't believe how suddenly he looks more intelligent and resourceful.

"I'm impressed. You kept concluding the same theory by just snooping around?"

"Well, you know, snooping is one of my special skills besides stealing. You'd be amazed how much info you can get out of a drunken dwarf, especially when it's one of the queen's guards," Ethan says, pulling out a small collection of unusual carved keystones from his pocket.

"What the heck is that?"

"I stole it from one of the guards. Besides, he didn't seem to care that he lost these keys."

"One of these days, Ethan, your luck will run short," James says.

"Ha, don't worry about that, my friend. I've been doing this for years; no luck will run short," Ethan replies.

"Like I said, you should take on another hobby besides your sneakiness," James persists.

Ethan laughs, but James notices that his expression hasn't changed. Suddenly, James walks toward the stone front door and stares at it. He extends his hand and places it on the door. Ethan walks slowly behind him, wondering if he should say something but deciding against it because it seems like James is concentrating.

James turns quickly to face Ethan with wide eyes.

"Someone or something is listening near us," James says quickly over Ethan's ears.

"What do we do?" Ethan asks with the same tone as James.

James turns to face the door and yanks it open with all his might, causing him to nearly tumble with the enormous weight. He jumps out, looking around wildly. Ethan joins him, his hand extending a short knife. They both look around, but no one is outside except for various birdlike creatures hovering in a circular formation over the city. They both stare at each other for a few moments and go back inside.

Ethan slightly closes the heavy door behind him and says, "What was that all about?"

"I'm not sure. All I know is that I felt a presence, just like what I felt when you were coming to see me. But the difference was that the presence was unfamiliar to me. I don't know how to explain it, Ethan."

Ethan stares blankly at his closest friend. "You're right, it's better you don't explain the magic. But can you do your magic thing and scope out the area to find this snooper?" he asks.

"I guess I can, but I don't know how or if it works that way. Radion said that Eva will begin my training when the time comes, whatever that means."

Ethan comes over and places his hand on James's broad shoulder. "Don't worry, buddy. I'll do the snooping for you. I don't like this magic stuff anyway. I believe in good old hard instincts."

They both nod. "Ethan, I'm glad you're here. Thanks for everything."

"No sweat. Just get a hold of me when you hear any news about the queen we are supposed to meet, okay?"

"And how am I going to do that with your 'magical' snooping technique?" James says.

"Hey, if I'm not around, just drop a note. You know, like the good old days."

James smiles. Ethan is referring to the times when he was in trouble back home, and James would draw coded notes or a special symbol they created to inform each other of things on the floor or wall.

Then Ethan pulls out from his wondrous pockets a small chalk and hands it over to James. They both clasp their hands, and Ethan quickly departs from the stone room. James is once again alone. After a few moments, he retires to his uncomfortable stone bed. He lies down on the hard surface, as the dwarf hadn't supplied any means of linen, which James imagines doesn't exist among the dwarf mountain.

As James starts to doze off, thoughts of his girlfriend, Abela, flood his mind. He misses her deeply, his heart aching with longing. He envisions her beauty and her soft lips, a smile crossing his face before a wave of regret washes over him for not making an effort to see her before the incidents back home in Lepersteed. Suddenly, a familiar sensation—a haunting magic—overtakes him. He quickly jumps off the bed, sensing someone outside, listening. It's the same feeling he experienced when Ethan was around. He hears a disturbance outside his small box window. He slowly takes out his short knife, ready to defend himself against any attack. Despite his doubts, James walks toward the door, using the technique Ethan taught him. He lets the stone doorknob open, and the door creaks slowly. He waits for the right moment and leaps outside with his knife, ready to face the stranger.

He sees a young dwarf warrior with long, braided black hair smiling at him. The stranger holds out his knife and says, "Ha, I heard you from the moment you came to the door. I could have slammed you with my foot."

James stops and stares blankly at the short dwarf with disappointment. "Funny," says James as he puts away the knife. "So why are you snooping, Sir Dwarf?"

"Snooping, hmm?" The dwarf is thinking as he uses his stubby hand to trace his long beard. "I don't understand," the dwarf replies. "But if you're referring to investigating, then yes, I am. If I may ask, what does the human king want with the mountain dwarves?"

Strangely, James senses that the dwarf is trustworthy. He extends his hand and says, "My name is James Lander. I am no king, just a farmer in a small human settlement not far from here. I was brought out here against my will, carrying some diseased magic thing inside me. My companions are here to help me through my ordeal."

The dwarf stares silently for a moment and then laughs roughly, doubling over like a child. James can't help but join in the laughter. He feels something good about this character, a feeling that they will be good friends. After a few moments, they resume their conversation.

"Pleasant humor," says the dwarf. "But I hear you are the descendant of the Destroyer."

"So they say," James replies secretly.

"The name is Kedar." The short, stocky dwarf shapes his hand like a fist and stands at attention, slamming his chest hard and slightly bowing.

James repeats the formal gesture that Kedar displays out of respect. "So, Kedar, why are you observing me?"

"Ha, so I was…" Kedar leaps into the air and lands right in front of James on the ledge of the rocky boulder. James is astonished at how well Kedar balances perfectly on such a thin ledge. "…wondering if I could be of any assistance to the mighty human king," Kedar finishes his sentence while throwing back his long, braided, black hair, which reveals small emerald bands on each side of his shining braids. The heavy golden necklace around his neck shimmers in the light of the moon above them.

James is still in shock at the quickness of this dwarf when he notices a couple of dwarves walking to his left, but they turn back once Kedar signals them to wait outside. Once again, Kedar leaps over James, using the rocky surface above him, and lands with one arm grabbing on to his large front doorframe. James hears a cluster of grinding from Kedar's hand, and then he lands on his enormous feet with a hard thump inside James's room. Kedar casually turns around, looking at James. James stands motionless, trying to comprehend how a dwarf could be so athletic, using his bare hands on an unsafe, chipped rock. He looks again where the dwarf stood and then above him, slowly searching for any indication of support that would allow this dwarf to get a grip so easily. There is none; the rock is completely smooth and has no cracks, except for the one Kedar made above his door, which indicates that he pierced the rock with his bare hands. The door now reveals three small, punched holes.

"Is there a problem, human king?" Kedar now moves about slowly with his large hands behind him, humming slightly, inspecting the entire room. James can now see a small cape behind the dwarf, outlined in the same colors as the golden necklace. The dwarf also wears a golden bracelet, indicating a crested moon and fist next to each other.

James enters the room and closes the heavy door behind him with a slight struggle. "So, are you the messenger of the queen?"

Kedar quickly snaps around as if James has insulted him, then quickly changes his attitude as if he has recalled something. "A messenger for the queen, ha! You are mistaken, human king. If my clothes have shown you any importance, you are misjudging due to your lack of knowledge of our culture. You see, I am merely here to...check your accommodations."

"I apologize for making a quick judgment, Kedar. You are right; I am not familiar with your customs," James says.

"Good," Kedar responds before walking over to a nearby stone chair and quickly leaping onto it with a thump that makes James squint his eyes as if he can feel the pain.

Kedar takes out a cigar and a stick, swipes the stick against the chair, and lights the cigar. He takes a deep breath and exhales a long stream of black smoke from his lungs.

"How can a human king with powerful allies be a farmer?" Kedar asks, enjoying his cigar.

"I thought you said you are here to see if my accommodations are well taken care of," James says, smiling.

"Yes, I am," Kedar says loudly. "I just want to...gossip, like you humans call it," he says after he settles down.

James stares at the well-dressed, clean dwarf, who seems to hold some important title. He decides to go along with Kedar's act to get a better insight into who he really is.

"Well, with all due respect, since you are here to accommodate me, I could use a more suitable bed to my liking. I can't sleep on a rock." James indicates the carved oval bed that has fist-sized boulders lined up horizontally and diagonally.

Kedar smiles, and the corners of his mouth reach each side of his perfectly round ears. His eyes glitter softly, and his clumped, bushy eyebrows lift slightly. Then he chugs on his cigar and laughs, and James can't help but join in.

"Understood, human king," Kedar says.

"Just call me James," James responds.

"Okay, Human King James," Kedar says as he leaps from the chair and approaches the large, rocky bed.

"Just James, Kedar."

"Ha, you say this is uncomfortable. It's not to your liking, King James? You're just not lying on it correctly," Kedar says, then starts stripping off his clothes.

"What are you doing?" James asks, staring in shock as Kedar sheds layers of clothing and throws them in a pile. In a few moments, Kedar is completely naked.

"What's wrong, King James? Never seen a naked dwarf? Ha, you humans are so vain. You have a lot to learn about us," Kedar says with a chuckle before leaping onto the stone bed. James hears another thump and a crackle, and as he observes Kedar's unusually hairy anatomy that covers his chest and down to just above his knee, he realizes how Kedar's body is able to adapt to the rock, which explains how he gripped onto the rock earlier. Just like a pillow, his skin maneuvers based on the rock, and his body adapts naturally. Although James is not sure why dwarves need to be naked to demonstrate how to sleep on the rock bed, he does not question it, assuming it must be their custom and natural way of how they lie down on their beds.

"You see, King James," Kedar says, purposely banging his head a few times on the rock and pausing his beard against the rock, then flipping over to his front with a thump. "Ahhh, why don't you join me?" says the dwarf.

"Umm, no thank you," James replies.

The dwarf looks up, surprised, and meets James's gaze.

"Bring your partner, then."

"Umm, no, he's not my partner. My partner is not here. I left her behind when we had to leave in a hurry...we were getting attacked...um, we had to go," explains James, "Kedar, now, would you please put your clothes back on?"

"Well, don't human kings have other mates? What difference does your biological stance make? I could bring some partners; they are outside, although when it comes to our females, they are not here in this section of this town," Kedar says.

"I'm sorry, Kedar, I will not participate. I'm not familiar with your customs," James firmly declines.

"You humans are so strange," Kedar remarks as he stands up and starts to put on his clothes. "I hear that you value monogamy, but I do respect your position, King James. Besides, my apologies for stepping out of conformity, but my Traversintul cycle is near, and the urge is sometimes uncontrollable."

"What do you mean by 'your cycle'?" James asks, curious about the dwarf's statement.

"Your curse, young Destroyer. The one your ancestor left us with," Kedar explains as he puts on his clothing. James realizes what he is referring to—the curse that James's ancestor placed on Kedar's people that altered their race forever. Their females are scarce, and new births are mainly males. Radion said that their race has become nearly endangered, all because of what happened with the orb souls of the Guardians' punishment. Their female population has become a rare biological need, and procreation is essential for their very existence to continue, but it is also a burden that they have to endure for their survival.

"I'm sorry, Kedar. I don't know how to fix this curse among your people."

"Fix? Ha, nonsense! Why fix something that has been naturally occurring for centuries? We are a happy clan and will not let fate stop who we are. We have developed magic that has maintained our existence. Even before your curse, we respected one another as equals, and we continue to do so as our ancestors did after the destruction. We will thrive once again!" the dwarf says, making a fist on his chest and pounding it hard. "Here." Fully dressed, Kedar hands James a single blue feather.

"What is this?"

"Ha! Just simply lay the feather on the bed," Kedar says.

"And then what?" James asks.

"I don't know; I'm not a human witch. But some sort of magic will develop, and you will be able to sleep well," Kedar replies as he turns around, walking toward the stone door. "I must depart, King James. It has been an engaging conversation."

Kedar pauses by the front door, turning about and staring at James, "I have to ask you, Human King James, how old are you?" His full features are illuminated in the candlelight. He waits for James's response. James observes him, seeing a well-liked young dwarf with a rough, weathered appearance that suggests a life of hard work and little rest. His skin is tanned, and his thick, dark hair is knotted and braided in various unique fashions, but well groomed. His eyes are bright and alert, darting around the room as if always on the lookout for danger. Despite his rough exterior, Kedar's clothing is clean and well maintained, with a hint of gold and silver threads woven into the fabric. Overall, James concludes that Kedar looks like a seasoned higher-standing warrior or sorcerer, someone who has faced many challenges and emerged victorious. He especially notices the various unique knives on Kedar's belt from the back and a small pistol, singularly made of stone and gold. He has heard that these dwarves are masters of weapons and have guns that shoot stones called pistols. He has never seen one before.

"I am eighteen, why?"

"I think it's fascinating that you look to be my age despite your much shorter lifespan. It seems humans your age don't get out much."

James feels a little insulted. "Why would you say that? I am a farmer, and my life was much better until I found out who I really am," he says defensively.

The young dwarf smiles. "Exactly. You do not embrace who you are, young king, descendant of Olen the Destroyer. You let your past mold you and dictate what will be expected from you as you meet your allies and enemies. You suppress the past with shame and guilt of something that was not your doing. In these parts, there are those who will embrace you and others who will seek to eliminate you, so centuries of tradition either do or do not change. You…are… inexperienced."

They stare at each other for a long time. James realizes that this dwarf is more than what he seems. James nods his head, as he has understood his warning, and Kedar does the same before leaving the room.

CHAPTER 19

Her Majesty

As THE HEAVY door closes behind him, James stares at the blue feather and the cigar that Kedar left by his stone bed. He studies the feather for a moment, trying to sense any magic or entity within it. Thinking about Kedar and the dwarf clan, he concludes that they are clever and very observant, something that Ethan has mastered as well. Despite this, James likes Kedar. He's not sure why, but his instincts tell him that Kedar is very loyal. James doesn't know who Kedar really is, but he knows he's not a servant. The way he presents himself and the absolute confidence he exudes give it away.

As James lingers in thought, he runs his finger over the feather. He decides that the next time he runs into Kedar, he'll introduce him to Ethan. Ethan will definitely get a kick out of him.

Just then, the door opens smoothly, and Eva enters with a smile. James notices that her outfit is simpler this time, with comfortable trousers and a top. Her long black hair is as well- kept as always. It's as if she's ready to go on a trek. James is a bit surprised by how different she seems when she's not at home.

"How is it that I can sense individuals when they approach my room?" James asks oddly.

"Not a hello or how are you, James, that's not polite…And it's called intuition, dear. Your soul is infused with the generational building of your ancestors' magic, which heightens your senses and warns you of other souls near you," Eva explains.

"Why can't I sense yours, Eva?"

Eva is now staring at James as she stands in front of him for a few moments in silence as he waits for her response. "That's because I'm trained to block those who have the capability of analyzing my presence. I find it very intrusive," Eva responds.

"I see. I'm sorry," James says.

"Don't be. This is all new to you. When we train, I'll help you keep your intuition under control," Eva assures him.

James sighs and stares away, lost in thought. She keeps saying this is so new for him. They keep telling him about training, but all he feels are senses. And everyone thinks he is dangerous. But now that his headaches are gone, how could senses be dangerous? He can't control things or perform that fiery substance that Radion mentioned when he encountered the Shadowlen or sense living things such as the trees, animals, and water, but it will be understood one day...after his training. He is so confused and doesn't understand what's happening. The Guardian of Water has asked him to meet her at her lair, which only adds to his fears and confusion.

"I know, my dear, all in good time," Eva says. James is taken by surprise, as if Eva were reading his mind.

Eva suddenly looks at the feather James is holding and lifts her right eyebrow, waiting for an explanation.

"It's a long story," James says.

"All right then, let's talk about the queen. She is very occupied, as are all royals, but her situation is unique, and she is constantly monitoring her kingdom for survival," Eva says.

"I see, but does she need to know about my dream within two days? Would it be imposing for her to arrange?" James asks hesitantly.

"The queen doesn't have time, nor does she care about affairs that are outside her kingdom. That task is usually up to the king. Her sole priority is her people and the offspring that continue to preserve their existence. As it stands, the queen usually doesn't like to send her people out of the kingdom unless it's for extreme measures," Eva explains.

"I know," James says sadly.

"What do you mean?" Eva asks curiously.

"I had a visit from one of the queen's guards. He seemed to be vetting who I was, making his own assessment," James says to Eva.

Eva stares at him, pretending she doesn't know what he's talking about.

"I see. And did this guard give you that blue feather?" Eva asks.

"Yes, he said it's magic, and if I place it on the bed, it will make me more comfortable when I sleep."

James can see Eva smirking slightly.

He lifts the blue feather, turning it about. It looks firm but simple, with hints of white lining around the feather.

"There's no magic on it, right?" James asks, feeling foolish.

"First lesson, James. What do you feel?" Eva asks.

James realizes Kedar was toying with him, and he smiles and places it into his pocket. "Nothing."

Then he looks past Eva and stares at the door.

"Someone is coming, Eva," James says softly.

"I know. The queen is ready for us. You need to follow my lead."

⊷══◑ ◑══⊶

In James's wildest dreams, he never imagined being so captivated by the enormous beauty of the queen's castle. Every room is sculpted to a specific meaning and reveals countless hallways that lead to untold corridors that are unfamiliar to him. The rooms possess perfectly carved and shaped articles on the floors and walls, and the carved stone and various integrated displays of countless arranged gems intermix and blend in. The stone tapestries are breathtaking, displaying various themes of the dwarf race and the various battles they encountered.

James constantly stumbles because he can't tear his gaze away. Besides the beauty, he can actually sense the flow of the magic elements, and Water and Fire run freely throughout the castle walls, floors, and fountains. Their presence seems to give life to the castle, a similar life that an expectant mother would give to her unborn child.

The castle has an inner illuminated glow that comes from the ceiling. The unusual fancy arches continue fantastically and spread out into smaller arches that pile high into the ceiling, which veils some sort of circle fixtures that allow the light to illuminate throughout the castle. The arched look reminds James of the small cathedral in his small town, but this one is fifty times larger.

With the castle being heavily guarded at every turn they make, what amazes

James the most, besides the beautiful articles and sculptures, is the fact that the castle is held up by enormous tree bark—particularly, to him, it looks like oversize roots. What James observes when he enters the grand fortresses of this castle is that the roots from above penetrate into a marble rock, and the dwarves used its support to carve out a castle for the queen. It is phenomenal. The columns are not all equally shape or partially sized, extending up high to the entire marble-like fortress that holds up the beautiful arches. He particularly agrees with Eva that these dwarves are the masters of stone. No wonder these soldiers ordered them to remove their shoes. James would never dare place his dirty shoes on such beauty.

Ethan joins James, who says, "It's about time you joined us."

"Well, if you had left a note like we agreed, I wouldn't have been scouting like a madman looking for you," Ethan replies.

"Sorry, I was caught by surprise. I didn't have time. Besides, I know you by now. You don't really need notes of my whereabouts. You're pretty sneaky anyway," James responds.

"Yeah, but not on unfamiliar grounds," Ethan says. "Nice-looking place," he remarks, with an unusual sneer on his face as he looks around the area.

"I wouldn't plan on snooping here, Ethan. Especially since making your fingers sticky will get you killed," James warns.

"Oh no, I wouldn't attempt anything here. But it would be nice to measure some of those gems and pretend that I can hold them," Ethan jokes.

Suddenly, there is a big thump that comes from the warriors who are leading the way. Soon the party is facing a grand stone way that clearly leads inside the royal palace. James takes the time to observe the beauty of the enormous oval doorway. The left side of the door seems to be carved to represent a glamorous staff. The right side reveals an oversize hammer. Both structures are carved perfectly and in such great detail that it looks as if they are mounted on the door. James notices that there are more carved spaces on each of the outlines of the door, which clearly represent the four elements of life. These symbols are throughout the city, as Radion explained it. A passive-looking waterfall the color of sky blue represents Water; a piercing, firing red rose represents Fire; an ancient-looking tree with an oversize sun carved behind it colored in lime green represents Earth; and a dark gray windstorm represents Air.

As James explores the chamber, he is captivated by several statues representing the Guardians of Life, each intriguing in its unique carvings and positions. While the other Guardians are clearly themed around elemental motifs, three statues stand out prominently. The Guardian of Death is depicted as a striking black opal stone carving, symbolizing solemnity and mystery. The dark body tone of the opal provides a perfect backdrop for vibrant flashes of color that dance across the surface, reminiscent of the fleeting nature of life. The figure is sculpted with intricate details, including a flowing cloak and a hooded visage, evoking a sense of enigma and authority. Nearby, a short and stocky female figure, resembling the moon in coloring, represents Void, embodied by an icy, diamond-like stone that glistens with an inner frost. Another statue, a tall male with elf-like features and an icy appearance, personifies Ice, sculpted from a clear, crystalline material that captures the essence of frozen landscapes. These Guardians embody their respective elements in distinct ways, reflecting the realms they govern. Darker gems representing elements of darkness adorn the lower surfaces of the statues. James ponders the stories he has read that could have inspired these depictions, feeling a sense of wonder and curiosity. Entranced by these sculptures, James is drawn out of his reverie as the door slowly opens to reveal the throne room, bathed in brightness and clarity.

In a crystal-like oval room against a massive mountain in the Dwarf Mountain, James and his party witness the breathtaking sight of silvery water cascading outside the throne room. The room is impervious to any outside noise. The crystal walls are adorned with magnificent decorations, and two solid columns stand at each end, seamlessly merging with the cold marble floor. As they approach the grand throne room, male guards in elegant attire are stationed throughout. On the left, there are male attendants near the thrones, while on the right, females stand grouped by their seal rankings, dressed similarly in vibrant outfits. Behind the crystal flowers, the queen with her staff and the king with his imposing hammer sit on a marble pedestal, observing their every move. There is constant murmuring around the queen as James and his party cautiously approach five fierce-looking warriors blocking the marble stairs. These warriors are dressed in war uniforms with steel-plated chests, reaching from their short necks down to their ankles. Like the rest of the kingdom, they are barefoot and have no head protection, but their hair is tightly tied up, revealing their stoic expressions.

Radion steps forward, triggering an immediate response from the warriors. They brandish their weapons and assume attack positions. Surrounding James and his party, the warriors close in, ready to strike. James is filled with shock and fear, unsure of what to do. His magic fails to help him, leaving him vulnerable. Suddenly, Eva touches his shoulder, urging him to stop. Warriors from all directions gather, mirroring the attack formation. Only the Malij assassins behind Eva prepare to defend. James feels his palms grow damp and notices Ethan's belt trembling in fear. Trying not to disrupt the tense atmosphere, James whispers, "What's happening?"

"It's just a precaution, dear. These specialized warriors, known as the Germatel Yemsal, or Protectors of the Beloved, are exclusively assigned to guard the queen," Eva explains confidently, devoid of fear and rather intrigued by the situation. "Through their unique training and proper magic, particularly involving the essence of Air, they can detect various types of magic approaching the queen and are ready to eliminate any threat to her safety."

"But we don't intend to cause any harm—"

"It doesn't matter. These warriors are mentally and physically trained to protect their queen, employing superior combat skills for that sole purpose."

Suddenly, the warriors encircle the group, assuming an attentive formation but remaining motionless. James looks ahead and notices the stoic warriors facing the queen and king in the same manner. The queen then signals for them to step aside by moving her staff to the right. With utmost respect, the five warriors pound their plated chests and stomp their left feet, producing a resounding echo throughout the room. They then move to the side in a perfectly straight line.

Eva interrupts James's gaze, still standing beside the queen. "If the queen faces any threat, it would be due to the king's actions or negligence. The warriors will not hesitate to kill the king. It's something you should be aware of, James, not that you pose any threat to her majesty, but it's a factor to consider when trying to persuade her."

"And would they kill us as well?" James inquires.

"Yes," Eva responds, firmly yet gracefully.

"Radion, representing Lord of the Rachar, come forward," the king's voice booms, resuming the background murmurs from the male and female attendants positioned on either side of the king and queen.

"No!" the queen suddenly interjects, her voice soft and sweet, her demeanor less bold and stern. Her straight nose and long, golden hair add to her delicate appearance. "Bring the human king and the woman forward," she declares, her thin, golden rod shimmering against her flowing golden robe.

"Come on, dear. Let's not keep her waiting," Eva urges James, attempting to guide him forward.

James feels his knees lock, and a wave of abhorrent fear rushes up his spine. He can sense and hear his heart pounding in his chest and temples.

"What should I say…I mean, I don't want to—"

"Just be yourself, dear. She won't harm you."

Both James and Eva are escorted to the front of the pedestal facing the king and queen. Radion stands a few steps behind, muttering angrily to himself, clearly dissatisfied with their decision. James notices Radion's furious gaze directed at Eva for unknown reasons.

The queen stands tall and imposing, her gaze piercing as she fixes her eyes on Eva. Her regal demeanor is accentuated by the crown adorning her head, its jewels glinting in the light. With a stoic expression, she exudes power and grace, her presence commanding respect. James and Eva kneel before her, their right hands pressed to their chests in reference to her authority. In this moment, the queen embodies strength and majesty, a figure to be both feared and revered.

"In your presence, Majesty, I am Mistress Eva of the Society of Rachar," Eva quickly introduces herself.

"I know," the queen interrupts, pausing as she gathers her thoughts, a frown on her face. The king turns to her, displaying concern for her behavior. However, a moment later, he smiles, seeming to lighten up within himself.

Eva stands, unfazed by the queen's reaction, patiently waiting. When the queen diverts her attention to James, his heart races even faster, unsure of what to say but feeling compelled to at least introduce himself.

"Your Majesty, my name is James Lander—"

Radion clears his throat slightly, attempting to signal him to use the formal title.

James stutters, saying, "My apologies, Your Majesty. I am still young and unfamiliar with your customs. My name is James Olen of Lepersteed, I mean, the human kingdom."

Suddenly, without warning, the entire room trembles as if violence is about to erupt. The king rises, shouting at the guards, while the Germatel warriors swiftly position themselves in front of the queen, ready to take action. Then, as abruptly as it began, the shaking subsides. Confusion fills the air, with murmurs spreading throughout the room. Even Radion sighs in frustration, as if things aren't going his way. However, Eva remains composed and unwavering, as if unaffected by the chaos that just unfolded.

"Reiler!" the king yells at the white-robed dwarf that is smoothing its hand on the large tree root. "Why is this happening?"

"Your Grace, I don't understand. She seems to be fine," Reiler says, fingering the enormous tree root and concentrating. "I sense anger, sorrow—" There is a pause. "And regret." He continues feeling around the large root and comes full circle.

"Yes, I also feel regret," the queen says.

The king turns slowly to face James, looking concerned and stern. "From the name of the king's blooded ancestor, she'll never forget," the king says sympathetically.

The queen instructs the warriors to move about and protect her while she fixes her composure and directs her attention to James. She waits silently as the entire room stands at ease, waiting for her next move. James thinks it is best that he start the conversation, since it was he who started this small episode in the queen's royal chamber.

"Your Majesty." James waits, remembering what Eva told him and how he must wait until she is ready to proceed.

"You may proceed, King James, for my time is very limited," the queen says.

"Thank you, Your Graciousness." Then James takes a few moments to gather his thoughts of how he should address this powerful queen with the request he needs.

"I am a descendant of Olen the Destroyer," James declares, causing the tree roots to tremble once again, although less aggressively. The king maintains his position as a protective presence, posing no threat to the queen and her chamber.

James continues, "My lineage has not been fully revealed to me, but according to the information I received, I must embark on a quest to find the sacred Orbs of Olen." Once more, the roots violently shake, resulting in a crystal light shade falling behind them. Ethan is startled and attempts to join James, only to be blocked by the Malij assassins standing nearby, who keep him at bay. Eva gazes gracefully at James and whispers, "Dear, please refrain from mentioning your heritage name. It troubles Eartha." James nods and proceeds.

"In our quest, we require your assistance in obtaining the orbs. I had a dream where I spoke with the Guardian of Water, who directed me to her lair and provided instructions for what I believe to be a quest," James quickly concludes.

"What is it that the Destroyer seeks my help with? The power that potentially surpasses my abilities?" the queen inquires.

"Your Majesty, if I may," Eva interjects.

The queen shifts her attention to Eva, offering a faint smile. "Yes, Ev—" She pauses, as if attempting to recall something. "Yes, Eva, you may."

"As the heir of King Olen has stated, we are in desperate need of your assistance. As you are aware, my king's reputation is not favorable in other cultures, particularly among our own kind. However, your esteemed people are our last hope. The bond between humans and dwarves predates the first war. Our gracious Guardian has conveyed a message through King James to your realm, which serves as the only pathway to access her lair. A request from the Guardian has not been made since the time of the Destruction. We must unite and uncover the purpose behind obtaining the lost soul orbs of the Guardians. While we are uncertain of their exact significance, many prophecies suggest that dark times lie ahead. If we fail to act appropriately, the orbs could fall into the wrong hands, and everything could be lost." Eva pauses briefly, and Radion abruptly interjects, as if his patience has reached its limit.

"Queen Montat," he says. "Please, if you understand the urgency of our mission, I implore you to assign at least one of your finest warriors to protect our quest."

"You are not to speak until I ask it of you, Radion!" The queen's voice fills the throne room with a commanding tone, shaking Radion to his core.

James notices the king casting a disapproving look at Radion, and Eva responds in the same manner, interjecting while glancing over her shoulder with piercing eyes.

"Radion, your behavior reveals your true nature," the queen continues, her voice returning to a normal tone. "You are a powerful wizard who belittles my culture. Besides your impatience and arrogance, you should understand that your presence holds no significance to me. Just like all the males of your kind, you assume that immediate decisions must be made. But you are in my kingdom, where your authority is worthless. If you cannot abide by our ways, perhaps you should join those who lack patience at the dwarf pub."

"My apologies, Your Majesty," Eva quickly interjects before the queen takes further action against Radion. "My scholar is under immense pressure, something that males of our kind struggle to control. We have approached King James's assignment with great patience, and due to previous difficulties with our king's family, we are constantly vigilant in protecting him from enemies that span multiple cultures. It is true that my scholar is a male, which may hold little significance in your eyes, but please understand that our quest is of utmost importance, and the inclusion of our wizard and all who join us is crucial."

"I apologize as well, Your Majesty," Radion adds swiftly. "I sometimes forget that my patience has its limits. I hope you can find it in your heart to forgive me."

The queen exhales, analyzing the situation while looking at both Eva and Radion. Then her gaze settles on James, intense and unyielding. James feels the weight of her scrutiny on his back as the queen narrows her distinct black eyes, her round face framed by long, blondish hair. He wonders how these female creatures differ so greatly in appearance from their male counterparts. The females, though distinct, possess a certain beauty that surpasses that of their male companions.

"King James, I am well acquainted with your arrival and the significance of your journey. We hold a favorable view of your kind, humans, more than any other race, and we appreciate the value of the friendship we once shared. Our history dates back a long way, but we suffered greatly at the hands of your ancestors. While we do not dwell on the pain, we cannot forget it. Although our gracious Eartha has forgiven, doubts linger. I am unsure whether I should assist you. The orbs, if found, have consumed your ancestors and altered races, including your own. I must prioritize the welfare of my people. Both our female dominance and my king are in demand. We face a shortage of children, and taking away my male at this time would add further strain. Unless you can provide a compelling reason for me to overlook our past and put my male in danger, I must decline your request for now."

James can hear Radion silently cursing and stamping his foot as the queen delivers her final decision.

James remains motionless as the queen waits for a response. He is unsure of what to say, hoping that Eva will take the lead. However, she continues to stare ahead, seemingly unaffected by the turn of events. Their hope begins to fade rapidly. Radion and Eva have insisted that they require the expertise of a skilled warrior from the dwarves to proceed with their quest.

"Your Majesty, if I may inquire," James finally speaks up.

"Yes, you may," the queen responds.

"I humbly apologize for any offense caused by my words," James says sincerely. "I have witnessed the possession of my best friend by these malevolent demons. The mayor of my town was ruthlessly slaughtered while bravely trying to protect me. Just yesterday, I had a harrowing vision of a city overrun by grotesque creatures I have never before encountered. Within me, a surge of power yearns to be unleashed, yet I struggle to control it. Your Majesty, you have demonstrated the profound importance of my mission and the survival of your kind. I stand before you not to intimidate you or disrupt your ways, but to lend my aid in protecting all those who strive for existence against this imminent threat. I wholeheartedly accept your decision, but I implore you to reconsider. My plea echoes not only as a king, but as a representative of a generation that has grown to cherish our land, our people, and all those who yearn for a peaceful coexistence."

At that moment, James remembers his enlightening encounter with Kedar and adds, "I have been enlightened to the consequences of these orbs. I solemnly vow that I will not allow them to consume us as they did our ancestors. Instead, I will diligently work toward resolving the pressing issues we face, seeking guidance from my allies gathered here."

As James concludes his heartfelt plea, he observes the queen's discomfort, her struggle to withhold something. Her battle against tears becomes apparent. James realizes that the dwarf females possess a heightened sensitivity compared to their male counterparts.

The queen casts a glance at her king, positioned at her right side. He remains resolute, his expression unchanging, his long white hair cascading over his regal attire. With his prominent nose and flat face, he remains an unwavering presence in the room.

"Very well." The queen surprises everyone with her response. "I will provide ten of my finest warriors, but I will not compel anyone to go. These warriors must volunteer willingly."

"Thank you, Your Majesty," James says, and bows.

When he looks up, he sees a male dwarf slipping out of view and walking beside the king. James is astonished; it's the well-dressed dwarf named Kedar who he met in his room earlier. This time, Kedar is wearing shining boots that cover the top layer of his foot. He is dressed in a bright golden-blue outfit that matches the attire of the king and queen. His hair is pulled back and braided, revealing his round face and spread nose. Kedar quickly gives James a smile, and a golden, heavy necklace gleams as he approaches the pedestal, positioning himself between the queen and king. He pounds his right hand on his chest and slightly bows.

The queen and king exchange slightly unsettled looks, clearly surprised by Kedar's sudden appearance before them.

"May I speak freely, my beloved queen?" Kedar asks.

The queen shakes her head as she looks once again for the king to answer. The king returns the look as to signal something to her and faces Kedar. "You may."

"I will accompany the human king and nine others," Kedar says.

"For what purpose?" the queen asks quickly.

"To protect our kingdom from any threat that may surface. It seems the human king spoke truly. We encountered a disturbance on the mainland. Elven Maspar from the north are taking form, and there is word that the Princess Argus is being hunted by the creatures released from the dark realm," Kedar says.

Then he turns to face the queen only. "Mother, I am better suited to understanding these creatures. If we are entering a new era of the coming of the Destroyer, we must prepare and train our Germtar and Demontrol in order to deal with any new threats we are not familiar with."

"My love, may I provide my resolution?" the king says to the queen.

"Yes, you may," the queen says.

The king sits stirring, fixated, and straightens up. "You have my blessings, my beloved son, but it is up to your mother." He turns to the queen and says, "He is best suited for this task. We need to help the human king and protect ourselves from any new threats, my beloved queen; it is our duty to save our kingdom from what lies ahead."

The queen looks distressed, as if she is being pushed against the wall. Kedar now faces the queen, clasping her hand, and says, "Please, my beloved queen. This task requires the safety of our people, a duty that is required by—"

"I know!" the queen snaps. "Kedar, you are my son. You shouldn't go. You can send another commander," she says with a sincere voice.

"Mother, please. I accept the responsibility. Give me your blessing so I may leave the kingdom," Kedar says.

"Very well," she says.

"Thank you, Mother. May I bring my sister too? She is one of the strongest warriors, and I could use her expertise."

"My child, my daughter may have special skills, but your sister needs to stay. It's the law."

"Mother, she is my twin. Our combined abilities can be useful."

"My queen, our son is correct." The king intercepts their conversation. The queen shoots a glare that conveys her disapproval of his being out of line, but she chooses to let the matter drop. "They are the firstborn twins of our generation. Their combined skills can balance the obstacles they face. With a powerful warrior combined with her brother's magic, they can be a unique match for enemies. Besides, they need to venture out to see the outside world to get a better understanding of what we are facing," the king explains.

The queen stares slightly at her son. Her long, blond hair hangs over the stone throne, every strand outlined in ribbons and gold. Her gown is strongly satin and red with gold outlines that set her apart from all her peers. She wears a small crown with red and white stones, diamonds that appear to glitter as she looks around at the bright touches around the throne room.

"Granted," the queen replies bluntly.

Kedar clasps his foot and pounds his right hand before turning around and walking up to the pedestal.

"Don't worry, Mother. We will be safe," he reassures her.

The queen leans forward and kisses him on the forehead. "My instinct tells me not to let you both go at the same time, yet duty tells me otherwise. You and your sister need to see for yourselves. Be safe, my son. Look after each other, and use each other's wits. You both are special. Go with the Destroyer, and bring back news and hope. Our bloodline and our people need to know if the time has come for redemption," she says to him.

Kedar seems perplexed by what his mother is telling him, but he simply bows and steps back.

The queen faces the party. "You will all use the eastern gate to access the great sea to our gracious Guardian of Water." Every dwarf in the throne room gasps and whispers quietly. Even Kedar is taken aback by the queen's request. James doesn't understand what just happened, but the entire throne room seems shaken by the words "eastern gate."

Then the king stands up. "Guards, locate the gatekeeper and escort our guests to the forbidden area at once." He bows to the queen. "Wonderful idea, my love. It will give our children a different perspective."

"I know," the queen says, and waves her arms to move the audience away from her.

CHAPTER 20

Portal

THE EVERGREEN LIBRARY in the ancient city of Kumartal buzzes with the lively sounds of insects and the scurrying of small animals, making it feel alive as Celestia waits for her cousin to finish her preparation.

"Okay, Celestia, are you ready?"

Celestia feels nauseous from the foul brew that her cousin has stewed up. It smells as if they are surrounded by a pit of human waste. Aberra claims it will soothe her transition into the ethereal realm and enable her to be guided safely. Celestia wonders how something so repulsive can be soothing and act as a deterrent for intruders.

Then Celestia glances over to her right and notices that Aberra has shifted a large, standing mirror next to her.

"Why do you need that?" Celestia questions, observing her reflection while tucking her long, brown hair behind her ear, the Argus stone shining against the light, giving her eyes a bloodshot appearance.

"Not many people know this, but that mirror serves as a two-way link between the living and the ethereal realm. It can assist us in various ways. It's complicated, but don't worry—I know what I'm doing," Aberra reassures her.

Uncertain but trusting Aberra due to her reputation and gifted talent to communicate with dead, besides her second cousin Netaha, Celestia allows her to proceed and adjust the mirror properly.

"Celestia?" Aberra says, looking sincere with her long, dark brown hair. She has grown into a beautiful woman, possessing the same oval Argus eyes. The Argus family resemblance is so striking that anyone could assume they are all siblings.

"Yes," Celestia manages to say as she tries to hold her breath.

"Okay, now I need you to concentrate. Think of something subtle, perhaps a peaceful place or a shared moment of silence and tranquility."

"I'll try." Celestia sits on soft grass cushions with her legs crossed under a massive oak tree in the library's research room. The breeze magically sweeps through, barely disturbing the scattered books and pages on the floor. Aberra thought this was a perfect place where they could find peace. It simulates an outdoor setting with abundant greenery, the large oak tree providing shade over rows of handcrafted benches in front of a wooden table. Birds sing sweetly, not a single insect disturbs them, and the sun shines gently without causing them to perspire.

The environment is incredibly soothing, but Celestia struggles, knowing her father might be dead and her mother is terminally ill due to an unknown sickness. There is so much sadness, making it difficult for Celestia to concentrate, but she forces herself to try. She recalls a moment when her parents and she had a picnic near the castle walls. Her father was dressed in short trousers and a lightweight shirt her mother had made. It was one of those occasions when her parents tried to blend in and forget about their royal background. Her mother had prepared a small arrangement of cut meats and fruits in a woven basket. They lay on the grass, soaking in the peaceful scenery of the garden and trees. Celestia played silly games with her father, and eventually, her mother joined them. It was the most cherished and loving time she had with her parents.

"I'm in," a voice echoes through her mind, startling her. "Calm down, it's just me. I've possessed your body," the voice explains.

"Can you hear my thoughts?" Celestia asks curiously.

"Yes, but I can't invade your privacy. I can only hear what you consciously think," comes the response.

"Isn't that invading my privacy, Aberra?"

"We don't have time for this. I won't possess you for long. Now listen up, focus on the Argus stone. Try to immerse yourself in the stone," Aberra instructs.

"You mean channeling magic into the stone?" Celestia inquires.

"Not exactly. You know how you search out your inner soul and call forth the magic? Try calling up your soul and forcefully push yourself into the stone. I will help guide you into the passion of the stone. If I encounter any danger, I will pull you out. Now, are you ready?"

"Yes," Celestia replies.

Celestia focuses on herself, feeling relaxed as she delves into her bloodline magic. This magic has been passed down through generations, since ancient times, when the Guardians roamed the earth. The inherent magic, known only to the Argus family, is still unfamiliar to her. It stirs gently within her and her family, like a milky substance bubbling inside. The life force surges upward as Celestia searches for the Argus stone. Its smooth, red surface calls to her, and she slips into the soul of the stone. Suddenly, everything goes black.

Celestia finds herself inside a long tunnel, blind but sensing the walls around her as if they are fingertips away. She realizes she is no longer in the library but in another dimension, somewhere within the stone. Gradually her vision begins to take form. The tunnel stretches out before her, with a beautiful golden light shimmering at the other end. It opens her heart, calling to her, and she feels no pain or anxiety—just a sense of freedom as she takes each step toward the radiant light. Celestia embraces her purpose, and the light eagerly plays with her mind, promising immense power and eternal life. She wants to run toward it, like a child being called to her mother, when suddenly a person blocks her path. She tries to push the man away, but he forcefully guides her in the opposite direction.

Frustrated, Celestia begins kicking him until the man picks her up, cradling her like a child. Her father's essence soon overwhelms her. She relaxes and realizes she is no longer a young lady but a two-year-old child. She sees her father's loving eyes gazing upon her as he continues to hold and comfort her. She can't speak properly, but she accepts his embrace—a hug she has missed from her parents.

Now she understands—her father is no longer present but trapped inside this stone. However, her father's gaze signals shock. No, he spoke to her like a baby, assuring her that everything was okay. Celestia feels confused as her father carries her further along the tunnel, away from the light, until he gently lays her down on the floor.

"My Celestia," he says, his voice full of determination and power. "So much will and power, so much like your mother. Go back; your presence here is not needed."

Celestia, now understanding the purpose of this journey, tries to speak to her father about the dilemma in the library, but only baby words come out.

"My dear, this is not a place for you. Don't worry; only a part of my essence is here. The stone is much more than you think. But be patient, my love, and learn of its power—a power that you have yet to understand. You know so little. You must go; your presence here disturbs the stone, and it seeks to take you with it."

Celestia can see a soft, shadowy figure taking form. The surroundings are vague, but she can make out other shadowy figures in the distance. The area feels peaceful and filled with evergreen sensations, accompanied by whispering voices, soothing rustles, and bird tweets. As she looks around, she realizes she is in a vast forest—or perhaps a garden. The figure draws closer, and she can discern the tall person with wild hair. It is her father indeed! *Is he dead?* she wonders. Could it be? Or is he in a state of mind between life and death? She recalls from her studies that the Guardian of Death sometimes influences the living, and there could be instances where a person walks into the realm of death. Once inside, the soul's destiny is determined, leading to righteousness or eternal suffering. The in-between, they say, is sometimes crossed when life is trying to thrive but death pushes into reality—a struggle.

Celestia starts to cry, but she refuses to accept her father being tormented by the struggle between life and death. This is the reason for the Guardians, where both entities, light representing life and darkness representing death, are balanced under the guidance of the Great Guardian.

"Your mother will explain when she is better. Seek her, my love. She misses you terribly. They are calling me; I must leave you. Remember, I will always be with you no matter what happens. The essence of your family's soul will protect you and could link to your bloodline, surrounding you in your love the stone will seek and protect. Remember, we are always with you. In time, I will be…"

Celestia realizes her father is trying to tell her something, but she can't understand what. She can visualize her father now—a handsome man with brown hair and wide oval eyes like the rest of the family. He has aged yet still possesses a youthful vibrancy. His features are smooth, but with subtle signs of aging. He wears the royal robe of the Arguses, a bright-red garment adorned with golden trimmings and embroidered with the family crest, a willow tree symbolizing the Guardians of Life.

Then her father starts to fade away, leaning forward to kiss her on the forehead. "I love you…Keep together, bonded…" And then he disappears, leaving silence in his wake. Another voice emerges from behind her—it is Aberra, searching for her. Celestia realizes her own body has turned, and she is far away from the enchanting glowing light. She seeks the source of the new voice, and suddenly she is pulled out.

Celestia is gasping for air as the sunlight of the research room shines above her. She places her hand on her chest, feeling her heart racing fast. She senses the residual warmth of the Argus stone slowly subsiding. Then she sees tears streaming down Aberra's face as she tries to support her.

Are you okay?" Aberra gasps for air.

Celestia clears her throat, finally relaxing as Jarin holds her and the entire family surrounds her.

She shows a hint of a smile and manages to say, "Yes."

"Sakeris, get some water," Larmari says, and then he dashes out of the room.

"I thought you guys were gone," Jarin says, kneeling and massaging Celestia's shoulders.

"No," Celestia replies, leaning over to hug her cousin. "Thank you."

Aberra returns the hug. "I'm just glad I found you. I was so terrified," she says.

"All right, so what happened?" Jarin asks eagerly.

"Relax, will you? Let her catch her breath," Aberra says, staying and cleaning the grass off her pants.

Aluiz and Dario come running toward Celestia, and they hug each other. "I'm okay," Celestia repeats to her younger cousins, reassuring them that she is unharmed.

Celestia and the party finally leave the room and return to the garden so that Aberra and Celestia can regain their strength. Soon after, Sakeris returns with a pail of water, and Aberra and Celestia feel refreshed and rested enough to proceed with their story.

Celestia then explains her experience in the ethereal realm in the stone.

"So your father hasn't said much, then," Jarin says, feeling regret.

"I'm not sure. He emphasized that I should protect our bloodline," Celestia replies.

"Well, he did say to stick together. Maybe we could form a wall of some kind, and the Argus stone will protect us all," Aberra suggests.

"That's worth a try," Jarin says.

"What about those who aren't in our bloodline?" Aberra asks.

"We could form some kind of circle chain, similar to a witch's prayer. We can keep Sakeris and the kids inside as long as we face the threat. Hopefully the Argus stone will protect us," Larmari says.

"I won't stay inside. I'll protect the princess," Sakeris insists.

Jarin sighs, "Really, brother—"

Celestia interrupts, walking toward Sakeris, who is quietly leaning in the corner of the tree after providing water to her. She notices that Sakeris is no longer the young, naive kid she once remembered. He has always been there for the family. Being the other older boy within their circle, they have a strong connection. They grew up together and ventured into many forbidden places their parents warned them about. She smiles, remembering how even then, he was so protective of her, as she was the youngest family member at that time. Now, looking at him, a grown man, he appears serious and deadly, like a malevolent, forbidden assassin. But as a family member, they all know, he has a heart like no other. "Sakeris, it's okay. I know your duty means a lot to you, but we are all family," she says to him.

"But you are a princess, and that puts us in—"

"Familial bonds are stronger than you think," Jarin interjects.

"Jarin, please." She returns her attention to Sakeris. "I know," Celestia says.

"Okay," Celestia says, turning away to rejoin her party. "I think we should hold hands in a circle. I have an idea too; give me a second to talk to Aluiz and Dario." She goes to find her younger cousins, who are playing with the animals in the Evergreen Library.

For the rest of the afternoon, the entire team discusses their plan. Celestia will lead the party, with each member of the Argus family holding hands. Celestia will be first in line, followed by Jarin, Larmari, and Aberra. They will form a protective circle around Sakeris, Aluiz, and Dario, shielding them from the creatures. If Aberra's plan works, the outer circle of the Argus family will be safeguarded by Celestia's stone as long as they maintain physical contact, creating a magical link. Jarin and Sakeris gather some supplies and food, just in case there are issues with the protective wall above the library or if it becomes corrupted.

As evening approaches, the party makes their way to the top floor of the exotic library. This floor consists of beds and benches where scholars usually retired when they'd rather not leave their studies behind. At the end of the dim bedroom chamber corridor, there is an exit door. The party approaches it eagerly, with Celestia in the lead, ready to escape with their lives.

"Are you sure this is a good idea?" Sakeris says, feeling cramped in the middle of the family with the two younger ones holding his hand on each side.

"Yes, just protect the kids with you. Don't worry, Celestia has powerful magic watching over her and the rest of us," Jarin says, looking at Celestia and waiting for her to open the door.

Celestia tries the door, but it won't budge.

"Great, we've wasted our time!" Jarin says, throwing up his hands.

"Just a sec, I think we have to ask properly to leave. If you recall, airhead, we had to ask to come in," Larmari says.

"Oh, that silly clause again," Jarin grumbles.

Celestia smiles as she turns to face the door. "I, Celestia Argus, Princess of Selcarth, command thee, Eartha Library, to release us along with my family and our beloved guest. We thank you for your wise reverence and gratitude for your comfort in your precious library."

Instantly, the door opens, and the group stays close, hoping to give the impression that they are Celestia's family. They all hold hands, relying on the stone to protect them as they step out. Celestia peers into the empty darkness, and the city lights brighten as the sun settles out of view. The smell of fire and smoke fills her nostrils. The cousins follow her, holding each other's hands. Jarin scans the surroundings intently, as do the other cousins. They form a circle, with the younger boys in the middle, including Sakeris. Sakeris objects, wanting to be at the front to protect them. However, they convince him that the stone will offer protection while they are in the circle.

Celestia quietly thinks to herself as they search for the portal. She had a secret conversation with Aluiz and Dario, instructing them to watch over Sakeris and ensure he entered the circle first since he was the most vulnerable. They both agreed and pretended to need protection from Sakeris so they could fulfill their duty.

As they walk slowly, closing the circle behind them, at least ten to fifteen wicked-looking creatures the size of cats suddenly leap over the ledge and start to pounce toward the party. Aluiz and Dario yell as they see the creatures' razor-sharp teeth, which drip with blood and bits of meat from recent feedings. Sakeris immediately huddles the boys to protect them.

Aberra lets out a yelp as a toad attempts to bite her head, but she remains unharmed. The Argus stone prevents any harm from coming to her. Then Celestia realizes their theory worked; she is face-to-face with three horrifying toads, their savage, distorted teeth trying to tear at her face and hair. She can smell the stench of decay and old blood on their breath, and their slimy saliva splatters on her face. But the invisible shield generated by the stone prevents them from making any contact. Strangely, she can feel the warm, rotten blood dripping from the creatures' skin, a trait she and Aberra share with all creatures. She senses hunger, anticipation, and death emanating from them all.

Celestia notices that these creatures are flesh-eating predators, with pieces of meat and body parts hanging loosely in their mouths. Other creatures pile on top of them, but the circle created by the group reveals a protective barrier of some sort. They can see oozing slime and blood from other victims slowly sliding off their shells. Thumps can be heard as more creatures appear, trying to push hard and break through the barrier, but it holds strong, assisting the group in moving forward without any strain.

The group pauses for a moment, their gaze fixed on the portal created by Professor Ref, located far away from their current position. It's a small portal, allowing only one person at a time to pass through. Celestia sighs as she searches for Jarin, who is positioned on the opposite side of the circle.

"Jarin, remember, the portal only permits one person through at a time," she informs him. She can sense Jarin's anticipation for a fight as the shield continues to endure relentless attacks from the creatures. They bite into the shield, but their attempts are futile as they fail to break through. The shield has transformed into a bright, solid substance, coated in a gelatinous liquid that sizzles with heat. The Argus stone continues to deflect any danger to the family as long as they tightly hold hands, maintaining their bond.

"We…," he yells back, but his voice is drowned out by the chaos.

"We can't hear you!" both Larmari and Aberra exclaim.

"We need to break the bond!" Jarin insists.

"Celestia, it's time!" Aberra adds.

Celestia observes her cousins on either side, ready to face the creatures without hesitation. No one would dare to challenge them. It's in their blood, a biological power that surges through the family when they step up to protect someone they love. Their magic manifests powerfully.

Celestia waits for the right moment, her eyes briefly shifting to Sakeris tightly holding their young cousin. Although the Argus stone prevents any harm, it doesn't stop the sinister creatures from making contact. As long as they hold hands, the creatures can spit their green slime and attempt to tear their skin apart, but the Argus stone shields them from harm. Celestia and her cousins swiftly move toward the back, leaning in closely to Sakeris, Aluiz, and Dario to maintain security within the protective circle they have formed.

Now there are over a hundred of these creatures, and their numbers are hindering their progress.

"I have to generate my staff to push them away!" Jarin yells, spitting at the same time.

"No! You will break the link!" Larmari screams.

"Jarin, try to repel them with your magic," Aberra says.

"Shit, crap! The shield won't let me use Air!" Jarin yells.

"I need room. Can you open your circle so I can throw my knives? They are magically toxic," Sakeris says, hovering over Aluiz and Dario.

Suddenly Celestia says, "Aluiz, Dario, you know what to do. When I say go, do it!" as the young boys hold on to Sakeris tightly, ready for action.

"Wait! What are the kids going to do?" Sakeris looks at them with surprise, seeing smiles in their wide eyes, filled with confidence. He is amazed at how strong their grip is, feeling a slight pain as they hold on tightly.

"Just trust me," Celestia yells back to Sakeris.

Sakeris shakes his head, not understanding the family's ways. His job is to protect the young ones, but he has a strange feeling that it is the other way around. He recalls Celestia talking privately to the boys, and when he inquired with Jarin if everything was okay with them, Jarin just smiled and said that she was giving them instructions for when they headed out, but Sakeris would be in the circle with them.

As they move backward, Celestia yells, "Okay, now boys!" as she waves back, signaling them to move.

To Sakeris's surprise, both Aluiz and Dario release their grip and leap onto him. Immediately, they are carried by the wind, soaring up to the large branches that hold the tree. It takes him a moment to process as the wind propels the young boys with a mighty swing, causing his body to lurch forward. Celestia swiftly releases her grip, as do the others in the group. Jarin magically conjures his ignited rod, while Larmari calls forth a watery substance with her hand, which then hardens into ice. Aberra leaps alongside the young boys.

In the midst of the chaos, Sakeris looks around, momentarily confused and ready to defend himself against any impending attacks. Celestia effortlessly lifts him up and pushes him toward the boys. The boys are already prepared with a sturdy vine that instantly wraps around Sakeris, while Aberra's hands guide the vines to secure him. The two boys pull him toward the portal. Sakeris tries to free himself, but they are too quick, and the vine forcefully pulls him. He tumbles into the portal, catching a glimpse of the grotesque sight of an oversize frog attempting to leap toward him. However, Jarin and Larmari, using their magic, push the creatures back with fire and water from their staff, effortlessly fending them off. Celestia and Aberra block the creatures' spittle with the surrounding tree branches under their command, shielding against the acid attacks.

As Sakeris passes through the portal, the vision slowly fades away. Immediately, he sees Aluiz flying alongside him, saluting him with jubilation, as they join each other on the other side. Sakeris finally relaxes as he materializes in a regal room, and the vines release him, realizing that he was the one in need of protection, an Argus without direct blood ties.

Celestia notices Dario preparing to join the fight, but the tree branches swiftly block his adventurous move, prompting Celestia to give him a quick glance.

"I know you're brave, Dario, but not this time," she says.

Dario salutes and smiles, walking backward toward the portal, acknowledging her command, and then disappears into the portal.

Jarin and Larmari wield their staffs, using fire, water, and ice to push the creatures back, causing explosions and the interaction of fire and water as they descend. Aberra subdues the creatures as they continue to climb the tree. Celestia commands the branches to slap the dragon frogs downward with each attempt as the four of them approach the portal.

"Jarin, it's your turn!" Aberra shouts.

"What? We should take them down!"

"Fire isn't affecting them! They seem to be in the realm of fire! She's right, you go first. We've got this," Larmari says.

Jarin leaps past them, soaring high on the branches and unleashing a powerful blast from his hand that engulfs the entire party. The explosion ripples beneath them, stunning and dazzling all the creatures. Then he swiftly jumps back toward the group.

"Fire always works." He smiles. "Hurry up then!" he urges, utilizing the guidance and force of the element of Air as he effortlessly leaps into the portal and disappears.

More birds come to their aid as the surrounding animals sense the family's danger. Celestia and Aberra block the creatures with the thick surrounding branches, but the creatures continue to break through the powerful blockages. Suddenly, a massive, reddish behemoth crocodile appears beside them, poised to leap, but it is intercepted by a sabretooth tiger that blocks Celestia and Aberra.

"No, you'll be killed!" Celestia yells at the sabretooth.

"Get out of here!" Aberra shouts at the sabretooth as well.

However, the sabretooth leaps toward the crocodile. Celestia and Aberra prepare to defend, but Larmari says, "No, it's too late for him."

Larmari uses the force of Water from the elements of Air to create a massive wall around them, which instantly turns into ice. Swinging her staff with force, she shatters the ice into thousands of sharp icicles that shoot toward the advancing dragon frogs, instantly killing hundreds of them, giving them a few moments.

"I don't know what Jarin is talking about, but a combo of dark and light elements can be very deadly." She smiles at her cousins.

"Larmari, go!" Celestia says as she places her hand on the surface of the tree. Within seconds, vines from outside grow and swiftly block the advance of other creatures by her command.

Larmari leads the way toward the portal, urging everyone to hurry as she disappears through it.

Suddenly, Aberra leaps into the air, carried by the wind, and slams her fist onto the surface of the Evergreen Library, creating a thunderous crack that forces

Celestia to cover her ears. The cloud above undergoes a wild transformation, and a massive tentacle shoots out from the sky, pointing directly ahead. With increasing intensity, it crushes and decimates anything in its path. Aberra skillfully employs the tentacle to repel the approaching spitting creatures that manage to break through the vine barrier. Swiftly, she conjures lightning tornadoes, intertwining with the tentacle's movements. The tornadoes electrify the air, ripping apart each creature they encounter, rendering them into scattered pieces.

"And of course, the element of Earth heads them all with your vine blockage, cuz," Aberra says, ready to help the sabretooth.

"No, cuz, go! I'll take care of him!" Celestia shouts as she witnesses the sabretooth tackling the crocodile, its fur torn by acid burns from the crocodile's attacks.

Aberra nods and embraces her cousin, summoning water to wash away the lingering fight between the oversize crocodile and the sabretooth. The water extinguishes the flames, giving the sabretooth a fighting chance. Aberra then disappears into the portal.

Celestia leaps toward the portal, harnessing the power of the wind. Suddenly, she spots Professor Ref near the library door, sneaking quickly toward it. Professor Ref realizes that Celestia is watching him. She gives him a serious look for a moment and then smiles. She goes through the portal and uses her command over the air to pull the sabretooth right after her.

⟶≡◎ ◎≡⟵

Professor Ref witnesses the sudden disappearance of the family, and the creatures start to dissipate. He notices the rock formation hovering in the far distance, leaps into the air, and heads toward the direction the group is heading.

Finally, it's his chance. His people, for centuries, have despised this human family. They believe they have unique abilities like the elves, but they are no match for the elven nation. His opportunity has arrived. The door to enter the sacred library of Eartha is about to close. He needs that relic.

Professor Ref finally enters the library, feeling exhilarated as the door closes behind him. Creatures of all kinds start appearing in the ethereal moment. He sees an enormous storeroom that he has been waiting for all these years to enter and retrieve the relic that the human dropped years ago from the other realm, believed to be where the Guardian of Earth is. A realm called Earth...how ironic. As he moves forward, the floor beneath him disappears, and he desperately grabs for anything to stay afloat as he plummets downward. He looks up and sees the creatures taunting him from above, mocking his fall to the ground.

CHAPTER 21

Comfort of Home

CELESTIA ENTERS A spacious living chamber, which is large and open, with earthy colors and windows that open to reveal the panoramic beauty in all directions. She hears the waves crashing against the rocks and the gentle whispers of the sea breeze entering through the open windows. This is her childhood home. As she looks around, she realizes that the portal was indeed a one-way transport to her family's sanctuary on Argus Island. It is their family fortress, a stronghold, and the root of her family's legacy.

She gazes out at the expansive open windows, where the sheer curtains sway gracefully in the light breeze. Her eyes are drawn to the majestic Grinda Tree, the largest of its kind, standing proudly in the center of the island. It is surrounded by the ancient Earthaean Castle, the birthplace and residence of the Argus family throughout history. This magnificent island, with its many wonders, is highly protected by the magic of fairies, creatures of both land and sea. It holds a vital place in the realm, and its preservation is paramount. The ancient tree and the island itself are intertwined with the magical destinies of the Argus family, who have been entrusted with its care for centuries.

Celestia's primary duty is to protect the human race in Selcarth, especially after their migration from the kingdom of Olen. However, her entire family, including herself, holds a deep devotion to the magnificent Grinda Tree that reigns over the island. Returning to this place brings back vivid memories of the day she first called it home.

She reflects on the creation of the portal, coming to the realization that it was the handiwork of the library, intended specifically for her family and their associates, rather than Professor Ref. Celestia briefly entertains the thought that

Professor Ref may have deliberately deceived them, with the intention of obtaining the valuable articles housed within the library for his own agenda. However, her smile returns as she recalls how they successfully evaded the realm of fire creatures by slipping through the very same door he was using. Deep down, she knows that the library will eventually take care of him, bringing a profound sense of relief.

Suddenly, she hears a low purring sound beneath her and notices the sabretooth tiger she brought with her through the portal lying in pain, gently licking its wounds. Celestia kneels down to assess the immense creature, which is twice her size. Its wounds are severe and oozing from the burns it received while protecting her and her family from the fire creatures. When she looks up, she finds a familiar face watching her intently, waiting for her to regain her composure.

"Uncle Cameo!" she exclaims, rushing toward him, her heart aching with a mix of emotions.

He receives her with open arms, returning her tight embrace. "Sweetheart, you're okay! We were so worried about you."

Celestia continues to hold on to him tightly, cherishing the familiar feeling that fills her with a sense of security and determination. The love she feels for her uncle is as strong as the love she received from her parents. She and her father's two brothers share a remarkable resemblance, along with a compassionate nature and an unwavering dedication to their family and their people. They all understand the importance of caring for their loved ones and giving back to the land, recognizing that these causes are greater than themselves.

Suddenly, Aberra enters the chamber, and Celestia embraces her, too, as her uncle finally releases his hold.

"Are you good, cuz?" Aberra asks with concern.

"Yes," Celestia reassures her.

Aberra raises her hand in the air, magically summoning a watery blanket, which she gently places over the sabretooth tiger that is still lying next to Celestia, tenderly licking its wounds. The watery blanket shimmers and glows slightly upon contact, releasing a soothing liquid substance that envelops the creature, providing relief. The sabretooth stands up, visibly comforted as the water sustains its healing properties and continues to glow as it works its magic, tending to the animal's burns and tears. Aberra then conjures another spell, creating a small cloudlike substance that hovers over the sabretooth, providing gentle warmth.

Celestia attentively observes her cousin's impressive magical abilities, captivated by the depth of power that flows through their entire family. It becomes evident to her that the mastery over the elemental forces of Earth, Air, Water, and Fire runs deeply ingrained within their bloodline. From the moment of their birth, they have possessed these extraordinary powers, with each family member leaning toward different elemental affinities.

Among them, Aberra shines with exceptional skill in harnessing the healing properties and strength derived from the Earth and Water elements. Her connection to the natural world is profound, and she exudes a sense of serenity and stability. Celestia admires her cousin's command over these elements, which seem to dance effortlessly under her control.

On the other hand, Celestia herself possesses a unique blend of talents, intertwining her abilities with the elements of Earth and Fire. She finds solace in the grounding energy of the Earth, drawing strength and stability from its roots. Simultaneously, the fiery passion within her ignites a fierce determination, adding a touch of intensity to her powers. It is a harmonious union of elements, complementing her nature and shaping her magical path.

But beyond their elemental prowess, both Aberra and Celestia share an extraordinary gift that sets them apart. They possess a unique sense and communication with all living creatures—a connection that extends beyond the realm of mere understanding. It is an ability known only to them, or at least as far as Celestia is aware.

As Celestia reflects upon their family's remarkable abilities, she realizes that their powers intertwine with their very essence, guiding them toward their destinies in ways only the elements can fathom.

Their family holds a unique position in the world, as they are the only humans known to be born with these elemental powers. The origins of their extraordinary gifts remain shrouded in mystery, intertwined with their enigmatic aging process. This remarkable trait allows them to effortlessly connect with the light elements. Moreover, their soulmates are also chosen by their inner-born magic based on their inherent magic, further perpetuating the significance of their extraordinary existence.

In contrast, other races, with the exception of the elves, are unfamiliar with such innate magic and are instead susceptible to the allure of the dark elements. The delicate balance of life is disrupted by these dark forces, which demand more from their hosts, requiring intricate spells, summoning, and consuming techniques. Remarkably, Celestia's family possesses the ability to adapt to these darker elements as well, seamlessly shifting between the elements of light and dark. This versatility and command over both sides of magic makes them an exceptionally powerful family, revered and feared by many.

Yet with this power comes immense expectations and burdens. The weight placed upon them originated with the tragic destruction of the kingdom of Olen, a pivotal event that forever changed their lives. The responsibility to maintain equilibrium and protect the realms rests heavily on their shoulders, shaping their destiny and driving their actions in the present day.

Celestia bends down and gently strokes the massive beast on its head. "Thank you so much, Oli. Next time, let us know what you're up to." She wishes the creature a speedy recovery, bidding it farewell for now.

Then she turns her attention to Aberra. "Where is everyone?"

"They are being attended to, as will you. We'll talk later. Right now, you need rest," Aberra responds.

"Yes," Celestia agrees, embracing Aberra once again. Aberra's magic lifts the injured sabretooth, suspending it above the ground. They exit the chamber, accompanied by a wispy cloud conjured by Aberra. The cloud floats alongside them, offering comfort and relief to the wounded creature with its gentle cushioning and soothing mist.

Celestia returns to her uncle's side, noticing the concern etched on his face.

"How many have died?" she asks, referring to her homeland, her heart heavy with sorrow.

"At least a thousand people have perished," her uncle replies, his voice filled with somberness. "Royalty, merchants, commoners—people from all walks of life, even animals. Our informants have revealed that there was an entity present before their deaths, one that does not belong to the realm of the living but emerges from the sinister underworld. However, we have yet to substantiate this theory."

Celestia's voice quivers as she speaks. "What is Raymul doing about this? Have you arranged for Father to be safely escorted out, Uncle?"

"I have covertly sent messages to your father's closest advisors," her uncle reveals. "I have made arrangements for a secret escape through your parents' underground labyrinthine tunnels. Uncle Jakat has informed us that Raymul is under the influence of the beloved Guardian of Death and has surrendered himself to her will. With your father's temporary condition and the inexplicable demise of our people, I took it upon myself to take action and protect those who are still alive and well. I have ensured their escape before all hope is lost."

Celestia is taken aback by her uncle's revelation. "My father's condition is temporary?" she asks, her voice filled with concern.

Her uncle sighs, his expression somber. "Your father has been ensnared by a spell, a spell crafted within the realm of the Guardian of Death," he explains. "We cannot comprehend the Guardian's motives for involving herself in human affairs, as her intentions have always remained enigmatic. But regarding your father, it seems that his soul has been forcibly extracted from his body, leaving him alive but devoid of his essence—a mere shell of his former self. It is as if he walks among the living, yet his soul remains trapped in the clutches of the Guardian. Our most skilled enchanters have tirelessly attempted to reverse the spell, even seeking the aid of the wizard elves and their formidable magic. Alas, all our efforts have been in vain. The Guardian of Death has chosen to keep his soul in her personal custody, an unprecedented action on her part. We have even attempted to commune with the dark realm, hoping to glean insights into the Guardian's motives and her involvement in our world, but our endeavors have met with failure."

Celestia's voice trembles with desperation as she clings to a flicker of hope. "But I saw my father through the Argus stone. Maybe we can reach out to him and find a solution?"

She pleads, her eyes brimming with determination, hoping against all odds that she can save her father.

Cameo looks at her with a hint of astonishment, trying to comprehend how she could communicate through the Argus stone. Celestia observes the uncertainty in his eyes and speaks up, offering an explanation. "It's a long story, but I was able to speak to my father."

"The Argus stone is indeed a unique artifact," Cameo affirms, acknowledging the significance of the stone. "If you claim to have spoken to him, I believe you. In the event of an Argus member's death, a portion of their essence becomes intertwined with the stone. This tradition was established by the first Argus, who married Olen the Destroyer. The wood fairies held deep affection for the Argus family and bestowed this stone upon them, meant to fortify and safeguard the Argus name. While it may be possible to harness the stone's power, I believe our focus should be on more pressing matters. Don't you think so, my dear? Your father would prioritize the safety of his people over concerns for himself."

Celestia feels a surge of realization, humbled by her lack of perspective. "I'm sorry, Uncle. I wasn't thinking," she admits, understanding the need to shift her priorities.

Her uncle embraces her once more, slipping a small vial containing a sleeping potion into her hand. "It's all right, sweetheart. You're young, and you've been through so much," he reassures her. Leaning closer, he whispers into her ear, "The stone also has properties like a reaper. Keep it hidden, and use it only in dire circumstances."

Celestia swiftly runs her fingers through her flowing hair, finding a discreet spot in the room to secure the small vial. The reaper, a term also associated with the Argus stone, traps spirits from their resting place, growing in power as it absorbs souls. Once unleashed, it absorbs both its captive and the environment before automatically returning to its original resting place. The memories of its ordeal remain intact within its ethereal consciousness.

"Have you tried the fairy folk, Uncle?" Celestia inquires.

"You need rest, Celestia. We will speak again tomorrow," her uncle responds, sidestepping the question with genuine concern for her well-being. "Your father is safe, and we will address the kingdom. Pennaldo is there, our trusted family informant and your cousin, and he knows what to do."

"Yes, Uncle," Celestia replies, suddenly feeling exhausted and in need of rest. Her uncle kisses her forehead gently and departs from her chambers. She gazes around her royal quarters, taking in the grandeur and artistic beauty. Intricate carvings of fairies and creatures unfamiliar to her adorn the walls, while vines of flowers cascade over the graceful windows. The spaciousness of the room is remarkable, almost resembling a garden rather than a closed-off chamber. She notices a protective spell that encircles the chamber, ensuring her safety and granting her privacy. The room is adorned with various items she has collected over time, reminiscent of her cherished moments with her family. There are small statues and a simple collection of rocks. She has always enjoyed collecting rocks during their family outings to the beach and picnics.

As she walks by the wide-open balcony, the air feels smooth and inviting, wrapping around her like a soothing embrace. Her eyes are drawn once again to the massive tree that dominates the landscape, its branches reaching intrepidly in all directions, seemingly protecting its surroundings like an ancient guardian. From the balcony, she observes the villages below, filled with chimneys puffing out smoke, and gentle wisps of it drift upward. The soft glow of light paints a warm picture against the darkening sky, creating a peaceful ambiance. In the distance, she can hear the joyful sounds of children laughing and giggling as they play.

In this moment, she feels a deep connection to this place, the island of Argus, where she was born and raised. The elements seem to harmonize with her spirit as the element of Air softly whispers its calming touch. The island's unique allure, with its mysterious creatures and natural wonders, has always drawn her in. As the evening sun casts a golden hue across the land, she takes a deep breath, cherishing the sense of belonging and tranquility this place provides.

Lost in thought, she contemplates the secrets held within the island's hidden caverns and the stories of magical creatures passed down through generations. It's a realm of both beauty and danger, yet it has always felt like home to her family.

Since the beginning, Argus Island has been said to be home to dark serpents, hidden caves, unnatural plants, and magical creatures unknown anywhere else. It's a place of beauty, grace, and peace, but it can be deadly for those who are not part of it. Her family was told that they were the first humans to set foot on this island. There are no records or explanations for this claim, but one thing is certain: it's an island of belonging, where the family always feels safe and protected.

Only those accepted by the family are allowed to come to this island. She, like her cousins and many before her, was born here. People of all ages grow up on this island, transitioning from birth to adulthood. Ancient libraries are available for them to learn about and embrace the beauty of this place.

The castle grew out of the earth, surrounded by protection from the family, creatures, and the power of the ancient tree that stands before her. She loves it here, and her heart overflows with happiness and contentment at the thought of returning home. This island is where she truly belongs.

With each passing moment, the gentle breeze carries the scents of the untamed flora, the blossoming of rare flowers with their alluring fragrances. The rustling leaves of the colossal tree create a symphony, and she marvels at the harmony between nature and the people inhabiting the island.

Celestia walks over to the bed, which has remained untouched for several years. As she approaches, the vines respond to her presence, gradually enveloping every opening and creating a cocoon-like sensation that brings comfort and tranquility. This practice, provided by the tree to the entire family since birth, is a unique tradition. The tree's tentacles adapt to the desires and needs of each family member, making it a deeply personal and cherished home for all. Its existence is everlasting, and it serves as a place of solace when a family member passes away.

Suddenly, she hears the sounds of waves crashing against rocks and a gentle breeze rustling through the room, preventing any sense of stuffiness. She lies down on the luxuriously soft bed, sinking deeply into its embrace. A profound sense of comfort washes over her as the room gently dims. Overwhelmed with exhaustion, she doesn't bother to freshen up or change her clothes. Tears stream down her cheeks as she drifts into a deep sleep, her thoughts consumed by memories of her parents.

⊷⇒◉ ◉⇐⊶

It has been a few hours, and Celestia suddenly opens her eyes. The Argus stone feels warm on her chest, and she knows someone is watching. She jumps out of her bed to find a huge creature with spread-out wings hissing at her. Its fangs are distorted, and its horns are hooked around as it materializes out of its camouflage. Its high legs are massive, and its scaly form is imposing. She yelps and stands her ground as the creature takes forceful steps.

"What are you, and how could you be here?" she asks, her voice trembling with a mixture of fear and curiosity.

The creature, a formidable and grotesque figure, stands before her. Its appearance is reminiscent of a stone gargoyle, with a muscular build and a menacing presence. Its hulking form is covered in a complex pattern resembling the texture of weathered stone. The creature's eyes, cold and unyielding, pierce through Celestia's gaze, revealing a deep sense of ancient wisdom.

Celestia instinctively calls upon her Earth essence, tapping into the primal forces of nature. Vines sprout from the surrounding environment, snaking their way toward the creature and ensnaring it in a tight grip. The young sorceress prepares to unleash her fiery magic, ready to defend herself against this unknown threat. However, as she looks into the creature's eyes, a realization washes over her, causing her hand to freeze mid-spell.

"Eila, what did he do to you?" Celestia gasps, her voice filled with a mixture of shock and concern. She suddenly recognizes the familiar essence that emanates from the creature. It is her dear friend, Eila, who has been transformed into this formidable servant by some unknown force.

In a swift and compassionate motion, Celestia withdraws her magic, allowing the vines to release their grip on Eila. The creature staggers forward, disoriented by the sudden release. However, the Argus stone, sensing the danger, unleashes a brilliant flash of light, creating a powerful barrier that pushes Eila back forcefully. The room is filled with the sound of crashing furniture as chairs collide with bureaus, momentarily disorienting the creature.

Undeterred, the creature regains its footing and resumes its steady approach toward Celestia. It tests the limits of the shield, probing its strength and searching for any weakness. Celestia's heart aches at the sight of her dear friend in this altered state, longing to reach out to him.

"Eila, please, can you hear me?" Celestia pleads, her voice filled with desperation and hope. She knows that deep within the creature's distorted form, a fragment of Eila's true self remains, struggling to break free from the constraints of this ancient magic.

The creature hisses loudly, again testing the shield and analyzing the situation it faces. It senses the powerful necklace around Celestia, which creates an ancient magic barrier, but it cannot simply grab her.

⟡⟡⟡

Aberra, Jarin, and Larmari dash down the winding corridors, their footsteps echoing urgently as they make their way toward Celestia's chambers. Just a few seconds behind, Sakeris joins them, slightly out of breath and struggling to keep up.

"I heard you all running. What's happening?" Sakeris pants, trying to catch his breath as he matches their pace.

"Celestia's room has been invaded by an intruder!" Larmari exclaims, her voice filled with alarm.

"What?!" Sakeris gasps in disbelief, his eyes widening with concern.

Ignoring Sakeris's reaction, they continue their rapid pace, determined to reach Celestia's chambers. The chambers are situated on the far eastern side of the castle. In a sudden burst of light, Netaha joins the group, having employed her teleportation magic while they were running. Sakeris, caught off guard by her sudden appearance, stumbles momentarily, struggling to regain his balance. Without hesitation, Aberra effortlessly lifts him up, a testament to the family's inherent strength.

"Tommy informed me that Celestia is in trouble; there's a Rockfear inside with her," Netaha explains as she passes Sakeris, running at the same speed as Jarin and Aberra.

"Who's Tommy, and what's a Rockfear?" Sakeris questions, his confusion evident.

"Tommy is a lost spirit within our castle, a young boy of our family who perished during the time of the Destruction of Olen," Netaha swiftly replies. She then notices Sakeris and offers a warm smile. "Oh, it's nice to see you, Sakeris."

"What?" Sakeris stammers, still trying to process the information.

"Netaha has a unique ability to communicate with the spirits of the deceased, a remarkable gift that draws upon both the forces of light and darkness," Aberra elucidates as they approach the door.

Jarin prepares to blast open the door, ready to take action. However, their plans are interrupted as a person materializes out of thin air and exclaims, "No!"

"Dad! That's—" Jarin screams, recognizing the figure.

The older man raises a shield of some sort, preventing anyone from advancing. Immediately after, the five royal Avions fly in through the open windows, joining the family. They are the fairy guardians, fierce warriors, and protectors of the island and its inhabitants. The Avions are adorned with shiny armor, their wings flapping powerfully. The tips of their wings are crafted from the strongest golden steel, sharp enough to slice through anything that dares to approach. Vetis, one of the female Avions, steps forward.

"The chamber is blocked by some kind of barrier; we can't penetrate it," she announces. "The mages are attempting to break the magical hold."

"Uncle, why are you doing this? Celestia is in there!" Larmari cries out.

"Yes, brother! What is the meaning of this?" Everyone turns around to find Cameo, Aberra and Jarin's uncle, as well as Larmari's father, standing with his sword at the ready.

The younger ones can feel the tension between the two brothers as Cameo approaches Jakat. Both brothers lock eyes, their gazes filled with intensity. As Arguses, they bear a striking resemblance to each other, but Cameo's hair is lighter in color compared to his brother's darker locks. They both possess distinct white insignias representing their ages. Their outfits also differ: Jakat wears a simple orange robe adorned with golden highlights and a long sash around his neck, displaying symbols of different forms of magic. Jakat is a seer, a rare person born into the magical bloodline of the family, who dedicates himself to foreseeing the future and protecting their existence. Cameo, on the other hand, serves as the family's warrior and protector of Argus Island.

"She needs our help, brother. Move aside!" Cameo pleads.

"I can't let you in, brother!" Jakat replies.

"Why?" Cameo yells. "It's Celestia in there, your niece, our family!"

"I know! She will be fine. The stone will protect her. She needs to do this alone. I can't tell you why, but she will be fine!"

They hear crashing in the other room, and everyone tenses up, ready to blast through. However, Jakat holds the shield firmly, which now transforms into a solid stone wall that seems impenetrable. But to the family, it's not impossible.

"How did the Rockfear break through our defenses?" Cameo asks Jakat, feeling uneasy and ready to strike through the wall.

"The family stone allowed the creature to enter her chambers," Jakat says sadly.

They exchange worried and perplexed glances, their brows furrowed in concern. Jarin's curiosity intensifies, unable to comprehend how the protective stone, which has always safeguarded her and their family, could allow such an intrusion into her chambers.

As they stand there, a faint yet eerie noise emanates from the other side of the wall. It sends shivers down their spines, a peculiar and otherworldly sound—a blend of hissing, growling, and an unsettling whisper, as if the creature were conversing in a language unknown to them.

Aberra steps forward, addressing her father. "Dad, are you certain about this? Are your visions warning against our intervention?"

"Yes, daughter. I cannot explain it, but she must be taken and guided by her destiny. All I saw was that the fate of our family hinges on her decision, and it must unfold without interference. She must be left alone," he replies with a somber tone.

"Your Grace, please allow us to enter. We must protect the princess," Sakeris implores, addressing Jakat.

Jakat smiles warmly at him, his gaze filled with love and concern. "I understand, and I cherish her as much as I do all of you. But you must trust me."

Cameo turns his attention to the eldest member of the group, Netaha. She is their second cousin and has dedicated her studies to both the dark and light arts. Her unique ability to communicate with the dead mirrors the intensity and power found within the family's eyes.

"Netaha, could you send one of your contacts to check on her? I'm certain your uncle's vision did not account for the intervention of the dead, as they cannot alter anything," Cameo suggests, seeking an alternative to ensure Celestia's well-being.

Netaha, feeling conflicted and not wanting to be in the middle of her uncle's dilemma, waits for approval. Her long, black hair covers one eye, adding to her mysterious allure. Sakeris notices that she looks graceful and elegant, just like the rest of them. They all look at each other, and Jakat nods in acknowledgment, giving permission to proceed. Netaha turns to her right and speaks to someone, and a shadowy, ghostly farmer boy materializes. He floats lightly in the air, emanating a playful energy. The boy bears a striking resemblance to Jarin and Aberra, sharing their features. He jumps around excitedly, swinging through the solid wall created by Jakat.

Moments later, a resounding crash reverberates from within the chambers, followed by a cacophony of sounds. The entire family surges forward, their urgency mounting, and Jakat releases the protective shield wall. They all rush inside, their hearts pounding with a mixture of fear and determination.

Upon entering, they quickly notice that the window has been shattered, expanded, and torn apart. Amid the chaos, they realize the Rockfear creature and Celestia, the princess, are already gone. Looking out the window, they see the Rockfear holding a glowing cage with Celestia trapped inside, disappearing into the far distance on the horizon. The eerie glow emanating from the cage casts an otherworldly light on her face. Tommy, the young and courageous boy, stands beside Netaha, conversing with her as she turns to address the rest of the family, her eyes wide with anxiety.

"Tommy explained that the creature created some kind of cage, and Celestia simply walked into it without hesitation. She smiled at Tommy, signaling that everything is all right, and they flew away," Netaha shares, relaying the information with a mixture of concern and relief.

Cameo, his gaze fixed on his brother, confronts Jakat with a sense of urgency. "Where did they go?"

"To her destiny's starting point, back home, where she will not be harmed." Jakat replies, his voice filled with a mix of determination and sorrow, knowing that Celestia's path has taken a fateful turn.

CHAPTER 22

Nest

So it begins, James thinks, *the untold tale of my legacy.* It has been two days, and James feels that his legacy is nothing more than a dreadful and confusing entity above him. The caves, since they entered, have become a somber and gloomy place. The walls, just as they were in the dwarf kingdom, are perfectly smooth, obviously carved by ancient dwarves at one time. James feels as if he is in some kind of enormous pipe where the distance ahead is so dark his eyes cannot penetrate it. The lanterns his party holds can only illuminate a few hundred feet, but the unknown still creeps up with every steady step they take.

The dwarves, carefully moving in and out of the abyssal darkness of the forsaken tunnels, inspect their party and constantly communicate with Radion. A few feet behind him are the Malij, now accompanied by two others who joined them before they entered the Tmoaly Tunnel of Sorkar. Right beside James is his faithful friend Ethan, looking content now, scoping the wall and examining the curious drawings laid before them.

One of the lead warriors, named Ulteal, is the formidable-looking twin sister of Kedar and a proud and fierce dwarf. They walk side by side, both brother and sister of the same height, but she wears heavy armor and wields a large mace, intricately adorned with gold and silver. Her body is much wider than her brother's, but they had looked indistinguishable when James first met them at the entrance of the cavern. She is accompanied by four other warriors, two females and two males, all wearing similar armors. Ulteal is a striking figure but shares the same humor as her brother. The siblings lead the team ahead with confidence, while her brother wields a staff containing a large blue gem that glows, lighting up the endless halls and corridors.

They stop momentarily as Ulteal sniffs unusually, touching the walls of the caves. "There is unease and unrest here, brother," she says in a raspy voice. "The walls are filled with tremors and fear."

"I felt them too, sis. Let's proceed cautiously," he responds.

James notices that the dwarves have a unique ability to connect with stone. He witnessed this when they arrived at the Guardian of Water's passage to her lair, which was completely sealed. When they arrive at the eastern gate entrance, a colossal wall, an older dwarf steps forward, touching the wall with some sort of ritual, feeling its grooves and speaking in a tone unfamiliar to James. To his surprise, his outstretched hand adheres to the wall. Ethan pushes forward, astounded and eager to see what the dwarf is doing. The older dwarf continues to turn his arm right and left in a combination, as if performing a sequence. Then his arm goes in further, slowly disappearing, and moments later, there is a loud click, and the dwarf withdraws his arm. Suddenly, the wall magically reveals a hidden doorway, pushing forward instantly as the air from the outside puffs in a cloud of smoke. A hollow sound reaches their ears, and the smell of decaying old must fills their nostrils. The cavern is now open. Ethan stands in front of the dwarf in amazement, staring at the keyhole that was apparently a locking mechanism only created by these highly skilled dwarves.

As James walks with the dwarves in the lead, accompanied by Radion and the Malij assassins behind them, he can't help but think of his friend. He feels a sense of sadness. Although Ethan has pointed out that he has no family to turn to, James still wishes that his friend was back home instead of standing by his side. He worries about Ethan's life and doesn't want any harm to come to him because of what James has become. James sighs with grief and turns his attention to Eva, who gracefully guides their way. She has changed dramatically, appearing plainly dressed, but she always walks with confidence and grace. Every so often, she glances behind her, checking to make sure that he is okay, like a hawk watching over her child to ensure their safety.

Again, James reflects on the legacy that lies before him—the legacy of his family and the mission that still awaits him. The queen of the dwarves granted the eight dwarves, the dwarf prince, Kedar, and his sister voluntary escort to James and his party to the ancient Lorgon of Waterdum, where the Guardian of Water awaits. The Guardian visited him in his dreams twice, pleading for him to come. In order for them to enter this secluded lagoon, they must pass through the ruins of Sorkar, a once thriving dwarf land that perished due to King Olen's seduction of the power of the Guardian orbs. It was this tragedy that caused the dwarves to excommunicate themselves from humans and the entire world—a pain that Radion explained could never be healed. So the legend of his legacy continues: James, the foretold new bloodline Destroyer, is reborn. He has no idea how to come to terms with his new position. Already the dwarves are highly skeptical of him. If it hadn't been for Prince Kedar, they would have never assisted in their cause.

James shakes his head, feeling the ache after staring into the abyss for so long. His neck is tired, and his back aches. There is still so much left to be foretold about his coming. He can feel the presence of a new entity beneath his heart—a magic so elusive, a magic that stirs with every emotion. It seems as if it wants to burst forth and go wild, but James, with every effort, tries to contain it. This magic, which obviously subsides quickly, came alive when the Shadowlen tried to possess his soul. James knows that this magic is somewhat different, though he is unsure why. It feels uncommon, as if it doesn't want to be with him, yet it accepts his existence. Regardless, he hates it and all that it represents. He despises who he has become, the foretold story and the legacy of a king—a descendant of a madman who killed thousands, even millions, due to the magic that seems to linger inside his soul. It is a foretold story that he must take on and prove that he is not like the evil King Olen, but rather, James Lander.

For a moment, Radion signals the group from behind to halt. He walks past them, urgency evident in his movements, though the pitch-black cave makes it difficult to discern. He reaches Ulteal and Kedar, engaging in a conversation before signaling the party to continue at a steady, slow pace. It becomes apparent that they are nearing the ancient ruins. James decides to join Eva and signals Ethan to stay back, seeking a private moment with his stepmother.

As they walk, James can't help but be mesmerized by the long, dissolving shadows on each side of the tunnel walls, separating the different layers like ridges in a language he can't decipher. He turns to Eva and asks about the water that once filled these tunnels.

"Eva, how long ago do you think the water was here?" James inquires, his gaze fixed on the smooth walls.

Eva follows his line of sight, studying the fading patterns on the walls. "I would estimate a couple of hundred years. Each of those ridges is probably about ten years apart, so based on that, I'd say around four hundred years in these tunnels."

James looks up and down the tunnel, counting the ridges. "So approximately seven hundred years. That's a long time," he remarks.

"This is just one of many tunnels, James. Remember, we haven't reached the opening that these tunnels lead to. I can only imagine how much time has passed," Eva explains.

Curious, James asks, "How do you know all this?"

Eva smiles at his curiosity. "Books, dear. I've read books."

Accepting her response, James gazes down the dark tunnel as they continue their journey. The tunnel stretches endlessly before them, its cold and eerie atmosphere intensifying with each step. The haunting sounds of their footsteps echo through the dimly lit space, accompanied by occasional hollow moans and cries that seem to emanate from the depths. It's as if the very air is heavy with a sense of anguish, wrapping around James like a suffocating shroud.

"Yes, dear," Eva replies softly, her voice carrying a tinge of concern. She observes Ethan picking up objects from the floor and discreetly slipping them into his pocket. A faint smile tugs at James's lips, appreciating his friend's resourcefulness even in the midst of uncertainty.

"Why do I get the feeling that I'm the only human known to be born into magic?" James finally voices his thoughts, curiosity and confusion lacing his words.

Eva's eyes meet James's, her slender gaze piercing the darkness. Despite the gloom surrounding them, her extraordinary features radiate a subtle glow, casting a glimmer of hope amid the shadows.

"Your magic is not the only magic born into existence," Eva gently corrects him, her voice carrying a touch of wisdom. She pauses, as if gathering her thoughts, before continuing, her words resonating with an air of mystery.

"The Argus family is another human lineage known to be born with magic. They are shrouded in legends, possessing the rare gift of being born with the elements of light. But your magic, James, is something altogether different. It is the essence of the four Guardians of Life, a power that may surpass even the magic of the elves and the Arguses. Your magic serves as a beacon to acquire the Orbs of Olen, unlocking a potential that sets you apart."

Eva's voice carries a mix of awe and concern as she delves deeper into the explanation. She emphasizes the significance of James's innate magic, rooted in his very soul, and the need to protect him. Her words paint a picture of a delicate balance between different races and powers, where James's unique abilities could be perceived as a threat.

"We must ensure your safety, James. Not only because you are the last bloodline of Olen, but also because your orb magic holds the potential to unsettle the elves and other races, including the Argus family that serves as protectors of the human race. Radion and I will do everything in our power to shield you from harm."

As their conversation comes to a close, James and Eva reach the left side of the cavern. James steals a second glance at the dwarves who have scattered ahead, their agile movements reminiscent of spiders scurrying when suddenly exposed. He marvels at their adeptness in navigating the rocky terrain, realizing how their bare feet have adapted to the stone as if they are one with it. It answers the lingering question of their peculiar footwear, akin to the adaptability of a hawk that clings effortlessly to the thin branches or bark of a tree.

In the midst of their observations, Kedar materializes by Radion's side, exchanging words before swiftly vanishing into the distant tunnel. Radion suggests taking a break to rest and gathers the head Malij for a conversation, setting the stage for what lies ahead in this mysterious and treacherous journey. Abruptly, James feels a sudden surge of familiarity welling up inside him, causing him to give a quick stare at the forbidding, dark tunnel that lies beyond his party. The memories of the dwarves' warning flood back, and James now understands why Eva urged him to stay close. She is prepared to instruct him in case they encounter any magic ahead. Kedar speaks to Radion, and after a few moments, Radion announces that they are ready to proceed toward the open cavern. Based on James's estimation, it appears to be late in the day. They pause briefly for rest and light meals, and James's stomach grumbles a bit as they enter the wide opening of the cavern.

The cavern is immense in height and width; although not as large as the dwarf kingdom, it is still of considerable size. Broken pillars that once stood tall now litter the area, various shapes and sizes protruding from the walls and scattered all around. James's gaze momentarily falls to the ground, and his heart sinks. Countless bones are strewn everywhere, remnants of dwarves of all sizes, mostly children. His heart begins to race, the bones appearing smooth and almost cleaned by the decades of water that filled the cave. As Eva indicated, the entire cavern is lined with ridges of different sizes, a testament to the years the water stood and slowly receded. It seems that various sea creatures found their way in, taking refuge before meeting their tragic fate. The horror of the scene becomes almost unbearable for James. The images of an area once bustling with life, where families kept their young ones safe, now drowned and entombed by the relentless water, haunt his thoughts. The sea had become a prison, offering temporary sustenance but ultimately sealing their doom beneath its depths. Overwhelmed with a sense of responsibility for his ancestors' actions, James struggles to comprehend how he can rectify such a tragedy.

Noticing Ethan walking over to him, James takes a moment to collect himself.

"I can't believe what I'm seeing," Ethan says, his voice filled with disbelief.

"I know. This was my family's doing. I feel so rotten now," James confesses, his voice heavy with guilt.

"You cannot undo what your family has done, but you can learn from their mistakes and work toward making things right," Eva interjects, her gaze fixed on the distance behind the cavern, searching for something.

"James, she's right. It's not your fault, buddy. You are not defined by the actions of your family," Ethan adds, attempting to console his friend.

"Since when did you become so wise, Ethan?" James snaps, frustration lacing his words.

"Relax, I'm just trying to cheer you up."

James sighs. "I'm sorry. Seeing all this is so unfair to these people. I have to find a way to make it up to them," he says, looking at the rest of the party. The Malij assassins observe in silence, taking note of James's words while they continue to press further into the decimated city. Radion stands alone, an unusual sight, his expression mirroring shock, as if he were witnessing the aftermath of a tragedy he had only read about in scrolls.

James tries to locate the dwarf group, wondering where they went. The party continues to move slowly, careful not to disturb the ancient bones that surround them. James can't help but shed tears, the overwhelming presence of the children's remains deeply affecting him. He notices Ethan sniffling too. The sheer number of tiny bones is staggering, outnumbering them by at least fifty to one. James covers his eyes and cries. Eva, sensing his anguish, reaches out and gently holds his arm, offering comfort.

"This is terrible, dear. Let the pain be released from you. It will aid in the healing process, especially for your magic, and help you focus on your journey," she reassures him.

James pulls away slightly, nodding in understanding.

Finally the group catches up to the dwarves, who are standing in a straight line, staring intently at their surroundings. None of them utter a word, as if they are lost in their own prayers or thoughts.

Suddenly Ulteal, wielding her impressive golden mace adorned with shimmering gems of various kinds, steps forward in a slow, deliberate manner. Her usually tidy hair waves wildly, and her fierce female figure radiates a sense of pent-up rage. She charges toward James, a deadly force ready to strike.

Without hesitation, Ethan swiftly retrieves his short knife and slips behind the enraged dwarf princess, poised to strike. The other Malij assassins draw various weapons, one with a red bow, and the others summon swirling currents of magical energy in their hands, preparing to engage. James feels a burning sensation building up within him, ready to be unleashed. But it is Eva who creates a shield of watery substance from thin air, pushing back the furious female dwarf who was moments away from attacking James. The burning sensation dissipates as Kedar grabs hold of his raging sister, pulling her away to calm her down. The other dwarf warriors, their anger evident in their eyes, watch but do not intervene.

"He did this, brother! Why are we assisting the Destroyer of the damn family that killed our children? They destroyed our legacy!" The dwarf princess rages, struggling fiercely on the floor as Kedar restrains her, creating a barrier with his strength, but to everyone's surprise, the barrier he conjures fails to hold her back. She breaks free effortlessly, asserting her dominance over her twin brother.

With a fierce determination in her eyes, the dwarf princess confronts her brother, her voice laced with a mixture of frustration and sorrow. "You know we are twins, Kedar! It won't work on me."

She breaks free with her strength and charges at them again.

Eva releases a binding restraint and holds her tightly. "Princess, with all due respect, we cannot fulfill the Guardian's request if you desire to kill the person she wishes to meet. You know it goes against your beliefs. Please refrain from your anger for now. I understand that King James's family has inflicted irreparable damage upon your culture, but I assure you, he is not the same as his ancestors. I have known him for his entire life. His family upholds the true essence of the Guardians."

Ulteal pauses momentarily, her eyes shimmering with a mixture of emotions. Finally, she nods and lowers her hand, causing Eva's magical bindings to disappear. It's strange that Eva's magic doesn't resonate with the Malij assassins, who use relics to aid them, but James lets the matter go, feeling his heart rate gradually decrease, the fear subsiding.

Ulteal joins her group as they all flow with Kedar by her side, engaging in conversation, singling out each member.

As they enter the vast chamber of the fallen dwarf cavern in Mount Rocksmear, which was once a thriving land with strong ties to Olen himself, Eva feels a peculiar sense of unease. She knows that this cavern has been deserted for centuries, and a powerful presence of magic lingers. "Do you feel that, Radion?" Eva funnels mind-control access to Radion.

"I thought we agreed that you would not do that," Radion responds in a mind meld, expressing his discomfort with having his mind exposed. Eva can feel Radion expanding the perimeter of his mind as they descend the rocky slope that leads to a vast dirt marble star cast into the unseen city beyond the abyss.

"Yes, Radion," she replies eagerly, dismissing his attempt to access her mind, a feat that Radion is unable to accomplish.

"There is an odd presence. Keep James close." Radion realizes the meld has ended.

Walking back to James, Eva quickly positions herself next to him, sensing his confusion and fear. The perimeter expands before them, and they begin descending slowly on the unkempt marble stairs.

With each step they take, Eva notices that magic is indeed at play, as the entire city is faintly lit by its presence. Raising her shield, she speaks slowly to James about the possible danger that lies ahead. If the exiled elves have somehow obtained magic, they will be very dangerous.

After observing the foggy city of the fallen caves, when they reach the bottom stairs, the city before them is completely ghostly and deserted. The smell of decay and rot quickly overwhelms Eva and her party. Everywhere they look, the homes, fountains, and streets have been destroyed or are barely holding up. Scattered throughout the perimeter are the destroyed scepters, symbols of pain and suffering, clearly all belonging to the dwarf. Eva sees the dwarves in their groups paying their respects, having possibly never seen such destruction in their young lives, possibly only being around a hundred years old.

CHAPTER 23

Kin

EVERY SO OFTEN, Eva notices Kedar shaking his head with a mix of anticipation and guilt. He slowly walks over to James, his large eyes and oversize nose making him appear ready to destroy anything, fearless and deadly. Staring at James with hatred, he says, "If I had known this is what the Destruction looked like, I would have never come!" He spits next to the human king, a comment that James does not expect but understands, given the dwarf prince's hatred for the bloodline that destroyed their once thriving city. A city that, from what James has gathered, had been a major ally and friend to King Olen and the human world. The city was rich beyond anywhere else, trading riches and weapons through these parts. And now it was all in ruins and destroyed.

"I'm sorry," James manages to say as the dwarf prince continues to stare at him intensely.

"That's enough," Eva cuts in, breaking the barrier between the two. "Kedar, you know your duties, and you cannot back out on your word. Remember, your people are at stake, and any information will benefit your people and your future. Besides—" Eva abruptly stops, her magical shield warning her of an impending attack.

A giant boulder of black energy comes hurtling toward Eva and her party as she recognizes the source of the dark magic. Quickly, she grabs James and instructs the rest to take cover. Radion, already countering the black magic, sends a blast of blackened red fire to intercept it, but Eva notices that it is a decoy. They are surrounded by thousands of deformed dwarf skeletons of all sizes and ages, ready to fight.

Eva conjures a blazing wind force that scatters the evil beings, sending them scurrying and tumbling in disarray. Ethan readies his short knife and hands it to James, who takes it without question. The Malij swiftly leap and flip with incredible power, skillfully dispatching their attackers. They use their black swords, their flexible bodies moving with lightning speed as they fight their way toward the enemy. Limbs are severed, bodies split in half, and magic springs from their hands as they seek to protect themselves.

James can't bear to witness the Malij assassins in action as they summon red-armored mammoths out of thin air, crushing the skeletal creatures attacking them. The other two assassins utilize dark elemental magic, channeling it through rings on their wrists and launching white fire missiles at the oncoming threats.

As James scans the battlefield, he notices that their dwarf group is nowhere to be found. Finally he catches sight of them in the distance, standing still and gazing at the approaching enemies as if entranced. He turns his head away and witnesses the dwarves, a group of skilled fighters who use stones and rocks to their advantage, adapting to their surroundings. Their unique fighting style involves seamless teamwork and mutual assistance. At one point, James sees Kedar, a particularly agile dwarf, twist and twirl, dispatching a nearby assailant with a swift, well-aimed blow. Other dwarves join in, confusing the relentless attackers and gradually overpowering them.

While James observes the battle before him, a scream jolts his attention. He looks up to see a new figure descending from above—a creature composed of bones, armed with weapons similar to those of the dwarves. It's as if all the damned dwarves of the city have been resurrected, ready to attack them. In a bold move, Ethan attempts to halt their advance, but Radion unleashes a blazing blue light that shatters the skeletal dwarves into pieces and swiftly joins Eva's side.

"What the hell is going on? I thought elves can't do any magic here," Radion exclaims, launching another fiery blast toward a group of attackers approaching from his side.

Eva, holding her ground, can't make sense of it either. "I don't know. It seems they have assistance. Someone with great magic tied to the element of Death has resurrected these creatures. We need to get away, Radion. We don't know what their intentions are," Eva says urgently.

As James and the others continue to assess the situation, they notice something unsettling. The scattered bones of the fallen dwarves begin to gather and assemble again, forming a formidable skeletal army. The eerie sight sends shivers down their spines as the skeletal dwarves take on a menacing and determined appearance.

The tricky and sinewy figures move with calculated precision, their empty eye sockets fixed on Eva and James. The resurrected dwarf skeletons seem to possess a malevolent intelligence, driven by an unknown force. The once-familiar faces of their fallen comrades now wear expressions of cold indifference, their movements devoid of any trace of humanity.

It is a chilling realization for the dwarves and their allies. The enemy they face is not only skilled in dark magic but also capable of manipulating the very essence of life and death. The odds are quickly stacking against them, and a sense of urgency fills the air.

Eva, Radion, and the rest of the group know they have to devise a new strategy, and fast. They can't let themselves be overwhelmed by this relentless skeletal horde. With determination in her eyes, Eva takes charge, rallying their forces to regroup and find a more defensible position. As they retreat, the dwarves valiantly fight the large, deformed skeletons, buying time and holding off the advancing skeletal army, but they instantly freeze in place, as if someone has used the magic of Ice. They need a moment to catch their breath, regather their strength, and come up with a plan to counter this unexpected and formidable opposition.

Suddenly, Eva unleashes a blazing blast of air toward another wave of skeletal dwarves, freeing their captive dwarves from their trances. As the dwarves regained awareness, they look around in horror, witnessing the macabre spectacle unfolding before them. The once lifeless city now teems with regenerated creatures, grotesque beings of various sizes, both children and adults, forming from the reanimated bones again. These abominations seize any available weapon, ready to launch an attack.

The dwarves are stunned, their shock evident as they stand frozen, unsure of how to proceed. Even the warriors among them, the protectors and leaders, appear lost and disoriented, akin to bewildered children desperately in need of guidance. Witnessing their own kind turned against them is disheartening, leaving the dwarves unable to muster the will to fight.

Eva focuses her mind, desperately searching for an escape route. As the Malij assassins unleash their shimmering blades and fiery arrows, some ineffective against the relentless skeletal dwarves, they find themselves overwhelmed. Amid the chaos, their dwarf allies are left behind, untouched, as the skeletal horde sweeps past them, recognizing their own kind and disregarding them.

Radion, determined to protect his companions, brandishes his fiery whip, lashing out at dozens of advancing skeletal beasts. Ethan tries to join the fray, but James, feeling an unexpected surge of energy, holds him back. In that moment, Eva, sensing the danger, swiftly creates a shield that envelops James and Ethan, providing them with a protective barrier. The skeleton dwarves relentlessly assault the shield, attempting to break through its barriers. Radion fights desperately as more skeletal reinforcements materialize, undoing the destruction caused by the group's magic.

One of the Malij assassins falls victim to a slashing blow from a skeletal dwarf warrior, tearing him apart. To James's dismay, Eva holds him firmly, refusing to let him rush into the fray. Although his desire to help burns fiercely, Eva's grip on him is unyielding. He struggles against her, pleading with her to release him.

"Eva! Let me go! I can help them," James exclaims, his voice filled with urgency and determination. "I need to help; Kedar and his sister are left behind. We need to go back," James pleads urgently, his concern for his friends overwhelming him.

"They are in a trance, James. They won't come. To them, their kin seek justice, and they will not interfere," Eva explains firmly. "Leave them!"

With unwavering determination, Eva unleashes a blinding light into the sky, causing the entire area to illuminate. The skeletal dwarves screech in agony, their eyes unaccustomed to such brightness after years of darkness. This is their chance to leave their comrades behind and save James. They vow to return for Kedar and his sister, even if it means rallying the entire mountain-dwarf army and their queen. Their plan set, they swiftly retreat, leaving the Malij and dwarves behind. James feels a pang of reluctance, but Eva assures him they will come back with reinforcements.

As they hurry toward the edge of the deserted city, they stumble upon a breathtaking waterfall. Radion uses his fire magic to set their pursuers ablaze, buying them some valuable time. Eva suddenly halts, her senses alert. Radion and Ethan approach her, curiosity etched on their faces.

"Eva," Radion calls out, "do you recognize this river?"

Eva's gaze falls upon the flowing water, and her astonishment is evident. "It can't be," she exclaims. "It's the Blacken River. How can this be? The gateway of death has seeped into the realm of the living."

"I don't know, but we must be cautious not to touch this water," Eva warns, her voice tinged with concern.

"Right, but how do we cross it? We need—" Before James can finish his sentence, Eva leaps lightly, defying gravity, rising above the blackened river. She turns to James and Ethan, her eyes filled with determination. "Listen to me carefully. Let your bodies relax, and don't resist what I'm about to do," she commands, summoning her magic. With her power, she effortlessly lifts James and Ethan into the air, while Radion feels a gentle breeze enveloping him as if the magic seeks to carry him. He surrenders himself to the sensation, allowing the magic to guide him over to the other side of the blackened river with ease.

Just as they cross, the light above them fades, plunging the environment back into darkness. Instantly, the skeleton dwarves screech once more, and one of them foolishly attempts to run across the wide river, forgetting the water that separates them. The liquid darkness engulfs it like quicksand, tearing at its bones breaking it apart. In vain, the skeletal remains try to escape the watery grasp, but they are consumed completely.

The remaining skeleton dwarf horde, seething with anger and hatred, abruptly halt their advance, their spears and knives poised for attack. Radion and Eva brace themselves, ready to defend against the onslaught. However, their ordeal is far from over. Before they can react, a scythe-wielding dwarf descends before them, launching a vicious attack on the remaining members of their party. Eva, determined to protect James and Ethan, swiftly unleashes a wave of powerful magic that disintegrates the skeleton dwarves, causing them to explode into fragments. Yet it proves to be insufficient. More dwarves emerge seemingly from thin air, overwhelming Eva and Radion. No matter how valiantly they fight, the dwarves keep coming. Soon, Eva and Radion find themselves surrounded by skeletal dwarves. Eva realizes that these soulless and mindless dwarves still possess the strength they once had, albeit now devoid of flesh. Without the aid of their own allies, Eva and Radion will inevitably be defeated and join their captive friends.

Immediately, James feels his magic surging within, a vigorously deepening intensity of unknown origin approaching. In the midst of their desperation, a sparkling light suddenly materializes before them, causing everyone to step back in astonishment and James's magic to subside. It takes the form of a small, radiant rainbow, dancing and shimmering in front of their eyes. Accompanying this mesmerizing display is a diminutive creature with large wings, resembling a dragonfly. James, initially taken aback, soon comprehends that this being is not human but something fantastical. The creature emits a sparkling light, its wings fluttering rapidly, like those of a dragonfly or a fairy. Its distinct features—pointed eyebrows, ears, and otherworldly appearance—leave no doubt that it is not of human origin. It possesses a striking beauty, adorned in glowing attire with a strong and muscular upper body. James's astonishment reaches its peak when he notices the creature's unruly sandy hair, an exact match for his own.

Suddenly, the fairy-like creature, with a mischievous glint in its eye, raises its delicate arms. A surge of magical energy emanates from its being, forming a sparkling sphere of light that expands throughout the cavern. The radiant sparkles dance and twirl, growing in intensity with each passing moment. In an awe-inspiring display of power, the sphere bursts forth, unleashing a torrent of energy that engulfs the advancing dwarf skeletons.

The blast is cataclysmic, tearing through the ranks of the skeletal dwarves with devastating force. The impact shatters them into countless pieces, scattering them in all directions. The echoes of the explosion reverberate continuously throughout the cavern, like thunder rumbling in the distance. The remaining fragments of the dwarf skeletons crumble into dust, drifting away on an ethereal wind.

The cavern is momentarily bathed in the aftermath of the fairy's spectacular display of magic. Silence ensues, broken only by the soft whispers of enchantment lingering in the air. Eva, Radion, James, and Ethan stand in awe, their hearts pounding with a mix of relief and wonder. The fairy hovers before them, its wings glistening with residual magic and a satisfied smile gracing its lips.

"May the echoes of this explosion serve as a reminder," the fairy's voice echoes gently in their minds. "You are not alone in this fight. Embrace the strength within you and the allies who stand by your side."

As the flying creature approaches the group, it smiles warmly, studying James with a mix of curiosity and familiarity. It takes a step back, raising its arms, and in an instant, the dwarf group that was stunned reappears alongside three Malij assassins. Returning to James's side and tilting its head, the creature's welcoming smile envelops them all. A profound silence descends upon the surroundings since the arrival of this enigmatic entity. James's eyes slightly sting as he remains captivated by the creature's delicate features. It speaks directly into his mind, bypassing the need for spoken words.

"The elders have sent me to alter the events that have already been set," it communicates in a sweet yet distinctly masculine voice. Drawing closer to James, it gazes into his eyes with an intense curiosity, akin to that of an inquisitive child. "Curious," the creature remarks, "why would existence—a magically born creature, reject the beauty of your true identity?" James is so astonished that he struggles to form a response, captivated by the creature's radiant aura. Sensing James's shock, the being pauses, humming softly for a moment as if awaiting a reply. Then, with an understanding smile, it communicates directly into James's mind. "Be swift on your journey, young one. Embrace your true self and fulfill your destiny."

Then it moves back a bit, its satisfaction evident in its demeanor. "We will meet again, young kin," it says before swiftly approaching each member of the party, embracing them warmly with joyful cheerfulness, a rare occurrence given the dire circumstances they find themselves in. As it reaches Eva, it slows down, lingering before her for a moment. With a radiant gleam, it smiles, its excitement palpable, as if it has received momentous news, and in a dazzling display of rainbow colors, it vanishes from sight.

"I can't believe a woodland fairy came to our aid. They are known to seldom intervene, particularly from a realm so distant," Radion exclaims, breaking the stunned silence that had settled over the group due to the unexpected visit.

"Yes," a new voice suddenly interjects from across the Blacken River. A hoarse, melancholic tone emanates from the other side of the darkened waters. An aged, wizened-looking woman emerges and makes her way toward them.

"You are indeed fortunate to have such a formidable ally by your side, young

Olen," she remarks, her words dripping with a mix of fascination and disdain as a slithering creature coils around her neck, hissing menacingly at the group when she reaches the very edge of the river. Her presence is truly intimidating, heightened by her cackling laughter that echoes through the air. As she laughs, her decaying, yellowed teeth are exposed, and her piercing black eyes seem to smolder with malice.

"So, it is you!" Radion's voice reverberates with anger and fury. "The vile swamp witch Gitma! What wicked machinations are you imposing upon the lost dwarves in these caves? You should not meddle in their lives but remain concealed within the depths of your wretched, diseased swamp!"

"What am I doing here?" she sneers, relishing her own wickedness. "I am granting them hope, a glimmer of possibility that no one else would extend. I have taught them resistance, how to defy their fate, and have bestowed upon them the knowledge of forbidden magic so they may stand on equal footing with their counterparts." Her laughter echoes through the cavern but then abruptly halts. "However, when I learned of your arrival, I knew I had to intervene, for he carries something that could disrupt my plan—a plan that requires only minor adjustments. Begone!" she shrieks, her voice filled with seething anger. "Leave this place! Never trespass in these caverns again, young Olen. Your presence reeks of the sickness that plagues the deceased, lying alongside your ancestors, and the exiled ones need no false hope from one who is destined to bring about our annihilation." With that final decree, she retreats, her laughter echoing in the darkness as she fades from sight.

As the witch departs, their dwarf comrades regain consciousness, their hands rubbing their heads in disbelief as they snap out of their trance. Kedar surveys their dazed expressions, his gaze landing on the scattered remains of one of the Malij, torn apart by the sudden onslaught of bones that now litter the area.

"What happened?" Kedar manages to utter, his voice filled with a mix of confusion and concern.

CHAPTER 24

Release to Death

THE KINGDOM OF Selcarth stands as the last stronghold of human civilization since the destruction of the city of Olen. Raymul stands by the large window ledge, gazing out over the lavish, bustling city below. The vibrant colors of blooming flowers surround the kingdom, untouched and meticulously cultivated by skilled gardeners. The intricate patterns of the gardens extend outward from the previous king's bedroom, overlapping in a mesmerizing display. Raymul feels a fleeting sense of ease before the pain coursing through his body abruptly reminds him of the turmoil present in the city.

Everywhere throughout the kingdom, smoke billows into the sky, casting an ominous shadow over the castle. The towers of the fortress, once symbols of strength, now blend into the chaotic cityscape. From his vantage point, Raymul observes the main marketplace in the distance, chaotic and filled with scared people running in disarray. Looters and bandits roam freely, reveling in the lawlessness that has befallen the streets. The disease ravages the unsuspecting populace, its nature unfamiliar to them but all too familiar to Raymul, who recognizes the signs of death accumulating with each passing day.

The burden of protecting the city falls on the shoulders of the general, who takes it upon himself to maintain order and guard the castle against any intrusion. With his guidance, the general organizes a team of elite soldiers to seek out the afflicted and isolate them in a remote corner of the kingdom. For those who succumb to the illness, their bodies are solemnly laid to rest in an attempt to contain the so-called disease. However, Raymul knows they are merely biding their time, for the ailment is nothing more than a manifestation of sinister demons from the underworld. But he has yet to uncover their origins.

He sighs, attempting to alleviate the pain in his back. It has been a week since he last slept, his mind consumed by thoughts of his beloved Guardian of Death. He awaits her next instruction, a promise of both power and destruction upon the forsaken land. A smile creeps across Raymul's face as he envisions himself as a ruler, one who controls all beings and magical entities. He needs but one command, a command that only the last stronghold of this kingdom can provide. A command that will unleash the powers of the Dark Guardians. He requires Princess Celestia to relinquish her hold on this kingdom, severing the bond between the Guardian of Earth and the arrogant generation.

Suddenly, a figure catches Raymul's weakened eyes. With a mix of excitement and anticipation, he recognizes the massive creature he sent away long ago. It has finally returned, bearing his desired prize. Raymul knows the creature would not have returned without fulfilling its obligation. Now, he must be careful, for once the Rockfear fulfills its duty, it could swiftly turn against him, their bond severed once the debt is repaid.

Raymul quickly reenters the king's bedroom, preparing his next plan. He swiftly exits into the living area, closing the thick, fortified bedroom door behind him. He steps out into the hall and instructs the guards to fetch General Pennaldo immediately, requesting that he bring one of his finest soldiers. The guards bow instantly and depart on their mission.

Returning to his solitude within the bedroom, Raymul notices the creature drawing closer. He approaches a beautiful black plant and instantly feels the presence of his gracious Guardian of Death, her influence weaving softly through his mind.

The massive iron doors of the bedroom balcony swing open, and the sinister demon soars through the air like an oversize lion, gracefully landing before Raymul. Just behind the demon, a cylindrical vessel hovers.

The chambers of the vessel open, and Princess Celestia Argus steps out slowly and confidently. She shows no fear, but Raymul can see the agony in her expression. Her gaze is fixed on him and the alien plant in her father's bedroom. The Argus stone, a visible symbol of her power, pulsates, protecting the princess as she walks toward Raymul. The creature screeches beside her, fulfilling its destiny, and yelps in pain as it slowly transforms into a fiery form before reverting back to its human shape. Celestia stares in shock as her loyal subject lies unconscious on the floor, unmoving. She isn't sure if he is alive or dead, but anger courses through her veins as she conjures fire in her hand, ready to attack Raymul and the sinister tree.

"Now, now, now, Princess, I wouldn't do that," Raymul warns, stepping behind the black tree and touching it.

Celestia isn't sure what she's dealing with, but she hears a slow, murmuring voice from the stone. It feels as if it's trying to tell her to stand down, and so she does.

Raymul smiles as he approaches the princess. "Now, Princess Celestia, there's no need to be hasty about this."

"What have you done?" she spits, her anger palpable. "To my faithful friend and my kingdom! Answer me!"

Raymul smiles, attempting to touch Celestia with his slender hands. Instantly, she smacks him so hard that he falls back, hitting the mantel and losing his balance. Anger fuels Raymul, and he conjures a harsh magic to bind the princess. But as soon as the magic touches her, it reverts and dissipates. The Argus stone glows vividly, awaiting the next attack.

"Don't you dare touch me!" she screams at him as the wind blasts through the room wildly.

Regaining his senses, Raymul realizes that the power of the princess and the Argus stone is too overwhelming to overcome. He calls himself and retreats to the door. The princess dashes out, yelling for the guards. Just before she reaches the throne room, General Pennaldo rushes in and grabs her, but before they can escape, Raymul sends a burst of magic toward the general and his companions, trapping them in an invisible bind that sends them tumbling to the floor. Celestia rushes to their aid but watches in anger and pain as they writhe in the invisible restraints. She has never seen this type of magic before. As she gazes at the black tree, she notices it's glowing with a dark aura. The magic must be emanating from the tree, she concludes. She attempts to break the hold on Pennaldo, but he continues to scream in pain, and she hears his bones beginning to crack.

"Release him at once, Raymul," she commands, her anger evident as she approaches him slowly.

"I will if you listen, my princess," Raymul replies, his voice tinged with a sinister tone.

"I'm listening," Celestia says, her voice filled with both fearlessness and impatience. She stares intently, her features mirroring the sternness of her mother yet radiating the sincerity and care of her father.

Slowly, Pennaldo's struggles begin to subside, and he relaxes. His eyes, fixed upon Raymul, display a mixture of defiance and anger. He breathes heavily, his focus on breaking free from the binding and helping the princess.

"Princess!" Pennaldo manages to say. "Don't do his bidding!"

Celestia realizes that Pennaldo is still bound; she can't grab his hand to protect him from the magic bind, his agony intensifying as he fights against the restraints. She witnesses his attempts to use magic to aid himself, but it proves futile for her cousin.

"Your Grace, forgive me for altering your servant, but it was for your own good. We need to attend to you immediately. As you can see, the land is in jeopardy, and my powers are forbidden from accessing the greater elements of Earth without your consent. Release your bond with your kingdom quickly so that I may save our people," Raymul implores.

"What are you talking about? You know I cannot do that. My legacy is forever tied to these lands, just as it was for my ancestors before me. I will not entertain such a notion! I will seek help and get to the bottom of this tragedy. Now release Pennaldo!" Celestia defiantly replies.

"Interesting," Raymul says, observing Pennaldo's futile attempts at breaking the bond. "I had no idea he was a member of your family."

Then Raymul directs a slight wave of magic toward another soldier who had entered the room. Instantly, the soldier clutches his chest and begins gasping for air. Despite the tightening hold of the binding magic, blood begins to spurt from his mouth as he falls motionless beside Pennaldo. His face turns deathly pale before slowly transitioning into a reddish-pink hue.

Celestia screams as she rushes to help him, but General Pennaldo pushes Celestia out of harm's way, attempting to protect her.

"Princess, we don't have much time. The Tree of Death is consuming the realm, and your beloved Pennaldo will die along with the entire kingdom. The bond you hold is from the Guardian of Death. There is no stopping it. You must release the kingdom to me now before the disease engulfs your realm! It is her right, and she demands it now, or she will destroy us all!" Raymul yells angrily.

Celestia watches in horror as the lifeless black tree shimmers with an eerie brightness while anguished moans echo both inside and outside the castle walls. The screams of the people grow louder, assaulting her ears. Yet the Argus stone around her neck emanates a brilliant light, its power pushing against the malevolence exuded by the lifeless tree, protecting the princess from its dark influence. Desperate to shield Pennaldo from the impending danger, she reaches out for him, hoping the stone's protective aura will extend to her beloved cousin. But the binding that holds him is not of this realm—it possesses a deep and ancient power, as Raymul forewarned. It belongs to one of the most formidable Guardians: Death.

Celestia stares at the soldier whose life force is slowly fading away. With the invisible bonds finally released, the soldier collapses lifelessly on the floor next to the bound general. Blood flows from every orifice of the soldier's body, a gruesome sight that fills Celestia with dread. The same fate awaits Pennaldo as he convulses just as the soldier had.

She can't bear the thought of losing Pennaldo, her family, her protector, mentor, and friend. Her heart aches with intensity, and though she can't understand why, she is determined to safeguard him. Pennaldo has been a constant presence in her life, someone she cherishes deeply. And she loves the people of Selcarth with the same fervor.

Celestia steels herself, feeling both resentment and fear as she faces the transformed Raymul, now infused with the essence of the malevolent tree. She senses a sinister presence emanating from the Tree of Death, its power encompassing elements of both light and dark, good and evil. Raymul has embraced and harnessed its dark elements, imprisoning his own malevolent soul to serve his wicked intentions.

Though Celestia knows this is a deceitful ploy, her father's words echo in her mind, repeating his last conversation with her. "Sweetheart, protect our people." The words resonate, urging her to fulfill her duty.

With a heavy heart, Celestia musters her resolve and addresses the sinister Raymul.

"I release my kingdom to you, Raymul; save my people" she declares, her voice filled with a mixture of sorrow and determination.

Suddenly, the earth beneath them begins to quake violently, as if struck by an enormous force. Celestia takes a step back, her gaze fixated on the world outside the window, which seems to darken ominously. Doubt and regret flood her mind. What has she done? By relinquishing the bond that ties her family to the kingdom, she has severed their connection, and now the screams of the people are replaced by the haunting howl of the wind. She is no longer intertwined with the fate of the kingdom.

Raymul erupts into wild laughter, raising his hand triumphantly, reveling in his newfound victory.

"Foolish girl!" Raymul yells with delight and excitement, his voice filled with pleasure and anticipation. As Celestia watches in shock, the small black plant within begins to grow wildly on the mantel. Its roots break through the walls and floor, expanding rapidly in a matter of seconds. The once-modest plant transforms into a massive, menacing tree, its branches reaching high and breaking through the ceiling, causing debris to rain down and destroying the tapestries that had adorned the room for countless years.

Celestia, overwhelmed by the unfolding catastrophe, thinks to herself, *What have I done?* She moves away from the room, her eyes fixed on Raymul as he lifts his arm, shaking it wildly with joy and accomplishment. The sinister tree continues to evolve, taking on the form of a colossal, ancient tree, its numerous twisted branches and blackened vines intertwining like a grotesque spider's web. Celestia berates herself for her failure. Her father would never have allowed this to happen. She willingly surrendered the precious bond between the Arguses and the benevolent Mother Earth.

Suddenly, Celestia feels a firm grip on her right arm, and General Pennaldo, her loyal protector, snatches her away with ease. Leaping away from the bedroom, Celestia, still in shock, feels the general's massive arm holding her tightly yet gently, ensuring she is safe. With one swift motion, he smashes through the arched wooden doors of the king's courtroom, evading the menacing tentacles as they snake their way through the royal halls.

At the end of the hall stands a magnificent ivory statue of Osele, the legendary queen who preceded Celestia's mother. The statue depicts a regal woman with a stern yet compassionate face, short hair, and a majestic crown atop her head. Her long gown trails behind her like a flowing wedding dress, a stark contrast to the attire of the current queen. The general quickly reaches for the statue and clicks a hidden switch behind its ear. To their surprise, the statue moves, rotating in a complete circle, carrying them within the wall. As soon as they walk away, the floor beneath them shifts, and the statue returns to its original position outside the wall.

While tightly holding Celestia with his right arm, the general reaches into his armor and extracts a small relic. Instantly, a blue light emanates from the relic, illuminating a concealed cavern entrance. Revealed before them is a small circular staircase that descends into darkness.

Celestia had no prior knowledge of this secret passage's existence. Her father always told her that the castle held many ancient secrets, and now she is experiencing it firsthand.

"You can put me down, Pen," Celestia requests, her voice filled with a mix of sorrow and determination.

Pennaldo obediently lowers the princess to the ground, his towering figure dwarfing her petite frame. He removes his armored helmet, allowing his long, black hair to cascade over his massive shoulders.

"I'm sorry, Princess," Pennaldo says sincerely, his voice filled with remorse. He gently embraces her, offering comfort in his strong arms.

"What have I done? I have forsaken a bond that has been with our family for generations."

Pennaldo tightens his grip slightly and moves her away from him, looking into her tear-filled eyes with compassion. "It wasn't your fault, my princess," he reassures her, his tone soothing and gentle, like a father comforting a child. "I'm sure Mother Earth would have preferred that you save our people and creatures. You were tricked."

"What do you mean?" Celestia questions, wiping her tears away with a mix of anger and frustration.

Pennaldo speaks with a resolute voice, his firmness shining through. "We had already moved our people out of the city when we realized an inexplicable epidemic was taking place. Demonic entities began manifesting in humans, attempting to steal their souls. The witches advised us to scan the healthy people to ensure they were not carrying these demons."

Celestia stands in silence, unable to comprehend what she is hearing. So many terrible things have transpired, and now her kingdom is in chaos.

"What happened to those who were sick?" she inquires, her voice trembling.

"We isolated them until they passed, and then we burned their bodies," Pennaldo explains, his voice heavy with the weight of the tragic reality. "The witches here told us it was the best solution to prevent the epidemic from spreading further."

Celestia falls into a momentary silence, her mind grappling with the unfathomable horrors unraveling in front of her. The dark cave envelops them in an eerie stillness, broken only by the haunting echoes of the wind that persistently circle around. Weariness is etched into her mentor's eyes, evident beneath the weight of exhaustion. Pennaldo, his face unshaven and marked by sleep deprivation, has undoubtedly witnessed unimaginable atrocities. Celestia can't help but wonder about the nightmares that plague his mind.

"Pen," she says softly, her voice laced with patience, awaiting his response.

Pennaldo clears his dry throat, his voice cracking as he speaks. "At least a thousand souls lost, though we lost count."

Celestia feels a surge of emotions coursing through her, transforming her sadness into a seething anger and a burning hatred. How could Raymul have allowed this catastrophe to unfold? She knows that his sinister machinations are responsible for the suffering her people endured. Her mother lies trapped in a coma, her father teeters on the precipice of death, and now her beloved land is being decimated. Celestia vows, in the depths of her heart, to never forget this day. She will seek justice for her people, obliterating Raymul and his malevolent deeds.

"Princess," Pennaldo interjects, breaking the tumultuous flow of her thoughts, "we must inform the family immediately."

Celestia's gaze hardens, her voice resolute as she responds, "Yes, but fear not for the family. They are aware of my safety." She touches the Argus stone hanging around her neck, feeling its faint vibrations resonating with the danger surrounding them. "I'm certain they've already sensed the disturbance in the elements. Besides, they will be preparing for the island's defenses. I will send them a message shortly. But first, we must gather the remaining survivors and ensure their safety. They need reassurance. Then, we shall journey to Argus Island. My uncles will provide shelter and care for them. Once I see our people secure, I will seek out the triplets and ask them for assistance."

"Triplets? You mean…," Pennaldo says with great concern and unease.

"Yes, the Hawthorne family. They owe our family a debt, and it's time to collect."

⊷≡◎ ◎≡⊶

In the meantime, Raymul revels in joy as the blackened tree finally takes root at the base of Castle Taeron. It has grown ten times in size, forming and embracing the entire bedroom. Its thick and dark tentacles of branches are extended, its bark deep and intricately patterned, exuding a strange beauty. The tree, once small and lifeless, now stands as a majestic oak, smooth and black as the darkest midnight sky Raymul has ever seen. The trunk consumes the entire royal bedroom and extends countless arms upward like oversize fingers, breaking through the ceiling and allowing the sunset light to reflect off its shining body. The roots intertwine throughout the king's chamber, pushing deeper into the ground. Raymul can feel the intense power coursing through the half-floor and roots as vines sprout and penetrate the floors and walls, caressing Raymul like an electrifying shock of sensations and unleashed love. Overwhelmed, Raymul's hair stands on end, and flickering images emerge at the base of the forbidden tree, images of the underworld.

A woman draped in a sheer black blanket, ethereal and almost see-through, gracefully approaches Raymul. Her face is pale, as if touched by moonlight, giving her an otherworldly allure. Raymul's heart races, excitement surging through him as this enchanting being draws nearer.

It is the Guardian of Death, regally tall, with delicate, pointed ears and piercing eyes that mirror the depths of the night sky. As she walks, the ground transforms into a midnight carpet, materializing from the depths behind her, a scene both familiar and foreign, beckoning Raymul into her realm. She smiles faintly, her countenance mysterious yet captivating, capturing Raymul's heart completely. He loves her intensely. Their lips meet, their mouths hungry for each other, and an overwhelming surge of passion courses through him. They kiss passionately, their connection deepening as they press their bodies together, their love intertwining like an inseparable bond. Their embrace is unstoppable, their lips and hands exploring every inch of each other. And in that moment, as they lie down together, they finally make love, their bodies merging in a passionate union that transcends boundaries. Their souls intertwine, a symphony of pleasure and fulfillment echoing through the enclosed space, as they surrender to the all-encompassing love they share.

She stops and pulls back, a mischievous smile playing on her lips. She teases Raymul, her radiant beauty captivating him as he stares at the most exquisite creature he has ever seen. Her face is pale, smooth, and flawlessly sculpted, with high cheekbones and eyes that hold a mysterious depth. Long, slender elven ears peek through her long, black, silken hair, which cascades down and gently brushes against her warm upper breasts, pressing lightly against his bearlike body.

"Raymul," she whispers in a voice that resonates with a sweet and alluring divinity. "I have been waiting for this moment for a long time, molding and feeding your innate power, and now, finally, you are perfect."

Raymul can't fully comprehend her words. Her radiant presence overshadows everything else. The vines continue to envelop them like a tender embrace, rendering her words secondary. All that matters to him is her, and the intensity of desire growing within him is so powerful that he struggles to fathom how it could be contained.

The Guardian of Death smirks, and in an instant, her black eyes transform into a captivating shade of crimson. As Raymul's insides churn with an explosive sensation, he feels as if his very essence is tearing itself apart, his flesh and bones quivering in an agonizing ecstasy. The Guardian continues her seductive enchantment, and with each passing moment, Raymul feels himself transcending mere humanity. Their passionate connection intensifies within the enclosed cradle of death, as Raymul wholeheartedly responds to her allure.

Dazed and bewildered, Raymul rises from the ground, attempting to regain his composure. Completely naked, he stumbles toward the broken door, only to be met by the stunning Guardian of Death, now adorned in a flowing, midnight-blue satin gown that trails behind her. A red emerald necklace adorns her neck, perfectly matching her eyes. She approaches him with grace, a smile playing on her lips, while a powerful energy pulses in the air.

Suddenly, Raymul feels his inner self shatter, bones cracking with excruciating pain, and his muscles contorting and expanding. He no longer recognizes himself, but he doesn't care. Whatever form the Guardian desires, he will assume. He belongs to her, craves her power. Slowly, Raymul grows to a towering height of ten feet, his transformation becoming apparent. His skin darkens to a deep midnight black as a hooved, snakelike tail emerges from his erratic, huge body. As he reaches a nearby mirror, he gasps in shock at his reflection. His features remain, but now he resembles a wolflike creature, with a fierce face and ram-like ears curling beneath his massive, bearlike chest. His elongated snout possesses heightened senses, capable of detecting even the faintest of scents, and his razor-sharp fangs could cleave through bone. His human body has been replaced by a powerful, muscular upper torso akin to a bear, with leathery black claws and sleek fur covering his lower body. His hind legs are robust, allowing him to leap and grasp with his formidable paws. A surge of magical energy courses through his veins, yet the details of his transformation elude his memory, fading away.

The creature senses an overwhelming need to protect, to guard, and to obey. It swivels around, searching for its master, and finds her standing before it. It understands its purpose—she is the one to be protected, no matter what means are required. It will obey or face annihilation.

The Guardian faces the creature, petting it with satisfaction, appreciating its presence. She looks around the realm, taking in the surroundings for the first time, and observes the effects of her plans. She touches her body slowly, reassured that her existence and her sister, Void, are now integral to a unique magical principle.

"My Belhemothar, sinister rogue and protector," she begins, her voice carrying immense authority. "It has been a long time. Your magical essence is intertwined with my existence and that of my sister, Void. You must protect this lair from any intrusion or harm. Both worlds must remain open to facilitate my dual existence. Prevent anyone from closing my realm, Belhemothar. Our success relies on both realms remaining accessible."

She pauses, her words imbued with overwhelming power, as the creature bows in submission. Its soul absorbs her command, understanding the gravity of the task at hand. The creature, now resembling a wolflike being, gradually backs away, allowing its master to walk back into the depths of the black tree. The Guardian retraces her steps toward the fractured threshold between the realms of light and darkness, entering her home realm of Death. Minions join her from the other side, gracefully holding her long gown as the creature watches her vanish into the darkness. The barrier between the two worlds appears like a translucent mirror as the creature howls to beckon other creatures to aid in protecting the shattered veil. The task bestowed upon it is of paramount importance—the duration during which both realms must remain open. Although uncertain of the Guardian's intentions, the creature understands the critical nature of safeguarding the broken veil.

Belhemothar now feels a hunger gnawing at its core, unsure of the last time it had eaten or why it has waited so long to feed. Despite possessing immense magical prowess and physical strength capable of tearing stone walls asunder, it can sense an untapped potential in its control of magic. It walks heavily, approaching a strange, lifeless being in the next room. Observing it curiously, the creature can't recall how this being met its demise, but regardless, it commands its magic effortlessly. Energy surges through its claws, causing the creature to convulse and breathe once more. It stands up, its visage similar to its master's but noticeably lacking in magical properties and exhibiting significant weakness. With another flicker of magic, the creature wildly transforms into a form that suits its preferences—a four-legged creature with increased speed and two heads, reassembling itself to facilitate coordinated attacks.

Belhemothar's voice resonates through the lair, commanding the creature to fetch more beings to bolster its ranks and ensure its sustenance. The creature responds with a wild howl, baring its massive teeth in a display of fierce determination. With an agile leap, it bounds out of the area, driven by the urgency of its task.

Satisfied with the creature's departure, Belhemothar embraces its duty to protect the lair. Bound by an unbreakable commitment, it remains rooted in its designated vicinity, unable to venture far. Settling down on the floor, it patiently awaits the return of its loyal minions, who will bring both sustenance and potential subjects.

With heightened senses, Belhemothar surveys the area, its powerful instincts attuned to detecting any form of danger. It can discern the faintest trace of life, the lingering presence of the deceased, and even the subtle nuances of magic. As the realm envelops it in an atmosphere of comforting, deathly air, pulsating with a sense of satisfaction, Belhemothar eagerly awaits its mistress's return, ready to serve her whenever she deems it appropriate.

CHAPTER 25

Unusual

RADION STANDS STILL, looking around, trying to sense something. James joins him immediately, while Kedar now appears perplexed as well. Eva joins the group, appearing calm, waiting for everyone's response to the sudden gathering.

"Something doesn't feel right," James says.

"Are they coming to attack again… the dead? We should get out of here now!" Ethan exclaims.

"No, Ethan, something feels off," James intervenes.

"Yes, I feel it too," Radion adds.

"The elements are disrupted. It seems the veil of the dark elements has been torn," Eva claims, calmly hovering over James like a hawk.

"Well, I don't feel anything. This is crazy; we should move on quickly," Ethan insists.

"I can feel the elements of darkness flourishing with love and needing to escape. It's an unsettling feeling," Kedar says, looking at his hand, playing with a light of some sort as it flows through his fingers.

"Enough of that, brother. You know as well as I do that love alters the elements. Don't be swayed by the elements. Rely on your physical strength and keep it at bay," Ulteal says, swinging her mighty mace behind her, revealing her muscular form as the other dwarves join them.

"She is right. Do not let your love cloud your judgment, young prince. The essence of love is a very powerful and unpredictable magic. It is probably the cause of the imbalance or the tipping point. We can't worry about this now; we must see the gracious Guardian of Water," Radion states.

James peers at Eva, confusion knitting his brows as she simply stares, listening but not engaging in the conversation. Despite the unexpected assault from the undead dwarves, she remains composed, her neatly pulled-back hair showing no signs of distress, not even a single bead of sweat.

"Love is a powerful essence, not an element that we know of. It can alter the balance of both light and dark elements to the user's bidding and enhance the effects of elemental magic. What you are feeling is an imbalance that love may have contributed to—a ripple or tear in the two realms of light and dark. It's a bit confusing; scholars still don't understand how love could affect properties of elements. But love is considered to be wild magic," Eva explains to James, who listens intently.

"I don't understand how love is powerful. It's just a simple emotion we all experience, isn't it?" James questions, seeking clarity.

Eva smiles and replies, "Love possesses a power unlike anything known to us. It encompasses feelings of passion that can bring fulfillment and immense satisfaction. Consider this, James: when one loves and receives love in return, it brings harmony. Conversely, when one lacks that love, it can lead to destruction and discord. The essence of love holds the ability to sway the balance, both in the realm of living beings and within the elements of light and dark. It can bring forth good or evil depending on the equilibrium of love. Love doesn't simply provide balance—it can also disrupt it."

James ponders, perceiving love from a different perspective. Love could extend beyond human connections and encompass even the love for the elements, which are governed by the Guardians. He feels a part of something he doesn't wish to be a part of.

He shifts his stance uneasily, a sense of weightiness and lightness conflicting within him. He recognizes the feeling without questioning its validity, but he notices he isn't the only one experiencing this unbalanced sensation.

"It will soon pass, James. It takes time for the balance to adjust to the new changes," Eva reassures him, sensing his discomfort.

Kedar suddenly speaks up, looking at Radion, his anger evident. "We must inform Mother of what we have witnessed. We need to alert our people. Everything has changed, Radion."

"Yes, I agree. Let them attend to their bidding. Our loyalty lies with our people," Ulteal adds, giving James a disapproving look.

"Our task lies with us, Kedar. You can't break away. It will only bring disorder to your queen," Radion reasons, his voice tinged with exhaustion from their arduous journey through the mountains.

James sits beside Ethan, waiting for Kedar and Radion to settle their dispute and decide on their next move. Eva retreats from the argument, paying no attention to the discord as she joins the two remaining warrior companions, tending to one of their fallen comrades.

"Crazy, huh?" Ethan remarks, squatting next to James, his gaze fixed on the massive cavern ahead. The interconnected bridges, tarnished and decaying from time, stretch from the bottom to the far top. The sight is an eerie glimpse into a catacomb-like network of treacherous walkways.

"Yeah, everything is strange. I never expected any of this. I wish—"

"Don't say that, buddy. Just accept it. Besides, you are the powerful and almighty Olen of the land," Ethan interrupts.

"Cut the crap, Ethan. You know I'm not."

"Hey, if I were you, I would embrace your inherent abilities and use your power to your advantage," Ethan suggests mischievously.

"You would do that, wouldn't you?"

"Heck yeah! I'd have everyone on their toes, getting what I need. With your powers, heck, I would be all over it." Ethan grins at James.

James smiles too, knowing his best friend is trying to cheer him up. It's working. Ethan is the only one here who keeps him sane, connected to his own home, feeling rooted and tethered. He's grateful that his friend joined him. He trusts him deeply—the only one he can truly rely on in this place.

It has been a few hours since their harrowing escape. Three Malij lost their lives, and they narrowly escaped the relentless skeleton dwarf warriors. Their lives were spared thanks to an unexpected intervention from the fairy world.

Radion explains that it is unusual for the wood fairies, as he calls them, to seek them out and involve themselves. According to Radion, these fairies are ancient and powerful beings, only found in a parallel subworld to ours. They are free to roam in both worlds, as they have been present since the creation of life itself—a life they oversee and govern with the assistance of the Guardians of Life. They ensure the balance of life and death through the magic that coexists in all things.

But it perplexes James. Why would the fairy refer to him as a brother and make him feel like a part of them? It unnerves him to see the enchanted, joyous face of the male fairy who rescued him. So small, with large dragonfly wings and colorful bursts of light emanating from its every movement. It feels like stepping into a fairy tale. Radion mentioned and concluded that the fairies seem to intervene when events are on the verge of incompletion. By saving them from the relentless undead dwarves and the malevolent tome, the fairies have effectively restored the intended path and purpose of their quest.

As Kedar raises his voice, James blinks and snaps out of his trancelike state. Kedar paces back and forth, his once well-groomed beard now disheveled. His clothes are torn, and his face is covered in dirt from their journey through the vast cave. They have followed Kedar without knowing his destination, eventually reaching a small gap on the far side of the cave. Kedar motions for his group to move out, and the entire party follows, unaware of where they were being led. Kedar stops near the gap, and the other dwarves position themselves at the side, waiting for their commander, Ulteal, to join them. She signals for them to guard the gap. Kedar turns to Radion.

"Here is a doorway that leads back to our kingdom," Kedar announces.

Radion scans the area. "I don't see a door, Kedar."

"Of course you don't!" Kedar replies. "We need a keymaster!" He pauses, realizing what is before him. With determination, he approaches a far wall that seems to be nothing more than solid rock. "I can sense an ancient doorway here," he says, placing his large hand on the wall, revealing the faint outline of an invisible door covered in cobwebs. Kedar and the other dwarves, with their heightened senses, can perceive the hidden doorway in these cavern walls.

Looking disappointed, Kedar faces the dwarf group. "We need to go back the long way. We are not trained in the arts of secrecy. Only a keymaster is adept at these skills, and there are only two of them back home."

"That's absurd, Prince Kedar," Radion interjects, walking toward the dwarf group. "You will be killed instantly once you reenter the witches' layer. We will find another way once we reach the surface. We're not far from it," Radion reassures him.

"I must inform my mother, Radion. My clan needs to know what has happened here," Kedar insists.

"I will not allow you all to be killed. You are not thinking rationally," Radion argues.

"Wait!" an unexpected voice interrupts.

Ethan pushes forward, leaving James puzzled about his intentions. Ethan approaches the prince, but Ulteal blocks his path.

"It's fine, sister. Let him," Kedar permits.

James stands up and approaches Prince Kedar, leaving everyone astonished. Wondering what his eccentric friend is about to do, James follows closely behind.

"I think I met one of your keymasters at one of your taverns, and he gave me this," Ethan says, pulling out his collection of keys. Attached to the chain is a crudely shaped stone key, noticeably different from the other metallic keys.

The other dwarves exchange glances and murmur in disbelief.

"That's impossible! You must have stolen it. No dwarf would give up their duty or responsibilities," one of the dwarf warriors retorts, positioning himself between Kedar and the scrawny Ethan, ready to knock him down with his massive arms.

"No, I didn't steal it," Ethan replies angrily, taking a few steps back as the dwarves glare at him with growing hostility.

James quickly intervenes, saying, "Ethan told me the same thing. He was given this key by one of your people."

Kedar pauses his warrior-like demeanor, and Radion interjects, "Tell me exactly how you obtained the master key, Ethan."

Ethan explains that the dwarf he encountered was drunk and insisted that Ethan take the key. He didn't explain why, but he believed Ethan was the right person to possess the dwarf's master key.

"Since I collect keys, I didn't press the issue any further. I accepted his generous gift," Ethan concludes.

Eva joins the group, seemingly at ease.

"Why don't you go up to that wall where Kedar claims there's a hidden passageway, Ethan? If you truly are the keymaster, your intuition should guide you," Eva suggests, straightening her outfit and wiping her delicate hands with a towel, seemingly unaffected by the tension.

"But I don't know how…" Ethan hesitates.

"Just do it!" Kedar impatiently exclaims, pushing Ethan and causing him to stumble before regaining his balance.

"There's no need for that, Kedar," James finally speaks up, his anger apparent.

Kedar faces James with a mix of anger and hatred. "Just as there was no need for the Destroyer to consume this once thriving city, a city where human greed tends to cloud your judgment." Kedar positions himself behind Ethan, waiting for him to discover the hidden passageway.

James chooses not to challenge the enraged prince. Since their arrival at the ruined city, Kedar's perspective toward James and the entire party has quickly shifted. James understands that witnessing the city's ruins and the lingering echoes of its inhabitants would change anyone's mindset. Right now, he needs the dwarf prince and his companions. James requires their expertise and skills.

The entire party watches as Ethan approaches the vast stone wall where Kedar claims the hidden passage exists. It appears to be an ordinary cave wall, much like any other within the perimeter. Ethan stands a few inches away from the wall, staring at it as if trying to decipher what to do. Moments pass, and he finally places his right hand on the rough, dirty surface, seemingly searching for an opening that isn't visibly present. At the precise center of his position, Ethan halts and gasps softly. Then, using his wide-open fingers, he moves his hand in a slow circular motion, almost as if he were calculating or inputting a combination without physically moving his hand.

After a few moments of pressing, everyone is holding their breath, especially the dwarves. Ethan's hand inadvertently causes the cave-in, and his fingers slip into the wall, disappearing magically. Ethan appears nervous and sweating, wiping his brow as he turns clockwise. Where his hand had been placed, he extracts a piece of the wall.

In shock, Ethan drops the stone he had held in his hand, revealing a small, narrow opening, easily passable for a human finger.

Without hesitation, Ethan retrieves his collection of keys and selects the long, strange stone key that resembles a cylinder, given to him by the drunken dwarf at the tavern. He cautiously inserts the key into the wall's slot and turns it clockwise. With a couple of loud clicks, the wall magically outlines a shapeless doorway, his hand suddenly sinking deeply to reveal a passage behind the massive rock leading into darkness.

"How did you know, Eva?" Radion snaps, looking intensely at her.

"Simple, my Radion," Eva replies. "Those who fell are those who will follow, as are those who once walked, and they are the loyal ones of the once-proclaimed Destroyer. According to prophecy."

"But I never would have thought Ethan would be one of them."

"Come now, Radion. Do you think Ethan, a simple local boy who enjoys getting into trouble and stealing, suddenly becomes James's best friend? You mentioned that he has unique abilities. Didn't you think to put two and two together?"

Radion persists, "Well, once again, Eva, you never cease to amaze me. Yes, I found it strange, but I didn't connect it to the prophecy."

Eva smiles faintly.

"What's going on?" James interjects. "What are you both talking about?"

Radion exhales, feeling increasingly annoyed with Eva's cryptic ways, and faces James, who looks as confused as a five-year-old child.

"During his journey and the ultimate defeat of the Dark Prince, Olen had powerful allies. One of them was a rare individual named Seli, a magical being born into secrecy. He possessed a unique magic that can unlock hidden knowledge. These traits are quite uncommon, as many people have abilities to unlock secrets, but it's rare for those with magic to unlock the unknown. Due to their extraordinary talents, they are often known to employ their abilities for personal gain, engaging in illicit activities to amass wealth."

"Thieves," James concludes.

"Yes, thieves. Although it was said that Olen's companion, Seli, a dwarf, was a loyal yet honest thief. He was the master of keyways and the gatekeeper of the dwarves. They are a rare and unique clan. They usually keep to themselves and are highly regarded by the royal kingdom of the dwarves. They protect dwarf homes from intruders by mastering the magic properties of Earth elements and bending the essence into mechanical techniques, creating secure doorways and locks that can only be opened by them. The prophecy states that when you are reborn, the companions who once walked with Olen will also be reborn."

"So Ethan is a descendant of Seli?" James inquires.

"Possibly, but it's intriguing," Radion ponders, attempting to analyze his assumptions yet remaining unconvinced.

"What is it?" James inquires.

Radion realizes he has been neglecting James. "Seli was a well-respected… dwarf descendant. The clan was lost since the Destruction of Olen," Radion says, looking puzzled.

"Who's Seli?" Ethan chimes in, approaching them with glee and excitement, causing his already long nose to appear even longer.

Radion stares hard at Ethan, and James notices a certain unease in Radion's gaze after the recent attack. His eyes look alert, his once neatly groomed beard is now untamed and wild, and the cloak that was once meticulously adorned is torn and tattered in several places.

"Do you know who your parents are, Ethan?"

"No, my aunt never speaks of them."

Then Kedar joins the group. Kedar's sister stands behind them as the other dwarves stand by the adjusted doorway, looking amazed. Suddenly, the outline of the ridged door reveals an ancestral magical structure, allowing the stone door, which is about fifteen feet thick, to easily open.

"Your ancestor was a dwarf, Ethan, and you possess a rare magic known only to my clan. You are a dwarf." Kedar says, and Ulteal simply smiles, looking at the skinny Ethan in amazement.

"Really?" Ethan exclaims. "I don't even look like one!"

Kedar gives instructions to two of his warriors to enter the tunnel and get word back to their queen.

In the meantime, James gazes at the thin, frail Ethan, with his disheveled hair and crooked nose that seems permanently bent. *How can my friend be a descendant of Seli?* James wonders, as Ethan appears to be the complete opposite of a dwarf.

CHAPTER 26

Journey

EMPRESS SAMATAR SKILLFULLY navigates through the winding corridors leading to an apparent dead end within the castle in the city of Kumartal. The hallway exudes a sense of antiquity, mirroring the age of the Guardians who once traversed these very plains. The walls are adorned with weathered, oversize stones, their formidable presence rendering them impervious to most magical attempts at breaching their defenses. The castle is fortified with a unique substance crafted by the enigmatic Guardian of Air, which possesses the remarkable ability to swiftly restore the structure in the event of an attack or intrusion. Although Samatar has never personally witnessed such an occurrence, ancient texts and prophecies allude to the Guardian of Air's affinity for this castle, where his persuasive powers were employed to manipulate individuals into carrying out his bidding—a characteristic inherent to the Air element.

Descending to the next level, the scent of musty dampness permeates her senses, and she feels a slight humidity in the air as she delves deeper. The stairs, long and old, maintain the presence of the Air element, as there are no signs of decay or damage anywhere. She scans the surroundings meticulously, ensuring that no one has followed her into the depths of the castle. Sensing no presence, whether of nonexistent or existing magic, she places her right hand on the stone wall, searching for the precise spot to input the secret combination her loyal dwarf companion had revealed to her. Instantly, the wall illuminates with a magical outline, and a hidden door materializes, swinging open to allow her swift entry into the dark chamber.

As soon as she enters, she raises her hand and magically seals her room so the hall becomes soundproof. Walking swiftly down the hall, the enchanted door behind her moves back to its original spot. Empress Samatar can hear her dwarf friend cursing as she enters a vast, sunken room filled with hundreds of vials containing various liquids and preserved animals. Quietly, Samatar walks around the old wooden table stacked with spell books and parchments, searching for Kerfort. She finds him by an ancient fireplace, meticulously holding an oversize black snake.

"There!" Kerfort exclaims, feeling relieved as the white substance finally drops from the snake's fangs and enters a large, old pot emanating a foul smell. With his powerful forearms, Kerfort carefully handles the powerful rare snake—an elven snake, capable of instantly burning one's insides and disintegrating the body like acid. Finally, Kerfort manages to place the snake into a large tank.

"Good," Samatar says when the snake is secured.

Kerfort starts, looking around. "Mistress, I didn't hear you come in."

"I did not want to disturb you, especially handling the Enyol snake." The dwarf appears well-groomed and healthy, his long, black beard neatly tied, and his wide face, with its oversize nose, exudes a sense of relief. It is evident that the tension has subsided, and Kerfort is now fully capable of handling his duty.

"I see that the spell worked," Samatar remarks, approaching the snake tank. She levitates it with her magic and places it neatly alongside other tanks containing various creatures.

"Yes, it did. I was able to trick it momentarily and extract its poison," Kerfort explains. "But they are clever; it quickly realized what I was doing."

"I did tell you to be quick. The spell only lasts for a moment. Now, how far along are we with this potion?"

"It's nearly completed, as you requested," the dwarf replies, walking over to an enormous bench and looking at an oversize old binder. Climbing a step stool, he quickly scans the opened page with his stubby finger. Then he looks up, perplexed.

"Mistress, why bother with this spell? It's very ancient and has never been proven to work. There are other substitutions, though not similar to this particular one you're trying to reveal."

Samatar smiles, knowing her inquisitive companion would be surprised by the substance she managed to acquire. From her long black cape, she extracts a small vial containing the blood of the Rockfear. Kerfort stares at the swirling red substance that seems to transition between black and red continuously. "How were you able to acquire this from the death realm creature? You know it's illegal. But how could you possibly obtain a substance that is nearly impossible for any sorceress to obtain?"

"Calm down, my friend. The Rockfear offered it," Samatar replies calmly.

He jumps down from the high stool, landing easily and smoothly on the stone floor with his large bare feet—a trait known to all dwarves.

"I never received any reports of a Rockfear. That would have been the first thing they told me when I returned. What's going on here, my mistress?"

Samatar simply walks over to the fireplace, where the large pot contains a simmering liquid and emits gaseous steam. She extends her right arm and pulls out a small knife from her cape.

Kerfort acts quickly, sending a wind-cast magic to intercept Samatar's movement. But she is already ahead, blocking his magic and sending the dwarf sprawling away.

Within seconds, two figures emerge from the darkness and seize the dwarf, casting a binding hold on his hands and feet before he can attempt another attack.

"I'm sorry, my friend. You have been so loyal to me all these years. But I know you are loyal to the school and the laws of this kingdom," Samatar says, her voice filled with regret.

"You don't know what the element of Void can do to that potion!" he yells as the magic restrains him in the air, preventing him from touching the stone. "It will alter its essence; it can take on another form. Don't use the precious guiding substance, Mistress!"

Samatar cuts a small slit on her hand, and warm red blood trickles down from her hand and enters the luminous potion. With her magic, she instantly heals herself and withdraws the vial.

"My Kerfort, do you think I would take such a risk? I researched for years, and with the help of a friend, I was able to develop my own spell. But of course, I needed the one element that can only be acquired from the darker side," Samatar explains. She opens the vial and carefully scoops up the potion from the ancient black pot to fill it, quickly sealing it. The substance swirls and turns into a milky, gray substance. Swiftly, she walks over to the large open binder and chants the spell quietly, searching for the right sign regarding the vial's contents. The potion bubbles and reverts to its red substance.

Samatar smiles, realizing that the spell has worked. Then she walks over to the suspended dwarf, who awaits his fate. The dwarf's sweat pours down his large face, his hair hanging as he scans the perimeter, desperately searching for an escape route, knowing that there is no hope.

The empress approaches the suspended dwarf, fully aware of her faithful companion's discomfort. As a dwarf, he detests being off the ground, but she has no pity for him—only one singular purpose.

"You know the Arguses will confront you, my mistress," Kerfort manages to say, attempting to move his long, black hair away from his wet face.

She smiles and replies, "They will also be preoccupied, since the underworld has finally breached the living."

The dwarf looks surprised. "Impossible."

"You can thank Lord Raymul for his selfishness and greed. Although it will take some time before the dark element surfaces, I imagine we will have plenty of visitors in the meantime to occupy the secluded and sacred grounds of the Arguses."

"Then the prophecies are true—the Destroyer walks among us."

"Yes, and I'm sure he or she will seek the aid of the precious Guardian for their orb to prevent the breach from fully opening. But it won't be easy this time; the Guardians are not that forgiving."

"It sounds like you want the Destroyer to fail. Whose side are you on?"

"Neither." She pauses for a moment, then replies, "Maybe one."

She pulls out the vial in front of the dwarf.

"You see, my friend, this elixir requires specific magical properties from the Death and Void. As you are well aware, it is extremely rare to obtain such properties, except from creatures that possess some essence in their realm. It so happens that the Rockfear contains some of those properties."

As she fingers the swirling white substance in the vial, she continues, "The possibilities I've envisioned with this potion, the one I've longed for so long to succeed, is to control one's mind while retaining their natural state and strength. Many types of magic or entities, such as the Shadowlen, can accomplish this, but the individual becomes mindless or already dead, merely following commands like a puppet without any intuition or common sense of their own. And of course, being a dwarf like yourself, naturally, your kind prevents any intrusion into your mind and soul. But with this…"

Then the empress opens the vial, and instantly a small fog escapes, swirling in the air like a snake uncoiling. She gently blows the fog into the open nostrils of her companion.

"The possibilities are unlimited. They will never know there is anything unusual about you, although you will be under my complete control."

Caught off guard, the dwarf shakes his head, trying not to inhale the substance, but it is too late. The fragrant yet woeful aroma overwhelms him, and the substance enters his bloodstream. He feels anguish as the substance courses through his veins, and a burning sensation spreads as if his heart is about to explode.

Watching the dwarf convulse wildly, the empress steps back to witness the slight transformation. The dwarf's veins slowly become visible under his large muscles, and then gradually, a new entity seems coil around the veins. The dwarf screams as the veins slowly disappear from his body, reappearing vividly on his upper head and eyes. Suddenly, his eyes turn bloodshot red, and the veins pulsate intensely as they enter his brain. Instantly, the dwarf stops screaming, gazing blankly into oblivion and closing his eyes as if the pain has suddenly escaped his body. The veins vanish and retreat back into his body.

Feeling satisfied, the empress commands the magic restraints to release him. The dwarf falls to the ground but stands up as if he is ready to attack.

"None of that, my Kerfort. You can relax now." Instantly the dwarf stands at ease, looking normal and staring naturally, waiting for his next command from his mistress as if nothing had happened previously.

"Good." The Empress, feeling grateful and satisfied, unleashes a blaze of dark magic and commands the items to be placed back appropriately. After spending a few minutes tidying up her potion room, she casts a dark spell, sending a subtly unstable wave of magic that will impose a slight curse upon the entire dungeon. With this, she believes her captives will be confined and unable to escape. If they attempt anything, a lingering curse will haunt them. Quickly, she gathers her precious spell books and a heavy, thick volume containing the rare prophecies, casting a spell to slip the weighty tome into her cloak. Satisfied, she turns to Kerfort, who has not moved a muscle other than waiting for his master's orders intently.

"Time to go, Kerfort. We have plenty to discuss and arrange before I depart, and we must prepare." Kerfort simply smirks evilly and nods in acknowledgment, following the empress back into the dark tunnel. As soon as they disappear behind the secret door, the spell in the room flashes brightly, causing the animals and inanimate objects to momentarily freeze and small particles of light to swiftly and slowly disintegrate, reinforcing the trap.

⊷⇒◐ ◑⇐⊷

Meanwhile, Castle Taeron in the kingdom of Selcarth, located in the far western land that once housed her home, stands high above the horizon, gleaming against the setting sun. Slowly, clouds hover over the castle, revealing what appears to be an overgrown tree, black as the midnight sky. It has broken through the castle's high pillars and transformed its majestic appearance into a distorted figure, overtaking the once-beautiful ancient landmark.

Below, Celestia, the temporary ruler of her land, sits quietly as tears slowly escape her eyes. Fires rage beneath the castle, scattering randomly and giving rise to unfamiliar creatures. From a far distance, she can see the scattered bodies of the fallen. Her father and mother are safe, but the people and creatures that perished below tell a different story. She managed to gather most of her surviving people and accounted for some of the survivors, but many had lost so much, leaving loved ones behind. This was the work of Raymul, converting the second land owned by the Arguses into a malevolent realm she is unfamiliar with.

Creatures begin to appear in the darkened clouds forming below, howling and scratching, sending shivers down Celestia's spine. Her skin tingles, and her heart races as her eyes catch sight of glowing red orbs, waiting for someone to venture too far into the cliffs. It was once a beautiful land filled with hope, green grass, and homes occupied by families. Now, it is overrun by unknown entities she has never seen before.

Celestia's heart ached as she witnessed earlier a doglike demon snatch a small child, reminiscent of her cousin Dario, and drag it away while another creature raced up to steal its meal like a predator. Quickly, Celestia turned her face away and silently cried. She had failed her father, mother, and her people. She had relinquished the sacred land to the evil Raymul.

Looking beyond the fertile, faltering farms, Celestia observes hundreds of people scattered like cattle, uncertain of which direction to take. Many clutch their children and carry boxes and bundles of their belongings, seeking refuge and guidance from their princess. Beside her, soldiers from the stronghold guard her while organizers work tirelessly to bring order to the weary masses who have just completed their long journey from the hidden underground tunnels of the city of Selcarth.

A massive grizzly bear begins its deliberate approach toward her, moving with an air of calm and assurance. Slowly, it graces her with its immense presence, allowing her to touch its fur with a gentleness that mirrors the grace of the encounter. This is Moonda, the evergreen caretaker of her realm and her home. In a language only they can understand, a language woven with innate magic, Moonda communicates with Celestia. She speaks of matters that only the two of them are privy to, her words an exchange of understanding and reassurance. Moonda's voice resonates, carrying with it a sense of concern, asking about the well-being of her cubs.

Celestia's gaze rests on the imposing figure of Moonda, taking in the sight of the handful of bears and their playful cubs. The bears' interactions with their father are a poignant contrast to the turmoil that now envelops their once serene territory. Among them, a few other creatures wander, their presence a careful dance that avoids disturbing the bear clan, the guardians of this sector.

One bear in particular, named Ragnor, stands out. As the leader of his sector and Moonda's mate in this region, Ragnor's a powerful warrior of their kind, watchful eyes fixed upon Celestia. There is a shared understanding between them as he inquires if all is well. Celestia nods in response, her thoughts racing. She knows that the Guardian of Earth has dispatched her Nimble minions, also known as squirrels, to investigate and authenticate the arrival of the life-aware, according to Moonda. The bear's words connect the dots, revealing that the Guardian of Earth has sent companions to bear witness to the impending arrival of the Destroyer.

Turning toward Moonda, Celestia's hand gently glides over the bear's exquisite brown, almost black coat, a mirror of the majestic trees surrounding them.

Gratitude fills her heart as she murmurs her appreciation for the information. With a final nod, Moonda rejoins her family, mingling with her cubs in a display of familial joy.

Left alone with her thoughts, Celestia ponders the significance of Eartha's actions. The fact that the Guardian of Earth, a presence that has been absent for centuries, has dispatched companions indicates that there is more at play than meets the eye. As questions swirl in her mind, a sense of urgency takes root. She knows that consulting her family is imperative. The weight of responsibility settles upon her shoulders, a testament to the role she plays in the intricate web of life and guardianship.

A firm hand suddenly rests on Celestia's red favorite cloak, and she looks up to find her faithful family member and close friend General Pennaldo staring at her intently.

"Princess, we are ready to move out," says General Pennaldo.

The princess simply stares into her older cousin's blue eyes, sensing the same regret for the city that once stood strong and powerful, now reduced to ashes. She has known Pennaldo since she was a little girl. He has been her father's closest advisor since their childhood, and they grew up studying together. They have shared many adventures, and these adventures are known to the elder Argus family. Legends tell of how the young Argus heirs often found themselves entangled with the outside world, and eventually, after setting things right, they returned to their own dominion. Celestia and her cousin are the youngest in the family, and somehow, they continued this cycle. Now she is leading her people out of their homeland to seek safety at Argus Island further southeast.

Celestia stands up, straightening out the casual clothing that Pennaldo's warriors obtained from the castle.

"Let's move to the outer rim; I don't want to draw any attention," Celestia says with a sense of weakness and regret. "Our family should be here shortly to aid in our quest back to the island."

"Let me guess, the animals sent word?" Pennaldo asks.

"Yes," she replies, gazing down below as two creatures with bright yellow and black spots walk beside her, fearlessly and gracefully. Their teeth are sharp and pointed, revealing fangs from both the upper and lower jaw. They move in perfect harmony and strength. As she pets them gently, they purr like majestic rulers.

Pennaldo observes the princess closely. She finally seems comfortable wearing simple garments she received from his warriors, wanting to blend in with her people. Everyone around her looks distraught, and she continues to provide comfort as other animals join the group from the forest. Bears of various types, deer, and small mammals all move alongside the people, playing with the children who have joined them. Everyone tries to take what they can, but many are left empty-handed or are carrying only a few belongings as they flee for their lives.

He finally speaks to Celestia. "My dear Celestia, your father would have done the same thing. There was no way of knowing that Raymul was behind this evil scheme. If I had known, I would have burned him and taken his life with my bare hands. Nothing, not even magic, would have been as satisfying."

"I know, Pen. I've thought about it, and my father's last words were to protect his people. I just wish my mother was here; I believe she would have sensed some sinister magic at work and noticed that something was amiss at our castle, especially involving the school. I would have expected the empress to be involved."

"This was long planned," Pennaldo says, now looking out at the kingdom covered by a thick black cloud of smoke, hanging over the castle like a magical blanket. "It seems we were all deceived. I'm sure if the queen had been with us a bit longer, her magic would have sensed it. Not even the witches were able to detect it, but your mother, being so powerful, would have. She would have destroyed Raymul and ripped the empress apart too with her own hands, given the time—damn that Raymul! If only I had known, I would have torn him to pieces!" Pennaldo blushes with anger and smacks his enormous hands together, like a boy wanting to challenge himself in a battle.

"Princess." Pennaldo stops, clasping his hands, realizing something important he must tell her. "I think you should reconsider your attempt to visit your mother. The journey to Asford is very treacherous and through wild lands. Besides, King Argus wouldn't allow it; he would want you safe within the walls of our island after the tragedy that struck our kingdom."

"I'm not concerned about my parents right now, Pen, nor am I concerned with the journey to Asford. Though I appreciate your concern, and I'm sure you would try every attempt to divert me, but after seeing my father in the Argus stone, my parents are okay," Celestia says, now touching the red stone that matches her red cloak, which hangs lightly on a thin platinum chain. "I am now in possession of the Argus stone. It will protect me."

"But it only protects you against magical harm and possibly nonmagical properties, and I'm sure our relatives can also protect you from the evil that's now among us. You'd be better off staying within our family's domain. You know better than I do that uniting with our relatives would make you safer within Argus Island's walls. You, the young one, should not run about freely, thinking you are invincible. Times have changed, my dear princess," Pennaldo says, slyly trying to convince her otherwise.

Celestia smiles; he knows her well. In the past, she had secretly taken part in some unusual events, just like Pennaldo and her father—small adventures with her cousins, a trait that seemed to run in the hands of the young Argus heirs. But Celestia thinks that this time, considering the unpredictable and sudden dangerous situation, she will not ask her cousins to join her. She knows that they would insist, and as a matter of fact, they would persist in coming along. She could utilize their unique abilities, such as Aberra's ability to speak to living creatures like her, but understanding the senses in plants, and Jarin's mastery of offensive magic in both light and dark elements. Sakeris, not being a blood relative but recognized as a family member, mastered the magic of dark arts, focusing on defense and magic, known within their cult. And of course, her elder cousin, Larmari, who enjoys exploring the unknown and hidden secrets of the old world and magic. Her abilities grant extensive knowledge of history and magical relics, making her a valuable asset if she came along.

Nevertheless, asking them would only complicate matters and put them in danger. "No, Pen, I will not ask them to come, but if you are eager to stop me, then you should join me."

Pennaldo, feeling satisfied with winning this personal battle, smiles. "Yes, Princess, I would be honored. Princess, if I may, I need to inform you of another peculiar event not far from our home that I thought might be important."

"Go ahead," Celestia says.

"Before our sickness started in our kingdom, word got back to me about a series of murders that occurred in the town of Lancaster."

"Odd in a small town, especially among farmers," Celestia says.

"Yes, I thought the same, and to worsen the matter, the mayor was murdered, and the town went into chaos."

"Mayor Zefer was murdered?!" Celestia exclaims, her eyes widening in shock—another family member, a second cousin from her mother's side. "But how? He was such a peaceful person, and in fact, the town is one of our most peaceful zones," Celestia says.

"I sent men to investigate, and the word was that some type of demonic possession took place there, possibly by a powerful witch. It seems the attention focused on one particular family. Apparently they fled, and the chaos subsided immediately. I sent out a search party, but they decided to confiscate the home since our warriors picked up residues of unfamiliar magic. It seems the family left in a rush, taking only what was necessary. One townsman and a friend of the family witnessed them fleeing toward Mount Rocksmear. Unfortunately, I stopped sending commands since the sickness worsened in our kingdom, so I couldn't further investigate this family."

Celestia stands quietly for a few moments, absorbing the series of events that took place. Finally, she looks up at the bearded soldiers with concern.

"Do you think—"

"I'm not sure, Princess," Pennaldo cuts in, knowing her next question. "The puzzle pieces fit, especially coming from our uncle, a seer, who once said that Eartha, the gracious Guardian of Earth and unforgiving Destroyer, will be reborn. The Destroyer is from Lancaster."

The princess simply stares at her cousin; he is a tall and burly man with a deep scar on his right cheek, yet smooth like the rest of her family. He is five years older than her but with similar traits, in that their ages slow down as they get older; his wide, deep blue eyes resemble those of her family, particularly her cousin Jarin. He reminds her so much of Jarin that sometimes she forgets they are not the same person. But Pennaldo stands out with his heavily built body, distinguishing him from Jarin. Pennaldo has been her closest family member besides her parents. She feels a sudden caring connection with him that feels different from others. She brushes aside her feelings and smiles as she gazes out at the once-pristine area; now the mountains and valleys that she once stood proudly upon are decaying due to her actions. Behind her lie a few hundred surviving humans, showing signs of distress and hunger, but standing behind her with hope and faith that she will lead them to salvation. Many of the animals also stand among them, not caring that she is not their princess, but waiting for their leader, the ruler of their land, to save them as well.

"Pen, see to it that you pick up the investigation where you left off. I would like you to send some men to both Lancaster and Rocksmear. And send a message to the underground network; I'm sure they have better clues than we do," Celestia says, preparing to set out.

"Princess, you know as I do that the dwarves don't welcome our kind."

Celestia turns to face Pennaldo, looking just like her mother, with those piercing, wide eyes like her father. The ruby oval gem around her neck flashes brightly in the sunset against the mountains to the east.

"Well, make it happen. If they won't cooperate, remind them of my family's ties with the fairies. We are very much involved with them as they are with us. If that doesn't work, speak to Professor Ref."

Pennaldo's eyes widen, his heavy eyebrows lifting one slightly higher than the other. "You know, Ref is affiliated with the UGSN organization. You know, the underground secret network."

"I know," she says. "I have my ways. Now, see to it soon, and let's gather our people. I would like to head east along the coast. I feel safer along the sacred coast of the Guardian of Water. Besides, my uncle is very close friends with Ref and very much involved with the system. Ref will lend a hand to his clan."

"Your Highness, you mean King Argus, your father?" Pen looks shocked.

"No, Uncle Cameo. He knows many people and befriends even the worst. How do you think our family gets around so easily? In every civilization, Pen, there is always an underworld network, similar to our life with the beloved Guardians of Light and Guardians of Dark. Always opposites that usually attract."

Pennaldo nods with realization that he is wasting time questioning the princess. "I'm sorry, Your Highness, I shouldn't question," he finally says.

"It's all right, Pen. I trust you as my father does. We are family. Now let's get moving."

"Yes, Your Highness," Pennaldo says, and salutes, hitting his chest hard on his golden breastplate, and heads off into the crowd.

Celestia watches as he yells out orders to the commanding officers, startling the young children playing in their tents.

CHAPTER 27

Witness

THE ENTIRE GROUP moves forward into the cave, entering an ancient, broken stone staircase that leads hundreds of feet to a small opening. Eva talks with James, explaining that this path will lead them to the land of the sacred Guardian of Water. Kedar has already assigned warriors to deliver the message to the king through the opening that Ethan provided for them. James is unsure how the warriors will reach the other side but assumes they are familiar with the opening cave, given Ethan's connection to it. Ethan stays close to his friend, walking in deep silence as they carefully step over the nearly broken and missing stairs, supporting each other along the way.

James finally catches up with Ethan and interrupts his thoughts. "You all right, buddy?" he asks, snapping Ethan back to reality.

"Yeah, I'm good. I can't believe they are claiming that I'm part of the dwarf clan. Can you believe that crap? Look at me; I'm just a puny guy and nowhere near looking like these dwarves."

James nods but notices Ulteal's gaze fixed on Ethan with interest and a sly smile as she gracefully guides them to the next set of stairs.

"I don't know, buddy, but I think Ulteal has the hots for you. She keeps staring at you with interest," James says, trying to amuse and cheer him up.

"What?" Ethan takes a quick look as the princess quickly shifts her eyes, pretending she wasn't staring.

"Umm, she's most likely intrigued, but I'm human, and she is a royal dwarf."

"Yeah, so what?"

"Cut the shit, James. It will never work," he says, and they both laugh.

"I know, buddy. I was just kidding."

They both continue their trek, with Radion following behind as they climb the stairs.

The dwarf clan members are astonishingly amazing, using every muscle and strength beyond any human's capability. They grasp each rock, whether small or large, leaping and slowly clinging to the treacherous wall, with each non-dwarf person on their backs.

As they proceed cautiously, James, holding on to Kedar, can see a small opening revealing a dim light outside. Apparently, once in this beautiful thriving city, the distant opening in the wall leads to the secret grounds of the Guardian of Water. During the time of Olen's madness, the powerful forces of the elemental Guardians destroyed every single bridge network. The sacred element of Water consumed the cavern and obliterated every bridge and magnificent structure, all due to one human's greed unleashing his madness upon the uncontrollable power of the elements.

James waits until they are halfway up to seize the opportunity to talk to Kedar. He feels uneasy as they cling to a sheet of rock, shadows lurking below them. Kedar pauses for a break while the other dwarves, not far from them, follow their leader's example.

Kedar uses an enormous, intricate rope that resembles a net, a method James has never seen before. He secures a metal stake and attaches the netlike rope to one end. With his powerful hands, he slams the metal stake into the wall, securing it on the other side. Kedar signals for James to get off and sit on the rope. James climbs off Kedar's back, feeling the firmly anchored rope, and sits facing the wall while Kedar does the same, looking away and drinking water from his backpack.

After a day of Radion trying to explain to Ethan that the legendary dwarf may be part of his ancestry, James finally has an opportunity to speak to Kedar.

"Your people are absolutely amazing. I would have never known the capabilities your kind possess," James says.

Kedar doesn't respond, just looks away and continues drinking his water.

"Kedar, I know my people and my ancestors are at fault, but that doesn't justify what the future holds now," James adds.

Kedar quickly looks at James, fiercely, more like a warrior than the gleeful dwarf from when they first met. "My father was right about you. Your kind is nothing more than greed, consuming all magic for its own purpose, without realizing the powerful love for the elements bestowed upon you. I will never forget what I saw. My parents knew the consequences. Now I understand. I'm only here to fulfill my word. After that, human, we are nothing to each other," Kedar says.

James, now referred to simply as "human," feels regret. He understands the grief, having witnessed countless bones and the suffering of dwarf children and adults, being used as puppets by the evil witch that now rules the area. He too would feel anger. James can't count the number of dead dwarves, all because his ancient ancestor took the magic of the elements to a different level, and it turned against Olen and everyone who stood with the former king ruling the surface world.

"Is there anything I could do to help heal the pain of your people? I know I can't do anything right now, but if given the opportunity, can I help in any way?" James asks.

"Yes, you can help by leaving my people alone. Once my mission is completed, human, leave me alone," Kedar replies, looking distressed and confused as he prepares to leave the rope.

Suddenly, a yelp echoes from below. Ethan is losing his balance.

"Ethan!" James exclaims. "Grab on to something!"

The entire party halts. The unburdened dwarf hurries to assist the one struggling to maintain his grip on the flat cave wall.

"Calm, Ethan! You'll get us all killed!" Radion yells, clutching on to one of the dwarves tightly.

Then the unexpected happens. Ethan falls just before the dwarf comes to his aid, and while turning, he yells loudly as his voice echoes through the cave. He descends rapidly into the misty abyss.

"Noooo!" James yells, losing control of himself as Kedar tightens his grip on James's back, using his immense strength as a dwarf.

Then, abruptly, Ethan stops in midair, confusion spreading among everyone. They realize that Eva's hand is extended, emitting a glowing blue mist. Instantly, James feels a surge of magic that leaves him astonished. He can't believe the extent of Eva's power, especially after witnessing her incredible abilities. It becomes clear to him that Eva is using the power of Air to hold on to Ethan.

Looking around, he can also see Radion and the rest of the party in the distance, trying to come back and assist. They too are in shock, witnessing Eva's formidable magic at work.

"Don't move about, Ethan! I can't bring you up if you resist!" Eva manages to yell, which is very uncommon for her.

"Ethan!" James yells, but Kedar silences him quickly.

"The Gloomspire found us, Ulteal!" Kedar urgently yells to his sister. "Secure him! The Gloomspire are here!"

"What is a Gloomspire?" James asks in a panic.

"Ancient beings," Kedar explains. "Creatures shaped by the Guardian of the Void, resembling entities infused with an intricate blend of human and Draconian worm. During the destruction brought about by your ancestors, it provided an opportunity for the Dark Guardians. They dwell deep below the abyss, their senses finely attuned within the cavern walls. My sister has sensed their presence abundantly. Your friend's cries near the cave walls drew their attention."

"Why now you say this, Prince?" James exclaims.

"What? I didn't know your companion would be quaking like—"

Instantly, Kedar, a powerful mage according to Radion, summons a magical rope that radiates an ethereal glow. He hurls it upward to where his sister is scraping the closest edge to meet them. "Sister, get the human!" Kedar yells.

Ulteal leaps into the air, effortlessly snatching the magical rope. James marvels at how the dwarf kin are so intertwined with the stone. Ulteal then flings the other end of the rope to her brother, its magic responding to its creator's will. It coils around Kedar's massive arm like a snake as it does the same on Ulteal's arm. The rope glows orange at the two connections, and instinctively know what to do as Ulteal swings past them, with Eva using her magic to try and hold on to Ethan.

The magical rope extends its length as Ulteal reaches Ethan. Ulteal effortlessly clings to the rocky wall with astonishing strength. Her power is unparalleled, and as her brother secures the rope's other end, the magic rope tightens, ensuring they are both connected.

With one hand, she reaches for Ethan, and the magical hold that Eva placed on him soon disappears. In an instant, Ulteal grabs Ethan in midair and presses him against the rock wall with her body. Ethan loses consciousness, and Ulteal, with her massive upper body strength, slings him over her shoulder, leaping swiftly as the cave below quakes violently.

The rescue party clings desperately to their precarious ascent toward the opening above, only a few hundred meters away. Then, an enormous worm, its tentacles writhing wildly, shoots out from below, unleashing ear-piercing screams that shake the entire cavern. Rocks rain down in chaos. James witnesses exactly what Kedar had described: a horrifyingly distorted worm, a colossal creature roughly a hundred feet in length. Its tentacles, a grotesque fusion of human and otherworldly claws, coil and clench around the rope with unnerving speed, maneuvering easily up toward their position. The worm has multiple sets of disconcerting, lidless eyes, at least ten or more, that observe their every move. It pounds heavily on the wall, trying to seize its prey. Its teeth are massive and disfigured, resembling a chaotic mix of human and other forms when he can discern them. James is both terrified and shocked to witness such a creature, which Kedar has described as the work of the gracious Guardian of Void!

Radion, already positioned at the cave's opening, continues to launch white fireballs at the creature. The flames have a noticeable effect on the creature, especially since its skin resembles that of humans and scales. The creature's piteous screams fill the cavern as it attempts to retaliate. The fireballs, however, inflict significant damage, causing it to recoil and retreat.

As they partly continue to ascend rapidly above, the remaining dwarf warriors adeptly manage to secure and haul themselves upward toward the cave's exit. They leap with remarkable agility. Eva manages to climb on her own without assistance, her protectors close behind.

Radion continues to unleash blasts to distract, which seems particularly effective against the creature, given its unevenly textured skin that resembles a mix of human and other scales. The creature's anguished cries echo as it struggles to capture them, but the fiery onslaught inflicts considerable damage, causing it to withdraw.

James and Kedar, now safely at the cave's opening, watch in awe and relief as the once-terrifying beast diminishes into a feeble, trembling shadow of its former self. The combined might of Eva and her fellow magic wielders have decisively turned the tide of battle, saving the rescue party from a grisly fate.

However, the brief respite proves short-lived. The wounded creature, desperate to escape, makes one final, desperate attempt to flee. It burrows into the cavern's walls, disappearing into the labyrinthine depths below. While the immediate threat has passed, the party knows their perilous journey is far from over.

Then Ulteal, with astonishing strength, propels Ethan toward the open doorway, resulting in a slight thump. Kedar reacts swiftly using his magic, shifting Ethan's body out of harm's way to prevent any more noise that might attract the Gloomspire. A warrior dwarf that is near the ledge is momentarily off balance and lets out a startled yell. A long, distorted tentacle from the creature, still hidden beneath, snakes out and ensnares his leg. Ulteal leaps into the air with powerful grace, reaching for the ledge and trying to stop the Gloomspire from taking the screaming warrior, who disappears instantly into the abyss as effortlessly as a burrowing creature through sand. Ulteal, Kedar, and the remaining warriors scramble into the opening, their clothing torn and revealing their muscled forms beneath.

Ulteal's enraged screams echo loudly as they continue downward. The landing where they stand shakes, sending up a small cloud of dust and gravel, as she vents her anger and frustration.

But nothing emerges to confront them. The Gloomspire has achieved what it wanted.

Ulteal faces her brother. "This is what our parents desired." Ulteal's voice trembles with sorrow. "This experience has only deepened our doubts about these humans. Witness the devastation they've brought upon our nurturing ground! Our young ones and their guardians…we bear the scars, the blood, and the bruises from this agonizing ordeal." Ulteal's voice cracks as she speaks, her words a lament that resonate through the cavern.

The other warriors turn to look at them, their eyes filled with tears. Kedar, too, gazes at his sister, tears welling up in his eyes as they share a moment of profound grief. Surprisingly, they suddenly cling to each other, attempting to conceal their tears, though they continue to flow. They have been holding in their emotions since they entered the cave. Both of them have only heard stories; never before have they witnessed their own kind subjected to such suffering brought by the potent magic of Water thrown off balance by the Destroyer. It is a searing memory etched into their hearts, witnessing the profound devastation in the nursery cave. Once a sacred refuge, the nursery cave shelters and nurtures young ones under the watchful guidance of guardian elders who educate and train them for survival and the arts. The sight of unimaginable death will take a long time to heal.

Kedar gently places a comforting hand on his sister's shoulder, and she turns to meet his gaze. They exchange a wordless look, their faces reflecting a complex mix of shock, anger, and a deep sense of helplessness. The remaining warriors stand alongside them, their silence reflecting the profound loss they feel.

The pain they experience isn't just for the loss of their fellow dwarf warriors; it is for the devastation of their nurturing ground, a place once teeming with hope and the abundance of their existence. It is a culture of life that has been disrupted, and now their kind stands on the brink of extinction.

The siblings exchange a deep bow, placing their wide foreheads together in wordless understanding and embracing each other tightly. Tears well up in their eyes as they struggle to contain the horror of what they have witnessed.

"I know, sister. Let's finish our task," Kedar finally whispers.

She gently pushes her brother's hand away and begins walking toward James. Her brother does not attempt to stop her, but when Eva positions herself in front of her, Ulteal hesitates.

"Don't," Eva says calmly.

"Are you or Radion his nurturing guardian?" Ulteal says.

"No," Eva says. "He is not accustomed to your ways, and he doesn't fully understand his ancestry. So your pain cannot be eased now. There will come a time when all will be made right."

Ulteal clenches her hand tightly, then turns away and walks toward the sunlight, her brother following in silence. The remaining warriors join their side as they move forward, leaving behind a scene of profound sorrow and devastation where the powerful magic of Water has wreaked havoc upon their world, unbalancing it in the wake of the Destroyer's destructive force.

As James, Eva, Radion, Ethan, and the Malij emerge from the tunnel, they step into a vast, open area filled with vibrant scenery that envelops them. It's a truly awe-inspiring sight, with walls adorned in artwork created by both children and adults, showcasing the boundless creativity of this place. Some of the symbols James recognizes as representations of the Guardians of Life, embodying both the light and the dark. These symbols, painted in a variety of shades, begin to radiate and glow as they come into view, a phenomenon that catches James off guard. He senses a formidable presence emanating from the ocean, causing a touch of unease to wash over him.

Eva, ever perceptive, notices his reaction and places a reassuring hand on his shoulder, inquiring, "What is it?"

James responds, "She's coming."

They stand there in anticipation as James immerses himself in the sheer beauty of the beach. The sand sparkles under the sunlight, and the ocean's reflection dances upon the nearby rocks, creating an atmosphere of serene elegance. The rhythmic sound of the waves weaves through their thoughts, imparting a sense of balance and harmony. The area is a breathtaking blend of beauty and the relentless march of time, where nature has reclaimed and transformed stone homes, giving them new meaning. As the sun begins its descent on the horizon, casting a warm, golden glow over the city, James can't help but be entranced by the picturesque scene.

Curious, James breaks the silence, asking, "What did Ulteal mean when she asked if you are my nurturing guardian?"

Eva patiently explains, as they bask in the grandeur of the shimmering surroundings, "The guardian of the dwarf clan is tasked with guiding the young ones until they reach adulthood. They ensure that the young ones grow up respecting their culture. Guardians command profound respect and protection, even from the queen herself, regardless of their gender. Typically, parents assign a guardian to a specific person at birth, and this guardian shepherds them from childhood into adulthood. The cabin we came from nurtures children from a very tender age. Where we are now serves as a training ground for young adults, honing their skills in arts, math, war, and magic. They spend ten years here deciding which path to follow, whether it's mastering magic, arts, or warfare. Each area offers a unique approach."

James gazes out at the multitude of tarnished cabins and various entrances high above the mountain, scattered throughout the area. The markings and tools left behind tell a tale that spans miles. Eva continues, "Many species have their distinct ways of nurturing their young. Humans rely on homes and schools, while dwarves have their own designated areas. Elves and Arguses have their unique methods on their respective northern and island."

Intrigued, James inquires further, "What about the Arguses? So they are similar to humans?"

Eva enlightens him. "They are humans born into magic, somewhat akin to elves but distinct in their own way."

Eva further explains, "This place serves as a transition into adulthood. Dwarf parents often visit during their children's years here, especially in this sacred area near the Guardian of Water. They spend quality time with their children as they grow up. There are also outdoor areas where parents and children can enjoy life together."

James, overwhelmed with a sense of remorse, turns to Eva and says, "So I destroyed all of this?"

Eva responds resolutely, "No, James, it wasn't you. It was your ancestor. Love and obsession led to its destruction."

Radion joins the conversation, adding, "Love is indeed a powerful force, capable of both granting everlasting life and plunging into darkness."

Eva interjects, "True, but it was love that disrupted the protection of this sacred place, a love between another Guardian, the Guardian of Earth, and someone she deeply cared for. When that bond was severed by your ancestor, love turned into destructive hatred. The sorrow and pain of that loss, attributed to your bloodline, affected all the Guardians, throwing them into turmoil and causing them to temporarily lose control. It was an anguish they had never experienced, leading them to relinquish everything they cherished, ultimately resulting in the devastation we witnessed. The Guardian of Water loves this place, the children, and the dwarves within, but the sudden surge of emotions—hatred and anger—overwhelmed her, unknowingly prompting her to unleash her potent magic in a fit of confusion and rage. It swept through the sea, obliterating everything in its path, even penetrating the caves. It took the entire smaller city within the mountain, the nurturing grounds, and nearly reached the dwarf major city before they managed to seal it off."

Radian responds thoughtfully, "That's a wealth of information, and it's not found in the scriptures. We can't even be sure if it's connected to the Guardians. How can you be so certain?"

Eva looks around with unwavering confidence, stating, "It doesn't need to be in the scriptures. The truth is plain to see."

Eva emphasizes once more, "James, it wasn't you. It was your ancestor's obsession with the power of the orbs, and love was the catalyst that drove Olen into madness and the Guardians into chaos. Love is unpredictable; it can be beautiful, sinister, given, or taken. It can bestow life or bring about death. It's an uncontrollable essence, one of the most potent and inscrutable forces in existence."

James observes Radion nodding in agreement as they continue to wait, their minds filled with thoughts of their next steps.

Ethan, ever the one to infuse levity into tense situations, chimes in with a playful comment. "So, what's the best way to greet the Guardian of Water? 'How's the weather in the mystical realm?'"

James chuckles appreciatively, thankful for his friend's knack for humor. Ethan has an uncanny ability to gauge the mood and know precisely when a well-timed jest can ease the tension. He is a constant presence in James's life, always there when needed most, offering a fresh perspective on the complex world they navigate together. Sometimes, it is as simple as a smile to accept the gravity of a situation.

As James casts his gaze around their surroundings once more, his attention is drawn to a peculiar sight behind them. The dwarves who have been leading them stand a few feet back, near the entrance of the cave, their forms bent in reverent obeisance upon the pristine, lightly tan sand that bears no signs of disturbance. They are kneeling. Their lower garments have been carefully removed to ensure they don't sully the sacred sand beneath their knees. James finds this display of respect for the Guardian both intriguing and deeply moving.

CHAPTER 28

Guardian of Water

INSTANTLY, JAMES FEELS a gentle breeze ruffling their clothing. Although the Guardian is not in sight, James understands that the dwarves went to great lengths to display their utmost respect by ensuring they didn't soil the sacred sand with any impurities while performing their prayer rituals without the clothing of their lower bottom.

He promptly removes his shoes and places them beside a nearby rock. As he steps onto the soft, yielding sand, he can't help but notice its comforting warmth beneath his feet. There are no small pebbles, only a reassuring, conforming substance that cradles his large feet. He rolls up his trousers and decides to approach the graceful ocean. Ethan, however, dashes up behind him and grabs him firmly.

"Where are you going?" Ethan inquires.

"I don't know," James replies, his voice filled with an inexplicable longing. "I just need to touch the water. I can feel something, something I can't explain. The water...I need to touch the water."

Ethan, visibly unsettled by the eerie surroundings and the dwarves' devotion, replies, "I don't know about you, but this place gives me the creeps. With all these strange surroundings and the dwarves praying as if they don't care if we get attacked, I think you should step back until we figure this out."

"That's not necessary," Eva interjects, approaching from behind with Radion.

Radion steps forward and addresses James, "Do you know what to do?"

"I'm not sure," James admits, his eyes fixed on the beckoning ocean. "I can feel something stirring inside me. I just need to touch the water."

Radian exchanges a quick glance with Eva, their unspoken communication clear. "Then go ahead," Eva encourages. "We'll wait right here."

Ethan protests loudly, but Radion swiftly escorts him out of sight, back toward the Malij assassins and the praying dwarves.

Eva waits until Radion has settled an agitated Ethan before turning her attention back to the perplexed James. "She is a powerful Guardian, and she can be persuasive. Be careful, dear."

James looks at her with confusion, wondering how she knows this.

Eva notices his concern. "It's just an instinct, my dear. A place so beautiful and perfect can reveal many things about a person, even a Guardian."

"How can I reach her?" James asks.

"I wish I could help you," Eva says, "but only you can know this. Just trust your instincts, and let your magic guide you."

James then turns and slowly makes his way toward the tranquil blue waters. With every step, he feels the intensity of the crystal blue ocean's rhythm grow. It is as if the ocean has anticipated his arrival, and it yearns to envelop him. The sand between his toes feels warm and silky smooth. With each stride, the sand yields gently beneath his feet, with no pebbles or critters stirring in the unusual natural beach sand.

Finally, he reaches the edge of the water. Instantly, the ocean responds, surging forward to caress his bare ankles, delicately avoiding his trouser cuffs. The sensation is unlike anything he has ever felt before, and the ocean seems to pulse with joy. James's magic stirs within him, urging him to immerse himself further in the circle of clear water.

James comprehends why the dwarves removed their lower trousers. The ocean, being a gift from the goddess, is considered sacred and pristine. Any contamination of their garments would be unnatural and forbidden in the presence of the perfect Water element. James rolls up his trousers, inching them up to his knees, and the ocean responds like a living, sentient entity. It rises like a vine, wrapping around his legs, exploring his body with a sensation akin to an octopus climbing up his legs, delving deeply inside his pants. This touch feels intimate and intrusive, almost unusually erotic, as it delves into his muscles, meticulously mapping his form from head to toe.

He struggles to maintain control as the ocean inspects every inch of him, every muscle, every sinew. The sensation is overpowering, and James can no longer contain his magic. It surges forth like a boiling pot of soup, uncontrollable and chaotic. His thoughts seem centered on the ocean, but he can't quite grasp why. There is something about his name that intrigues him. The ocean is connected, somehow, to love, to the act of lovemaking, to the union between him and this eternal, exotic entity.

Suddenly, an overwhelming surge of energy overtakes him, and he feels a tight knot of desire stirring deep within him. It explodes out of him, and at the same time, he utters a name that feels unfamiliar yet significant: "NAECO!" James realizes it is "OCEAN" spelled backward. The ocean reacts violently, as if it has been forcibly invaded. It slaps James's face with a forceful and angry intensity, and he feels the ocean retreating, a shocked and wounded presence. Its power focuses on pulling away, like a whip lashing against James's skin.

The ocean withdraws from his body, along with his magic, and he is left gasping. James can feel the burning sensation on his skin, the aftermath of the ocean's furious departure. It seemed to invade him, examining every aspect of his being, only to be repelled when he uttered that enigmatic name. James stares out at the ocean, still unsure of what has transpired, but he knows that this encounter has forever changed him.

As the sea waves gracefully in the distance, a translucent figure emerges from the water, effortlessly walking on the fluid sea surface. The waves crash more aggressively against the sandy shore, and sea creatures of various sizes and unknown species leap from behind her, following the rhythm of her movement, causing the coastline to sway in harmonious splashing. The light blue sea shimmers in the bright sunlight, reflecting a vibrant rainbow of colors. Dolphins and whales join in behind her, leaping from the sea, celebrating the emergence of the Guardian's powerful presence. The Guardian of Water seamlessly blends with the waves as she gracefully walks toward the shore. The sun's radiant glare reflects off her form, creating a shimmering rainbow that dances around her. Gradually, she transforms into the appearance of a human elf, her hair flowing as white and wavy as the sea itself. Her enchanting beauty and fluid movements evoke the essence of the ocean as she walks along the beach in her nakedness.

But as her feet touch the sand, a subtle transformation takes place. Gracefully, clothing of silk materializes around her, draping her chest in elegant angles. Her hair forms a small crown adorned with pearls and diamonds.

James, observing from a distance, notices humanoid, fishlike creatures emerging from the sea, their eyes fixed on the Guardian. With a wave of her slender right hand, she commands them, and the warriors obediently return to the depths of the water. James, still entranced by the intense magic of the ocean, squints his eyes, struggling to regain focus. A faint lightheadedness washes over him as he observes a fluid silhouette approaching.

In an instant, oddly, he recognizes that the powerful Guardian of Water has finally revealed herself. As she stands before him, her form is solid yet liquid at the same time, beautifully shaped like that of a human. Actually, royal-blue-painted toenails connect seamlessly to the ocean behind her, as if a bond as strong as a tethered rope ties her to the sea. Small jewels adorn her arms and lengths of various types of sea-colored items that glitter in the sun, and these jewels go up her shoulders, perfectly matching her small crown.

Silently, James moves closer to her, his gaze fixed on her perfectly sculpted form. He kneels quickly before the powerful Guardian of Water, whose human-like legs grace the shore. He gazes upon the exquisite and ethereal being before him. She is stunningly beautiful, her fully human form displaying a subtle transparency. Sunlight gleams through her, casting a myriad of iridescent hues around her perimeter. Her long, now emerald-green hair sways gently in the breeze, reminiscent of the tranquil ocean's movements. Her lips are perfectly small, matching the color of her toenails, and they form a faint, enchanting smile. Her facial features are breathtaking, with cheekbones slightly higher than Eva's, revealing a gentle, stern, and immaculately beautiful countenance. James's heart races, not from fear or anticipation but from the sudden respect, love, and grace that radiate from her presence. Her transparent form glistens like ivory, adorned with small, sky-blue veins that point upward toward her small elven ears.

The rest kneel in reverent silence as the Guardian looks at them: Eva, Radion, and Ethan, along with the other party. They remain quietly still, not interfering. They kneel as the Guardian begins to look at each of them, starting with Eva, who oddly makes a small nod, perhaps a gesture of acknowledgment of the woman in the lead here.

"You may stand now, my beloved Olen," she says with a voice that echoes melodiously and smoothly, as if born from the voices of dolphins and whales. Every word resonates, creating an echo that sweetly lingers in the air.

James stands still, unsure if his attire is suitable for such an unpredictable encounter. The ocean shifts slightly behind her, and James suddenly spots dolphins and even whales leaping with joy. Now standing upright, he notices that she is slightly taller than him, and his face reflects his astonishment. He gasps as his eyes finally meet hers, both pairs wide and of the same deep sea-green hue.

"Uh," James stammers, struggling to find the right words for an introduction. Her beauty captivates him to his core. "My name is James Lander," he eventually manages to say.

"So, it is true, my Olen." Her voice echoes sweetly, ignoring James's introduction. She extends her hand toward his chest, nearly touching his clothing. A blue, glowing light forms between her fingers, flickering like a gentle flame. His own magic responds instantly in a warm sensation, but not threatening. Yet it remains under control, flowing naturally through his body like a gentle current. She lowers her hand, tilting her head with a somewhat puzzled and concerned expression.

Suddenly, James feels a surge of energy climbing up his spine, reaching toward his head. His own magic tries to intervene but is overwhelmed by the foreign energy. It feels like the Guardian is probing his mind, attempting to understand who he is. Moments later, the energy subsides.

Finally, she smiles. "My sisters and brothers won't be pleased," she remarks. With a graceful movement of her hand in a slight circle, she conjures a radiant, liquid-like throne chair before her. Seating herself, she crosses her naked legs in a ladylike fashion and then waves her left hand. In an instant, a one-legged table appears, holding a purplish, liquid-filled, elegant crystal glass. The chair appears exceedingly comfortable, and as she settles in, she lifts the glass to her lips, taking a sip of the mysterious substance.

The rainbow reflections that glitter off her body move with her, a sight James will never forget.

James now notices that the ocean has crept up around him, revealing all types of fish and creatures within it. None seem to take notice of him or dare even to touch him.

The Guardian waves her slender hand. As she does this, the watery appearance sways, and another crystal-like substance appears before James, floating in a spiraling motion like water, holding the glass in front of him. "Please take," she says, as the water starts to climb, creating a small table with a crystal-like wineglass filled with a yellow substance. She takes her crystal glass, which is obviously different from the one she's offering, and she stares at James, waiting.

With respect, he walks toward the small table that is now sprouting like a little water fountain, holding the crystal in place. He takes it, and he slowly drinks. He feels a vibrant sensation entering his whole body; weakness and tiredness vanish instantly. Every scar and scratch obtained through his adventures to get here is completely healed. He feels as if he has rested, becoming alert, with wide eyes. Feeling his strength return, he is rejuvenated, surrounded by the enchanting area. He is filled with hope and newfound vigor. The glass slowly disappears in his hand like water. He says, "Thank you," and the Guardian nods, withdrawing her hand.

Similar tables appear in front of the others. They hold the same substance. Even the dwarves, loyal companions on this journey, drink from the crystal glasses. Everyone shows their respect for the Guardian by taking a drink. However, Eva, with a graceful gesture, sips once and places the crystal back on the watery sprout, acknowledging the offered substance. The crystal disappears from their hands as they experience a surge of strength and healing. The scars vanish, and even the kneeling dwarves, still in the same position, are rejuvenated, with newfound strength coursing through their bodies.

James moves slightly forward toward the manufactured throne room.

"My beloved Olen," she says. "You may call me by my name, my beloved; you used to do that all the time, or should I say, your entity once did."

James does a bit of a double take; she keeps referring to him as "beloved," and he assumes it is some kind of connection with his ancestor Olen.

"NAECO, Guardian of Water, with all due respect, my name is not Olen; I am a descendant of his, the cursed carrier of the primed Destroyer."

The Guardian looks at him intently and speaks sternly. "You question me?" Her voice carries a weight of authority, but then her expression softens into a knowing smile. "Your ancestors did the same, always challenging me."

"What do you need from me, Your Grace?" James asks.

James waits in respectful silence, observing the Guardian as she appears lost in her thoughts. Her eyes shimmer like the sea, sparkling and flowing with grace. Her hair moves in a manner reminiscent of ocean currents, though no wind is present. Her face is flawless, with elven features, yet is somehow more majestic than the fairy he met in the caverns. She stands taller and exudes power, her gaze making James feel smaller in comparison. When she speaks, it is as though her words are a humming melody that resonates directly in his mind, as if she is addressing only him.

Finally, she responds, "I'm not sure, my beloved."

James feels a sense of perplexity and asks, "Do you need me to stop the darkness or the Dark Guardians?"

The Guardian's response is measured. "Is that what you think, my beloved? Do you assume it was my cousins, the takers of life, who caused all this? Don't be quick to judge based on appearances. What you see may not necessarily reflect the true essence of things. My cousins played a role in assisting your ancestors to restore balance. Your species often rushes to label the dark as evil and the light as good. We, the Guardians, are tasked with maintaining balance, nothing more, and love, with all its complexities, can tilt the scales in either direction in our realm of both light and darkness. It was the Dark Guardians who attempted to restore the equilibrium."

Her gaze shifts toward the mountain, a sudden sadness overtaking her. She now stares at the kneeling dwarves, their heads bowed in utmost respect for the presence of the Guardian. "My sister tried desperately to change what was preordained, her doing. It was in her nature, and she sought our assistance. She discovered a way to intertwine small fragments of our souls, the givers of life, in the hope that it would restore balance. However, it backfired terribly. My beloved," she says, her voice full of sorrow, "your ancestors' goodness and beauty were consumed by the greed for love."

A solitary tear, unlike anything James has ever seen, trickles down her cheek as she looks at the group of dwarves. The tear resembles a crystalline rainbow and falls to the floor, solidifying into a gemlike structure. Yet she says nothing.

With regained focus, the Guardian turns back to James. "I need you to retrieve my soul," she says abruptly, catching him off guard with the urgency in her tone. "I need you to find it and return it to me."

James is genuinely confused. "I don't understand. I don't have your soul."

The Guardian's expression grows stern. "I will guide you to it. My soul is nearby, but you must be willing to return it to me."

James hesitates but then asks, with humility, "Can't you use your powers to retrieve it?"

In an unexpected turn, the sea surges, a colossal wave rising as though propelled by a mighty force. It crashes behind the Guardian, causing a tumultuous commotion before settling. James realizes he has crossed a line by questioning the powerful Guardian's abilities.

"That is your task," she declares firmly. "I know you possess other means to work with my soul. Once you obtain it, return here, and we will discuss your next journey and how to recover the other souls for my siblings. My sisters and brothers will be eager to see you. But my elder sister, Eartha, is not present here and has no desire to meet you. To reach her, you'll need magic from another realm. That, my Olen, is something you must discover on your own."

"I'm sorry, Your Grace. I was out of line. Please forgive me. I will do as you ask. I will find your soul and bring it to you as you wish."

The Guardian simply looks at him, taking her wineglass once more without moving her head, and then smiles. After taking a small sip of her wine, she smiles again and places the glass back on the watery formation table she created. It dissolves back into the silvery oceanic floor, and she stands up, causing everything she conjured to dissolve in a similar fashion.

"Of course, I forgive you. Surface beings don't understand the beauty of the elemental forces above them. Many surface dwellers can't appreciate the true essence of these elements. For them, these forces exist only to be exploited," the Guardian remarks.

She then moves gracefully toward James, her hair swaying beautifully as it catches the sun's glow. A scent of sweet pine and flowers seems to emanate from her body, an intoxicating and sensuous fragrance that James has never encountered anywhere before.

She places her hand on his unshaved beard. James can feel the electrifying softness of her hands, silky and moist, an experience he has never felt before, something incredibly beautiful.

"So," she says, her fingers gently brushing his beard as she smiles, "you need the sword to hold my soul and the souls of my sisters and brothers. This sword was crafted centuries ago by the skilled dwarves of the kingdom that brought you here. It is the one tool that will harness the precious souls of our entities,

entities that can aid and alter the forces of the dark entities of life. But why should I help you with such power, a power that already grows within you? A power that was misunderstood and abused by my beloved, who is no longer here to accompany me."

James simply stares at her; her face is so breathtaking that he almost can't hear her melodious voice. He can't help but wonder how anyone could resist such beauty. He can only surmise that this Guardian had been deeply loved by his great ancestor, Olen. He decides to keep this thought to himself for now; he has to provide an answer to this Guardian.

"Your Grace, I am an individual who cherishes the entities of our world, the entities that give us life and death. They are precious to me, and I believe in giving back rather than constantly taking away. Before I became aware of my ancestral background, I was a farmer, and my culture taught me to give back to life, whether it's a small mammal or the streams that flow into the sea. I hold life's existence above all else. I may not fully understand my task, a task and magic born within me that suddenly emerged through my bloodline. But I assure you, I will accept my destiny, whether I like it or not, learn from any mistakes my bloodline has made, and I will take all that I hope to accomplish to create a better world for all beings, both surface and non-surface."

The Guardian stares quietly at James, her fingers gently leaving his face. Contentment seems to wash over him as if he were being comforted like a newborn child. The Guardian smiles, her face radiating purity and innocence, nearly bringing tears of happiness to James's eyes.

"Spoken like a true king. Your blood is strong, and the magic that lies within you, my partial magic, is growing stronger. Be careful, my young king, for my beloved once had the same determination but was quickly seduced by the sweetness of unfamiliar and alien magic that he once possessed. However, I foresee a different outcome for you, Olen the successor. The magic is born into you, and it is very different from that of your ancestors. This has never happened in my entire existence, a unique and fascinating fusion of our souls merging with yours. Perhaps your destiny could indeed be fulfilled. But beware, my young king, and never underestimate your magic or the entities that made it possible for you."

Feeling satisfied, the Guardian waves her hand, and a massive wave emerges from behind her. It crashes down before hitting the beach, growing larger and more imposing by the second. It hovers menacingly over their heads, appearing as if it were made of glistening, steel-like waves, eager to snap at them. But it passes over them without touching, creating a cushion of air beneath James's entire party. The wave lifts them up like a blanket and, with one swift motion, gently lowers them toward the waiting Guardian. Just as quickly as it appeared, the wave vanishes, leaving them standing beside the graceful Guardian, completely dry.

James and his party are left stunned by the enormous wave and the powerful entity that conjured it. It is so overwhelming that even Ethan passes out before the wave subsides.

"So, who have you brought for your journey, young king?" the Guardian inquires, waking up the shaken dwarves, who are kneeling awkwardly.

"Ahh, I brought my stepmother and...," James begins but then clears his throat, still somewhat shocked by the recent episode. "Sorry, Your Grace," he continues, walking closer to the Guardian. "Allow me to introduce you. These are the Mountain Dwarves, led by Prince Kedar and his sister, Princess Ulteal, who have chosen to accompany us on our quest. This is Radion, and Eva, the magic bearers. The one on the floor is my closest friend, Ethan, and these are the Malij."

The Guardian smiles warmly at the dwarves and gestures for the dwarf princess and prince to stand. They simply bow without making eye contact with the Guardian. She gently touches their faces as they both stand firm, not flinching.

"Ah, the loyal protectors of all Guardians, including those of the witchery clan in the powerful realm, well respected throughout these lands," the Guardian remarks. "I'm surprised you accepted this particular task, considering your kind usually guards your precious nests. My sister Eartha would not be pleased, I'm sure. My other siblings wouldn't care. But I am intrigued by your sudden actions." She pauses, her gaze fixed on the wide-eyed dwarves. The dwarves do not move or blink; their eyes remain focused and sincere, a display of respect and an unusual change that James hasn't witnessed in Kedar before.

"My regards to both of you and your noble clan," she says gently and continues to stare deeply into his eyes, as if reading his thoughts. "He is loyal and trustworthy, my dwarf friends, but I know it takes more than just words to forgive the forsaken tragedy that once befell your beloved people." She withdraws her hand from the dwarf.

The Guardian then kneels down to meet the dwarves eye to eye, touching each of them with grace and sadness. It seems as if she is communicating with them telepathically. They all nod in gratitude and quickly bow down. The Guardian waves her hand, and the teardrop-like diamonds she created earlier float toward her and the dwarves. The Guardian lifts the two tears, which have now transformed into larger forms, to the size of her palms, and hands them to the prince and princess. The two dwarf royals accept the Guardian's gifts with grace and humility, holding the diamond-like tears against their chests as if cradling a precious child.

The Guardian finally stands up and says, "Let it be known that in your home, the heartfelt sadness of my tears shall be placed at your entrance. Your home shall no longer be abandoned; it will be filled with joy. Gather all the remains of those who perished because of my actions by the sea. The Destroyer shall seek a way to reverse the curse that was upon your deed. For now, I will take all those who suffered and perished to my realm so they may rest in peace. Their souls shall come to protect your home from my elements once you place my tears at the entrance by the sea. Their souls will return whenever a threat to your realm arises."

"Yes, Your Grace," Kedar finally manages to say, clearing his voice. "We will do as you have asked. Thank you for your beautiful gifts and blessings, and for allowing the souls of those who suffered and perished to be a part of such a momentous acceptance into your realm. We never asked for your forgiveness, as we all understand that Your Grace had no ill intentions. It is a great honor for our clan to be part of this majestic alliance with your realm."

She smiles and nods her head slightly to both the princess and prince.

CHAPTER 29

Purpose

THE GUARDIAN OF Water approaches Radion and Eva with deliberate steps, moving gracefully away from the waves until she stands directly before them. Her gaze fixes upon Eva, not with a glare but with an intent, as though she's trying to read her mind. Several moments pass in silence before the Guardian offers a faint smile and a nod in Eva's direction, without speaking a single word. Then she turns to face Radion.

"Where is Socrater, the magic taker? I thought he would be the first in line to accompany young King Olen," NAECO says.

Radion, still bowed, looks up. "Gracious Guardian of Water, the ancient legacy of Socrater no longer walks upon your sister's ground. He passed away over three hundred years ago, a misfortune for his followers, although it was said he lived to be 176 years old."

"Has it been that long? It seems like only yesterday that I was standing in the same spot with his followers, guiding them on their journey with my—"

"Yes, but I will not be looking after him, as my role is to assist Sorceress Eva. My task will be simply to confront any obstacles that may interfere with our mission," Radion says.

"Good." The Guardian feels satisfied and uplifted. "A female species of your kind will be better suited. Especially one who can guide those who do not truly understand the essence of self-being. I wasn't satisfied with Socrater's decision when he decided to take the task upon himself. Maybe if a woman had taken on such a task, you would not be standing here with his heir to the Olen throne, taking on the task again. Nevertheless, I presume the cycle must have taken place for a greater purpose yet to be foretold. You and your followers have my blessing,

Radion, Summoner of King James Olen." She nods in agreement with Radion and then walks past Eva, inspecting each individual as if she is examining them, before finally looking down at the skinny Ethan.

Ethan stands up, regaining his bearings, and simply stares at the Guardian before him. He can't help but admire her beauty and her perfect breasts.

Suddenly, waves rush past their party like flying knives hurled from a distance. In an instant, the Guardian's arms, resembling a whip made of water, wrap around Ethan's neck and lift him at least five feet high, choking him. Ethan's eyes widen, his face turning red as he struggles to grasp his neck and gasp for air. Immediately, James and the Malij leap forward to aid Ethan but are abruptly blocked by what appears out of nowhere—leathery-looking shackles that snap if they attempt to get closer. Eva instinctively grips James to shield him while Radion signals the Malij to stand down. The dwarves remain transfixed and mesmerized in the distance, frozen and unmoving, witnessing the Guardian's wrath and wishing for the situation to de-escalate.

"You disrespected my statue! How dare you, creature of the surface!" The waves crash wildly, their fury evident. The sea roars, rising ominously and threatening everything in its path. Dark clouds gather rapidly, merging with the sea's tempestuous rage. The once-graceful and rainbow-hued Guardian has transformed into something unknown, murky, and foreboding. Her elegant presence dissolves into a swirling maelstrom of chaotic energy.

The sands beneath their feet respond to this ominous transformation, mingling with the Guardian's essence. It is as if the very earth trembles in her anger. The sea, once calm and serene, becomes a relentless force of nature, resembling a monstrous typhoon. Towering waves loom menacingly, ready to engulf the Guardian and the entire party.

As the Guardian's wrath manifests, creatures of the deep, normally concealed in the ocean's depths, answer her call. Deadly sharks, their jaws bristling with razor-sharp teeth, and other enigmatic sea creatures surge forth from the churning waters, drawn by the Guardian's fury. They circle around her, ready to defend and aid in the destruction of anything that threatens her.

James, usually unshakable in the face of adversity, is now overwhelmed by sheer terror. He feels crippled, unable to stand against the overwhelming power and wrath of the Guardian and the elemental forces she has unleashed. Sinking to his knees in submission to the raw power of the sea, he watches in awe and fear as the world around them transforms into a realm of darkness and chaos, uncertain of what comes next.

He can't understand why the Guardian is accusing Ethan of something he hasn't done. All he did was look upon a beautiful woman, a normal act—even he couldn't resist her beauty. Then something occurs to James; it was back home in Lepersteed, in the town garden. The Guardian must have read Ethan's thoughts and remembered when he taunted the Guardian's statue, playing a joke and acting like his usual self. The Guardian took this offense seriously, and now she's about to kill him, with no one daring to help his best friend except for the sinister Malij. James thinks quickly.

"You Grace," he finally manages to yell, barely breathing and gasping for air. "Please, do not take his life! He is not worthy of your effort. He is my servant, a loyal companion, you may call it, who follows my lead and listens to my direction. He did not know that your precious statues would have any link to your existence. I plead with you, please, release your power. I will do anything for you." James thinks quickly, wondering if he has said the right thing.

Suddenly, the Guardian releases Ethan, and the waves, along with the ominous-looking black shackles, recede into the water. The creatures and the surroundings return to their normal state, with the Guardian slowly reverting to her graceful appearance. Ethan falls to the ground, gasping and coughing for air.

Immediately, the Guardian of Water lifts him up again with the simple aid of the water surrounding him. The water cradles him closely to the Guardian, and they lock eyes. Ethan looks frail and weak in the presence of such beauty and grace as the Guardian lifts him with her water command. Suddenly, Ethan nods his head in acknowledgment. A conversation unfolds between the two, and abruptly, the water subsides, dropping Ethan to the floor again. He scrambles quickly to bow repeatedly, heading toward the dwarves, who are kneeling. The dwarves do not object since they are in agreement with the Guardian's wishes, whatever she may have communicated to him.

James gasps, unsure of what transpired in the mental conversation between the Guardian and Ethan. He is relieved that his best friend was not killed on the spot by the fearsome water creature. He simply takes a step back as the Guardian watches him intently, the hurricane-like water subsiding behind her, and her silken water drapery gracefully returning her attention to analyzing the entire group. James is ecstatic that his friend has survived yet another day.

The Guardian then approaches Eva. Oddly, they stare at each other for a few moments, neither uttering a single word. Only Eva bows in respect as she examines the Guardian from head to toe. Once again, a silent understanding passes between the two women. They share a similar aura of regal highness and beauty, their features exuding grace. The overpowering presence of water generates ripples and motion that seem to emanate from the Guardian as she gazes at Eva. Viewing them side by side, one would see power and goddess-like beauty in one, and the other a queen.

Finally, Eva nods her head, and the Guardian steps away. The water that looks silky, with gentle ripples, flows between the sand, glinting like a never-ending veil that gracefully envelops her.

The Guardian walks away, manipulating the water with a wave of her hand. From a distance, a huge fish swims toward them and leaps into the shallows. Strapped to the fish are sea creatures, each a captivating blend of human and fishlike qualities. Their scales are thick and shimmering, with a mesmerizing blend of golden and silvery hues, rippling like muscles beneath the water's sheen. They are both strong and powerful-looking, and James can't distinguish whether they are male or female. Each has a unique characteristic that sets them apart: one with long, flowing hair, and the other with intricate patterns etched into their scales.

Their upper bodies are nearly humanlike, boasting well-defined and armored torsos. The transition from fishlike tails to human torsos is seamless, with scaly skin that adds an otherworldly charm. These beings exude a powerful and enchanting aura as they gracefully present the wrapped item to the Guardian. James can't help but notice the unusual weapons they carry. They appear to be crafted from a combination of sea materials and metals he has never seen before, a testament to their remarkable craftsmanship. With a quick bow, they retreat into the ocean, disappearing into the rolling waves. A few moments later, James watches in awe as an enormous blue fish leaps out of the water, and the fishlike creatures join it, both vanishing on the horizon where the sun is about to set.

James finds the Guardian of Water right next to him, not showing his amazement at the beautiful fish creature that has just appeared.

"They are called merfolk, not mermaids, as you may know them on the surface," the Guardian explains. "They are my personal servants in the fortress city of Necoksertm. Don't worry, my known king." She smiles gracefully, warming James's heart. "We will learn together because I know you are eager with questions."

Then she brings forth a wet-wrapped, silk-lined sheath the color of the deep blue ocean, and slowly unwraps what appears to be a silvery, thin sword. The blade gleams brightly as the sun's light caresses its long edge, emitting a faint, melodious hum as the Guardian solemnly hands it to James.

"I present to you the gracious Sword of Olen, the Vertmor, a creation of my fairy folk, given to me by the merfolk," she says, adding an extra layer of significance to the weapon. "Will you accept the task set forth in your bloodline and carry out its pledge for the journey and the stories yet to be told, King James Olen, successor of the ancient King Nathen Olen, and bring back my soul?"

James is shaken as he stares down at the beautiful handcrafted blade. It feels so light that he can actually lift the sword with one finger. The craftsmanship is unlike anything he has ever seen. The handle seems to be oval and open, revealing what appears to be four empty silk pockets. The carvings are intricate, depicting the four elements of the Guardian—Water, Earth, Fire, and Air—outlined in diamonds. They resemble the markings he saw on the dwarf throne's door. The entire handle features various creatures, including a fairy, a unicorn, and the sun, all coming together in a triangular shape, forming the image of the moon. The silvery blade appears to be made of some platinum-like material, with outlines of fire and water running down from the blade, touching an oversize tree, with the swirl of air illuminating the leaves and creating what seems to be a tornado. This sword feels more like a treasured artifact than an ancient killing weapon, a fact James has learned from legends.

James turns the blade around and examines the other side, which is simpler and plainer. However, the color seems to shift from silvery to gray, catching James's attention. He holds the sword by its cross handle, and the tip conceals a ruby diamond that sparkles. He looks up at the Guardian, who watches him patiently as he observes the exquisite craftsmanship of the sword.

He doesn't know how to answer her. Twice he has felt like she has tricked him—first in his dreams, by seducing him, and then by telling him he must join her in her city after the task. He thinks carefully about how to respond but isn't sure. The task, which he has yet to understand or predict, remains shrouded in mystery. All he knows is that he had to come here to speak to this Guardian, and now she is giving him a task he can't fathom.

James recalls a previous conversation with Radion and Eva where they emphasized the need to restore balance to the world, although he remains uncertain about what that entails. Eva and Radion emphasized that the world is undergoing changes and needs to be brought back into balance. This task was attempted by James's great ancestor but ultimately failed due to the greed or love from Olen, as the Guardian's souls were overtaken by the magic of a sword, preventing the restoration of balance. To James, it seems that the task was never truly accomplished, and he suspects that the magic recognized this failure, transferring the responsibility to him. This new responsibility may involve a greater task that he is not yet aware of. James also considers the possibility that the Guardian he's encountered is probing his mind, expecting answers or insights from him regarding this newfound role and the mission ahead.

James pauses and then thinks of something.

"If you reveal the whereabouts of your previous orb and show me how to control it while I visit your kingdom, I will accept your whichever task, even the ones you provided in my dreams," James says.

The Guardian smirks and, for some reason, looks at Eva and then back to James, chuckling. "Interesting," she replies. "But be wary, young king, that you can't always have your requests granted just because of your charm. I'll accept the bargain I've already set. Ensure that you come here, alone, once the task of obtaining my orb is completed. I'll inform you of the next task and provide the necessary training."

She moves away toward the sea, and as she turns to James, nodding, an enchanting transformation unfolds. As the Guardian approaches the sea, the ocean seems to respond to her presence. The sand behind her starts to revert back to its normal state, its surface smoothing out as she touches the sea with her slender bare foot. She glimmers and begins to emanate an illusion that blends her with the sea. The ocean opens, and a large wave approaches them. The wave swells and roars, but it seems to recognize the Guardian, cradling her gently as she becomes one with the sea.

Her form dissolves into the water, and for a brief moment, it appears as if the ocean itself has embraced her. She becomes a part of the sea, her presence and essence merging with the vast, undulating expanse of water. The waves continue to crash around them, but the Guardian's connection with the ocean is unmistakable, and the sea acknowledges her with a tranquil, rhythmic dance.

The entire party, including James, watches in awe as the Guardian's transformation continues. The sea and her body become one, an ethereal and surreal spectacle, a testament to the ancient magic she possesses. The ocean seems to accept her, and she becomes a living embodiment of the power of the element of Water. Suddenly, she disappears with a large splash, causing the waves to ripple wildly. The ground beneath James shifts from sandy beach to rugged old pebbles, and the glowing writings on the walls vanish, revealing a dingy, seaweed-covered cave. The salty sea air rushes in, and James can smell the deep, briny ocean, as if he were back home fishing.

The entire party lets out a collective sigh of relief. The dwarves, who have been kneeling since they entered the chamber, finally stand up and begin searching for their trousers. Ethan leaps in front of James, asking if he is okay, while the dwarves hover around each other, observing the artifact placed on top of the cave's entrance. Eva pulls out her pan and cooking utensils, preparing another evening meal as the sun begins to set.

"Okay, you okay, boy?" Radion says.

"Did you and Eva know about her soul and her plans for me to obtain it?" James asks with concern.

"The Guardians never like to interfere with the surface world, although occasionally they must intervene to accomplish a goal known only to them. I'll tell you one thing, boy, she is a fair and loving Guardian. History tells us that she adores the surface creatures and is very fond of humans."

"Did you know she had an affair with King Olen?" James asks.

"There are no definitive written indications about the personal relationship between the Guardian of Water and the Destroyer. However, rumors have swirled for centuries suggesting that the Olen monarchy visited this particular area, and the allure of any Guardian can be captivating. Why do you ask? Did you suspect any specific behavior?" Radion asks curiously.

"No," James lies. "I was just wondering." James starts to think of the dreams he has had of the Guardian. They were vivid and intricate; sometimes he found himself falling over the translucent Guardian. In other dreams, he realized it was another person inside of him, who he believed to be King Olen's spirit dwelling deep in his heart. Nevertheless, his feelings were unusually strong in the Guardian's presence, a connection he can't explain. He decides not to share his experience with his party.

"Are you alright?" Ethan says while fingering his neck that is now bruised from the Guardian's wrath as he joins the group. The dwarves are now gathering themselves and quickly join Ethan. James notices that they are actually unusually calm after their encounter with the Guardian of Water. The two remaining guards stand side by side next to Ethan, as if preparing to attack, but their hard gaze is on James, not Ethan. He is taken aback. Eva's warriors are also standing beside her, seemingly transfixed, as if a new revelation was revealed to them, empowered by the Guardian's offering, ready to take on anything, but more protective of Eva than themselves.

"I told you not to touch her," James finally says as his friend stares at him strangely.

"Well, I didn't know that the statue is linked to the Guardian," Ethan says.

"It wasn't," James says. "She read your filthy mind while you were staring at her body. You probably were comparing her to the statue back home." Now James looks at Radion. "How come you never told me she would invade our minds?" he asks.

"James, you have to remember, she is the powerful Guardian of Water. Besides controlling the elemental nature and all those that benefit from its resources, her element represents purity and solidarity. In nature, she seeks and provides purity in any living being through her own natural ways. For example, she instinctively seeks the pure essence of a person's mind—the truth. She is the Guardian of this element and can nullify our magical essence of Water. Even the guidance of any other magic, she is too powerful to control. Remember, she is in a class of a goddess. As far as I know, only an ancient fairy from her line can overturn her power, although some rumors suggested that one ancient wizard, Socrater, was a powerful match in magic for all the Guardians."

James continues to observe the dwarves as they hover over Ethan. His best friend appears rejuvenated and repurposed, embodying a newfound energy that James finds unfamiliar.

Kedar presses forward, surpassing his sister and warriors to stand in front of James. The prince of the Dwarf Mountain, alongside Ethan, now stands before him. James peers into Kedar's bruised eye, taking note of the prince's five-foot stature, which belies his massive, muscular body. Despite his shorter height, Kedar's powerful structure rivals that of the other warriors.

"I'm truly sorry for what happened to your clan. I had no idea," James manages to say to the prince and princess.

"I know. I still stand by what I felt when we first met. I understand it was not your doing. But there will be others who want to see you dead, or those who do not believe. My kingdom does not trust humans."

"Is that what your sister was going to do, kill me?" James asks.

"Maybe, or she just simply wants to have a battle with you to ease her pain. I don't know. I don't speak for my sister."

Kedar stays silent, glancing at Ethan and exchanging a quick, incomprehensible interaction with him. "We are leaving now. And Ethan will be staying with us," Kedar declares.

"What! Why? What's going on?" James exclaims.

Ethan interjects, and strangely, the dwarf warriors once again advance, watching either him or James, the uncertainty lingering. Ethan says, "Hey, buddy, it's okay. It's a directive and order from the Guardian herself. I am tasked with aiding the dwarf kingdom in seeking a new haven where the destruction occurred and gathering the dead for the Guardian."

James stares at Kedar, who cradles a beautiful diamond covered slightly with clothing, treating it delicately, like a child. The diamond, a symbol of some promise according to the Guardian, meant that the atrocities of his ancestors would never happen to the dwarf kingdom again.

The Guardian had handed the diamond tear-looking stones to Kedar and Ulteal, which glittered warmly. She explained that it would serve as a promise, a protection against the recurrence of such events, bestowed upon the dwarf clan and families. They were tasked with gathering all that lay in ruins and bringing them to her, to the sea, to join her fortress, a ritual of sorts. Now Ethan was entwined in this task, perhaps a penance for disrespecting the Guardian's essence.

"So, you're saying what you witness here will help you rebuild or that what I have done will be over?" asks James.

"I don't know. What I feel I need to do now is rebuild, starting with caring for our dead first. These are the wishes of our Guardian," Ethan explains.

"I don't understand, Ethan. You are just going to leave us? Or what?"

"I don't understand it either. All I know is that the Guardian put this task on me and directed the dwarves to meet me through. I am their key to access the lost haven that we sealed during the Destruction."

James stares at his best friend, aching for the first time as sadness overcomes him. The Guardian's wishes or any thoughts of punishment for disrespecting her crosses his mind. His friend, with whom he shared everyday routines on the farmland, is now being sent off on his own. It feels as though a piece of his life is being torn away, but he has no choice but to accept it.

Finally, Kedar joins the conversation after seeing James distressed.

"We need Ethan. He's our only means of expanding our search for other, smaller cities. He can feel hidden passages. There are only two others in our city, but they're old and frail. Ethan is a descendant of our kin; the gracious Guardian of Water made it clear to us. He will be our means to fulfill our obligation that the Guardian is seeking. Ethan is the key. He needs to come with us. He needs to help us open up all the passages so we can continue to seek our dead, put them to rest, and rebuild."

"But you just said that you don't like humans either. Will he be killed there? I won't allow that."

"He will be fine. He is half dwarf."

"There's no way of telling. Look at him. He doesn't even look anything like you guys."

Eva interjects, "James, he definitely has dwarf in him. No other race or species could do what he does. Ethan has the capability to make keys and open up pathways with the stones. It seems to me that his father was a dwarf."

"But I have to tell you, he will be killed. Your kingdom will kill him if he doesn't look like you guys," James protests.

Ulteal steps forward and smacks Ethan lightly on his shoulder. Ulteal, the princess of the dwarf kingdom, hovering only four inches, looks up to Ethan with a gleaming smile of pride and soothing assurance that James can't figure out. She says, "I will protect him. No one would dare hurt him in any way." She looks up at him slightly and smirks.

Ethan simply stares at the group, not knowing what to say. Finally, he says, "Hey, buddy, I have a strange feeling that Kedar is right. Something is telling me it will be fine. I don't know why, but it's a good feeling, a gut feeling. Also, I want to know more about the dwarf community. After all, if it's true and my father is half dwarf, I would like to know who he is or who he was. I want to have a better understanding of who I am. It could be a great opportunity for me to understand these prophecies and help you further in your quest."

Kedar looks at James, staring at him deeply, and says, "I know you will return after I have your friend. We still need to seek a cure for our kingdom."

James looks at him hard. "You're keeping him hostage," he says to Kedar sarcastically.

"We'll catch up later. I will join you later on your journey to find a cure for my people."

"It's still a hostage. You're taking him not of his own will."

Kedar looks at James and says, "I don't think so. The Guardian wishes it. Besides, I guess you can call it reassurance of your return."

James looks over at Ethan, who seems not stressed at all. Something is definitely going on between those two since the Guardian of Water was prominently in their presence. He isn't sure but decides not to push the issue. He needs to move on and get this task he has to do for the Guardian as well. It seems the Guardian has her own way of manipulating the situation that seems to benefit her. Ethan as a hostage while he obtains the Guardian of Water's soul and brings it back to her. Then follows another task, and he has no idea what it's all about. He isn't even sure why any of them are even here. Eva, tagging along and acting strangely. Radion watching his moves, and even the Malij assassins, why they are tagging along too. He has so many more questions than answers.

"Okay, fine," he says distantly, and shakes his best friend's hand. His grip is tighter than usual as he pulls his friend close, and in that embrace, they find solace. Time seems to stretch as they cling to each other, the weight of the impending journey settling between them. Quietly, he whispers into his dear friend's ear, his words carrying the weight of a promise, "I will be back, buddy, and once this is all over, we will go back to our home."

Ethan finally pulls his friend back, the nod between them sealing an unspoken pact. But as they lock eyes, a subtle unease lingers beneath the surface. In the depths of his friend's gaze, Ethan can sense a haunting uncertainty, a silent acknowledgment that the place they once knew might be forever altered, if not lost entirely.

At that moment, James notices a monumental spectacle unfolding in the distance. A massive procession meanders along the shoreline, silhouetted against the dying embers of the day. Are they tribal beings or a mirage painted by the whims of the sea breeze? Unusual and furry, the figures move with an otherworldly grace.

James stares with a mix of awe and curiosity. "It seems the Guardians have sent their guides to us."

They all pause, the world around them seemingly holding its breath. The enigmatic procession continues, a trail of creatures accompanying them in a strangely orderly formation. Furry beings, their features obscured in the fading light, walk alongside various cats in a surreal spectacle.

CHAPTER 30

The Plans

NOW, FAR TO the west of the Atlantea Ocean where the events involving the Guardian of Water unfolded by the eastern shores, Celestia's fingers trace the smooth oval surface of the Argus stone, feeling its cool, unyielding texture. As she does, a subtle warmth emanates from the heirloom, as though it recognizes her touch. The red stone conforms to her grip, resonating with the soul energy passed down through generations. Her stone is not in the same fashion as her cousins'; they are unique in their own way. Their stones aid in finding loved ones when they are lost. Celestia's stone shares similar properties, but it protects; it's an ancestral stone.

There's no record of how the stone was first created; it's simply known by all born into the Argus line. This energy is not merely an ancestral link; it carries unique magical elements of protection—safeguarding all magical elements assigned to the bearer. Celestia learned that by keeping her extended family close, the stone not only protects her but also her family. Its unique power symbolizes the leadership of her lineage—a birthright of extraordinary essence encapsulating her family's ancient soul, passed down when the eldest Argus passes.

This knowledge is preserved in their ancient library, a piece of their love handed down to the next holder. No one knows how or why, but the stone is now hers. Lost in thought, she continues to run her fingers over the precious stone, her mind dwelling on her father's legacy. The Argus stone, a prized possession of her family, is more than just a decorative gem; it holds the essence of her ancestors. Each generation contributes a piece of their soul to the stone, forming a protective bond with the current bearer.

Beyond the stone, Celestia and her cousins now shoulder the responsibility of leading the human kingdom, a role they had never assumed before. However, this duty became imperative after the destruction of King Olen's kingdom—a crucial charge for safeguarding the human race. The interconnectedness of her family, fortified by the Argus stone, their uniquely born magical elements, and the bonds with extended kin, forms a formidable force—an embodiment of the culmination of their ancient soul magic in the face of adversity.

She has learned the importance of proximity and connection. She glances around and sees her cousin, Aberra, standing nearby. Without hesitation, she reaches out, and their hands intertwine in magic. She now realizes the energy of the Argus stone seems to amplify, and the collective strength of their family pulses through their intertwined hands. Celestia finds herself immersed in deep contemplation, memories of her parents blending with the present reality. The touch of the Argus stone serves as a powerful reminder of her roots and the shared strength derived from generations of familial bonds and protection.

As they settle in, preparing for the challenging journey ahead, Celestia's gaze lingers on the remnants of her once-beloved kingdom of Selcarth—a realm erected after the destruction of Olen. From a far distance, she can see and smell the harsh smoke, a grim reminder of the fires that have engulfed the castle she once called home. Strange batlike creatures fly and circle the castle, casting an eerie shadow over the land. Above all this, a dark cloud hovers over the kingdom, a dense shroud that floats in a specific location, unmoving and ominous, like a drape of despair over the heart of the fallen realm.

Celestia finds herself lost in contemplation; her thoughts are consumed by memories of her parents again. A gentle touch on her shoulders brings her back to the present, and she turns to discover Jarin offering her a piece of freshly baked loaf. The aroma fills her senses, and her stomach rumbles in response. Jarin, along with Aberra and Sakeris, have come to her aid, while the other members of the family remain behind to prepare for their arrival and salvage what's left of her kingdom.

She hesitates, pushing the food away, and utters, "Give that to the people; they need it more than I do."

Aberra joins in, insisting, "A princess must take care of herself to look after her people. Please, Celestia, take it. There's plenty for everyone."

Taking the lead, Celestia accepts the offer. The realization of her hunger strikes, and as her cousins stand by patiently, she begins to eat. The day wears a gloomy facade, and nightfall approaches. Sky knights attend to her people, offering comfort and preparing them for the arduous journey back to Argus Island. The animals, too, sense the impending change and make their own preparations.

"We should investigate who this Destroyer is." Aberra speaks up as Celestia completes her bread and food, her cousins waiting patiently to eat.

Celestia agrees, "Yes, we should." Finishing her bread, she casts a sorrowful glance over her people. The weight of the situation overwhelms her, and tears well up in her eyes.

Her cousins gather around, offering solace and reassurance. "Don't worry; things will get better," they whisper.

Amidst the emotional embrace, Celestia expresses her regret. "I just wish I had been here sooner. I had no idea the kingdom was in danger."

Jarin chimes in, "That's why we didn't engage. Dad was right; we had to let you go to confront this terror. But I prefer that Dad should have told us. I hate that his magic does this. I know it's for the sake of the family, and his intentions are always for the greater good, but damn, Dad, I wish he could have provided some clue."

"Let it be, Jarin," his sister comforts him, placing her shoulder on him. They are identical, sharing the same hint of extreme similarity in features—a trait similar to Celestia, who smiles at them.

Celestia sighs, acknowledging the complexity of the situation. "Uncle always knows," she murmurs.

As they console Celestia, she suggests, "I agree; we need to find out more about the Destroyer. Have you heard anything beyond what I told you?" There are more rumors circulating among the animals.

Jarin interjects, "I think it's more than that. My sources tell me he's at the Guardian of Water's lair."

Aberra, intrigued, asks, "Really?"

Jarin confirms, "Yes."

Celestia's eyes widen with realization. "He's after the Guardians' orbs again, as it was foretold. There's so much history tied to those orbs. We cannot let him obtain the others," she declares. The group falls into a momentary silence, contemplating the challenges that lie ahead, their collective focus on the preparations unfolding before them.

Celestia finally speaks, directing her words to Aberra and Jarin. "Both of you should go; take Sakeris with you. The three of you need to witness this Destroyer and gather more information. I'm going to accompany my people and guide them back to the island; the Sky Knights will stay with me and provide assistance, along with the bears. Once everything is settled, I plan to visit the triplets."

Sakeris, who has been assisting a small family nearby, pops his head up like an excited child and exclaims, "Are you talking about the three evil witches?" His expression shifts to fear. "Those wicked-looking creatures? I've heard so many rumors about them. Supposedly, they carry around a single eye and switch out people's eyes to see through their vision," he says.

"And I heard they eat the eyes too," Aberra joins in.

"Yes, and they eat you too," Sakeris says in fear.

"Yeah, I heard that too!" Jarin teases, playfully punching Sakeris on the shoulder. "Don't be silly; those are stupid rumors. Don't listen to my sister." The three of them chuckle lightly at Sakeris, who feels a bit embarrassed. Aberra gently pats him on the shoulder, offering reassurance.

"Of course, the triplet witches and their mothers are not evil," Aberra interjects. "Actually, they are a beautiful family; they are one of our closest friends, going back centuries. We have a long history with one of the brothers. They are not evil, nor are they ugly. The young ones are, in fact, powerful dark element wielders, very similar to our family, element of light born."

Celestia comforts him, saying, "Don't worry, sometimes stories can be misleading. It's not your fault. There's misinformation about the simultaneous riddle of the Hawthorne family. The family is always in three parts—the sisters and their partners. One had triplets, our closest friends."

Then she changes the conversation.

"I am going to visit with them again. Emma owes me a favor. They could help me understand what happened to my kingdom, and perhaps guide us to the next steps to find the next Orb...of Earth."

Aberra chimes in, "Actually, we could get a head start to one of the orbs. The crows told me that the fancy door at the library seems to be a portal to another realm. They kept saying their goddess went to 'Mass Hall,' and the squirrels were telling me they heard the Guardian saying something about 'Saman' or 'Salem.' I'm not sure if they're pronouncing it correctly. Sometimes the squirrels are particularly rambunctious and tend to mumble; you know how they fumble with their words. But if we reach the Guardian of Earth first, that will give us the upper hand."

"How is that possible you guys can understand other creatures?" Sakeris asks.

Celestia smiles and affectionately touches the unkempt beard of her dear friend, who is like a brother to her. He has grown so much, yet he remains the same boy she has always known, with the same smooth, brown face. "It's a special family trait, born into us. It's more of an instinctual understanding, but for Aberra and me, we can actually speak to them."

Jarin interjects, "Okay, but I sensed from the Guardian's watchers, while we were at the library, that a man came through by accident a few years back. They said it seems he was in a battle and yelling for someone, then lost his memory and dropped a relic that I was telling you guys about. That was strange. Do you think if we go through that portal, we could lose our memories?"

"It seems to be ancient magic, a protective mechanism for anyone transporting without the permission or guidance of the Guardians, to maintain balance between the realms," Aberra explains.

Sakeris proposes, "Well, can we ask the ev—" then quickly corrects himself, "the good triplets?" They all share smiles and laughter.

"Good idea," Jarin and Aberra say in unison. Sakeris smiles, feeling embarrassed again. He doesn't know why, but his heart always swells with love for this family—a trait he remembers since his young days spent on the island, when they were all young and adventurous.

Yes," Jarin adds, patting Sakeris on the shoulder with respect and love, "we could ask them for guidance in this realm. Also, if I am not mistaken, this place mentioned by the watchers, this other realm behind that portal, is a segregated magic realm kept underground, revealing itself only to their own kind, along with creatures alike, keeping them separate from the unmagical reality world. Very different from our cohesive world."

"We must be very careful to keep our identity and elemental magic in place, then," Aberra cautions.

"You're right, sis. Okay, so that's the plan right now, and we will do as you said, Celestia. We will find out and identify the Destroyer and meet you back at the triplets' homes," Jarin declares.

Sakeris questions, "Where are they? Where is their home?"

"Witch Mountains to the south," Celestia replies.

Sakeris expresses doubt. "There's nothing there but desert."

Celestia explains, "They and all their ancestors prior to that are from the in-between, a neutral world. There are several in-between worlds, similar to the Miser Forest where the fairies live. The forest exists as an entrance with secret passages to the in-between worlds; they only reveal themselves when they are in need. I guarantee you we are in need, and since we are good old friends going back to our ancestors, we always help each other. They are powerful, resourceful, with ancient literatures, and will aid us."

"Celestia, maybe you can ask the triplets how we can control the nightmare minions," Jarin suggests while observing the people and children crying near their parents.

"Nightmare minions?" Sakeris asks, looking confused and trying to discern what Jarin is gesturing toward in the crowd. All he sees are distressed people and animals scattered, trying to find a safe place as they wait for instructions, attending to their young ones.

Jarin responds as he turns to face Sakeris. "Since the human kingdom is now obstructed, the gracious Guardian of Dark is free to employ more actions, ignoring some of the agreements and laws placed between the Guardians themselves. The nightmare minions are scrawny, little ice-elvish creatures governed by the Guardian of Ice. I know what you're going to ask me, bro—why ice? He not only is the element of Ice but also has the capability to manipulate and drowse your mind, and his minions are able to touch and explore any creature's mind at his pleasure. It's one of many attributes of the Guardians of Life, their minions, but it can be further exploited if the barriers between the light and dark are open, which seems to be the case. I could see these little, long pointed eyed creatures playing in the children's minds, with the footlong fingers touching the children, who are the most vulnerable right now."

"Wow, I had no idea. I'm sorry I asked. Is there anything you or the family can do?"

"No, Sakeris. It's out of our jurisdiction; the power of the Guardian of Dark is very different from the light. Although our powers can block such intrusion, we do not have the expertise to block a direct power of the Guardian himself, especially one of the three powerful dark elements. Perhaps Uncle can look into it; he has experience," Celestia says. "But yes, Jarin, I see them too. Shiny little nightmare minions skip happily as they crawl their fingers into the childhood of the most vulnerable, playing with their fears and laughing. They are taking advantage of the moment. We need to clear out of this domain so these minions can return to their original portal. I could ask the triplets; they are the only powerful beings born into the art of dark elements. They would know what to do. I will try, Jarin.

"Okay, then it's settled," Celestia says. "We will leave at dawn. You guys should go on foot, lie low while you head to the Guardian of Water's area. I assume they are heading toward the old ruined city of Olen."

"Please make sure the Sky Knights and Pennaldo are with you, Princess; it's dangerous and…" Sakeris stops.

Sakeris stares at the princess's stone, pondering its powerful significance. He knows that each member of the Argus family wears a special necklace, but Celestia's stone is uniquely different. Recalling a few days ago when they left the Evergreen Library, Sakeris reflects on how the family seemed to be protecting him and his younger cousin. However, upon deeper reflection, Sakeris realizes that the family's protection was actually tied to their shared bloodline, with Celestia's stone meant to safeguard her family—not Sakeris. Jarin nudges him lightly when he notices Aberra and Celestia gazing at him with wide eyes and evident frowns.

"I mean, umm," Sakeris finishes his statement as he gets lost in thought, the others looking at each other oddly, "they need to help you protect the people; you don't need any protecting. Ha, if they cross paths with you or any of you, you know, that magic stuff…" He smiles awkwardly.

They smile and laugh together suddenly.

Then the family gathers and starts hugging. Sakeris stands alone; Jarin looks up at Sakeris. "Really? Get your ass here," he says, and Sakeris joins in, smiling and feeling the comforting warmth of an unexplained connection.

Empress Samatar, accompanied by Kerfort, traverses the ancient Witch Mount, descending various corridors of the castle. They head into the vast dungeons of the abandoned low mounts deep within the castle. After passing through several corridors, they reach a mutual area adorned with old, tangled tapestries depicting ancient wars. These tapestries were once used to keep various prophecies, and beyond them lies another chamber concealed behind a large steel door, heavily chained. The door hasn't been opened in years, but with her impressive magical abilities, Samatar unlocks the various locks, revealing a simple doorknob. She instructs Kerfort to stand guard and prevent anyone from entering. He smiles eagerly, enchanted by her spell, as she enters the dark room, closing the heavy door behind her.

Inside, she brings out her small staff, which emits a magical glow, illuminating the room. It's old and cavernous, with five long hallways leading to alcoves that seem to beckon. These alcoves are active portals that predate the castle, composed of a mysterious substance akin to mirrored magic, capable of leading into the unknown and erasing one's identity upon entering the other realm. Stories of the Guardians utilizing these chambers are both told and hidden. This particular one is safeguarded by the Guardian of Fire, a formidable entity tasked with protecting the entrances to these realms.

The room is vast, devoid of windows, with an ancient wall adorned with unusual textures and inscriptions unfamiliar to Samatar. She needs to understand how the system works and gain access to the innermost layer and the ancient book she seeks.

She waits patiently. As midnight approaches, the instructions become clear: on this day, the Guardian of Void will appear and provide her with the means she needs.

Moments pass, and suddenly the central hall flashes, accompanied by a swell of fog. Instantly, a burst of flame materializes at the front door, momentarily blocking Samatar's view as the intense heat fills the room. Then, as quickly as it appeared, the flame dissipates, revealing the majestic Guardian hovering above her.

Samatar is struck by her grace; though slightly shorter, the Guardian's beauty is breathtaking, with features reminiscent of an elf but with a more substantial stature. She gracefully extends her hand to Samatar, who bows in return. The Empress then presents a vial of ghastly green substance to the Guardian.

"I am sorry, Your Grace," Samatar says. "I tried to have Eva come as you asked me to, but she refused." She pauses for a moment, waiting for the Guardian of Void to say something—punishment, or anything of that sort. But the Guardian remains cool and gracefully calm, a smirk of some sort seeming to indicate satisfaction as her features remain as smooth as stone and her piercing elven eyes awaiting a response, her head tilted in anticipation.

"As you requested, Your Grace," Samatar continues, reaching into her long cloak. "The vial contains the essence of Eartha's life tree from Miser Forest. It cost us many lives, but we succeeded. The fairies of Miser Forest fought valiantly, and we prevailed, extracting the blood of the ancient tree."

The Guardian accepts the vial, acknowledging its significance. "Though not from the ancient tree itself, it is a sister to one that resides within the Argus Fortress," she states. "Be warned, my sister will be displeased with your actions. She will seek retribution upon her return, spreading your soul over her garden to nourish her precious flowers and herbs."

Samatar's heart begins to pound heavily at the Guardian's warning. She feels shaken by the realization that the Guardian of Earth might one day seek revenge and use her as fertilizer. Despite this unsettling thought, she acknowledges the warning, affirming that the sacrifice is justified by the greater purpose. With the exchange agreement secured, the Guardian presents another vial, this time a deep blue hue that matches her gown, and hands it to Samatar.

As Samatar gazes at the Guardian, she notices the complexity of her features, reminiscent of the sky itself. The Guardian's voice, though light, carries the weight of ancient wisdom.

"Be warned," the Guardian continues, her voice carrying a weight of solemnity, "I perceive your intentions regarding the in-between family." Samatar realizes that the Guardian of Void is referring to the Hawthorne family, a formidable, ancient lineage deeply intertwined with the enigmatic in-between realm—a realm of solitude, neutral to all forms of magic. The Hawthorne family's power rivals that of the Argus family's, yet they are uniquely attuned to the elements of dark, contrasting with the Argus's affiliation with the elements of light. Both bloodlines are inherently bound to magic, a mysterious twist that Samatar seeks to understand through access to their ancient texts. Residing solely in the in-between realm, accessible only to those with unique abilities,

Samatar is determined to tap into their rich history of relics and books, having obtained a toy or doll from one of their descendants. With the assistance of the Guardian, she endeavors to forge a connection with this elusive family.

"Interfering with any of them, especially the children, will bring forth consequences far greater than my sister's wrath," the Guardian cautions, her tone grave. "They will seek retribution upon discovering your intrusion into their minds. Should they learn it was you, you will beg for my sister to take your life." With a final warning, the Guardian fades into mist, and flames erupt before she disappears completely.

As the room darkens and the scent of arcane musk lingers, Samatar contemplates her choices. She understands the risks but also the potential rewards of her actions. She decides to proceed with her plans, knowing the challenges ahead.

With determination, Samatar leaves the chamber, her mind set on the intricate scheme to gain control over one of the female members of the Hawthorne triplets to whom the doll belongs. It's a plan that will require patience and precision to avoid detection, but she's willing to do whatever it takes to achieve her goals.

CHAPTER 31

Unexpected

THE JOURNEY TO Olen Fortress is short. James lies on a simple, hay-like cot, comfortably cozy and warm in the specially constructed hut, with the soothing sound of the sea splashing nearby. As he rises, he notices a few dozen cats hidden in plain sight, their slightly glowing eyes fixed on him intently, watching his every move. It's an eerie feeling to be surrounded by these catlike people in the tribal village. They share stories of their past; once human, they were transformed during the destruction brought by his ancestor, Olen. How exactly this occurred remains a mystery. Some say that in the city, which once thrived in riches just north of the Dwarf Mountain, areas were populated by feline cats, lions, and tigers. The Guardian of Void, she unpredictably transformed these animals into humans, infusing them with magic or physical abilities. This is the essence of the Guardian of Void.

Their guide's tribe appears peaceful, outwardly bare, with the Ferlines, as they are known, barely clothed, their bodies adorned with various colors from head to paw. Their clothing is adorned with seashells and ornaments, but they carry weapons, deadly looking yet intricately crafted. The warriors of the Ferline tribe are a sight to behold, their appearance both striking and formidable. They stand tall and proud, their muscular frames honed through years of training and battles fought. Each warrior carries themselves with a sense of confidence and purpose, exuding an aura of strength and determination.

Their clothing, or lack thereof, is a testament to their connection with nature and their feline lineage. Adorned with various colors, from earthy browns and greens to vibrant blues and purples, their bodies are a canvas of intricate designs and patterns. Their attire is minimalistic yet practical, allowing for ease of movement in combat while still retaining an air of elegance and grace.

From head to paw, their bodies are adorned with ceremonial markings and tattoos, each telling a story of bravery and honor. Symbols of protection and strength intertwine with images of nature and wildlife, reflecting their deep reverence for the natural world and their place within it.

Their weaponry is as deadly as it is beautiful, crafted with precision and skill passed down through generations. Swords with blades forged from the finest metals, adorned with gemstones and intricate engravings, gleam in the firelight. Bow and arrows, meticulously crafted from the wood of ancient trees and tipped with razor-sharp arrowheads, are slung across their backs, ready to be unleashed with deadly accuracy.

As they move with purpose through the village, their every step is accompanied by the soft clinking of jewelry and the faint rustle of fur. Despite their fearsome appearance, there is a sense of camaraderie and unity among them, a bond forged through shared hardship and triumph.

Upon entering the village, James finds cats everywhere, considered their guardians and companions of the in-between world they reference. The Ferlines and their Cublits, childlike in appearance, are unusually playful, climbing over him and sniffing him to discern his intentions. It's unexpected but oddly comforting. After sharing supper with them around a large firepit, with various tigers watching from a distance and the tribe surrounding him, it becomes clear they've accepted their fate and seem content.

As James exhales, the cats continue to watch, and then a male Ferline enters his hut, fully bare save for some pearls and earrings adorning his body. His face is a mixture of human and cat features, his smile revealing fangs like a lion, fur cascading down his back decorated with jewels and shells in a bow tie fashion. He walks toward James confidently, placing a clay mug beside him.

"Tea for your comfort, it will be," he purrs, urging James to drink the tea to make himself comfortable.

James sits up, noticing the cats moving quickly around, feeling uneasy.

"Worry not, protection will be," the Ferline reassures him.

James nods, thanking him. He doesn't want to be rude, so he drinks the tea. It's bitter and sweet, oddly pleasant. The Ferline male bows slightly and leaves the hut. James can hear muffled noises and scratching. He feels comfortable now, perhaps due to the tea. Radion says they need to rise early; the entrance to the Guardian of Water's orb is nearby, according to the Ferline tribal leader. The leader was clear; it's a short distance, and they are allowed to enter the protected cave that the tribe has guarded for centuries, in the direction of the Guardian. Suddenly, James feels content and at peace. He buries himself in his hay-like pillow, his thoughts drifting back to his girlfriend once more. Oh, how he misses her—dreaming of holding her close and inhaling the scent of her rosy hair, longing for her even more. Eventually, he falls asleep.

⊶⫘⫘⊷

Eva sits within her private hut, a spacious and adequately comfortable abode. Among the Ferline, renowned for their meticulous hospitality and well-maintained tribal customs, such a dwelling is standard. The earthy aroma of clay and dampness permeates the air, but the addition of lavender and herbs, brought in as a gesture of respect for her status, transforms the initial scent of decay into something soothing and comforting. With deliberate movements, Eva retrieves her brush, intending to untangle the knots in her hair while contemplating plans for the coming day. Suddenly, an ancient, familiar presence materializes swiftly within her sanctuary. She reluctantly lowers her magical defenses, allowing a moonlit figure, slightly shorter yet ethereally graceful, to approach.

"Welcome, Echot, my gracious Guardian of Void. To what do I owe this unexpected visit?" Eva inquires, her tone a mixture of curiosity and caution. "I am uncertain how you traverse the earth now. I assume the ethereal Guardian of Fire granted passage. I hope it does not involve further meddling in the affairs of Montor tribals, for they already endure much suffering," she adds, her voice tinged with concern.

The Guardian speaks, their words soft yet resonant within the confines of the hut. "You know well that our interventions are not always of our own volition. My involvement was beyond my control, influenced by forces beyond our understanding. Even my brother, Borters, ruler of the dominion of Ice, has been occupied with the aftermath of the catastrophic freezing of the Elven Nation. However, they have adapted admirably, as have the tribal clans here."

Eva nods, acknowledging the complexities of celestial duty and consequence. "I understand, though my heart aches for the races. Forgive me, Your Grace, but what brings you here, and how may I assist you?" Eva replies, still uncertain why the Guardian has come to see her.

"I come bearing troubling news," the Guardian says softly and gracefully. The voice sounds distant yet vibrates against the essence of her Void.

Eva's brow furrows in perplexity.

"You are part of the prophecy," the Guardian says. "I regret that I cannot provide detailed explanations. You must simply accept what is to come," the Guardian replies cryptically, their expression inscrutable.

"I don't understand; why I am part of the prophecy?" Eva challenges, her gaze unwavering.

"Because your destiny is intertwined with this course of action, and it must be fulfilled," the Guardian declares with an air of finality.

Eva's heart sinks under the weight of the Guardian's words. Her perplexity deepens at the unexpected turn of events. "And what is this prophecy you speak of? What role am I to play?" she inquires, her mind racing with uncertainty.

"I'm sorry, I can't explain. I will ensure it's not invasive, and you won't feel a thing," the Guardian insists, their tone powerful as the surrounding ambiance darkens and hollows, the gravitational energy slowing enough to make the hut's walls creak. But Eva stands her ground, preparing to unleash her own magic, if need be, against one of the most powerful entities.

"And why would I accept anything without knowing what is expected of me?" Eva counters, her voice tinged with frustration.

"Because you are intertwined with fate, and it needs to be done," the Guardian replies, their gaze unwavering.

As the Guardian raises her hands, Eva attempts to resist with her own magical prowess. Yet she finds herself immobilized, her efforts futile against the overwhelming power of one of the most powerful Guardians. With a radiant glow enveloping her form, the Guardian begins to merge with Eva, their essences intertwining in a profound and irreversible union. Eva's protests fade into silence as her consciousness is engulfed by an inexplicable force, her mind descending into a void of uncertainty and darkness, feeling her soul being displaced into the void realm of her world.

⟡

"James." A soft whisper echoes in his mind, a familiar tone that causes his eyes to open. He feels so comfortable, yet everything he sees seems slightly shadowed as he tries to locate the source of the voice. A young woman approaches him, and he rises steadily, gasping when he realizes it is Abela, his love. But how can this be? Yet she stares at him, a small smile playing elegantly on her lips, and he recalls their time together. He rushes toward her passionately, feeling the warmth and familiarity, exciting him even more. The magic within him begins to feel impatient, a sense of urgency overwhelming him. He's not sure what's happening. How can she be here? Is this some sort of trick? He tries to pull her away, but his heart aches to keep her close. The roses and flowing essence around her overpower his excitement. Finally, he gently pulls her away, staring into her blue eyes intensely. It is her! She has traveled all this way to see him. It must have been a tremendous effort on her part.

"Abela...," James finally manages to say. "How is this possible? You journeyed so long and found me."

She smiles, hugging him tightly, whispering in his ear as her long hair brushes his face, urging him to embrace her fully. "My love, all I want is you," she simply says.

Instantly, she begins to remove his garments, and James follows suit eagerly. They kiss passionately and intensely. Something deep inside him screams, but the passionate love overwhelms him, plunging him into a heavenly passion he cannot resist. She pulls him closer, taking control, and they spin out of control, falling onto his hay bed. He feels immensely happy to have her here, but he notices the odd looks from the cats peeking into his hut, causing him to snap back momentarily. However, she continues her love, and he becomes lost in her trance.

James wakes up to the distant sounds outside his hut, panic seizing him. He jumps out of his cot and runs outside, watching the tribe members going about their business. "Where is she? Abela!" he calls out loud, looking frantic. Was it a dream? What is going on? Radion comes over, looking perplexed at James, putting a hand on his shoulder.

"Boy, do you need to bathe or something? You should be quick; we need to be on our way."

"What?" James returns the look, seeing Radion well rested and in clean garments provided by the clan, looking prepared for another journey. Radion signals James to look down, and he follows, realizing he is completely naked and exposed. Though everyone in the clan walks with bare parts covered in fur like a feline lion or tiger, Eva stands nearby, not taking notice as the others look at him perplexedly. James quickly retreats back to his hut, feeling embarrassed, as he prepares for their departure, the memory of Abela's visit lingering vividly in his mind.

⊷≈⊙ ⊙≈⊶

They have been walking for a few hours now as the forest, dense and shattered-looking, becomes thicker. Scattering animals quickly escape as the company of Eva moves forward, with Radion and two of her warriors hidden on the side and two dwarves accompanying James, as directed by their prince, Kedar. The dwarves are half his size, named Mistril and Templier. Mistril seems to be more observant as she meticulously looks around, scanning for any signs of danger, features typical of her female clan, which are very few and mostly protected by her race back on Dwarf Mountain. She hasn't spoken a word since their encounter with the Guardian of Water. She appears dangerous. Templier, on the other hand, is a sociable individual. They engage in small talk, but he is careful not to divulge much information, especially anything related to his people. He walks comfortably, not as bound as Kedar but strong and fit, with a leisurely outfit as he confidently moves with a bow slung across his back.

James notices the forest starting to feel denser; scattered, abandoned, ancient-looking cottages overwhelmed by nature can be seen, overtaken and consumed by vines and trees, and now home to various creatures. The Ferline group leads them slowly into an area where they all have to slog through the trees that dangle, making it difficult to walk. James sees Radion using magic to cut through the vines with Eva's help as they make their way deeper into the outskirts of the ruins of the kingdom of Olen, once thriving with human inhabitants and other magical communities for trading and education. Eva had mentioned early on in their adventure that Olen was the most powerful kingdom, with races from all over visiting, including fairies, dwarves, elves, and humans, sharing ideas, trading, and educating. The Olen kingdom, just above the Dwarf Mountain, was the closest ally to the dwarves. The dwarves were a massive clan, thriving once, until King Olen destroyed their kingdom and everything around them, pushing the dwarves to near extinction, throwing the elven nation into chaos, and causing a world that became an unbalanced altar of all living things.

James's heart sinks. He doesn't understand how he could change what was so badly damaged. The dwarves look at him as the reborn Destroyer, his bloodline destined to end all their lives. While Eva and Radion find hope in the restoration of balance, he feels lost and confused. Eva tries to comfort him by reminding him that it's okay to let his feelings go, trying hard to hold back his tears. Radion tries to reason with him, explaining that the Guardian's intention is to help him restore the balance, and the return of her orb will be a beginning process of good things to come.

All he wants to do is go back home. He feels the magic weighing heavily on his chest. It begins to tingle and comes alive again; he knows he is getting near the Guardian of Water's orb, her soul calling out to him. The ache becomes stronger. His magic feels different compared to Eva's and Radion's. He doesn't know how to ignite it; it feels like pressure and an entity deep inside, waiting for a vessel to latch on to. James wonders if the sword that sits constantly behind him is that vessel. The Guardian insists it will be necessary to use the soul for the orbs, but he doesn't know how.

＊＝◎═＊

James's mind wanders back home as they continue on a downward track where he can hear a nearby river. The forest is dark and deep, the trees tall and forbidding, casting shadows that cover most of the heat and light from the sun. He feels a chill and huddles a bit more. How he wishes he could just be with his friend now. Ethan would know what to do. He smiles as he recalls some of their crazy adventures in town, often getting into trouble and chased by locals on

Main Street. Then he thinks of Abela. He can still feel her presence last night. It felt so real; he can still feel her body on top of him. It was beautifully surreal to dream of her. The overpowering smell of her body made him so happy that they were together again. But it was just a dream; his heart sinks, wishing it weren't. He dearly misses her so much and feels guilty for not seeing her during the catastrophic event a few weeks ago at the town hall. He feels responsible for everything and has yet to fulfill the Guardian's task, which he doesn't even want.

They are halted by the tribal clan. The lead Ferline female, resembling a tigress, with decorated headpieces that seem to be some sort of sorcery, uses a staff to wave at thick, thorny vines, which move and untangle themselves as if responding to her command, revealing a cave. Then the female Ferline speaks to Eva and Radion and slowly backs away from them, waiting for the party to move forward into the dark cave.

James notices that the entire perimeter starts to untangle slowly as he moves toward Eva and Radion, revealing what was once an open area. The cave seems to be where a small fortress or shrine stood, or perhaps a chapel of some sort. The area around them opens up now, seeming to be a gathering place with tall trees surrounding them.

Stepping into the expansive chamber, they feel as though time itself bends around them. A musty scent hangs in the air, hinting at centuries of neglect. The dryness whispers stories of abandonment, as if the chamber has been frozen in time since the moment of its destruction. Yet oddly, a faint glow emanates, casting soft light upon the walls as they venture deeper, revealing a massive carving. James is struck by a sense of familiarity, reminiscent of his visit to the Dwarf Mountain. Before them rises a towering, thick tapestry stone wall, undoubtedly depicting the entrance to the Garden of Water he saw weeks ago in the dwarves' home.

Turning to Templier, who tightly grips his bow, and his companion, poised with her hammer, James asks, "Is this similar to the portal in your homeland?"

"No," Templier responds, tension evident in his voice. "I've never seen anything quite like this. The carving bears resemblance, but it's not of our craftsmanship."

As James observes the warriors cautiously inspecting ancient artifacts scattered throughout the room, Radion runs his fingers over a marble surface, exclaiming, "Elven craftsmanship! I recall seeing this in the ancient texts of the Northern Kingdom."

Surveying the room, James senses a frozen moment in time, as if it had once been a gathering place for scholars or council meetings. Eva stands a few feet away, lost in thought, her disengagement palpable. Something troubles her, a distraction from their exploration. James moves to approach her when a sudden flash of light erupts, revealing a river-like flow materializing from the tapestry, illuminating the chamber further. Everyone tenses, ready to act, and James instinctively draws his sword, though he's never fought in any wars in his life.

Books, parchments, and scrolls litter the floor as the riverlike substance snakes along the wall, its source shrouded in mystery. Radion beckons James over, pointing to a glowing plaque near the flowing liquid. James hesitates, his gaze lingering on Eva, who remains rooted in place.

"Eva, aren't you coming to see this?" he inquires.

"No, go ahead, dear. I'll stay to ensure our safety," she replies, her voice distant.

Examining the intricate writing on the tapestry, James finds its ancient script both foreign and captivating. Radion translates, "It's Elvish. It reads, 'Blood of the one true heir of life, let it be known.'"

"Do you have a knife?" Radion asks.

"Yes," James responds, producing a small blade.

"Prick your finger and let a drop of blood fall into the stream," Radion instructs.

"And what do you think will happen?" James questions.

"It will open an entrance," Eva interjects, finally joining the conversation.

"Yes, it should open an entrance or portal," Radion confirms.

With resolve, James pricks his finger, allowing a drop of blood to mingle with the flowing liquid, anticipation building as they await the outcome, with Radion stepping back to give him room.

As the water stream, originating from an unknown source in front of the wall, captures his blood, James is suddenly engulfed in a fiery blast. He staggers backward, with Radion instinctively rushing to his aid. The flames soar skyward, emitting an intense heat and a vivid orange glow, causing James's sweat to evaporate into steam. Had he not pulled away quickly, he would have been reduced to ashes.

"I don't understand; shouldn't there be a door?" James queries, bewildered.

They all exchange puzzled glances, but this time Eva steps forward, her presence comforting as she approaches James, who stands uncertainly.

"I'm so sorry, my dear. They always seek to resurrect the past," Eva says softly, her graceful smile offering solace, reminiscent of the warmth she exuded while cooking and caring for him, the only mother figure he has ever known. But why now?

James remains perplexed, watching Eva closely as she continues, "They still won't forgive her, after all these centuries."

As Eva approaches the wall with the waterway, she extends her hand, a tiny pocketknife in the other, and carefully pricks her finger, allowing a drop of blood to fall into the stream. Instantly, the water surges upward, cascading over the wall like a reverse waterfall, forming solid, towering hands clad in glowing, substantial steel, armed and formidable. They clench into fists before gradually shifting to fit the formation below, their massive strength evident as they pull on the rock tapestry with incredible force, even in midair.

As the large water hands exert their tremendous power, the thick rock wall begins to yield, trembling as massive stones dislodge and fall. James and the others scramble for cover, but Eva remains motionless, her gaze fixed on the unfolding spectacle. Ignoring James's attempt to assist her, she shoots him a sly look, indicating that she is unharmed and needs no help.

With a resounding shock, the chanting wall begins to split apart, rocks raining down as the powerful water hands tear through. With their giant, steel, watery hands, they rip open the barrier, revealing another room shimmering with an ethereal glow. The armored steel of the water hands dissipates into droplets, heavy with impact, as the entire water system vanishes instantly.

Eva faces everyone, her expression a mixture of confusion and amazement at the revelations she has just shared. They all look at her, unsure of what to say, as she stands before them, gathering her thoughts.

"This is not solely my mother's fault, yet it is entirely her doing," she declares, her voice tinged with both sorrow and determination. James is puzzled, struggling to grasp the full meaning of her words as she continues, her tone somber.

"Mother fell in love with Pedre Argus, the first of his family. You see…" Her gaze shifts from one companion to another, observing their dazed reactions. "It was her nature of life and love that fiercely took over, but her partners were unprepared when she became pregnant. The revelation shook them to their core, even angering the dark elements that she broke the rules. She tried to rectify the situation, seeking assistance from her siblings, but only one, aligned with dark elements, offered aid. Despite her efforts, my twin brothers perished due to overwhelming magic, leaving me as the firstborn, imbued with wild magic. My mother's partners, including those closest to her, distanced themselves, unable to accept our existence. Alone, she remained, until her first beloved's passing, continuing to guide our family lineage and placing powerful magic upon them to ensure their survival. However, I was different, wild and untamed, staying by her side as she sought refuge in the Witch Mountain, which you all know as Kumartal, delving into mysteries within her library."

A sense of foreboding hangs in the air as Eva recounts the turmoil that followed, the consequences of her mother's actions triggering war among those displeased with the breach of law.

At that moment, Radion drops to one knee, followed by the warriors, leaving James startled. What are they doing?

"You mean you are the daughter of…"

"Yes, Radion, I am the daughter of the Guardian of Earth."

Gasps fill the room as everyone kneels and bows in reverence. James stands frozen in shock, his gaze locked with Eva's, now transformed with a deep green hue he has never seen before. As his knees begin to weaken and tremble, he struggles to comprehend the magnitude of her revelation.

"Eva is my nickname; I am Eventra Eartha Argus. Though unknown to the Argus family, I am a descendant of the firstborn essence of the Guardian. Centuries have passed for me, while for you, it is but a few decades. Born from my mother's life essence and given more, my existence is intertwined with the fate of our home of Terra. After me, my mother had another set of twins, Peda and Pendo Argus. As I said, she instilled a special substance of her life essence into them to extend their lifespan beyond that of a typical human, along with unique magic to maintain their existence, and they had children of their own. The Argus family continued to grow with unique properties, overseen by both the Guardians of Light and Dark in watchful agreement to help maintain a balance in Terra's elements and healing the realm had started.

"Centuries later," Eventra continues, now facing James, "it was your bloodline that fell in love with one of the Argus, Terbara. The magic orbs that the Guardians of Light provided to your ancestor were meant to stop the Guardians of Dark from exploiting a mistake my mother made when she tried to ask for forgiveness. The Guardians still weren't forgiving, even after the agreement. However, the orbs inadvertently drove King Olen mad. He struck down Terbara, an Argus connected with the souls of the Guardians of Light, causing chaos in this realm and allowing the elements of dark to enhance their essence into chaos as well. My mother was distraught and forbade your bloodline from intervening, requesting it to be destroyed. It was I and Socrater, human and frail, who convinced her to watch and protect your line. She refused, but eventually, she agreed, as it was another Guardian's request to keep your bloodline alive.

"James," she says, "I pleaded with my mother to let me watch over and protect your bloodline, despite her initial refusal. It was a decision made out of love and a sense of duty—a pact forged by another Guardian to preserve the balance of life.

"I begged Mother not to destroy the child born of Olen, influenced by the ill will of his father and the power of the Guardian orbs that drove him mad. She finally agreed, always seeking to rectify the terrible mistake, though it was not entirely hers."

Addressing the room, she continues, "Love's essence is uncontrollable magic, capable of both great good and great harm. For a Guardian, it can be unpredictable. Love overpowered my mother's essence; she desired to hold on to that love. But when she became pregnant—against the rules of her task—the balance was disrupted. My mother was a victim of her own love. I was with her every step of the way, her companion in both light and dark. The Guardians are forgiving but will not forget the turmoil that my mother caused out of the simple essence of love. It was not her fault. They are still angry with her…It was believed that your bloodline, James, born out of my mother's love for a nonmagical creature, could restore the balance of the realm. But an agreement was made for the Arguses, born into the light elements of magic, to watch over humans, while the dark elements would assist those willing to learn their dark arts freely. Eventually, my mother agreed to the pact, though she felt embarrassed and distraught, leaving the realm in search of forgiveness and redemption. Years of wars followed."

Her gaze fixes on Radion, who appears stunned and shocked. "And it continues to this day! Spread the word, write it down—I don't care! I'm done with these Guardians!" James feels the weight of her words, sensing the frustration and aggression boiling within her, emotions she doesn't usually express.

The room falls silent, awaiting a response. No one dares to speak.

"Now that it's all out in the open…," she says, her tone calm and reassuring, which puzzles James and the others. They exchange confused glances as they listen to Eva addressing them with composure. "I appreciate your understanding. Let's stay focused on our mission; otherwise, our efforts here will have been in vain, and there are dangers at stake."

CHAPTER 32

Orb of Water

JAMES FINALLY MANAGES to speak as he stands by the rugged entranceway.

"What do I call you? I don't know who you are or what you are," he says cautiously, facing the ancient person Eventra before him.

"I am the same person as always, dear. Nothing has changed. I am the same person who cradled you when you were a baby, who bound your bruises, who watched over your play outside. I am the one who read you stories that intrigued you so much and sought out and protected you from the foes and evils that waited without your knowing. I am here to see you through your quest and mold you into the man you are—honest, caring, and strong-minded—to face what is expected of you. Your parents knew who I was and urged me not to tell you so that you could have a normal life as a child and enjoy your youth. I am sorry that it has come to this, my dear James. It was the only way I could watch over you. As for calling me, you know better. Eva is my preferred name."

"Then the orb is meant for you, since you are the one true bloodline."

"No, it is for you, James, an answer to you only. I was the revelation key to lead you to it. Now, shall we?" Her tone changes.

They move forward cautiously. Radion, still in shock, doesn't know how to proceed but simply bows lightly as he passes her. Eventra simply stares deeply into his eyes and says nothing while the rest of the party walks into a vast opening that shimmers with a blue glow.

The cave is massive in every direction, but the entrance and exit are the only doors. Nothing seems out of the ordinary, but an eroded pedestal of rock at the far end of the cave is illuminated brightly, causing the room to shimmer. Eventra directs her warriors to stay by the entrance as they place their arms against their chests, acknowledging her newfound royalty. Both dwarves are now halfway through the room, not sure what they are seeing, simply staying halfway from the middle of the room, wary, not daring to come close to the glowing pedestal. James walks slowly as the pedestal continues to glow. He sees it holds a golden-looking basin with a swirly, milky water that slowly moves as if someone is stirring a stew. He stares down at the basin and looks at both Eventra and Radion for any advice.

"What do I do?" he says.

Radion stays quiet, still in shock, as if his thoughts have been taken away because of Eventra's revelation.

Eventra finally says, "Call to her. Let her know who you are and what your intentions are, dear."

James clears his throat. He is shaken because the basin looks to hold only the liquefied blue substance and doesn't reveal any source of relic or item to retrieve.

"Um, my name is James Lander. I am here to take you back to your owner. Um, the Guardian of Water." Nothing happens; it's quiet.

Finally, Radion says, "Use the sword, boy. Maybe it needs to connect to it."

James retrieves the sword and looks at the polished relic. He notices now that it has four small compartments on the steel handle, and one of them starts to glow, indicating something should go in there. It takes him by surprise.

A scream suddenly interrupts everyone's gaze as they see a huge creature materialize in thin air, heavy bones all over its body, killing one of the warriors. The dwarves instantly start hammering and shouting at the creature.

"Stay here! Eventra, we need to slow them down!" All of a sudden, the entire entrance is filled with icy cries, darkness, and shadowy figures starting to appear near one of the dwarves as it merges and takes over Templier's body, who tries to fight the creature inside him. James quickly turns, but Eventra stops him short.

"No, stay here and try to get the orb. They are here to stop you! We will handle this!" She quickly joins Radion as he tries to block the creatures from emerging from the doorway with some sort of shield, as the possessed Templier, screaming like a man possessed, kills his partner with arrows as Eva blasts him back with energy from her hands. The creatures overwhelming the protected wall from Radion are pushing through, causing it to crack and crumble as both Radion and Eventra continue to fight against the creatures, their skills unmatched, especially Eventra, swaying her hands; none of the creatures can penetrate her magic, but Radion and the warriors are struggling.

"James! The orb!" Eventra screams in the distance. James, shaken in shock, wants to aid them. Something is holding him and preventing him from doing so.

He turns around, and a single spear is hovering over the basin with the same swirling movement. James pulls out his sword to capture the floating spear, which is the size of a coin, but its animated movement brings it closer to James, startling him as he tries to pull back. The spear continues to animate, coming closer and is now up against his face. James feels his heart start to pound in his chest with fear, but his magic seems to surge inside him, and he feels an overwhelming essence deep inside him spiral out of control.

James barely gets the sword up against the spear, but it smacks against his face and body unexpectedly. He feels lost and starts to fall, everything flashing in his mind. He sees himself with the Guardian in a flash of memory, inside or on a beach somewhere, looking up as water swirls above him and creatures swim. He is magically kissing the Guardian, partially, but it's not him—it's Olen! This memory is in the Guardian Kingdom, a place he doesn't know. The flashes continue: He finds himself in a beautiful, shining castle, engaged in a heated argument with the Guardian who suddenly smacks him hard, pushing him away. In another flash, he's standing in a room, gripping a now-glowing sword, within the confines of a royal bedroom. Then another vivid image emerges—a haunting flashback of a woman, likely one of his ancestors, with a sword piercing her body. He realizes it's a vision of King Olen killing his wife. The woman, dressed in a nightgown with flowing hair and wide, fearful eyes, screams in agony. Overwhelmed by the pain of this memory, he is suddenly thrust back into reality. He feels a surge of unexpected power rejuvenate him, feeling invigorated and confused by anything that stands in his way.

He sees the struggle: Radion is on his knees; only the two of them exist now, and Eventra is overwhelmed with various unknown creatures.

"Nooooooo!" he yells with power, and the water from the basin shatters the pedestal. The water rises, engulfing him like a wave, forming into swirling garments that harden tightly against his body. The water enters through his nostrils and mouth as the smooth substance gives him a sense of impenetrability from within. All aches and pains are instantly wiped away as the water transforms into a steel armor that covers him from head to toe, feeling as light as cloth. The sword transforms into a scimitar within his grasp. The water carries him with ease, as he is needed to end this fight. He smashes into the middle of the creatures, causing them to scatter away from Eventra and Radion. They both move away to give him room as they continue to fight.

James swings the sword with ease, creatures trying to entangle him, but he feels nothing, ripping them away like feathers and slashing wildly, not knowing how to use the sword. More creatures come into the doorway, and without knowing how, he raises his free hand, his arm transforming into a tentacle-like appendage with spores, grabbing a dozen or more creatures with their horns unable to penetrate the tentacle arms. He smashes them against the cave wall, instantly splattering it with black blood, and they die.

James feels more agile and energetic than ever before. He uses the tentacles again, and this time, they enter the mouths of the creatures, feeling their insides, and with a surge of energy, he annihilates them from within, causing all the captive creatures to burst into pieces of black nothingness.

He can hear a distant scream; Eventra is calling to him, but he sees no danger near her. Now more creatures, this time icy-looking elves, burst through the door, shooting at him. These beings, with flowing white hair and blue skin frozen for years or centuries, come in with ease. Nothing is piercing his armor; he struggles to block it. But it is not working. His frustration increases, and suddenly he needs to release a power housed inside of him; his armor extends above the ceiling, and the water turns into various sea creatures, one of them a huge deadly shark with madly grinning teeth, ready to consume the elves into their doom. Eventra touches him and says, "No, James!"

He snaps out of his trance, and the creatures instantly revert back into water, splashing their entire company and the elves on the ground. The elves, in fear and shock, run from the cave. James falls to the ground as the water subsides from his mouth and body, coughing, and next to him, the sword's small compartment opens, and the orb slowly retreats into the cavity, closing and disappearing.

James breathes heavily as Eventra cradles him. Radion, barely able to walk, comes to them.

"It's okay, dear. I am here. It's over; you saved Radion," she says.

James looks perplexed, gazing at Eventra, who seems undisturbed and calm, while Radion lies flat, looking up, breathing heavily.

"What happened to everyone?" James says.

Eventra doesn't say anything, trying to help James up. The entire cave is damp and wet; the water seems to have subsided into the walls to somewhere he doesn't know. The sword in his hand glows as he can feel a new entity emerging, which the Guardian of Water's soul is occupying.

"Let's get moving," Radion says.

"They are dead because of me, right?" James says, his anger rising.

Eventra takes him by his arms and says, "You are here to get the orb back to the Guardian of Water, dear. They came to help you see this through. Kedar expected this when the Guardian spoke with them directly. They knew the consequences. They know that one day you will bring things back to order and help their clan thrive once more. The Guardian revealed this to Kedar and his clan. He purposely decided to take your best friend, Ethan, with them as a guide to help them, but in reality, it was to protect him from what might have happened if he joined you. Their deaths were not in vain here. They came to save their race from becoming extinct. Now please, let's go. You need to go with Radion back to the village and return to the Guardian of Water's lair so her companions can guide you to her fortress to return the orb to her."

James finally feels exhausted, the energy of the orb overpowering him unexpectedly and powerfully. He doesn't know what he is doing, but he wants to protect Eventra and everyone, yet he has failed. Eventra seems not to need protection, being the daughter of the Guardian of Earth, indicating that he saved Radion. He wonders if this is just a showcase for them, if the creatures knew of her and played along. He lets the matter drop and then realizes what Eventra said.

"What do you mean, Radion and me?" James says, now on his feet, staring at Eventra.

The same look she always gives, a passionate display of maternal care as she strokes his overgrown beard. She smiles, the same smile as when she helped with breakfast a few weeks ago. She exhales with ease, and small tears start to drop from her face as she tries so hard to hold them back.

"I need to do something; my task here is done," she says.

James is ready to protest, but she places her finger on his lips, not allowing him to interrupt.

"Please know, I am so deeply sorry for everything…everything. You are so important to me, but I promise we will meet again. I cannot tell you when."

She looks up at him and exhales hard. It seems she wants to tell him more, but again, the secrets are there, not meant for him to know right now.

"Let's go, dear. You need rest at the village," she says as they exit the fortress, now destroyed by the raid.

As they walk out, the Ferline warriors emerge from the woods without a word, as if they dare not interfere with their ordeal.

One of the warriors is now looking up at a tree. James follows his gaze.

Three individuals are positioned high up, intentionally visible. They appear to be youngsters, perhaps in their teens, observing intensely. One boy holds his hand against the tree, staring directly at him, his eyes wide with intensity and his features smooth. Meanwhile, the other, a female, remains comfortably leaning against another tree bark, watching from the corners of her eyes. The third, a burly boy with dark skin, stands behind the one being observed, seemingly taking in the entire scene, though uncertain of what he's witnessing. He appears to be a companion, while the other two seem closely related, evident in the striking similarity of their facial features.

"Those are the Argus clan," Radion says as he stares up with James.

James continues to stare back at them; they seem fearless and waiting.

"Why won't they come down? They should have helped. After all, aren't we distant cousins?" James says to Radion.

Radion chuckles. "That's Jarin and his sister Aberra. Believe me, we should be in danger from them. I am not sure why they are just waiting. I guess they want to witness you. Now that we know the history, I wonder if they do and if they are abiding by the truce of the Guardian to protect the humans. I believe they didn't want to intervene because of your history, of your ancestors."

"From me? I will not hurt anyone."

"I know," Radion says. "Eventra saw to that and has molded your generation for centuries and has done a wonderful job." Radion turns around, looking startled, which causes James to ask, "What's wrong?"

"She is gone," Radion says.

James looks around the perimeter and confirms that Eventra did leave. He doesn't know how, but after all, she is a descendant of the Guardian, and he's sure these woods are an easy task for her to disappear in.

James looks up again, but the watching party is now gone. He knows his so-called stranger cousins will eventually meet up with him again.

⟡⟢

It has only been an hour since Eventra left James, her heart heavy with the weight of leaving him behind. There is so much he needs to know, but the timing isn't right; he needs to learn on his own. She closes the hidden portal behind her; her mother and she always traveled between the network of ancient trees. You need to know which ones; the ancients' trees were her mother's oldest companions, deeply integrated into Terra, nurturing and protecting the realm from harm. The trees know her; the willow back at James's home recognized her will and kept her connected to her mother. But she wasn't here; she had come to James's ancestral home, assuming a different persona, watching over him and his ancestors since her mother's departure.

She recalls her last connection with her mother, "My Eventra," she commented through the trees. "I seek knowledge and must attend to those who need me more now."

"What are you talking about, Mother?" And she left, as cold as she had always been, but in nature, she knew it was the way of the Guardians of Life— always nurturing all forms of life around her, a task given to her and all her descendants, including those governing the dark elements.

Eventra searches through the network of powerful, ancient trees. The elder one, Eltor, reports that she is nowhere to be found in Terra. Eartha, her mother, no longer loved, afraid of the consequences of excessive love. Eartha sheltered her love, which seemed to spiral out of control and disappear into another realm. Feeling saddened, Eventra finally reaches her destination and waits.

She stares at the cottage, smoke rising from the chimney, surrounded by peaceful and beautiful gardens. She sees a big man chopping wood, his dark skin glistening as he works. She waits patiently, unwilling to intrude. She remembers this place, the history that spans decades, even centuries. This family, based on knowledge, the witches of three, always three. They are also an ancient family, like the Argus. Eventra is familiar with the family and how they have intertwined for centuries, going back to the days of the Guardians. These witches are intertwined in destiny, whether one of them has children of three or all, always in three, gifted by the Guardians. They are witches of knowledge, as powerful as the Argues. Always concealed away from civilization, always to themselves, tight-knit and insular, much like these children and their family—the Hawthorne family secluded within society, separate from everyone else, in the in-between realm that had once been hidden from her, completely to themselves. Eventually, the Hawthorne family opened their realm to her, inviting her to enter.

Suddenly, Eventra hears a scraping noise beside her, and a young boy, no more than ten years old, sits down beside her. He is well groomed but barefoot, with dirty, ripped pants that are torn at the lower part of his legs. He is picking berries that have grown in her presence. He looks up to her and smiles. She hasn't met him yet. It's been a long time since she was here. The boy says, "It took you long enough." Then a girl appears next to her on the other side, the same age, and with identical features as her brother—ponytail hair and an elegant dress adorned with various flowers. She skips along in front of Eventra and says, "Oh, just leave her alone. She's so cute. I can't wait until she's born, Eventra. Oh, goodness!" She looks at Eventra and says, "Oh, I'm sorry. Did you—you didn't know?"

Eventra smiles and replies, "It's okay, Emma."

Another individual, sharing similar features to Emma, appears behind Eventra. This person has a more eccentric appearance, wearing colorful clothes, sporting nicely groomed hair, painted nails, and bright purplish hair. He asks, "Does she know?"

The first boy, sitting down, replies, "Of course she does."

The girl adds, "Not really, she suspects, but she should know her. She's going to be beautiful, for love."

The flamboyant boy behind her comments, "Cunning too."

The boy sitting down chimes in, "And unique."

The girl then says, "Mom said you will be with us for a while."

The boy sitting down reassures Eventra, "We will protect her."

His sister affirms, "Yes, we will," while the other brother adds, "We'll be very close to her."

"Don't worry, Eventra," they all say simultaneously. "She'll be protected." Eventra thinks to herself, noting how they speak just like their mother—and their two aunts—the three witches with their penchant for riddles, powerful seers with potent magic. She waits patiently as the family of three, these powerful triplets, wield the dark elements and more, inheriting their abilities from their mother, who is also one of a triplet with two other sisters. It's said that triplets born possess unique abilities across many realms and hold great power in this land.

The two boys—Esler, sitting next to her, and the other, Emer—and the girl, Emma, are the children of one of the witches of the three. She was carrying triplets that continued the legacy of this family, a process that they all linked together, uniquely protective and understanding of both human and nonhuman lives. Very powerful. Eventra has to get used to this again. She looks at the children one by one—they all look alike, with similar features. The daughter looks like her father, and the two boys look like their mother but with extraordinary features and beautiful, just like their parents.

Then Emma says, "Dinner is ready," and Esler turns to Eventra, saying, "Mom made your favorite," while Emer adds behind her, "Stew, just the way you like it."

Eventra's stomach starts grumbling. She's been craving that stew since she walked in this area. The barrier between here and home still holds up strong, and Esler, still eating his berries, says, "You know you can just walk right through. There's no way the barrier will refuse you."

The girl says, "You're always welcome here, Aunt Eventra," and Emer behind her says, "Why are you waiting here?"

Eventra simply says, "Just out of respect," and the three kids chuckle and grab her hand, leading her to sit with them.

Emma says, "You know, the princess is coming too. She's very close friends to us, but we will hold her off until the time is right."

Eventra looks at the girl and says, "I appreciate the news."

"Of course," she replies, while Esler says, "As you wish."

The boy still sitting down says, "Why are you still here? Let's go! Don't be silly. Come on," and they guide her through the visible barrier. As soon as she passes through, everything surrounding her smells of beauty—graceful, peaceful birds chirping and the aroma of stew immediately filling her nostrils, even though they are a few hundred feet away from the cottage, a cottage that has been there for legacies.

The children stand before her in formation—Esler in front, Emma next to her, and the other brother, Emer, behind her. Eventra realizes that they are protecting her, or rather, not just her but also her unborn child. She doesn't fully understand why, but she doesn't question it. These powerful young witches, the triplets, are the most powerful beings, and receiving protection from them is comparable to receiving protection from the entire Argus family. One Hawthorne youngster may be difficult to overcome, but the triplets as a whole are nearly impossible to overcome. They are known throughout the realm and even to the Guardians as formidable foes you do not want to cross paths with—respectable, following the rules, but not to be crossed. The question of why they are so interested in Eventra's unborn child lingers in her mind for now. This family always looks out for the best interests of others, something that she obviously can't ignore, and the triplets have now been assigned to protect Eventra and her unborn child.

As they approach the pleasant-looking cottage, Eventra doesn't understand how the cottage could accommodate such a big family—three sisters, one married with these three children, another partnered with someone else, and the third single. She knows the cottage holds deep secrets, rumors of underground areas, relics, ancient history, and books known only to them. Some say there's a society within their underground world, unseen by anyone else, governed solely by them —an in-between world, as she calls it. As she enters the cottage, she sees many people around the room. She reflects on how different realms portray the sisters—some depict them as evil, with one sharing an eye with another, while others portray them as a beautiful family. Regardless, they are worshipped in either light or dark, always a clan that protects the existence of life and death. They are revered for their knowledge and respected across different parts of the realms.

As she approaches, her dear friend embraces her deeply, while the other sisters join with their partners and the rest of the family. It may not be her parents' cottage, but it's close enough. She's finally home.

End of Book 1

This concludes Book 1: Destroyer, Guardians of Life series.

Coming Next

Book 2: Creator, Guardians of Life Series. It will feature a map of the Terra Realm, (a parallel realm of Earth).

Acknowledgments

Gratitude to everyone at Elite Authors for their ongoing support, especially to the initial team members for patiently addressing my questions in a complex literacy industry. Special thanks to the editors for their excellent reviews, insightful input, valuable comments, and suggestions that brought my creativity to life. Also, thank you to your team for preparing, formatting, and expanding upon my daughter's design.

My heartfelt thanks to Sheila Segarra, my wife, for listening to my story and being an early reader of my manuscript, despite it not being your typical genre. Your unwavering support and love made it all possible.

A special thanks to Caitlin Segarra, my daughter, for creating the cover of my manuscript. Your unique skills beautifully captured the essence of my vision, reflecting the magic we've shared in understanding stories together since you were young. Your assistance in analyzing my ideas and your attentive interest in listening to my story have greatly contributed to making my book possible.

Thank you, Benedict Dawn-Cross, for your support. Your background in acting has given me confidence in your insight.

Thank you to my entire family for your inspiration over the eighteen years, while balancing home, job, and education, which it took to write this first novel. Your unwavering support is the backbone of my book. With the foundation set, I promise that the rest of my story won't take another eighteen years to unfold.

A most special thank you to my readers, for embracing my story and bringing my realm to life!

Made in the USA
Columbia, SC
07 September 2024